ABSYNTHE

ABSYNTHE

BRENDAN P. BELLECOURT

DAW BOOKS, INC.
DONALD A. WOLLHEIM, FOUNDER
1745 Broadway, New York, NY 10019
ELIZABETH R. WOLLHEIM
SHEILA E. GILBERT
PUBLISHERS
www.dawbooks.com

First Printing, December 2021
1st Printing

This one's for Bill Mattocks.
Thanks, old buddy. For the good times, for your service,
for speaking truth to power.

ONE

On a crisp spring day in 1928, Liam Mulcahey found himself sitting in the back of a sleek maroon Phaeton, headed for the grand opening of the new flashtrain line.

As the Phaeton navigated the roads of the Chicago suburb, the driver glanced into the rearview mirror with his glowing blue eyes. "Are you quite certain it will be all right for me to attend, Master Aysana?" His voice was slightly garbled, the speaker built into his faceplate in need of repair. In the driver's seat was a mechanika named Alastair, the chauffeur of the Aysana family, whom Liam worked for.

Sitting beside Liam in the back seat was Morgan, son of the famous rail baron Rajan Aysana. "I'm certain," Morgan said with a placating smile. Alastair had been giddy with excitement for days at the prospect of seeing the new flashtrain debut.

"Because I can stay in the car if it would be too much of a bother," Alastair went on.

"No, no, Alastair, you're most welcome." Morgan was twenty-eight, the same age as Liam. He had a round, freckled face and straight black hair with long bangs he was often flicking out of his eyes, a source of frustration for his doting mother.

"Well, then, that's fine, sir." Alastair couldn't smile as such, but Liam had been working on him long enough to note the signs of his contentment. He sat straighter in his seat. His head momentarily jiggled from side to side. "That's fine as raspberry wine."

Liam didn't like crowds—a predisposition that had only deepened since war's end in 1918—yet he had to admit, he was excited too. Rajan Aysana's accomplishments deserved recognition, but more than that, Liam wanted to pay back the kindness and generosity that Rajan and his wife, Sunny, had shown him over the years. So while the grand opening promised to be cheek-to-jowl, Liam had vowed to stifle his discomfort and raise his voice in celebration.

Besides, Leland De Pere, the President himself, was set to give a speech. He had been an Army officer during the war against the countries of the St. Lawrence Pact: Germany, France, Great Britain, and Canada. Liam had served under him, though all he recalled of the man was a speech he'd delivered to Liam's class of soldiers, fresh out of boot camp, at Fort Sheridan. Liam doubted very much the president would remember him, but what an honor it would be if he did.

Soon they were pulling off the main road and entering the jammed parking lot of the gleaming flashtrain station. Attendants waved them toward the front of the lot, where a line of long-nosed limousines were letting out the VIPs.

The station itself was a small but impressive structure of rough stone, frosted glass, and highly polished steel. Red, white, and blue bunting was everywhere. A crowd of men, women, and children waited near the entrance, cordoned by red velvet ropes into a long, snaking line. Hundreds more had already been let in. Liam could see them standing along the edge of the platform two stories above. He swallowed hard while staring up at them; it was going to be *much* tighter than he'd envisioned.

As the Phaeton reached the back of the queue, Liam realized Morgan had been staring at him.

"You can stay in the car if you want, old buddy," Morgan said.

"No, I'll be fine." Liam had meant the words to sound more convincing, but he could tell by Morgan's sympathetic reaction he'd failed miserably.

"Or Alastair could take you home if you're not feeling up to it," Morgan said. "I'll tell you all about it tomorrow."

Liam shook his head. "I wouldn't dream of robbing Alastair of the chance to see the President speak."

Alastair glanced at Liam in the mirror. "Oh, don't worry about me, sir."

"No," Liam said firmly. "We're here. Let's celebrate."

Morgan paused, weighing Liam's sincerity, then smiled. "We won't stay long." He squeezed Liam's shoulder. "I promise."

The Phaeton pulled to a stop, and waiting attendants opened the passenger door. After stepping out and being patted down for weapons by two serious-looking government officers in black uniforms, Liam and Morgan headed up the nearby ramp. When they reached the elevated platform, practically every square inch was packed. And not just the near platform; the westbound platform was half-full as well.

Feeling his breath growing shorter, Liam used one of the few tricks that helped to calm his nerves: he studied his surroundings. High above, an arched roof of steel girders and frosted glass shaded all from the bright, noontime sun. Many of those in attendance had dressed up. They wore fine suits and bowlers, frocks and cloche hats, but there were others with simple coats and dresses, not to mention a few button-down shirts that showed a wrinkle or two. Liam didn't feel at home, precisely, in his simple woolen pants, pea coat, and tweed flat cap, but neither did he feel out of place.

Set near the tracks was a decorated wooden stage with stairs and a raised speaking platform. Cordoning the area around it were more stanchions and velvet ropes. Standing behind the ropes were men wearing black suits with the initials of the Central Intelligence Corps embroidered onto their breast pockets. More were situated at the edges of the crowd. To a man, they stood at military ease, their legs spread shoulder-width, their hands clasped behind their backs as they scanned the crowd for signs of danger.

As the seconds passed, Liam's heart slowed, and he breathed a short sigh of relief.

"One minute!" roared a burly cuss of a man, a porter with a push-broom mustache. "One minute remaining!"

Like the other porters, the man wore a long black coat, white gloves, and a red cap, though in his case the cap was pulled so low one could hardly see his eyes. The way he barked—indeed, the very timbre of his voice—summoned memories of the war, of drill sergeants. Curiously, his loping gait was accompanied by a faint, mechanikal whirring, likely from one or both of his legs having been replaced with prosthetics.

Liam was frustrated by his inability to remember more of the war, but he'd long grown used to it. The head wound he'd suffered during one of the war's final battles had erased most of his memories of his time in uniform. What was odd, though, and made it all the more frustrating, was the fact that the erasure wasn't absolute. Every now and again, something would spur a memory, but the moment he tried to reach for it, it would fly away like a startled goldfinch. Such was the case on the train platform as Liam tried to recall who the porter's voice reminded him of.

He gave it up as useless just as Alastair, having parked the Phaeton, joined them. Liam, Morgan, and Alastair were all of a height, just shy of six feet, but Alastair was necessarily thinner, the minimum amount of weight being critical for extending the life of the power source inside his gut. "Have I missed it, sirs?"

"You're just in time," replied Morgan.

"Very *good*, sir." Alastair might be a mechanika made of steel and brass, but at the moment he looked like an overexcited child—restless feet, eyes constantly moving, his metal fingers tenting before him. "Look!" he called in his garbled voice, pointing. "There it is!"

Heads turned. Necks craned. The porter stormed along the platform's edge shouting, "Behind the yellow line, now! Behind the yellow line!"

Standing on tiptoes, Liam saw a glint of silver to his right. Beyond it, visible over the treetops, were the towers of downtown Chicago. The silver shape grew, the sleek engine and its trailing cars becoming more discernible.

"Hold your hats!" shouted the burly porter as the hum of the train's engines grew louder.

Liam pinched the brim of his cap just in time. The platform vibrated. The flashtrain blurred past. Liam felt himself tugged forward in the vacuum of its wake. Then a gust of wind washed over the crowd like a wave off the sea. Dresses lifted, exposing knickers. More than a few hats flew into the air, sucked into the flashtrain's mighty draft. Many laughed in excitement. Others stared in awe as the train dwindled into the distance. A few rows ahead of Liam, a red-haired girl sobbed in the arms of her mother.

As the train's thunder faded, the crowd hummed excitedly. Many of those in attendance would never have ridden on a train. Now they'd seen a wonder of the modern world, a train so fast its speed rivaled the bi-planes from the war.

"So that's it, then?" Liam shared a wink with Morgan. "Time to go home?"

Morgan let out an affected sigh. "Yes, yes, I suppose it is."

Alastair looked from Morgan to Liam and back, somehow managing to look heartbroken. "But the President . . ."

Morgan smiled sympathetically. "Sorry, Alastair. It was only a joke. Father wanted to demonstrate the train's top speed. It'll be returning shortly."

"I see." Alastair's eyes went dark several times, his equivalent of a blink. "Did you think your joke was funny, sir?"

A laugh burst from Morgan. "No, I suppose I didn't."

The hum of conversation had only just started to die down when the crowd shifted their attention to the westbound track. Moments later, the train glided to a stop ahead of them. Behind the sleek engine were three passenger cars, each bearing Aysana Lines' bright yellow logo, a circle with the letters *AL* inside it. Curiously, the third car had no doors at all— apparently, it could only be reached from an adjoining car—and its windows were blacked out, blocking any view of the interior.

To Liam's right, the burly porter dragged a truly massive sandwich board toward the edge of the track. It read, *Forest Park Welcomes President De Pere!* After setting it down near the last car, the porter turned to face the crowd. "Ladies and gentlemen," he roared, "I give you the President of the United States."

To a round of applause, the first car's doors slid open. Revealed was a strikingly handsome man in his late forties with hazel eyes and golden blond hair parted to one side. Standing behind him were Morgan's parents, Rajan and Sunny Aysana, a handsome Vietnamese couple who'd met in

Chicago after emigrating to the States some forty years ago. They departed the train car together. As Rajan and Sunny smiled proudly, De Pere shook a few hands, waved, and sent smiles over the crowd, then he took the stairs to the top of the waiting stage.

Liam recalled a much younger Leland De Pere, the striking officer who'd given the speech in Fort Sheridan along the shores of Lake Michigan. It had been a hopeful day, but for some reason, seeing De Pere working the crowd gave rise to another of the few memories Liam had of the war, one of a broken battlefield, of holding a Springfield rifle, of trenches crisscrossing the shattered terrain. It had been dusk, the air both chill and damp. Ahead, a thick bank of fog had approached Liam's position, and somewhere inside it, rhythmic booms pounded the earth. Red lights swept the fog's thickness, ruby scythes cutting wheat.

Liam could never remember how he'd wound up in that terrifying place. He'd trained and served in the 128th Infantry, a grease monkey outfitting and repairing the battle suits used by the U.S. Army. How he'd landed on a battlefield, holding a bayonet-tipped rifle, he wasn't sure. His best guess was that desperation had driven the Army to reassign him. It had been a critical battle, after all, the last major offensive of the war. He must have been reassigned to help in it.

Liam was suddenly drawn back to the flashtrain platform when Morgan elbowed him and said in a low voice, "What do you think happened to him?"

"Who?" Liam asked.

Morgan pointed to the shadows of the passenger compartment the President had just left. "The President's aide, Max Kohler."

Watching from within shadows was an impeccably dressed man whose face was hidden by an iron mask. Much of the mask was the dull color of pewter, but its filigreed swirls shone like oxidized brass. It was all soft curves, with no human features to speak of save three slits, where the mouth and nose would be, and two eyeholes—one a circular red lens, the other oval-shaped, revealing a bright blue eye. As the President spoke, Kohler studied the crowd warily.

Liam stared at him a moment. "I've no idea."

It was likely Kohler had sustained some terrible injury during the war. His demeanor was off-putting, as if he distrusted everyone and everything around him. Leaning as he was against the luggage rack, his jacket hung open to reveal a sidearm, a Webley revolver, in a black leather holster. Like the burly porter's barked commands, there was something familiar about the cocky way he was surveying the crowd.

For a moment, Kohler's lone blue eye met Liam's browns. He stared at Liam hard, as if he too were having a moment of recognition. Or maybe it was Liam's imagination. In all likelihood he was only sizing Liam up for threats to the President. Soon, his gaze passed over to others in the crowd.

What followed was the sort of speech a public official gives at a ribbon cutting. That De Pere was a one-time military officer and a West Point graduate was clear. You could see it in his posture, in the precise way he spoke. He praised Rajan Aysana's accomplishments as an inventor, an innovator, and an industry leader, but he gave compliments to his wife Sunny as well, who was bright, funny, and an ever-present fixture at all of Rajan's public appearances.

"So it is," De Pere said while waving to the red ribbon behind him, "that I bestow the honor of opening Chicago's newest commuter line to the woman who supported her husband each and every step he took to becoming a giant of American industry."

Sunny and Rajan climbed the stairs up to the platform where Sunny, her eyes crinkling with pride, picked up a massive pair of scissors from a pedestal. The scissors looked comically large in her small hands, but Sunny didn't seem to mind. It took her a few tries, and her efforts were accompanied by a smattering of good-natured laughs, but eventually she managed to cut through the ribbon. Then she, De Pere, and Rajan were walking onto the roof of the train car, linking hands and raising them in triumph.

The crowd along both platforms cheered.

Eventually it was quiet again, and Rajan and Sunny took the stairs down. De Pere remained and walked to the edge of the stage, where he spread his arms wide and cast his gaze over the crowd.

"Good people of Illinois," he began, "there's another reason I came here today. As you're well aware, open hostilities between the United States and the nations of the St. Lawrence Pact ended ten years ago, but just because mechanika are no longer pounding over the Heartland doesn't mean we have achieved peace."

A pall fell across the crowd. Faces, so recently jubilant, turned serious.

"News of some of the heinous acts committed by the SLP have no doubt reached you. But for every one you've heard about, there are four more that, for reasons of national security, must be keep secret. The most devious among these amount to nothing less than the poisoning of the water supplies of dozens of townships and villages across New England."

Liam had heard mention of it on the wireless a few months back, but it had been a single location in Vermont, not dozens of townships and villages, which made him wonder just how many incidents had been suppressed.

At some unseen signal, the doors of the second passenger car slid open. Revealed was a table with more bunting. Behind it stood three nurses in caps and white aprons with red crosses over their chests, a common image from the war. On the table were clipboards and ordered ranks of paper cups filled with a sky blue liquid.

"The accomplishments of men like Rajan Aysana are awesome in their potential benefit to our nation." De Pere waved to the table. "But just as awesome are the achievements of our Surgeon General and his team of doctors. Among many other accomplishments, they've developed a preventive cure for the poison the SLP are attempting to inflict upon us. Mark my words, Germany and the other members of the SLP will pay for what they've done. In the meantime, we must protect ourselves, protect our *children*. The serum the nurses have ready has been tested and fully approved. Supplies are limited. Those on the East Coast are clamoring for it, but I reckoned that you, those most harmed by the SLP's final offensive a decade ago, should be among the first to receive its protections."

At this, the nurses raised the clipboards high.

"What we are offering is purely voluntary. But those who accept will have the gratitude of their government and will receive regular follow-ups from our team of doctors." De Pere paused and took in the line already starting to form in front of the table. "Well, bless your hearts, I see there's no shortage of patriots in Illinois!"

"Hooah!" cried many service members in the crowd. Others clapped.

"I thank you. Your country thanks you." De Pere gave a crisp salute. "And may God bless the United States of America."

He stepped down the stairs to applause, the loudest yet. As he made his way through the no doubt carefully selected group that surrounded him, the volunteers began filling out their forms. The first to take the offered serum, a muscular fellow with a crew cut, made the sort of face one makes on downing a spoonful of castor oil. Those who followed did the same, but were quickly clapped on the back by others. That the serum was unpleasant only seemed to enflame the crowd's enthusiasm; the lines were growing by the moment.

"What do you think?" Morgan asked, tipping his head toward the lines.

In truth, part of Liam was tempted. The SLP were ruthless enemies. But there was something about his time in the service that gave him pause. Looming in his mind was another of his scattered wartime memories: holding his arm out to a nurse dressed very much like those standing behind the table. In the memory, the nurse gripped his wrist, then injected his right arm using a syringe. He felt the pinch, then a cool sensation along his forearm as she depressed the plunger. A lightheadedness followed, then the memory faded. It was immediately replaced by a similar vision of another nurse injecting in a slightly different location along his arm. More visions flashed, one layering over the next like a flip book, as if he'd received many such injections.

Liam was doing his best to hide his dismay, but Morgan still paused, taking on that familiar look of sympathy that was one part endearing, two parts embarrassing. Liam hated being viewed like he was broken.

"I'm fine," Liam said. "You go on."

"You sure?"

"I'm sure."

Morgan nodded. "Okay, it won't take long," he said, then headed toward the back of the line.

Liam wandered to the far edge of the platform, where he wouldn't feel the crowd so acutely. As he inched closer to the down ramp, a commotion rose up in the crowd. A pretty black woman wearing a corseted woolen dress was fanning herself. She looked woozy. Then her eyes fluttered, her knees gave way, and she collapsed to the platform.

The crowd parted. Several women fanned her with their hats.

"Give her space!" shouted an elderly man. "She's only fainted."

As one of the nurses from the train headed her way, Liam heard a faint popping sound, followed by a hiss. Liam knew that sound well. It was the sound of an acetylene torch being lit.

The rail car with the nurses was ahead of him. To its right was the massive sandwich board the porter had dragged into place near the last rail car. The porter himself stood beyond the sandwich board, largely hidden from view. Shifting a few paces to his right, Liam saw the porter hunched over, close enough to the car to kiss its stainless steel side. The hissing sound grew more pronounced, as if he were welding something against the side of the car—or cutting *through* something. A few seconds later, the sound was cut suddenly short, after which Liam heard a faint, metallic clatter and saw the porter stuff his hand inside his coat pocket. Most strangely, the porter suddenly leaned to his right with a heaving motion, the sort one might use to slide a cargo door open. Except there *was* no door—he was standing at the only car that didn't have one.

Then the porter did something that made Liam feel as if he were losing his grip on reality. He walked *through* the steel.

TWO

Liam approached the rail car with wary steps, worried the porter was going to burst from it like Athena from the head of Zeus. When he was close enough, he held his hand over the steel but stopped just short of touching it. He wasn't sure what he was afraid of, but the fear was building by the moment.

"You're acting like a fool," he said under his breath, then pressed his fingers to the gleaming steel.

It was cool to the touch, and solid as could be. He moved his hand, pressing several places, while the wild memory of the porter slipping *through* the side flashed like images in a spinning zoetrope. In the years since the war, he'd had visions, like the broken battlefield, of things that wouldn't have happened to a simple mechanic. He'd often wondered if they were dreams, events his wounded mind had somehow made up. He was beginning to worry this was more of the same, that his affliction had progressed to the point he was seeing things.

Maybe the porter *hadn't* walked into the car. Maybe he'd walked away. Maybe he was in the crowd, maintaining order in the mild, celebratory chaos.

Liam turned and scanned the crowd, but the porter was nowhere to be seen. In that moment, he felt a buzzing sensation along his fingertips, which were still pressed against the steel. It felt like the Van de Graaff generator exhibit he'd touched at the World Expo last year.

He turned his attention to it, and the feeling grew stronger. Suddenly, his hand was slipping *through* the steel, just as the porter had, with the sort of tickling sensation that came with lowering one's fingers into water.

"Hey there!"

Startled, Liam snatched his hand back and turned to find Max Kohler, the man in the iron mask, headed his way.

"What are you doing there, friend?" Kohler asked. This close, his lips could be seen through the narrow breathing slits.

Fortunately, the sandwich board had blocked Kohler's view. He wouldn't have seen . . . whatever it was that had just happened.

"Nothing." Liam cringed inwardly at how pathetic that lone word had sounded—he'd never been very good at lying.

Kohler's visible eye continued to tickle a memory at the back of Liam's mind as it took in the rail car, then looked Liam up and down. "Then why were you touching the President's car?"

Liam fumbled for the right words. He considered lying but the very thought of crossing this man made him go cold.

Kohler's blue eye narrowed. With slow, deliberate care, he pulled his jacket aside and placed his hand on the butt of his Webley revolver. "I asked you a question."

"There was a man," Liam said quickly. "The porter."

"And?"

Liam had no idea how to say it. "This is going to sound mad."

"Try me."

"I saw him step into the car, *through* the side."

Liam thought Kohler would laugh, or demand that Liam explain himself. Instead, he drew the revolver in a motion that was almost too fast to follow. With a glance back, he whistled sharply. Immediately, three of the black-clad men in CIC uniforms began closing in.

"Get back," Kohler ordered Liam.

As Liam complied, Kohler faced the car and gripped the pistol with both hands. "Could it be? My old friend, Clay? I *thought* I recognized you."

Many in the crowd were inching closer, to see what was happening, until more CICs in black uniforms corralled them away.

Kohler, meanwhile, stared at the gleaming steel before him. "Come on out, Clay." His tone was light, almost playful. "There's no need to be shy."

From inside the car, the porter scoffed. "You know me better than that, Max. The last thing I am is shy."

A muzzle flashed through the suddenly semi-transparent steel as the report of a firearm pierced the noise of the crowd. The round caught Kohler dead in the chest. He flew backward, arms flailing.

As Kohler fell onto the platform, grasping at his chest, the porter named Clay emerged from inside the car, *through* the steel, and a collective gasp rose up from the crowd. Clay held a tommy gun in one hand. His other arm was wrapped around a wooden box marked with a red cross. Liam hadn't noticed it earlier, but a soft hiss accompanied Clay's movements, like a leaking air pump. Pointing the gun at the platform's frosted glass roof, Clay squeezed the trigger. The gun kicked as it fired round after round, shattering panel after panel.

As glass rained down, the crowd screamed and tried to push to the edge of the platform, out from under the shards. They rushed to the exit ramps while three agents in black whisked the President to the safety of the first train car.

Clay, meanwhile, spun and pounded over the platform toward the end of the train.

The three nearest CICs lifted their sidearms and fired. One round pierced the box Clay was carrying, causing wood and blue liquid to spray from the point of impact. Several more bullets punched through the tail of his long black coat. Another hit him in the center of his back, accompanied by a spark and a sound like a bullet ricocheting off metal, as if he were wearing armor.

At the end of the car, Clay leapt to the tracks and began tearing along them. Liam was confused until he spotted, fifty yards ahead, four men in gray clothes crouched along the tracks. Like Clay, they gripped tommy guns with round ammunition drums beneath. No doubt they were members of the Uprising, a group whose stated goal was "to expose the evils the government had committed, both during and after the war." Near the four men, a pair of ropes snaked down from the elevated track—their planned escape route, apparently.

The CICs emptied their pistols from the chaos of the platform. They fired at Clay and his Uprising allies, but the men on the tracks shot back. A hail of bullets—buzzing, whining, pinging—streaked over the crowd.

Their aim was conspicuously high, however, as if they were purposefully avoiding hitting anyone.

Suddenly Morgan was at Liam's side. He had a Browning pistol in his hand, which he proceeded to unload in wild fashion, firing over and over at the men crouched on the tracks.

In response, one of the men adjusted his tommy gun's aim until it was pointed straight at Morgan.

"Morgan, get down!" Liam grabbed him by the back of his coat and yanked hard.

Morgan tipped over and fell in an awkward heap.

The man on the tracks let off round after round. Liam could almost feel the bullets ready to punch into his flesh, or Morgan's, but they never struck. Something had blurred past them. It was Alastair, now kneeling in front of Morgan. Bullets tore into his chest. Sparks flew as they careened off his steel skull. One punched through his left arm, causing red hydraulic fluid to leak, a mechanikal analog for blood. The arm went slack.

By then, Clay had reached his allies. All four of them began an ordered retreat down along the ropes. Gunfire continued for a few more moments, but it became more sporadic, then stopped altogether, both sides abandoning their efforts when they realized the conflict was over.

"Were you hit?" Liam asked Morgan.

Morgan looked himself over, as if he wasn't quite sure. "No."

"What on earth made you *do* that?" Liam asked. "And why the hell are you carrying a gun?"

"For *protection*, Liam!"

"Well, your *protection* nearly got you killed."

Morgan looked angry, but then his eyes shifted to the place where the Uprising agents had been crouched. He took in the shattered glass spread all across the platform with a look of shock, as if the sheer recklessness of his actions was just beginning to dawn on him. He spotted his parents approaching a moment later. After shoving the Browning pistol into its shoulder holster under his jacket, he stood and met them halfway.

Liam thought surely the President's man, Kohler, was dead, but he wasn't. He was conscious and probing the hole in his vest where the bullet had struck. Beneath the fabric, Liam caught sight of some darker material—bulletproof armor of some sort. A moment later, he was helped to his feet by the nearby CICs.

"I'm *fine!*" he roared, and shoved them away.

Favoring his left side, Kohler made his way into the first train car and order slowly returned. The people who'd begun flooding the ramps in hopes of escape had been stopped. The security personnel assigned to the President had prevented them from leaving. Liam reckoned they were planning on questioning everyone about the attack.

One of the CICs, a red-cheeked Scotsman, motioned Liam toward the train. "This way."

Morgan and his parents were nearby. The couple appeared shaken. Sunny nodded and smiled her crinkly smile, her way of offering Liam solace and encouragement. Liam nodded back, then scanned the crowd for the pretty black woman, the one who'd fainted, but she was nowhere to be seen.

Liam was led to a compartment within the first car. It was open and spacious, with only a few leather seats spaced about. The compartment's lone occupant was President De Pere.

Liam, feeling intensely nervous, took off his cap. "Mr. President."

De Pere had one leg crossed over the other in a casual pose. "I hear you witnessed our enemy break into the last car."

"That's correct, sir."

De Pere motioned to the empty chair across from him. "Please."

Liam took the chair and rolled his flat cap up, feeling more than a little inadequate. "They were part of the Uprising, then?"

"Oh, most assuredly." De Pere smoothed down his pant leg. "Tell me what you saw."

Liam did so, going into detail as De Pere asked very specific questions. By the time he was done, he felt like he'd explained every single facet of it.

"You seem to know a lot about firearms," De Pere said casually. "You serve?"

"A corporal in the 128th Infantry. Yes, sir."

De Pere smiled. "My very own. You see time in the trenches?"

"No, I was a grease monkey. Serviced clankers, mostly. A few hoppers. The odd wallbuster."

De Pere smiled the sort of smile serviceman shared only with one another. "You were assigned to Fort Sheridan, then?"

"Yes." Liam shrugged. "Maybe elsewhere."

De Pere looked confused. "*Maybe* elsewhere?"

"I took a wound to the head, sir, near the end of the war. Most of it's a blur now."

De Pere stared at him hard, and Liam suddenly felt as if he'd been placed under a microscope. "Well," De Pere said, and the feeling vanished, "your country thanks you for your service. Tell me again how the man, Clay, broke in through the door of the last car."

Liam paused. "As I said, sir, he *didn't* break in through the door. There *was* no door."

"Mmmhmm." De Pere nodded as if he weren't at all perturbed by the contradiction. "Tell me about it, the door."

Something strange happened in the moments that followed. Liam found himself questioning his own memories. He thought back to the train car, to Clay standing beside it, his body blocking whatever sort of torch he'd been using to cut through what Liam assumed was a lock. He thought of how Clay had stepped into the car, and realized it wasn't through the wall, but a proper, sliding door, just like the other cars had.

Liam thought he should be surprised at this strange turn of events, but found that he wasn't. Not in the least. How could someone have gone through solid steel anyway? He'd clearly seen it wrong.

"The doors were the same as the other cars," Liam found himself saying, "except they were padlocked."

De Pere nodded. "Go on."

"The porter used some sort of miniaturized acetylene torch to cut through the lock, then he went inside."

"And when he re-emerged?"

"He caught your man, Kohler, unawares, standing in the shadows as he was."

They continued like this, De Pere asking clarifying questions, Liam becoming more and more certain that Clay had entered the car through a sliding door—indeed, that the door had been there the entire time.

He was dismissed a short while later. He returned and spoke with Morgan and his parents. He spoke to others nearby as well about the strange assault. Some, as Liam had been, were certain Clay had emerged through solid steel, but the President was speaking to more witnesses. As others emerged from those interviews, they corroborated Liam's story. More and more, the crowd came to understand what Liam already did: that this was a tragic attack perpetrated by the Uprising, and that nothing untoward, nothing bizarre, had happened beyond that.

As Liam got into the Phaeton with the entire Aysana family, and Alastair, wounded arm and all, drove them toward the Aysana estate for the planned celebration, it was with the feeling that justice would be done, that the government would catch the perpetrators of this terrible crime, and all would be well in America.

THREE

Five days later, Liam stood in the workshop of the Aysana estate's expansive garage. It was a warm, humid day. The nearby door, propped open with a brick, revealed massive white clouds and a sky so blue it made the heart ache. He stood before a repair cradle, tightening the last bolt on Alastair's new arm, which was made of pristine brass and polished steel. The new arm looked out of place, what with the deep gouges and dents left by the bullets on Alastair's chest and skull plate, not to mention the small scuffs and scratches that naturally came over time. Adding to the discordant feel was the five-barrel Gatling built into the forearm. Rajan Aysana was no fan of guns and had long been loath to add the Gatling to Alastair's kit, but he'd asked Liam to order the part the day after the attack during the ceremony.

"Almost there, Alastair."

Alastair didn't respond. He *couldn't* respond. His eyes glowed softly blue, on and off, the indicator that he was in his quiescent state, which was used to recharge his power cells and for the occasional repair.

On a shelf above, a wireless filled the workspace with the bold sounds of new-era jazz. The song faded to a hiss, replaced by the scratchy, nasally voice of the station's newscaster.

"Breaking news, Chicagoans! Less than a week after the harrowing attack in Forest Park, the CIC, your Central Intelligence Corps, has apprehended two of the perpetrators of the attempted assassination of President Leland De Pere. Both men have been identified as members of the hated Uprising, who of late have intensified their attacks on freedom, justice, and the American way."

With a glance toward the wireless, Liam paused in his work. The attack hadn't been an assassination attempt, but a theft. The Uprising's agent, the porter named Clay, had taken a wooden box, presumably filled with the serum the nurses had been administering to the volunteers. But it wasn't only that that was giving Liam pause. There was something odd about his talk with President De Pere, something that wasn't quite right, but for the life of him he couldn't put his finger on it.

The newscaster continued with breathless verve, "Your capital of Novo Solis—indeed, these entire United States—needs your help more than ever, citizens. Stay vigilant. Stay loyal to one another. Report any and all suspicious activity to local authorities or the CIC immediately."

After taking a deep drink of the tart lemonade Ms. Aysana had brought, Liam finished connecting the hydraulic tubes and began the bleeding process. When he was done, he wiped away the excess oil with a rag and reconnected the braided electrical wires that powered the arm's sensors. When he was satisfied, he pressed the series of buttons inside Alastair's chest that would initiate his startup sequence.

"We take a moment to mark the one-year anniversary of the abduction of famed inventor and neo-medicine pioneer, Stasa Kovacs," said the announcer. "We pray for his safe return and hope that his kidnappers will be brought to justice."

A brief pause.

"And now we bring you George Gershwin's latest, 'Someone to Watch Over Me,' courtesy of Kovacs Power and Light."

As violins eased the listener into the song, Alastair's head twitched and his eyes lit solid blue. With a whirring sound, he unhooked himself from the repair rig. He flexed his arm at the elbow, then gave his fingers a pianist's roll. He spun the barrels of the Gatling until they whined. "Having a weapon feels most strange, Master Mulcahey."

Liam knew what he meant. It felt peculiar to have heavy armaments so *at the ready*. "The arm feels good, though?"

"Yes, I suppose it does." His gaze shifted to the opposite arm, then to his chest and legs. "Almost too good. It makes the rest of me feel old!"

Liam smiled. "I could rough it up for you if you'd like."

"Oh, no, sir." Alastair twisted the arm back and forth as if he were admiring a new pair of gloves. "I'd rather *something* on me remain unblemished."

Liam's smile faded as he tried and failed to stifle his memories of the war. "I know what you mean."

Liam had just finished the button sequence that would save Alastair's current state to memory when Morgan walked through the door.

"Well, *someone's* looking better," Liam said.

"*Feeling* better too!"

Morgan had been dealing with some sort of stomach bug the last few days. It was curious that the symptoms had started the day after the fire-fight at the flashtrain ceremony—the day after he'd taken the serum the government nurses had been administering—but fortunately he seemed to be on the mend. He was almost back to his old, energetic self.

"So it's done?" Morgan asked as he leaned against the nearby work-bench and crossed one ankle over the other. "Our Alastair's fresh as a new-minted nickel?"

"Well, I don't know about *that*, sir," Alastair said, "but I can certainly return to duty immediately."

"Smashing!" Morgan clapped his hands and rubbed them together vigorously. "We'll be heading into the city tonight, Alastair."

Alastair's eyes brightened. "A special occasion?"

"Indeed!" Morgan goggled at Liam through his long bangs. "We're celebrating Liam's birthday."

"Oh, very good, sir." Alastair headed toward a doorway, which led to the open space where the family's cars were kept. "I'll prepare the Phaeton."

When he was gone, Morgan put on a hopeful smile. "*Please* say you'll come."

Liam began wiping down his tools. "My birthday was four weeks ago."

"True, but you had conflicts and postponed. And then we had the at-tack. It's well past time we celebrated properly."

"You've been sick all week," Liam said as he sleeved the wrenches into their pockets in his old canvas bag.

"Yes, but as we've already established, I'm feeling better. And besides, I seem to recall Dr. Ramachandra advising you to get out more. I believe the words, 'It'd do you good,' were used."

Dr. Ramachandra was the Aysana family physician. After Liam had admitted to feeling a bit *too* isolated, Morgan had arranged for Liam to see him.

"I know," Liam said, "but—"

"I also seem to recall you asking me to *push* you into following his advice."

"Yes, but the attack . . . It has me on edge. And you know how crowds get to me."

"Which is why our dinner reservations are at the Blackstone. It's always quiet there. Then we'll go to a speakeasy. The best one in town. They have this quiet corner. We'll make camp there. We'll listen to a little jazz."

"We'll drink a little absynthe . . . ?"

"Absynthe. Whiskey. You can have whatever you like. And *Geraldine* is going to be there. You can finally meet her!"

As always, Morgan's eyes lit up the moment he started talking about Geraldine, Mayor Burgess's daughter. Morgan had been wooing her for months.

There were times when Liam felt uncomfortable with Morgan's generosity. He often acted like the big brother Liam never had, except he *wasn't* Liam's big brother. They were the same age. They'd grown *up* together. If anything, Liam was the voice of reason to Morgan's impetuousness.

He cares for you, a voice inside Liam said. *Is that so bad?*

He supposed it wasn't, but just then the thought of going to a speakeasy— the oppressive smoke in those places, the low lights, the *noise*—made him feel defenseless. "Another time," he finally said. "I promise."

For a moment Morgan looked like he was going to argue, but then he stopped himself, clapped Liam's shoulder, and nodded. "Another time."

Morgan had always been generous with his time, money, and affection. But just then his sympathy was too much for Liam. "See you tomorrow," he said, then slung his bag over his shoulder and left the garage.

Alastair often drove Liam to and from the nearby train station in Evanston, but Liam could just as easily walk. At the center of the village, he hopped on the flashtrain and took it to the small Irish community of

North Town, just outside Chicago's downtown. From the corner grocer he bought a small bag of potatoes, a head of cabbage, butter, parsley, and a smoked ham hock, then headed up to the tiny three-room apartment he shared with his grandmother.

"Colcannon, Nana?"

Liam's parents had died on the return to New York from their one and only trip to the Emerald Isle, their steamer sinking off the coast of Newfoundland in a freak storm. He had lived with his Nana from the age of fourteen. After the war, it had been Liam's turn to take care of her. Though her real name was Ashling, Ashling Mulcahey, most called her Grandma Ash. To Liam, however, she was and had always been Nana.

He heard creaking floorboards from down the hall. A door opened, and there came the familiar sound of shuffling. Nana appeared in her pink robe and slippers, looking not chipper, exactly, but not exhausted, either. Most days Liam would call that a victory, what with the gout and asthma that plagued her, but there was a darkness in her eyes, a grimness in the crooked set of her mouth.

"What's wrong?" he asked.

"Not what's wrong with me, sonny boy," she said in Irish. "It's what's wrong with *you*."

He took a deep breath and set the stock pot under the tap to fill. How she always seemed to sense his moods he'd never know. After lighting the stove and putting the potatoes on to boil, he sat across from her.

Her look pierced him, accused him. Part of Liam felt that Nana's insights, her strange empathy, should bother him, but it had been like this since he'd moved back in with her after the war and begun the slow recovery from his head wound.

"I didn't want to go, all right?" he finally said, the note of defensiveness in his voice stronger than he'd meant it to be.

"Live a little, Liam. No sense you staying here with an old woman who's got one foot in the grave when there's free whiskey in the offing."

"You need care, Nana." He waved to the ham on the cutting board. "Who's going to make you food?"

She made a disgusted noise, then tore a crust of bread from yesterday's loaf and began nibbling on it. "So make the food and go. Be with your friend." She leaned forward and snatched his left hand, the one holding the cleaver, ready to chop the ham. "Damnation, boyo, I willn't *break*."

As her hand began to warm his, he was whisked away to that dark field, the one that haunted him so.

It was the beginning of a battle, a turning point late in the war. He wore a doughboy's uniform, complete with helmet, trench coat, leather boots, and leggings. The Springfield rifle with its bayonet had a hefty sort of balance that felt familiar, as comforting as his grandmother's colcannon. But now he was strapped into a hopper exoskeleton. Hoppers were battle suits, the sort of equipment he'd been trained how to *fix*, not operate. It had locust legs, blue canisters peeking over his shoulders, and reinforced hydraulic tubes running everywhere. He felt like a creature straight out of an Edgar Rice Burroughs's Mars novel.

Liam and his squad mates crouched low in a long, winding trench. He'd always assumed his picking up a rifle and fighting in that last battle had been born of his military commanders' desperation, but these didn't feel like people he'd just met. They felt like men and women he'd go to hell and back for.

A name drifted up from his subconscious: the Devil's Henchmen, a squad that had trained together for months in anticipation of this, the major offensive they'd been expecting from the SLP.

Coils of barbed wire and massive steel girders—crow's talons, meant to slow the advance of armored vehicles—complicated the battlefield's muddy landscape. Past that battered wasteland, occluding everything that lay beyond, loomed a thick bank of fog. Pounding came from deep within it. Red lamps, distant but growing larger and brighter by the moment, made it look as though the gates of hell were cracking open and demons were spilling forth.

Liam gripped his rifle, prepared to rise from the trench when the signal was given. He heard a familiar whirring as he adjusted the stance of his powered armor. The earth shifted beneath his feet. A low pounding rattled his bones. The red lights continued to expand, devouring the fog as it billowed, consuming the broken landscape.

Not a single soldier along their line made a sound. All were ready, tense, a host of hornets ready to swarm the enemy.

When the first of the enemy goliaths lumbered free, a voice echoed inside Liam's head.

—*Ready, you cheap, dime-store motherfuckers?*

It was the voice of his CO, calling to Liam and his fellow Henchmen through the power of telepathy.

—*Yes, sir!* came the response from Liam and the rest of the squad.

United, connected, each member was an individual but very much a part of the whole. The Devil's Henchmen were a machine, no less than the goliaths pounding toward their position.

Silhouettes, tall as grain towers, loomed in the fog. Massive armored heads with red lamps for eyes were the first to break through. They had cannons for right arms, Gatlings mounted where their left forearms should be. They plodded forward. Their crimson gazes swept the landscape, their heavy Gatlings following.

They were German mechanika, sent by the SLP to lay waste to America's lines. And yet, for all their power, they weren't prepared for what Liam and the others were about to unleash upon them. Not by a country mile.

—*Now!* their CO ordered.

As one, the Henchmen rose, twenty of them in all. They swarmed ahead, bounding over all obstacles, prepared to deliver death. Giving the legs of his hopper a boost of power, Liam flew toward the nearest goliath.

The cleaver slipped from Liam's hand. It clattered against the cutting board, scattering ham everywhere. Slowly, the world of the small apartment returned—the delicate furniture, the quaint, framed photographs of his family.

His hands shook as he retrieved the cleaver and picked up the fallen ham. The beat of his heart was so loud he was sure Nana could hear it. It sounded like the rattle of a distant Gatling.

With sadness in her eyes and a melancholy smile, Nana said, "Go. Tie one on with Morgan."

Liam managed to slow his breathing. He bunched his hands into fists, steadying them. He couldn't understand why, but these odd spells of memory had become unbearably more vivid in the days since the firefight at the train station.

Trying to restore some normalcy, he said, "How would you know about *tying one on*?"

A twisted smile broke out over her crooked mouth, revealing the imperfect lines of her teeth. It was a devious look, one that, strangely, did much to calm Liam's nerves. "What you don't know about me, boyo, could fill a fecking library!"

"Nana!"

A rare laugh, a tumble of bricks. "Go, sweetpea. Loosen up for a change."

"Can't," Liam shot back, starting in on the ham again. "Morgan's already gone."

Leaning back in that creaking chair of hers, a Cheshire cat grin spread across her face. Seconds later, a high-pitched whine filtered in through the nearby window—the familiar sound of Morgan's Phaeton. Liam stood and drew the curtain back as the chrome-laden sedan rounded the corner grocer. The neighborhood boys stared as it pulled up in front of Liam's building, its horn emitting a sequence of notes tuned to Sidney Bechet's latest jazz hit, "Cake Walking Babies."

Nana was always doing things like this, knowing things she had no business knowing. "How, Nana?"

Nana winked. "Nana knows more'n you think, doesn't she?"

"That she does." He could see Alastair at the wheel. Morgan, meanwhile, stepped out onto the curb and waved up. Liam nodded to him while saying to Nana, "What about the colcannon?"

He turned to find that she'd already turned off the now-done boiling pot of potatoes, shifted the cutting board around to her, and taken up the cleaver. "The day I can't make a pot of colcannon is the day they put me in the ground and throw dirt on my face, sonny boy."

Liam kissed her on the head, then hurried off to change into his best suit.

"I was just headed downtown," Morgan said sheepishly as Liam stepped out of the apartment building's criminally narrow entrance hall. "I thought I'd give it one last try."

"Fine," Liam said. "You win. Let's go see what this speakeasy of yours is all about."

"You won't regret it, I promise, but"—Morgan looked him up and down—"is that what you're wearing?"

Morgan was decked to the nines in an impeccably tailored brown pin-striped suit, rich leather wingtips, and a navy blue homburg.

Liam shrugged to hide his embarrassment. "This is all I've got."

"No, no, no, it just won't do." Morgan stepped aside and motioned to the open car door with a theatrical flourish. "I never got you your birthday present. We're going to make amends right now."

Liam didn't know what to say. He felt foolish, a shy boy faced with his first day at a new school, but Morgan's smile was infectious.

"If you insist," Liam finally said.

"I do! Now let's hurry. We're painting the town red tonight!"

A momentary vision of the goliaths, towering, lumbering from a red-rimmed mist. Part of him wanted to understand how he'd become a member of the Henchmen, how so much of the war could have been lost to him, but that was a problem for another day. He blinked the vision away and hopped into the car, but not before giving the staring neighborhood boys a wink.

As the boys laughed and gawped, Morgan filed in, pulled the door closed with a satisfying click, and slapped the front seat twice. "Onward, Alastair."

"Very good, sir," Alastair said. With a satisfied purr, the Phaeton accelerated.

A block behind the maroon Phaeton, a black delivery wagon pulled away from the curb. Within were a pair of serious-looking men, no longer in the CIC uniforms they had worn when the flashtrain ceremony had been attacked.

The wagon stayed behind the Phaeton all the way to the streets of downtown Chicago.

FOUR

The Phaeton delivered Morgan and Liam to the Aysanas' personal tailor. Liam entered with woolen trousers and a coat a bit threadbare at the elbows and left wearing a chestnut three-piece. His new wingtips were the finest things he'd ever owned, made of a leather so lustrous he worried with every step he was going to scuff them. The only thing he kept was his tweed cap—he needed *something* to keep from feeling like he was living a complete lie.

Dinner at the Blackstone Hotel came next. The meal was easily the best thing Liam had eaten in years. His baked potato was crisp on the outside, fluffy on the inside, and topped with a mouthwatering combination of sour cream, chives, and crumbly bacon. As undeniably delicious as it was, it couldn't hold a candle to the massive, juicy porterhouse that came along with it. Liam had been tense on the ride into the city, but by the time the plates had been cleared and he and Morgan were enjoying cups of coffee, Liam found he was actually relaxed.

Morgan, on the other hand, had seemed fine at the tailors but now looked poorly.

"Stomach bothering you?" Liam asked.

"Yeah, but it'll pass." Morgan pressed a hand to his belly as the hum of conversation cocooned them. "It gets worse with rich food."

A poor decision in hindsight, Morgan had opted for the veal marsala with buttery mashed potatoes. Rich food or not, though, Liam was concerned about the underlying cause of Morgan's sickness.

"Did you call the number the nurses gave you?" Liam asked.

Morgan rolled his eyes. "Mother did. They said it might be the flu, but that a bit of cramping isn't uncommon with the serum. They said to call again in a few days if it hadn't passed." Suddenly pensive, he began twisting his gold-rimmed cup in its saucer. "I know it hasn't even been a week since the attack, but I swear, it feels like a month."

Liam shook his head, remembering it. "You should have seen yourself, standing there blasting bullets like a raw recruit."

Morgan laughed, as if he couldn't quite believe it himself. "I don't know what came over me. I was just so angry they'd ruined the ceremony Papa had worked so hard for."

"Where'd you get that pea shooter anyway?"

Morgan pulled the right flap of his coat aside, revealing the butt of the Browning. "You mean this one?"

"Yes, *that one*." He'd spotted the shoulder holster at the tailor's. "You sure you know how to handle that thing?"

Morgan pretended to be aghast. "I was in the Army, sir!"

"Behind a comms desk."

"Well, yes, there is that." Morgan relaxed, then shrugged. "But one can't be too careful these days." He scanned the dining room in mock suspicion. "The Uprising are everywhere."

Liam paused, feeling suddenly self-conscious. He hadn't planned on mentioning his talk with the President, but since Morgan had already brought it up . . . "Does anything feel strange about your talk with De Pere?"

"Strange how?"

"My memories are all a-jumble, like a puzzle that's been pieced together poorly. It feels as though it didn't happen like I recall."

Morgan frowned. "What do you mean?"

"Sitting with De Pere. The porter. The rail car." Liam shook his head, feeling more than a little impotent. "Something about it feels off."

"It was a wild moment. Chaotic." Morgan's look turned sympathetic. "But no, nothing feels strange about it beyond the suddenness of it all." Morgan glanced up at a passing busboy, waited for him to pass, then lowered his voice. "Things have been better, haven't they, with your head wound?"

For years, Liam had not only had trouble remembering the war itself, he'd had trouble putting things in the right order. Memories seemed to rearrange themselves in his mind. It made him feel broken, as if *he* were the puzzle that had been pieced together poorly.

"Yes, it's been better," Liam said.

"The laudanum helps, doesn't it?"

Dr. Ramachandra had prescribed it after Liam's consultation. "It helps me sleep, which helps me think."

"And have you been taking it?"

"Thank you for asking"—Liam downed the last of his coffee in one swallow—"but I already have a grandmother. Now, I believe there was a rather respectable jazz establishment we were about to visit."

"Jazz . . ." Morgan cleared his throat with a wide-eyed, Buster Keaton glare. "Yes, best we get to it!"

Night had fallen over the city while they were dining. With the jazz club only a few blocks from the Blackstone, they decided to walk off a bit of their meal. A few turns and several gusty streets later, they arrived at an importer-exporter's office. Inside, standing behind a long counter, was a rakish fellow wearing a chalk-striped suit and a strong five o'clock shadow. As the door jingled shut, he gave Morgan a deferential nod. "Mr. Aysana."

Though it was clearly pro forma at this point, Morgan pulled a card from his billfold and held it up for the man to see. Printed on the cream-colored paper was a stylized design of a woman firing a bow and a name: Club Artemis.

The man behind the counter gave it no more than a cursory glance. "Enjoy your evening, gentlemen."

With a tip of his homburg, Morgan led Liam toward the back of the office and down a sloping tunnel. At the end of it was a baby grand of an attendant sitting on a stool near a rolling door. "Welcome back, Mr. Aysana."

He stood and patted Liam—only Liam—down for weapons, then heaved the door aside. Revealed was Club Artemis, Chicago's most exclusive speakeasy, a place that rivaled even the famed Room 21. The main room, a converted wine cellar with walls of Cream City brick, had rounded ceilings, arched doorways, and elegantly curved supports on the chairs. Glass globes hanging from the ceiling emitted a low diffusion of golden light from their corkscrew filaments. Arched wall niches held bronze statues sculpted in the Deco style.

A lively hum pervaded the place, with clutches of smartly dressed men and women talking, sitting, drinking. The women wore flapper dresses or formal gowns, most fringed or beaded or both. Some wore tiaras, others complex, feathered headdresses. A couple, a pair of real Oliver Twists, danced to the lively number played by the jazz quintet in the corner.

Morgan was greeted by several people. He gave them each a wave, a quick word, but all too soon he'd herded Liam and a handful of friends to a small, quiet table in the far corner. Liam and Morgan sat on a blue velvet sofa, the others on tufted chairs. Throughout the evening, the men—Liam, Morgan, and a lanky banker with dirty blond hair and offset eyes named Charlie—mostly ordered whiskey and water. Elle, the daughter of a shipping magnate, and her pretty friend, Violet, had Gin Rickeys and Sidecars and some drink called "the Mary Pickford" that'd been making the rounds in New York, Boston, and Philadelphia. They drank. They talked. They smoked cigars, even Violet and Elle.

Though Liam was wearing his new suit, it was clear after only a few minutes of conversation that he couldn't rub elbows with these people. The conversations kept drifting toward stock market trades and polo and pleasure trips to Martha's Vineyard or America's renamed capital, Novo Solis. But Morgan, bless him, always steered the conversation to topics Liam could participate in. Stock market trades became talk of finding hidden gems at antique markets, which Liam liked to frequent. Polo shifted to conversations about horses, which Liam had always had an affinity for. And talk of travel naturally drifted to the transformations seen in the Midwest in the decade since the armistice had been signed. The war hadn't taken Liam particularly far, but he shared a bit about Milwaukee, where he'd been stationed—how it had gone from an up-and-coming Midwestern city to a bombed-out husk and back again.

"Oh, we're *much* too glum!" Violet chimed in. "I resolve we have no more talk of the war. Do I have a second?"

"Seconded!" shouted Charlie, who'd already had rosy cheeks when Liam and Morgan arrived.

Violet slapped the table soundly. "All in favor?"

Ayes all around, drinks raised, then laughter.

"Motion carried!" Violet said. She proceeded to launch into a pitch-perfect rendition of "I Wish I Could Shimmy Like My Sister Kate," the jazz tune the quintet was playing.

As everyone listened, Liam leaned toward Morgan and spoke softly, "I dare say, old chum, you've chosen your friends well."

Morgan reeled. His mouth fell open. His bangs hanging unruly over one eye, he looked Liam up and down as if he couldn't believe his ears. "Liam Mulcahey, are you telling me you *like* them?"

Liam shrugged. "Maybe."

Morgan goggled his eyes. "Are you having *fun?*"

The smile that had been threatening to break over Liam's face finally did. "So what if I am?"

Morgan clapped him on the shoulder with a laugh.

Liam surprised even himself when Elle convinced him to sing a song. He led them in a rendition of "Whiskey in the Jar," a song his grandmother had taught him as a boy. It was one of his earliest memories of her. When he was done, they all clapped, and Morgan proceeded to murder "A Drink in the Morning."

As Morgan's song was winding down, a woman stepped into the main room from the darkened entrance tunnel, and the entire speakeasy seemed to take note. She wore a golden dress with silver and rust-colored beads in a design of butterflies and cherry blossoms. The dress's long, flaring skirt was connected to a bracelet she wore on her right wrist, creating a bold curve whenever she lifted her arm. Her blonde hair was aggressively waved and held in place by a pearl bandeau, and her lips were painted red, almost violently so, yet somehow it only served to enhance the creamy complexion of her skin.

She waited at the bar for a drink that Liam was sure she hadn't bothered to order, a martini with a lemon twist, then wandered toward a high-top table and kissed cheeks with a handsome, dark-skinned fellow. As she spoke, her gaze swept over the room. Morgan waved to her. She waved back.

Then her eyes met Liam's. And time froze.

Her expression was pleasant, giving little away, and yet Liam had the unmistakable feeling she was seeing him, *truly* seeing him, just as he was—not as the shell of a man who had returned from the war but the one who'd entered it, bright-eyed and hopeful, ready to defend his homeland with his life if need be. As he had during his talk with President De Pere, Liam felt exposed, but where De Pere had seemed predatory, this woman seemed merely intrigued, as if he were an enigma in need of solving. It was an absurd notion, he knew, but there it was.

"Her name is Grace Savropoulis," Morgan said. "She's an heiress from the east coast who comes to Chicago from time to time."

As Morgan spoke, Grace broke away from the man she'd been chatting with and sashayed toward their table. "I see the gang's all here."

"That we are"—Morgan suddenly shifted on the sofa, creating space between him and Liam—"but we're woefully incomplete." He waved to the open space on the cushions. "Won't you join us?"

Grace's thin eyebrows rose as she took everyone in, effectively asking the group's permission. "I won't be intruding?"

Elle stood and took Grace's hand. "You're joking, of course. You've done us a favor." She led Grace to the open space on the sofa between Liam and Morgan, then pressed her gently back until she'd sat down. "There, you see? Now we're even. Three boys, three girls."

Liam felt his cheeks warm, but thankfully Violet launched into a story of a recent boating expedition in Lake Geneva, giving him time to recover.

They drank more drinks, sang more songs. Violet even led Charlie out to the dance floor, where Charlie, against all probability, threw off his drunkenness and made a passable go at the Charleston. Morgan, still hoping to see Geraldine, kept glancing at the entryway.

For Liam's part, he was acutely aware of Grace. He felt her shifting on the cushions, felt the heat of her arm next to his. She mostly talked with Elle and Morgan, but at a pause in the conversation, she turned to Liam. "Morgan tells me you're a mechanic."

Liam tried to hide his surprise that she knew anything about him at all but was certain he'd failed miserably. "Strange, I don't recall him mentioning it."

Grace flashed a smile. "Not tonight. I saw him a few nights ago, and your name came up." She leaned in and spoke in a low voice. "You might not have noticed, but Morgan has the gift of gab."

Though somewhat annoyed Morgan had gone out for drinks while sick, Liam couldn't help but laugh at Grace's comment. "I don't know that I'd call it a *gift*, exactly."

"What *would* you call it, then?"

"An affliction." Liam jutted his chin toward Morgan, who was regaling Elle with a retelling of the firefight, entirely overplaying his part in it. "The man can hardly help himself."

They listened to Morgan's tale for a few moments, then Grace, with a sip of her martini, turned back to Liam. "Rumor has it you had a conversation with the President himself."

Part of Liam wished Morgan hadn't mentioned it, but he was hardly surprised. The attack was all Chicago seemed to be talking about. Plus, his heart had swelled to twice its size the moment Grace started talking to him. He didn't much care what they talked about, so long as they continued doing so. "In all honestly," he finally said, "it felt more like a deposition."

Grace nodded. "De Pere can be a rather intense man at times."

"You know him?"

She smiled wryly. "Our paths may have crossed once or twice."

Just then, the barman, a roguish fellow with a handlebar mustache, stopped by and whispered in Morgan's ear. Morgan's face fell, then he whispered something back. The two exchanged a few more whispered phrases, then the barman nodded and left.

"What's wrong, darling?" Elle asked.

"As it happens, Geraldine has been detained."

Charlie immediately perked up. "Time for our flight, then?"

He meant the flight of absynthe, Liam understood.

Elle slapped Charlie's arm. "You're such a boor when you're half under. Can't you see Morgan's in pain?"

With great effort, it seemed, Charlie cleared his throat and focused his gaze on Morgan, "And for that I am most sorry, but it's all the more reason to retire to the back."

Elle slapped him again, and this time Violet joined her.

Whether they'd meant it to or not, their defense of him made Morgan laugh. "It's all right. I've told the barman to get everything ready." He turned to Grace. "I hope you'll join us?"

"And take Geraldine's place?" Grace took in the whole group. "Now I really *do* feel like an interloper." At the chorus of boos and shaking heads, Grace smiled and nodded gratefully. "Well, then I thank you. I don't mind if I do!"

As everyone stood and made their way to the red door at the back of the speakeasy, Liam tugged on Morgan's sleeve and spoke in a low voice. "I'm sorry about Geraldine. I really was looking forward to meeting her."

Morgan patted him on the back. "Another time," he said, then headed after the others.

Liam, meanwhile, paused as the barman pushed through a set of swinging doors that led to the kitchen. For just a moment, before the doors swung shut, he saw a black woman, the spitting image of the one who'd fainted on the flashtrain platform.

"You coming, Liam?" Grace called.

Liam nodded to her, then gazed back at the doors. As their swinging slowed then stopped, he got one last look into the kitchen, but saw no one.

Just your imagination, Liam thought, and headed toward Grace.

FIVE

The barman, apparently having gone through some other entrance, opened the red door from the opposite side. "Welcome," he said, and waved them all in.

Charlie, Elle, and Violet went first. Liam and Grace came next. Morgan, bringing up the rear, paused when the barman spoke to him in low tones. A moment later, Morgan nodded and handed him his Browning pistol. Liam felt relieved—flights of absynthe weren't known for being violent, but one never knew.

Beyond the doors was a long, narrow room. In the near corner hung a collection of brass cages that contained a veritable flock of clockwork chickadees. With soft tweets and clattering wings, they flitted on delicate bronze branches, seeming to watch Liam as he passed by.

The birds might be relics of a bygone era, but they were a nice complement to the room, which was decorated as extravagantly as the front, only along different aesthetic lines. Wrought iron artwork, bent into the shapes of vines with leaves and budding flowers, adorned the rough brick walls. Fluted pedestals were spaced about. Atop each was a clutch of empty wine bottles, candles burning in their mouths. If the front room had the feel of an architect who'd built it with painstaking care, this one had the feel of a gardener who'd coaxed it into existence.

In the center of the room was a sunken area, a conversation pit complete with a curving wooden bench, a host of red velvet cushions and pillows, and in the center, a round table. They sat on the cushions, the six of them palpably giddy with excitement. The bartender, meanwhile, having briefly left the room with Morgan's gun, returned with a large silver tray, upon which was a bottle of green liquor, a pitcher of ice water, six empty glasses, and a cellar of sugar cubes. He placed the tray on the table and, with all the flair of a carnival showman, set to work placing the glasses in an arc before him. When done, he placed a slotted silver spoon on each glass, then a sugar cube into the center of each spoon. Finally, he poured the absynthe over the sugar cube, making sure to douse the sugar completely each time.

Everyone watched, rapt. The air blossomed with the scent of fennel and anise. With a slow wave of his right hand, the bartender drew their attention to the glass closest to Violet, who had been eyeing the bartender while talking in low tones with Elle.

The bartender flicked his thumb.

Elle and Violet gasped. Liam blinked.

How he was doing it, Liam had no idea, but there was now a flame flickering at the end of his thumb. He touched it to the sugar cube, which burned with a low, blue-green flame. Like molten emeralds, the flames dripped into the glass and lit the well of absynthe, making the eerie flames rise even higher. The sugar began to melt, then bubble and caramelize.

Violet, laughing and clapping her hands, leaned into Elle beside her, but her gaze was for the bartender alone. He winked at her with a smile. One by one, he lit the other five sugar cubes. When done, he shook his hand, extinguishing the flame at the end of his thumb, then took up the pitcher of ice water. With practiced ease he poured a measure of water into each glass, dousing the flames and turning the drink to cloudy swirls as the cold water mixed with the absynthe.

After swirling each drink with the spoon atop its glass, he bowed and took up the silver tray. "Enjoy," he said, this time being sure to eye Morgan, the man paying.

Morgan took up his glass. Everyone else followed suit, all save Liam, who suddenly wished he'd gone home. The legend that had built up around absynthe was strong. Euphoria. Hallucinations. A feeling that the world was larger than it really was. He didn't need that. He knew too much about the world already. And he certainly didn't need help inducing hallucinations.

Goliaths trudging over the broken landscape. Sympathetic vibrations that spoke of savagery. The sound growing louder and louder while Liam bounded forward in his hopper exoskeleton, rifle at the ready, screaming alongside his squad, his fellow Devil's Henchmen.

"Come on, Liam," said Violet, breaking the spell.

Beside her, Elle giggled. "He's so dreamy." Liam wasn't sure if she meant his penchant for drifting away or his looks.

Morgan, meanwhile, stared at him sympathetically. "You don't have to, Liam."

More to clear his mind than in answer to Morgan, Liam glanced at Grace, who was watching him closely. She seemed expectant, as if she'd been looking forward to his joining her on this flight.

You're reading too much into it. You're hoping *she feels that way.*

He was well aware he'd only just met Grace, and yet he found he didn't want to disappoint her. Shaking his worries away, he picked up his glass and, with all the cheer he could muster, said, "To all the days here and after, may they be filled with fond memories, happiness, and laughter."

They raised their glasses high.

Even with the stories that swirled around absynthe and its effects, the liquor was stronger than Liam would've guessed. As before, they drank, talked, and laughed, but it quickly changed. The laughter came less often. As did the conversation.

Together, they took a spiral staircase to a patio on the roof, which was decorated similarly to the room below with pedestals, wine bottles, and candles. Laid out before them was the city, Lake Michigan beyond, an endless slab of slate abutting the golden, ordered lights of the city streets.

Liam felt . . . strange. Not drunk, but more aware—of *what* he wasn't sure. The others stood by a railing at the edge of the building. Some stared down at the street below, others gazed across the city, their faces lit in wonder, their eyes roving as they took in whatever vision their dose of absynthe had delivered.

For Liam, Chicago's lattice of golden lights transformed into a field of wheat, its glittering stalks tipped with soft brushes, ready for harvest. Gusts of wind sent waves over the field's surface, occasionally revealing the furrows of dark earth beneath. A short distance ahead, the wheat parted, and a silver, hourglass figure rose up. A woman he realized. Elle. Her hands cupped his cheeks as she leaned in and kissed him. He felt her lush, warm lips, her hands on his face. Part of him wished *Grace* were kissing him, but it had been a long while since he'd kissed *any* girl, and Grace surely wouldn't be interested in a man like him, so he let those worries go and kissed Elle back. For several beautiful moments, the sounds of the city faded to a susurrus, and his world was reduced to the sound of Elle's breath, the touch of her lips.

As their bodies pressed tight, Liam heard something new. A moaning. He tried to ignore it, but when it came again, he realized who it was and immediately sobered.

He pulled away from Elle, their parting lips making a soft smacking sound. He waded through the stalks of grain, separating the rows until he found Morgan on the ground, holding his stomach.

The vision faded, delivering him back to the roof above Club Artemis. "Morgan?"

Morgan looked up, his round face in such distress it nearly broke Liam's heart. "I'm not feeling so well," he said.

Liam nodded and helped his friend to his feet, then guided him back toward the stairs. Vaguely, he realized the moon, visible through the light cloud cover, had crossed half the sky. They'd been up here for *hours*. Was that even possible?

He had no time to wonder about it. As a light drizzle began to fall, he helped Morgan down the stairs. The others followed, including Elle, who was silent as they wound their way down toward the candlelit room with the pedestals. Charlie and Violet were together. Grace, however, was nowhere to be seen.

"Anyone seen Grace?" Liam asked.

Everyone shook their heads no.

As he eased Morgan onto the cushions in the conversation pit, the clockwork chickadees began chirping loudly. They flitted about their cages, moving with frenetic energy and a speed that bordered on violence. Outside the room, there came a loud bang. Then voices raised in alarm.

Something, or some*one*, Liam realized a moment later, rushed past him. The bartender Elle had been flirting with. He reached the red door, slid an eyehole open, and immediately snapped it shut.

"This way," he said, motioning everyone toward the darkened passageway in the far corner.

"Who's there?" Elle asked.

"Not sure." The bartender looked terrified. "Uprising, maybe. Just follow me." And then he was ushering them toward the rear exit.

"Morgan can't move," Liam said.

The bartender stared down at him. "Leave him or stay. Your choice." He was suddenly gone, with Violet and Charlie following him down the passageway with languid movements.

"Charlie!" Liam called.

But he only kept doddering after Violet.

It's the absynthe, Liam thought. It was the only thing that might explain their strange behavior. Liam still felt rather peculiar himself, as if his mind had been placed in fetters in some ways, while expanding in others.

As he dropped to Morgan's side, Elle strode regally in the other direction, toward the red door.

"Elle!" Liam hissed. He wanted to stop her, but he couldn't. He had his hands full getting Morgan to his feet and ushering him toward the exit. "Elle!"

She seemed oblivious to him as she unlocked the door and pulled it wide. The sound from the front room rose up. People shouting orders, others reacting with fear or anger. The birds were going mad. One cage crashed hard against the concrete floor, but the birds continued their ruckus, djinns in a bottle, billows of chaos and brass. Elle held her hand up in greeting and addressed someone Liam couldn't see from his angle.

"I'm Eleanor Ginsberg," she proclaimed in a regal tone, "the daughter of the city's comptroller."

"Elle!" Liam shouted, terrified for her, though he knew not why.

He'd just managed to get Morgan off the concrete bench when a large revolver lowered into view. The man holding it had yet to step through the doorway from the front room, but on the cuff of his gray sleeve Liam caught the sign of the Uprising: a hand with three fingers raised.

In that moment, Liam heard mumbled words—what they were he couldn't make out, and where they might be coming from he had no idea.

While facing whoever held the gun, the features of Elle's delicate face turned hard. "What are you—"

She never had a chance to finish.

Thunder filled the room. Elle's head jerked back. A spray of red splattered the wall behind her, the brass cages, and the chickadees within.

SIX

Liam nearly called out to Elle again, worried for her though he knew she was already gone.

As the gray-clad gunman stepped inside, Liam's old instincts kicked in. He'd been trying to guide Morgan out, letting him walk on his own with help, but now he squatted low and heaved Morgan across his shoulders in a fireman's carry. Morgan moaned. He was shivering badly.

Liam climbed the short set of stairs from the conversation pit and made for the back exit, but he hadn't gone three strides before the gun reported again. The sound pressed in around him as a bright line of pain seared across his right leg. He stumbled. He tried to lower Morgan as gracefully as he could, but it was impossible. Morgan tumbled away. The hollow thump of his head against the concrete was heart-stopping.

"Jesus fuck," Liam rasped.

He scrambled to Morgan's side and reached into his suit jacket for his pistol, only then remembering that the bartender had taken it before pouring the absynthe. Desperate, Liam got to his knees and grabbed a nearby pedestal. Wax dripped in waterfalls. Wine bottles fell and shattered as Liam lifted it in both hands. He turned to find the man in the gray coat advancing on him. Again Liam heard mumbling. The man leveling the gun at his head didn't speak a word—his mouth was set in a stark line, unmoving and grim—and yet Liam *felt* his intent.

Liam shifted the pedestal a split second before the gun roared. Stone shattered. The man reared back, catching a spray of scree in his face. He stumbled backward, retreating far enough that Liam couldn't easily attack him. Liam immediately began dragging Morgan away by the collar of his coat, hoping to make it into the hallway at least, but the man in gray recovered.

Spots of blood welled in cuts along his face. Blinking fiercely, he lifted his sidearm. Just then Liam heard a metallic pounding behind him. The man's attention shifted, and his eyes went wide as headlights. He adjusted his aim while backpedaling. He fired one bullet, squeezed off a second round and a third, giving ground as he moved closer to the red door behind him.

The pounding kept coming, along with an all-too-familiar whirring. From out of the darkness came a blur, a skeletal form of brass and steel. Alastair's blue, catlike eyes were eerie and depthless as he charged forward. As the man in gray unleashed another shot directly into Alastair's face, Alastair crashed into him. Hard. The man in gray flew through the air with a wheeze and a deathbed moan. He fell against the cement floor, limp, and slid another fifteen feet until he met the wall near the sliding door with a meaty thump. There he lay, unmoving, blood trickling from a deep gash to his nose and cheek. Liam couldn't tell if he was breathing or not.

Alastair turned, eyes aglow, his silhouette infinitely more aggressive than Liam had ever witnessed him having. "It's time for you and Master Aysana to go," he said, his voice oddly inflected, echoing against the room's harsh surfaces. He whirred forward, helped lift Morgan up and balance him across Liam's shoulders once more. "Wait for me in the alley, sir. I'll be along shortly with the Phaeton." He gave Liam a shove—just enough to get him moving. Liam's final look back showed Alastair stepping into the front room, the massive door ramming closed, and sparks flying near the latch as Alastair used the torch built into his forearm to seal the way shut.

The hall ahead of Liam was painted black and lit with dim red light bulbs, making it look as though it were dripping with blood. Liam had made it halfway along when more shots rang out. Shouts of surprise followed, a man yelling at everyone to back up.

Breathing hard, Liam made it to an exit door that was already ajar. He kicked it open and entered the back alley. The ground glistened, slick from the light drizzle. Ten paces to his left, Charlie tottered near the mouth of the alley and onto the main street. He swung his head this way and that, confused, perhaps having lagged so far behind the others he'd lost them.

Another man appeared, also dressed in gray, with the Uprising's three-fingered design on the cuff of his sleeve. He was an ox of a man with thick red mutton chops, and he was holding a shotgun. "You with them, boyo?" he said as he stepped onto the alleyway's bricks, the shotgun leveled at Charlie. "You in the back room, imbibing that *filth*?"

Charlie spun about to face him. His eyes filled with horror. His hands lifted in a sign of surrender. He shook his head several times while his jaw worked soundlessly.

And then Liam heard that same disembodied voice, this time much clearer than the previous two times. It was something that felt familiar. Something from the war? God, his memories were too fractured to remember.

—*He's not the one.*

The words came from nowhere. From everywhere. A voice inside his head.

"No!" Liam screamed, once more feeling someone else's intent.

The moment slowed—almost, but not quite, frozen in time.

The man's face, hard and angry.

The shotgun, belching fire and smoke.

Charlie, his already-wide eyes going wider.

The light from the explosion transformed their faces into obscene caricatures. For a moment they were motionless, stone-like, two buildings set ablaze.

The explosion dimmed as a hole the size of Liam's fist burrowed its way into Charlie's chest. Back he flew, arms flailing, until he collapsed against the curb.

The man with the shotgun turned and set his merciless eyes on Liam and Morgan.

—*The one being carried. He's the one.*

The voice . . . Before Liam could so much as try to speak up, the man leveled his shotgun at Liam.

—*No! We need the scourge unharmed.*

The man nodded as he lumbered forward. Liam was just beginning to turn when he saw Grace fly out from the speakeasy's blood-red hallway.

Knowing in his gut she was destined for the same fate as Elle and Charlie, he hoped he might step in front of her, but Morgan was too heavy. He wouldn't make it in time.

Then a miracle happened.

Grace flung her hands forward—as if flicking water from her fingertips— and a mirror image of her *flowed* forward. The image moved translucent, dreamlike, while the other, the one that appeared solid, came to an abrupt halt.

The ghostlike image flew toward the street. The man with the shotgun tracked the illusory Grace, fired when she came near. The blast gouged a hole in the mottled brown bricks of the opposite building, but the ghost was unaffected and continued to run, her golden dress flowing in her wake.

With the flip of a lever, the man cracked the shotgun open and pointed the barrel up. The two spent shells dropped against the concrete with soft clucking sounds. Liam, meanwhile, set Morgan down and charged forward, his footfalls as silent as he could make them.

The man spun as Liam reached him. He swung the butt of the shotgun across Liam's path, aiming for the side of his head, but Liam ducked and came up with a fist to the man's jaw, then a sharp jab to his stomach. When the man staggered back, Liam followed and delivered a sharp cross to his temple.

The man's knees buckled, and he dropped like a sack of potatoes.

Grace, meanwhile, the real Grace, had reached Liam's side. She grabbed his arm, trying to lead him away, but Liam refused to budge.

"Where were you?" Liam asked.

"The lady's room."

"What did you just *do*?"

"Never mind that. We have to leave. *Now.*"

"Why?"

"Because they're after Morgan."

A tall delivery wagon was rumbling up near the end of the alley, along the main street. Its headlights cast a yellow light, illuminating the falling drizzle in two expanding columns. It looked vaguely like a police wagon but was unmarked, black—the vehicle Death himself might have taken up in the modern age.

Grace tried to pull Liam away again, but he refused to move. "Why do they want Morgan?"

"Not here . . . I'll explain everything once we're safe."

Men in gray clothing spilled from the wagon—six of them plus the driver, each holding a shotgun or a revolver. So far, they seemed not to have noticed Liam or Grace, or Morgan lying on the ground.

—*Orders?*

Liam felt the other presence—somewhere close, though he couldn't pinpoint it exactly. Downtown, maybe. As before, he felt *intent* building from several of the men, particularly the driver. Desperation welled up inside him. He needed to do *something* to stop them, but what?

A memory came: the ground exploding from a cannon shell, the Devil's Henchmen all turning toward it. A split second later, a hellacious boom came from somewhere further up the street. The sound was accompanied by a burst of light that lit the stone facades of the buildings across the street. The men in gray stared in shock, mouths agape. A moment later, they ran toward it in a loose pack.

As the pressure inside Liam eased, Grace stared at him, her green eyes wide with awe. "Liam . . . ?"

She said it like she'd just met him. No, like she'd just *recognized* him. Liam felt completely out of sorts, like he should know *her* too.

Grace's brow glistened from the evening mist. She looked as if she were about to speak when the purr of a Phaeton came loudly from the alley's opposite end, fifty paces distant. Morgan's car rolled to a halt, headlights off, and Alastair hopped out. After opening the passenger door, he clanked toward Liam's position.

Grace was silent as Alastair arrived. Morgan, thank God, was conscious again, and moaning. Working together, Liam and Alastair carried him toward the sleek car.

"Liam, wait!" Grace called. "We have to talk."

Liam stopped, nodded for Alastair to continue with Morgan. "I'm leaving in that car," he said to Grace. "If you want to talk, you'll have to come with us."

"I can't do that." The rain was falling heavier. Grace stood, licking her lips nervously as streams of rain traced lines along her face. She looked so forlorn Liam nearly reached out to embrace her.

"Why can't you?" he asked.

Her hands were bunched into fists. "*Please* come with me."

There was something about her manner, her desperation, that made him want to trust her, but how could he? He'd be risking not only his own life, but Morgan's as well. Without another word, he turned and headed for the Phaeton.

"Morgan will die without our help!" she called after him.

It was as if she'd read his thoughts, but he refused to give in to fear. Morgan needed a doctor. Grace said no more as Liam reached the car. When he climbed inside and closed the door, the Phaeton's headlights blinked on and the engine hummed to life. As they pulled away, he looked down the alley one last time.

Grace was gone.

SEVEN

Dr. Ramachandra's medical office was a set of three cozy rooms occupying the lowest floor of his posh brownstone. Although the hour was late, Dr. Ramachandra arrived quickly at the door when they knocked. Liam's experience with the man was limited, but his unflappable manner and calm authority had already done much to build trust.

Dr. Ramachandra rushed Morgan into his examination room. As he listened to his breathing through a stethoscope, his bristly beard and the sapphire-blue dastar wrapped around his head bobbed—an affectation, it seemed, as if Morgan's heart were set to a ragtime beat.

"Breathe deeply," Dr. Ramachandra said. His Punjabi accent was barely noticeable.

With a grimace, Morgan drew in a deep breath. His shirt was off, exposing clammy skin much paler than normal and a physique that had become noticeably softer since his army days. Morgan was far from well. The shot of morphine Dr. Ramachandra administered took the edge off his pain, but he still looked miserable.

"Again," the doctor said as he moved the chest piece lower.

This time Morgan's breath was accompanied by a heavy rasp. Not since the war had Liam seen a man look so scared. When Morgan glanced over, Liam shared a confident nod with him. Morgan returned the gesture, though it was filled with more misery than hope.

After removing the stethoscope and wrapping it around his neck, Dr. Ramachandra spun his chair toward a desk and began writing.

"In the dream," Morgan said, continuing the story he'd started when they arrived, "I saw a field of wheat."

"So did I," Liam said, more than a little surprised.

On the car ride over, Liam had been tempted to tell Morgan about his absynthe-fueled dream, but Morgan had been in so much pain he'd decided to remain silent. He quickly gave Morgan the broad brushstrokes: the field, Elle kissing him, Morgan lying between the rows.

Morgan huffed in disgust. "At least you got a kiss out of yours. All I got was a horror show. There was a naked man between the rows of *my* field. He was pitiful and chilling. Black pits for eyes. Pale skin with blue veins. Shivering with palsy and gaunt as a war prisoner."

It was curious that their dreams were so similar, but the naked man was easily explained—it was surely Morgan's own pain manifesting in his dream.

Morgan seemed eager to get the dream out, to have Dr. Ramachandra interpret it for him, but Dr. Ramachandra rejected the very notion. "Dreams echo our hopes and fears," he declared flatly. "They have no bearing on your physical condition."

Liam had been about to broach the subject of the strange, disembodied voice, the orders being passed, but given the way Dr. Ramachandra had just reacted to Morgan's dream, he thought better of it. Dr. Ramachandra would probably just laugh at him.

Later, he promised himself, *when Morgan and I are alone.*

As Dr. Ramachandra went on to check Morgan's blood pressure, Liam pulled back the heavy green curtains of the nearby window. Alastair had insisted on standing guard on the doctor's front stoop, and Liam reluctantly agreed. His presence would likely draw curious eyes, but with sunrise still hours away, few enough would notice him. And whatever attention might come, a mechanika looming on the stoop like a mafia foot soldier was worth it. The men in gray uniforms. The attack. Liam's hands were still shaking from it.

After drawing a sample of Morgan's blood, Dr. Ramachandra wrote a series of instructions on a piece of paper, wrapped the instructions around the syringe, and placed both into a pneumatic canister. Then he popped the canister into a messenger pipe, clamped the pipe shut, and pressed one of several buttons on the wall, the one marked "Lab," and the canister was whisked away with a *thoomp.*

"That'll be a day or two coming back." Dr. Ramachandra sat and took several more notes. "Tell me again what you drank."

Morgan shrugged. "Whiskey, mostly. A few mixed drinks. Then ab-synthe."

"Any of it moonshine?"

"I don't know," Morgan said, looking perfectly wretched, "but I doubt it. Club Artemis is clean as they come."

"Plus," Liam broke in, "Morgan was already experiencing symptoms. Ever since taking the government serum."

"It's doubtful the serum is to blame here." Dr. Ramachandra looked back and forth from one of them to the other, clearly choosing his words with care. "I'm not going to berate you for imbibing alcohol. I leave that to your parents and God. But I will admit I'm concerned. Your symptoms are similar to several cases of poisoning I've heard about."

Morgan blinked. "Poison?"

Dr. Ramachandra nodded. "The making and running of alcohol have become major sources of income for the Uprising. They've been waging a war against the traditional bootleggers, and it's escalated in recent months. There are reports of people being poisoned, others being abducted or killed when they threaten to finger the ones who did it. These days, getting in-volved with alcohol in any way, shape, or form is dangerous."

Morgan frowned. "But the Uprising were the ones who attacked us! Why attack a place where they'd already poisoned the booze?"

"To sow even more chaos. Or perhaps to make a statement to other bootleggers that Chicago is theirs. I don't know the minds of criminals, Morgan. My concern is to see your health returned to you." He went to a glass cabinet and retrieved two small brown bottles. "I'll make inquiries. In the meantime, take these." He shook one of the bottles. "This to help you sleep, two spoons, just before you lay down." He shook the other. "This one twice daily, with food. It should help you fend off the worst of the symptoms until I can learn more. And Liam, you'll let me know straight away if you have similar symptoms."

Morgan accepted the bottles, but Liam was concerned. "And the gov-ernment serum Morgan took?" he asked.

Dr. Ramachandra gave him a noncommittal nod. "I'll contact the Bureau of Health and ask them about it. But the serum is hardly new. Whatever President De Pere might have said at the ceremony, it's been distributed fairly widely along the East Coast. If there were major concerns over it, I would have heard about them by now."

"All right," Liam said. "Thank you for checking."

Morgan, meanwhile, was staring at the bottles Dr. Ramachandra had given him as if one was poison, the other the elixir of life, and he didn't know which was which.

Dr. Ramachandra put his hairy hand on Morgan's shoulder. "You've a strong constitution, Morgan. You always have had. Take those, and we'll soon learn more. I'll send word the moment I know." He squeezed Morgan's shoulder, then patted it twice. "We'll see you through."

Morgan nodded tentatively, then pulled his shirt back on. In short order, he and Liam were in the Phaeton and Alastair was driving them north through the streets of Chicago's posh Wicker Park, heading for the Aysana estate.

In the rear, Morgan and Liam were silent, both dumbstruck, worried, scared. Outside, the tall brownstones gave way to staid homes spaced farther apart. In the distance, through the light rain, Liam could just make out the flashtrain line, the very one he took to work every day. A train streaked toward the glowing Deco towers of downtown. The air in the car smelled musky, some new scent Morgan was giving off. It wasn't altogether unpleasant, but it was worrying just the same, yet another of the strange symptoms Morgan had been exhibiting since the firefight at the train station.

When the Phaeton began taking the easy curves of a road through a forest preserve, Morgan said, "I can't believe Elle and Charlie are gone."

Their final moments, so bloody and violent, flashed through Liam's mind. "We should count ourselves lucky Geraldine couldn't make it."

"True"—Morgan made a miserable attempt at a smile—"but her absence wasn't some random fluke."

"What do you mean?"

"She had a better offer is all. Her message said she was detained because

President De Pere himself was staying for dinner. Geraldine's father, Walter, apparently had a meeting with him that went long. Her mother offered to host him for dinner, and he agreed." Morgan paused, his gaze going distant. "It *was* a bit odd, though."

"What was?"

"She said I should head home, that she'd call me tomorrow to explain."

Liam was stunned. "Head *home*?"

Morgan nodded. "It was the bartender who passed me the message, so it might've gotten a bit mangled, but apparently she wanted me to head home straight away."

The moments that followed were filled by the Phaeton's purr, the hiss of the tires navigating the wet road. Liam was trying and failing to understand why she would have said it. "So she gives you a warning like that," he finally said, "and then the attack happens?"

Morgan looked affronted. "Don't be ridiculous. She couldn't have known. It's just a coincidence."

"What did she mean by it, then?"

"Isn't it obvious? Leland De Pere, our president, a famous teetotaler, was in her *home*. She was worried that my being associated with Club Artemis, or *any* speakeasy, for that matter, would implicate *her*. Her father only gained the mayor's seat a few months ago. If De Pere finds out she's been tipping back Gin Rickeys all over the city, Walter would instantly lose favor."

Liam shrugged. "You're probably right. It's too bad it turned out like this."

"It's fine. She's going shopping for flowers at the market on Wednesday. Decorations for the President's final night in Chicago, apparently. I'll see her then, assuming I'm well enough." A hint of a smile broke across Morgan's face. "Speaking of sweethearts, what'd you think of Grace?"

For a moment Liam felt like the same fool he'd been on seeing her enter Club Artemis, though the feeling was all but smothered by the memory of Grace summoning an image of herself to save him from the man with the shotgun.

Morgan, perhaps interpreting Liam's silence as embarrassment over his attraction, said, "She asked about you, you know."

Liam stared at him, confused. "When?"

"Three nights ago at Club Artemis. I was talking about the firefight at the flashtrain station. She said she'd heard someone say he'd witnessed the porter shooting Kohler point blank with the tommy gun. She seemed to know quite a bit about the incident already. And you. She described you and what you were wearing before I'd even said your name."

Liam frowned. "How could she have known?"

Morgan shrugged while glancing out the back window. In the distance, a pair of yellow headlights trailed them. "Who knows? There were plenty of witnesses."

"Do you know where she's staying?"

"No"—Morgan's smile broadened—"but there are only so many hotels a woman like Grace would stay in." Though amused moments ago, Morgan's smile collapsed the longer he stared at Liam. "What's wrong?"

The very notion of hearing voices in his head still seemed mad—so mad Liam nearly told Morgan it was nothing—but he needed to talk about it, and if he couldn't trust Morgan, he couldn't trust anyone. "During the attack, I heard someone speaking to those men, someone issuing orders. It wasn't from anyone in the bar, though. It felt like they were coming from far away. Did *you* hear it? A voice in your head?"

Morgan stared at him doubtfully, clearly thinking it was a poor sort of joke.

"I'm not kidding, Morgan. I heard a man's voice telling them who they could kill and who they couldn't. Elle's death was authorized. As was Charlie's. But not yours . . . They wanted you alive."

"But you said it was a voice inside your head."

"It was."

"And that it was coming from far away."

"Look, I know it sounds wild—"

Morgan released a pent-up burst of laughter. "God, you had me going there for a minute." When Liam didn't immediately back down, he went on. "Don't you get it? It was the *absynthe*. None of us had come down from it yet."

"I know, but it felt too *real*. Like you and I talking now. It was nothing like the dream in the wheat field."

"You think the wheat field is the only sort of hallucination you can have with absynthe? I've felt myself falling apart and then being rebuilt by dwarves. *Dwarves*, Liam. Little ones with long beards and golden hammers. I've had extended conversations with alpacas, and they did most of the talking. I've felt myself inside a dozen people at once. Then none at all, which is a lot scarier than you think. Every flight with the green fairy is different. Depends on who's there with you. Your mood. *Their* mood. The provenance of the liquor—an *unknown quantity*, as Dr. Ramachandra would say."

"The voice said they wanted the scourge unharmed."

Morgan's next words died on his lips. "What did you say?"

"The voice I heard, it was talking to our assailants, directing them. It said, 'We need the *scourge* unharmed.' It was talking about you, Morgan."

Morgan's eyes spoke volumes.

"What is it?" Liam asked.

"The naked man I saw in the wheat field. He was whispering a lone word, over and over. *Scourge*."

A chill ran down Liam's spine. "What the hell's a scourge?"

Before Morgan could reply, Alastair's warbly voice reached them from the driver's compartment. "Sirs, I don't wish to alarm you, but there seems to be a squad car following us."

Morgan and Liam turned to look through the back window. The yellow headlights he'd spotted earlier were close now. The car looked to be a long-nosed sedan of some sort. As it shouldered into the curve behind the Phaeton, a red light on its roof blinked on and off while a brass bell on the hood rang over and over, hammering a sequence as manic as a firehouse drill.

"Sir, we're not far from the estate," Alastair said into the rearview mirror.

"Let's just see what he wants," Morgan said. "Likely we'll get home with little more than a tip of the hat."

Morgan's reasoning was that his father, one of the wealthiest businessmen in the Midwest, was granted certain protections, and that those protections extended to Morgan as well. He wasn't wrong. Liam had seen it for himself over and over again, from being let go after being stopped for speeding to sobering him up at the police station and discharging him in the morning, scot-free. Still, Liam didn't like it. His stomach twisted into knots at the mere thought of stopping the car in the middle of nowhere, and the more the Phaeton slowed, the worse it got.

As they pulled to a stop along the road's gravel shoulder, the police car did as well. All seemed calm for a moment, the cop car sitting there, idling. Liam tried to peer through the windshield, but the lights were too blinding. Beyond the glare he saw only darkness and the red lamp as it flashed. For long moments, no one exited the vehicle.

"What's going on?" Liam asked.

"He's probably using the wireless to report to the station."

"I don't like it, Morgan."

"Just stay calm. We'll talk to him and we'll be back home soon enough."

On the driver's side of the police car was an unlit spotlamp. Presently, it swiveled up and around, the lens rotating until it faced forward. A series of blue lights flashed from it, so bright Liam and Morgan both cringed. The faint popping sounds that accompanied each flash made Liam feel sick to his stomach.

Liam turned forward when he heard a thumping, rattling sound. In the driver's seat, Alastair shook terribly as if he were having an epileptic seizure, then he simply slumped forward across the wheel, his weight engaging the horn. As the Phaeton blew one long, ceaseless note into the muggy night, the driver and passenger doors of the police vehicle opened.

EIGHT

Two uniformed men emerged from the squad car and closed the doors with an unhurried calm that sent Liam's fears soaring. They were well aware of what they'd just done to Alastair—the strobing light had been turned on for a reason—and now they were walking with the confidence of men who were sure they had the situation under control.

One had his hand on his sidearm as he approached the Phaeton's passenger side. The other, the driver, wore a sergeant's uniform, including the high, rounded helmet with the station's insignia, which, if Liam pegged it right, was from downtown, nowhere near the Aysana estate. The badge on his black wool coat gleamed red in the Phaeton's taillights. He had a policeman's baton in one hand, which he swung in circles, catching it with a snap as he sauntered forward.

On Liam's door was a switch that would lock all four of the Phaeton's doors. He pressed it and heard the locks engage. Alastair was still leaning against the wheel, the horn blaring. Liam reached an arm through the sliding window that divided the rear seats from the driver's compartment, pulled Alastair away from the wheel, and allowed him to slump sideways along the front seat. The horn fell blessedly silent. There were no guns in the car, only the Gatling built into Alastair's new forearm. If Liam could reach it, trigger the firing mechanism . . .

Slow down, Liam. Aim before you fire. Don't do anything rash.

From a metal hoop on his belt, the sergeant unhooked a long black flashlight. It blinked to life with a bright, glacier-blue beam. He shone it inside the cabin, taking a good look, first at Morgan, then at Liam, before using the head of the flashlight to send three sharp knocks against the window. "Mr. Aysana, I'm Sergeant Holohan of the Chicago P.D. Would you care to step out of the car?"

"Don't do it," Liam whispered.

"What?" Morgan rasped. "I have to!"

"No you don't. Tell him you're taking the car to your father's estate, and he can meet you there."

"It's the police, Liam."

"And they just deactivated your mechanika. Do as I said, Morgan."

The policeman knocked again. "Mr. Aysana?"

Morgan turned away from the window. "Liam, this isn't a game."

"Exactly my point. If they are who you think they are, what's the worst they'll do? Give you a stern talking to on your father's estate? Hand you a citation? But what if *I'm* right?"

"You think they're with *them*? The ones from the speakeasy?"

"I don't know, but it's not worth the risk."

The sergeant adjusted his tall helmet, then spoke in a booming voice. "Sir, I'm going to need you to step out of the car."

Morgan rolled down the window, but only a crack. "If you don't mind, sergeant, I'm not feeling very well. It's been a long night. I'm only trying to get back home."

"Back home?"

Morgan pointed. "It's just up the road."

The sergeant spun his baton, leaned to one side, and shone the beam of his flashlight into the driver's compartment. "Seems like that'll be difficult without a chauffeur. How about I take over the wheel for you? Officer Carolan here can take the squad car. Can't you, John?"

"Surely." Officer Carolan had a thick Irish accent. "I'll follow just behind."

"No," Morgan said quickly. "We'll be fine. But I do need to get moving."

The sergeant swung the lamp back to Morgan. Coming in as it was through the crack, unblocked by the tinted windows, it was positively blinding. "Well, what's stopping you?"

Officer Carolan approached the door on Liam's right and rattled the handle, trying to open it. Finding it locked, he walked casually to the front passenger door and tried that one as well.

"For the third and final time, Mr. Aysana," the sergeant said, "step out of the car and we can talk about this like the gentlemen we are."

To Liam's horror, he heard Morgan's door latch click, after which Morgan pushed his door wide and stepped out into the night. Liam heaved a sigh. He knew he couldn't leave Morgan out there alone, so he followed, making sure to flip the switch to unlock all the doors, not just Morgan's, before he did so.

"Well now, that's better, isn't it?" The sergeant had a pleased expression on his face, the sort employed by schoolyard bullies after they've cornered the class pipsqueak in the bathroom. It was in this moment that Liam heard the mumbling, just like he had in the speakeasy. The voice was little more than a tumble of vowels at first, impossible to make out the words, but then it coalesced.

—*believe he's a Henchman. Take utmost care.*

Again, Liam *felt* where it was coming from. It was definitely downtown . . .

—*Delay. Ensure the scourge is unharmed. Help is on the way.*

The sergeant glanced at Liam, but then seemed to forcibly drag his attention back to Morgan. "You said you're feeling sick. Why?"

"A touch of bad food," Morgan replied.

"Bad food is it?" the sergeant said reasonably. "And where, exactly, did you eat?"

"At the Blackstone Hotel," Liam said. "I had the porterhouse, but Morgan had the veal. We think it was bad."

The sergeant swiveled his head toward Liam. He shined the flashlight directly in his face as Officer Carolan walked around the front of the Phaeton and stood easily, his thumbs in his wide black policeman's belt. With the head of the flashlight, the sergeant poked Liam in the chest, stared at him like a junkyard dog. "What's your name?"

"Liam Mulcahey, sir. The Aysana's mechanic."

"Well, I didn't ask *you*"—he poked Liam in the chest, harder this time—"did I, *Liam*?" He turned back to Morgan. "Any other stops tonight, Mr. Aysana? You can get stomach bugs in the strangest places these days."

"No other stops," Liam interjected.

Morgan looked worried over Liam's challenging the police. He also looked like the morphine was wearing off. Either that or his sickness—or the effects from the poisoned absynthe, if that's truly what it was—was getting worse.

Again the sergeant swung his gaze to Liam, but this time he sidestepped until he was face to face with him. He was a big cuss, the sergeant. He loomed over Liam like an old oak. But Liam gave no ground.

The billy club came with a suddenness that surprised Liam. It took him hard against the ribs. Even so, he'd been expecting it. He grabbed it tight and twisted sharply. The sergeant lost his grip, but the billy club was still wrapped around his hand by the leather cord, so Liam yanked again, harder this time, and the cord snapped.

By then the other copper was reaching for his sidearm. Liam lunged and brought the billy club down against his fingers as he was pulling the gun out. The gun fell to the slick street, and Liam kicked it across the road. A splash could be heard as it fell into the rain water rushing noisily along the ditch. Seeing the sergeant reach for his own weapon, Liam spun back and sent three quick strikes of the baton against his hand and wrist.

The sergeant hissed as he dropped his pistol. Liam gave him a strong shove in the chest. Before he could recover, Liam had the pistol up and in his hand.

"Morgan's sick," Liam said loudly, "and I'm taking him home."

"No, boyo," the sergeant said, "that's not how this is going to go. That's not how this is going to go at all."

Liam ignored him. He pressed Morgan back toward the rear door. "Get in, Morgan."

"Liam—"

"Get in the fucking *car*, Morgan."

Morgan finally complied, the door clicking as he shut it behind him. The coppers spread out. Liam held the gun at the ready and they kept their distance, but he could tell they were readying an attack.

—*Thirty seconds.*

At this both coppers glanced down the street. Liam did too. In the distance, a set of four bright blue lights, most decidedly *not* the headlights of a car, were headed their way. They formed a rectangle—two up high, two down low—and seemed to be bouncing along the street like a kangaroo.

It's a hopper, Liam realized. *They've sent a hopper, and it's going to be here in moments.* Holding the gun steady, he reached behind and opened the Phaeton's driver's door.

"Can't let you do that, Liam," the sergeant said.

"Try and stop me, then."

The sergeant lifted his hand to his hat, as if he meant to tip it. As he had with the men in the speakeasy, Liam felt *intent*. He had no idea what the danger might be, but he dove inside the Phaeton anyway and tried to pull the door closed. Too late. The sergeant's fingers touched the brim of his hat. The moment they did, the station insignia in his helmet brightened into a sickly yellow sun, its light wavering like a mirage. Something struck the driver's side door, slamming it shut. The windows were bulletproof, and yet both his and Morgan's windows shattered into a kaleidoscope of refracted light as the strange, wavering flash dimmed and finally went out.

Liam worked his jaw. He blinked. His ears rang, high-pitched, getting worse by the moment. Ahead of the Phaeton, the yellow and white lines on the rain-slicked street crossed one another like dancers in a chorus line. The engine was still running, he realized. He'd managed to lose the sergeant's gun. It might've dropped onto the asphalt as he leapt into the car, or maybe it'd fallen onto the floor of the car. Before he could think to look for it, a fist crashed against the left side of his face. In the rearview mirror, the blue lights bounced ever closer.

Liam slipped the Phaeton into drive as the sergeant drove another punch to the side of his head. The other copper, Officer Carolan, was fishing in the water running along the drainage ditch. He came up with his gun just as the Phaeton was pulling onto the road.

"Down!" Liam shouted.

He had no idea if Morgan heard him—he couldn't see him in the rearview, and Morgan made no sort of reply. Two shots shattered the humid night, the copper trying to take out the tires, maybe, but the Phaeton had run-flats and kept on purring.

The sergeant, standing on the running board, tried another punch, but Liam ducked the blow, then opened the car door and shoved hard. The big policeman lost his footing and swung out, dangling above the road. Using a leg to keep the door wide open, Liam accelerated and guided the Phaeton onto the road's left shoulder.

"I'd drop now if I were you," Liam said.

When the copper saw the stout wooden post of a speed limit sign rushing toward him, he did. He dropped and rolled, his legs slamming hard into the post, sending him spinning wide of it and into the ditch. In the rearview, Liam saw him rise and limp back onto the gravel shoulder. In that moment, the blue bounding lights landed just next to him, and Liam finally got a good look at it. The hopper was twelve feet tall, with long, grasshopper legs. A soldier was strapped into its chest, his legs swallowed by the hopper's metallic thighs. He wore a rounded helmet, army issue, with goggles that glowed the same cerulean as the cylindrical tanks strapped to his back. A thick, camouflaged plate protected his torso and neck while lighter armor covered his arms.

As the hopper bounded high into the air, Liam realized how intimately he understood the capabilities of its armaments, the fog that had once lain so thickly over his memories continuing to lift after his odd meeting with President De Pere. Shortly after his reassignment to the Devil's Henchmen, he'd gone through weeks of training as a hopper pilot—all the Devil's Henchmen had. So when he felt the same strange *intent* coming from behind and high above, he slammed on the Phaeton's brakes.

The tires squealed as the Phaeton decelerated sharply. An explosion blasted the asphalt just ahead of the car. For a moment, the relative darkness beyond the windshield was replaced by an avalanche of asphalt and stone. Fragments struck the windshield's reinforced glass, cracking it in three places. The right headlight flickered, then winked out altogether. On the heels of the first explosion came two more, each ten yards ahead of the other. They struck in a line, the three grenades fired from the launcher built into the hopper's right shoulder.

The hopper landed about fifty yards ahead, then came to a lurching, drunken sort of halt. It turned, and the gaze of the soldier's glowing blue goggles came to a rest on the now-slowed Phaeton. It was a thing out of nightmares, Spring-heeled Jack reborn, bearing all the armaments that modern warfare might offer him.

The soldier, wrapped in the hopper's exoskeleton, lifted his rifle, aimed at Liam, and fired five times in rapid sequence. The impact from each bullet cracked the windshield a little bit further. Liam ducked to one side while keeping one hand on the wheel, and gunned the accelerator as more bullets tore through the compromised windshield. The dark cloth of the seat beside him exploded again and again, white cotton padding filling the air like dandelion seeds.

"Morgan?" Liam shouted. "Morgan, you okay?"

"I'm okay," came his weak reply.

Liam reached down, hoping to find the sergeant's gun somewhere along the floorboard, but the floorboard was empty. Again he felt a desperate need to *do* something, an urge, he realized now, that had been drilled into him years ago. Drilled by whom, and for what reason, he wasn't certain.

His memories flashed to a weapon developed by the neotech division during the war, a yet-to-be-perfected cannon that had arced wild whip-strikes of lightning from a glowing white rod mounted to a modified tank chassis.

A split second later, a bright white streak appeared to the left of the hopper. It sizzled down from the sky to strike the base of an elm tree along the side of the road. An earth-shaking sound followed. The lightning arced, faded, then arced again, dividing the sky in two. White sparks flew from the tree. It began to tip, the ponderous top of the elm tilting toward the street. And the hopper.

As Liam sat up and pulled the wheel hard to avoid the crashing tree, the hopper leapt up and away, lost to the night and Liam's blindness as the tree collapsed against the road amid sharp cracks and a terrible, rolling thunder.

Liam skirted the road's gravel edge. At one point the Phaeton slipped off and onto the shoulder. The entire car twisted, sliding closer and closer to the wet ditch. He adjusted the wheel into the slide and gunned the engine to regain his bearing. Gravel, then dirt and grass, flew in rooster tails from the back wheels as the Phaeton edged slowly back toward the street.

The rear tires hit the street with a sizzling sound. The sedan fishtailed as Liam fought the wheel. The long, powerful vehicle wove back and forth, fighting to maintain speed and regain a proper line.

He'd finally managed to control it when something came crashing down hard against the hood. Two long, spindly legs obscured his view of the road. Each had a thin canister glowing sapphire blue along the back—the legs' piston tanks. The soldier's body lowered into view, his blue eyes staring through the Phaeton's wreck of a windshield. In came the rifle through one of the many gaps, but Liam was ready. He grabbed the barrel with his right hand, refusing to let it aim at him or Morgan.

The soldier fired again and again, emptying a magazine. The barrel became blistering hot, but Liam held on, knowing that to lose control now would cost not only his own life, but Morgan's as well.

He heard a clattering sound. Saw a gun magazine, lit blue by the hopper's glowing canisters, fall to the hood, then rattle and slip to the right. Liam tried to swerve, to throw the soldier from the hood, but the hopper's feet had punched through the metal hood. It was there to stay.

Unless . . .

Liam glanced over to Alastair and spotted the right arm with the high-powered Gatling attached.

With a great shove to the soldier's rifle, Liam let go of the steering wheel, leaned to his right, and grabbed Alastair's arm. He lifted and pointed it at one of the glowing blue piston tanks. Outside, he heard the clack of a new magazine setting home, the clatter of the charging handle being pulled back.

He aimed Alastair's arm through the window. Pulled back the rod that would release the hammer.

As more shots tore into the compartment, Liam released the rod. A high-powered round blew bits of the windshield outward. Liam pulled back on the rod again, firing over and over, aiming for the piston at the back of the hopper's leg. On the fourth round, the canister exploded. The sudden release of pressure caused the leg to give way. The soldier still managed to release two more rounds—the second grazing Liam's left shoulder—but then he was tipping sideways, arms flailing. His rifle went flying as he tried to use his articulated arms to blunt the landing, but Liam had regained the wheel. He pulled the car sharply to the left to send him careening over the side.

The soldier in his insectoid armature went down hard against the street, moments before the Phaeton's back wheels thumped over soldier and armor alike.

The car bucked, twisting wildly as Liam fought to right it. Finally the exoskeleton was dragged free, and he was speeding down the street, green coolant bursting in a steamy plume from the holes gouged into the hood where the hopper had landed.

Watching the rearview carefully for signs of pursuit, Liam drove into the night.

NINE

Three days after the attack on the Phaeton, Liam was legging it along the rundown streets of Bucktown. His cap was pulled low, his coat buttoned tight against the pouring rain. Clouds hung pendulously in the sky like endless tufts of steel wool. The heavens had opened up the day after the attack on Club Artemis. It had been raining pitchforks ever since.

On reaching an old pneumatics garage, Liam turned off the street, tackled a set of weatherworn stairs, and entered the spare room above the garage. The single-room apartment wasn't a place a man like Morgan was accustomed to, given his means, but after abandoning the Aysana estate as too dangerous for everyone involved—Morgan's family included—they'd decided they couldn't trust any of the hotels where Morgan might have been able to call on his father's credit. They couldn't so much as trust the downtown streets. Morgan might not have been a widely *recognized* public figure, but he was still a public figure. And so, after sending a telegram to the Aysana estate, making it clear Morgan was safe and sound and would return as soon as possible, they'd resolved themselves to staying away until they could decide their next steps.

The attic had a bed and a couch for sleeping, a bathroom to bathe in. For now, that was plenty. Preferable, even. The garage was owned by a man named Sean. He occasionally supplied parts for the various equipment and mechanika Liam serviced on the Aysana estate. Liam had come to know him well, at least well enough to know he was a man who could be trusted to help a friend in a pinch.

"And why not?" Sean had said in his thick Kerry accent when Liam had asked to use the room. "Anything for a lad from the old country." Despite the sentiment, he'd given Liam a look, the sort an uncle might give to his mischievous nephew. "Is there anything I should be knowing, Liam?"

"Just a bit of work going on at the flat," Liam had said. "I haven't been able to sleep."

"Your nana's not bothered by the work?"

"Grandma Ash?" Liam hadn't had to fake a laugh. "She can sleep through anything. It's like she's dead to the world!"

"And what about your friend?"

"A bit of trouble with the missus is all."

"A bit of trouble with the missus . . ." Sean's tone made it clear he found Liam's answers sorely lacking, but he dropped the subject after that.

Liam shook the rain off his coat and hat and hung them on the nearby wall hooks. After locking the door, he headed across the dusty, musty attic. Morgan was lying in a fetal position on the apartment's small bed, sleeping. Liam went to the table beside the window and dropped his weight into one of the two wooden chairs—a little too freely, as it turned out. His shoulder was still tender from the bullet wound.

As he sucked air against the pain, Morgan opened his eyes. He looked terrible—sallow skin, eyes heavy with dark bags beneath them. "Any luck?"

"No." Liam had just returned from his bank a few miles away. It had a telephone its clients could use for a fee. "I rang seven hotels. Grace wasn't registered at any of them."

Morgan shrugged. "It was worth a try."

Liam had been kicking himself for not asking Grace how he could contact her, but the moment had been too wild, too chaotic. Now that he'd had time to think, he desperately wanted to know what information she'd planned on sharing with him, and why she seemed to think Morgan was in so much danger.

Outside the garage came the sounds of clopping hooves. Wincing from the burn his fingers had suffered from gripping the soldier's gun barrel, Liam pulled the window curtains aside. An old mechanikal horse hove into view. A delivery boy with a wide-brimmed hat and an oilskin coat rode on its back. With practiced ease, he pulled up near a stoop across the street, slipped down to the curb, and opened a hinged lid in the horse's side. Cool steam misted out, consuming the boy's legs and ratty leather shoes as he took out two quarts of milk in glass bottles. After setting them on the nearby stoop and grabbing the empties, he returned to the horse, stored the bottles, and was up in the saddle in a flash.

"The owner of Club Artemis knows me," Morgan offered as the horse trotted away. "You want me to reach out to him?"

Liam shook his head. "It's too dangerous. I don't want any contact with the club, not until we know more."

Liam's gaze slipped to Alastair, who was propped up in a chair in the corner, inert. He'd tried to revive the mechanika several times, but all his attempts had failed. As near as Liam could tell, Alastair wasn't *dead*, just deactivated by that strange pulsing light the coppers had used.

If they even were coppers.

Liam wasn't convinced. Chicago police, even the ones downtown, didn't have access to hopper exoskeletons like that. And no squad car he'd ever heard of had lamps that could deactivate mechanika. Nor devices that could stun a man like the sergeant's helmet had done.

Liam hadn't felt so vulnerable since the war. The attack by the hopper stank of the military's black-ops labs, the unit that had given birth to all of the Army's mechanika, though why *they* might be involved, he couldn't begin to guess. He only wanted Morgan to get well again and for things to go back to normal.

Morgan, clearly uncomfortable, shifted on the bed, grabbed the large glass of water from the night table, and downed several swallows. "The morphine hardly helps anymore."

"If Dr. Ramachandra was right about the absynthe being poisoned, it'll take time to pass through your system."

As he lay back down, a bit of the old Morgan returned with half a smile. "Well, I wish it would shake a leg already."

Liam made a miserable go of returning the smile. Morgan looked scared, almost childlike in his fear. The morphine had worked well the first day, but the pain had grown steadily, and Morgan had been taking more to stave it off. The seven-day supply they'd started with was only going to last another day or two, which made it all the more imperative that they speak with Dr. Ramachandra.

"And what if *you* were right?" Morgan asked. "I mean, *you* had the absynthe and *you're* not sick. What if it was the serum I took at the train station?"

"Dr. Ramachandra will check on that too."

The attack had happened on a Friday. They'd decided to give Dr. Ramachandra three days—the weekend plus Monday—to learn more. Tomorrow morning, bright and early, Liam would go see him.

Morgan's gaze went distant. "At the flashtrain ceremony, the porter absconded with that wooden box, the one with the red cross on it. It had to be the serum the nurses were handing out. That seemed to be the only reason they were there, right?"

Liam shrugged. "I suppose so."

"What I don't get is why? What's so important about the serum that the Uprising would go through all that trouble to get some vials of it?"

"There are rumors the Uprising are being sponsored by Germany and the other members of the St. Lawrence Pact," Liam said. "If what De Pere said is true, that the serum really *is* an antidote to the poison the SLP have been spreading, maybe they wanted a sample to learn more about it."

The memory of the porter standing on the platform, firing the tommy gun at the platform's curving glass roof, was bright in Liam's mind. The vision was suddenly replaced by another memory of the same man, Clay, but in a different time and place. He wasn't holding a tommy gun, but a Springfield rifle, and he wasn't dressed like a train porter, but as a soldier. He was strapped into a hopper exoskeleton. As Liam was. As their entire squad was.

Morgan, sensing Liam's consternation, propped himself up on one elbow. "What is it?"

But Liam hardly heard the question. His squad, the Devil's Henchmen, had been patrolling along the edges of Waukesha, a village west of Milwaukee. Though the air was bitterly cold, they'd been out for a good hour and Liam was sweating from it. They crested a low hill and the village itself came into view. Bustling only weeks earlier, it had been abandoned after being bombed by the SLP. It was eerie seeing the gutted, red-brick buildings, the empty streets. The church at the center of it, with half its roof caved in, only intensified the feeling, as if God himself had abandoned the village as well.

"Let's get a move on!" called Nick Crawford.

Lagging behind the squad was Clay Graves, who alone among them went by his first name. "No one calls me Graves," he'd told Liam. His last name being what it was, Liam hadn't had to ask why—soldiers were a famously superstitious lot.

As they headed down the hill toward the nearest of Waukesha's crater-pocked streets, Liam shivered at the sound of a small explosion. Something whistled past him—a rocket-propelled grenade, Liam realized. It streaked toward the church and crashed through the steeple's stained glass window, the sound of it reaching them a split-second later.

Everyone turned to look at Clay, who was staggering in his hopper a bit, regaining his balance after what had just happened. He stared at the church, then the squad, then the church again, his eyes wide as a barn owl's.

Liam felt a bright, burning anger coming from their sergeant, a handsome fellow with bright blue eyes. It felt important that Liam remember more about him, remember his name, at least, but for the life of him, he couldn't.

"What in the name of fuck just happened?" the sergeant asked as he lumbered toward Clay in his own hopper suit.

Liam felt Clay's embarrassment flare as he realized the precise degree to which he'd fucked up. "It just went off," he said.

"It just *went off*?" echoed the sergeant.

In addition to Liam's own irritation, he felt exasperation building in the men and women of his squad, as if he were experiencing not just his *own* emotions, but the entire squad's. Earlier, Clay had reported one of his practice grenades as having bent fins. The grenades had no explosive warheads, but they *did* have propellant—in addition to patrolling, they occasionally took time to test the range and accuracy of the weapons.

"So leave it," Crawford had said.

"Nah," Clay had said with a broad grin. "I'll fix it."

Clay had clearly been trying to do just that, but had accidentally triggered the launch mechanism.

Clay's gaze alternated between the sergeant and the broken window. "It was an accident," he said lamely.

"Accidents happen, but they always seem to happen around you, don't they, Clay?"

"Sometimes." He stood there in his shame, then jutted his chin toward the church with a lopsided smile. "Pretty good shot, though, wasn't it? Hit the bulls-eye on my first try."

"You think that's funny"—he took one loping stride forward and shoved Clay hard—"desecrating a house of God?"

The fact that Clay recovered from the shove only seemed to incense the sergeant further. Liam felt a bright, burning anger coming from him as he launched his hopper into the air, twisted backward, and kicked. His hopper's broad feet landed against Clay's reinforced chest plate.

Clay flew backward. The snow and dirt that had built up along his hopper's legs arced skyward as he struck the frozen field. Clay lay there a moment, wheezing, his breath coming out in a white fog. Then, using a maneuver they'd drilled endlessly to right themselves, he kicked himself to a stand. "What'd you do that for?"

It was then, as the sergeant was staring knives at Clay, that Liam finally made the connection. The blue in his eyes was an exact match to the lone, visible eye of the President's aid, Max Kohler.

Kohler had led the Devil's Henchmen, Liam realized. He'd commanded Liam himself. *For how long? And, dear God, what else have I forgotten?*

Crawford stepped closer until he, Clay, and the sergeant formed a tight triangle. "Look, it was an accident. And there's no harm in it. The whole *town's* empty."

Nick Crawford was well known for innocent good looks and a smile that lit up a room, but just then he looked hard, determined, a man ready to defend his comrade. It was only natural. He and Clay had been friends since before the war. Hell, they'd entered the *service* together, signing up the very same day.

"Did either of you ever stop to think," Kohler replied, "how much danger stupid shit like that will put us in when the fighting starts?"

Clay backed away, then began lowering his hopper legs so he could reach his rifle, an awkward maneuver at best. "We're *miles* from the front."

A bright flare of emotion rose up from Kohler at Clay's defiance, at Crawford's defending him. "Hold it right there, soldier!"

In the moments that followed, the entire squad stood there, stunned. A vision of Kohler's intent had cascaded through them all. He'd pictured lining Clay and Crawford up against the church wall. He'd pictured lifting his own rifle, sending a bullet through their foreheads. He'd pictured their bodies slumping as blood and brains dripped slowly down the white clapboard siding. The image reverberated through their minds, fading as Kohler's shock—at realizing everyone had seen it—slowly registered.

Clay, who'd stopped just short of grabbing his rifle, pulled himself upright. He blinked several times, unsure what to say, what to do in a moment like this.

The spell was broken by Reyes, whose attention had been drawn toward the church. "Uh, guys?"

He needn't have bothered—what *he'd* seen, they'd all seen.

From the church's front entrance, several people were exiting. Some stared up at the broken window. Others cast their gaze over the open field, at the Henchmen in their hopper armor.

"Here's what's going to happen," Kohler said, his emotions obscured, almost muted, now that he wasn't so lost in the moment. "You and Crawford are going to exit your armor. You're going to walk to that church and clean up the mess Clay made. Then you're going to ask how you can help make their lives better. Only when you've done that are you going to retrieve your armor and return to base."

Liam felt Clay's mind working. A thought came—of defying Kohler's orders just to spite him, of heading toward the shattered remains of the village and only *pretending* to comply with Kohler's order—but he rejected it as soon as it had come. They were mentally linked, and the effect wouldn't fade for hours. Kohler would *see* whether Clay and Crawford had complied. They all would.

Clay stood there, a battle of wills playing out, but the outcome was never really in doubt. He folded the legs of his armor, unstrapped himself, and hopped down to the ground. As he retrieved his rifle, Crawford joined him on the snow-covered ground.

"Fall in!" roared Kohler.

As Clay and Crawford jogged toward the church, their footsteps crunching over the snow-covered field, the rest of the squad hopped across the grassy terrain, heading back toward base.

"Liam?"

It was Morgan, in the room over the pneumatics garage. He looked worried.

Liam blinked, shook his head, and slowly the musty dimness of the attic returned.

"A new memory?" Morgan asked.

Liam nodded. He'd told Morgan how, ever since meeting with President De Pere, more of his memories from the war had been returning.

Morgan considered it awhile. "He gave that address when you graduated from boot camp, right? Maybe it's that, seeing him stirring up all sorts of old memories."

"Maybe," Liam replied. "Did I ever mention anything to you during the war about what I did? Or where I was stationed after basic?"

"You sent me a few letters, but they were carefully worded, and sometimes sections were blacked out. I don't think you ever really tried to tell me, but the Army's censors made sure no one learned where soldiers were assigned. You know that."

"What about the Devil's Henchmen? Did I ever mention them?"

"No, but that was normal, too. We weren't supposed to talk about where we were assigned, or what our duties were."

Liam took a deep breath. "I feel like I'm going mad, Morgan."

"Not mad," Morgan said evenly. "You took a knock to the head is all."

"Did I *actually*, though?"

Morgan's eyes narrowed. "What do you mean?"

"That's just what I was *told*." Liam tapped his forehead. "Until a week ago, the last several years of the war had been lost in this fog. All I remembered was basic, a few months learning the ins and outs of being a mechanic, then waking up in my apartment with Nana months after the armistice was signed."

"You've mentioned the goliaths, though."

"Right, and now more memories are coming back, like ravens spilling from a tree."

Morgan shrugged. "I wish I had answers, Liam."

Liam laughed. "Where's a crystal ball when you need one?"

"I know. All our problems would be solved!" Morgan's smile was warmer now, but the feeling soured as he cringed and put a hand over his stomach. After several seconds, he leaned forward and grabbed the bottle of morphine off the night table next to the bed.

"Morgan . . ."

"Sorry, Liam," Morgan said as he twisted the cap off. "I need it."

Liam was tempted to argue but let it go. He would ask Dr. Ramachandra for more in the morning.

Morgan swallowed another dose, then lay himself down. Soon he'd closed his eyes, his breathing lengthened, and he fell asleep. For a time, Liam stared out the window. He felt exposed as he peered through the narrow gap in the curtains. He expected a hopper to come bounding over the tops of the two-story homes, or a black-and-white to pull up outside in the falling rain. Or maybe it would be a wagon full of gray-suited Uprising men, ready to storm their small room, kill Liam, and take Morgan away.

No sooner had the grim thought come than Liam heard a creaking up the back stairs. The door was locked, yet he heard it groan as it was opened, heard a thud as it closed. He might have been alarmed—part of him thought he should be—but he wasn't. He suddenly remembered leaving a note for his grandmother two days ago, then hiding a key beneath the mat outside for her to get in.

Feet shuffled along the narrow hallway. Into the dimly lit room came Nana's crooked, aged form. She wore a patterned dress, white stockings, and her old, worn slippers, the ones she said helped her gout. She clutched a shawl around her shoulders. And she was dry as a bone, not a lick of rain on her.

"Nana," Liam said.

Nana headed toward the small table, but paused to glare at Alastair's still form. When she reached the table, she scraped out a chair, sat across from him, and curled her lips into something like a greeting. He could tell she was in a bad mood, but he didn't mind—she was at her creative best when *the wrath* was on her.

Nana poured two helpings of bathtub gin from the jar between them, then set one near Liam with a hard clack against the table. She spoke in Irish, her voice rough as a concrete barrier, "'The *scourge*,' they said. Said they wanted him unharmed." She downed her small helping, bared her teeth, then poured another. "Military's got to be involved somehow."

Liam took a swig of his harsh gin. "I don't disagree, but *how* are they involved? And why?"

"Don't know." Her mouth worked as if she were teasing a canker. "They said to take utmost care with *you*, though. Why, boyo? What is it they think you can do?"

"It's got to be the Devil's Henchmen. The abilities we had." Liam recalled the explosion in front of Club Artemis, the lightning strike on the tree when the hopper was chasing him and Morgan. "The military did something to us."

"We need more than that, Liam. I feel them closing in. You do too. And they've got well more'n we do."

Liam thought back. "Something was done to us. To *all* the Devil's Henchmen. But I don't remember what."

"Maybe not, but Grace knows something. She did the same thing you were able to do. She'll have answers."

Liam nodded. "You're right. I'll keep looking for her, but Morgan's in trouble. Dr. Ramachandra's our next move."

Nana considered this, her face pinched so badly she looked like she was sucking on a lime. "Didn't Morgan say Ramachandra was a surgeon in the Army?"

"Yes. So?"

"*So*, the coppers who chased after you came on awfully quick after you left his office. And an Army-issue hopper was sent as reinforcement."

Liam thought it over. "You think Dr. Ramachandra called someone?"

Nana laughed. "You think he didn't?"

"He might've," Liam admitted, "but I still need to go."

"Fine"—Nana's stare turned hard as nails—"but you can't go light."

Liam twisted his glass on the stained wooden tabletop. "No, I suppose I can't."

"Here's what we'll do." She laid out precisely how she wanted things to go, finishing the jar of gin as they worked through the details Liam hadn't thought of yet. When they were done, Nana stood and shuffled away, but paused at the hallway that led to the door. "And Liam?"

"Yes?"

"I know you'll want to, but you'll not be holding back. Hear me, boyo? Whoever's after you is the enemy, as much as the goliaths were, as much as those bastards in the trenches."

"You're right," he said. "I won't hold back."

She nodded, her face as pinched and angry as he'd ever seen it. "Good." And then she was gone.

TEN

It was still dark when Liam reached the sidewalk opposite Dr. Ramachandra's office in Wicker Park. The air was chill and oppressively humid. Rainclouds hung over the city, threatening another day of rain.

Through the low-hanging branches of an elm tree, Liam peered through Dr. Ramachandra's windows, watching for movement. He felt grim, ready for anything. Then suddenly the tops of the facing brownstones were lit golden. In the east, the clouds were drawing back like a defeated host, breaking to reveal the sun, stunningly bright after the accumulated days in darkness.

The street, the parked cars, the lamp posts, and the benches were still wet from the morning rain. As they glistened, dew-like beneath the bright morning sun, Liam took a deep, cleansing breath.

Dr. Ramachandra, as Morgan had said was his habit, came to the front door early and unlocked it so that his assistant, Nurse Harris, could let herself in. After taking one last look along the street, Liam pulled his tweed cap low over his face, like a gangster, and headed for the doctor's front door.

As he climbed the steps, he unbuttoned his double-breasted Ulster, allowing it to fall open. Inside the flaps, two sawed-offs hung from belt clips. A pair of Colt .45s rested heavy in their shoulder holsters. Heavier still was the single-shot hip cannon hanging from the back of his belt. It was a thing he'd kept squirreled away for years, a highly illegal bit of surplus he'd procured after the war in a fit of paranoia. After the hopper incident the other night, Liam thought it more than worth its cumbersome weight.

He opened the door without knocking. A small bell rang as he stepped into the foyer. After closing the door quickly behind him, he locked it.

"You're early!" called Dr. Ramachandra from the back room. Then a pause. "Nurse Harris?"

Liam strode into the waiting room, then through an archway to the small kitchen, where Dr. Ramachandra brewed tea for his patients. He wore a coal-gray suit with a bright red dastar. At Liam's entry, he turned from the breadboard, where he'd been buttering some soda bread, then started, staring wide-eyed at the .45 pointed at his chest.

"Remain calm, Dr. Ramachandra. No shouting. No sudden movements."

The doctor swallowed hard. His frosty beard waggled as he motioned to Liam's gun. "What makes you think you need that?"

"Today, *I'll* be the one asking questions. Are we clear?"

Dr. Ramachandra nodded. The look on his long face might not have been calm, but it wasn't hysterical, either—the instincts of a war surgeon kicking in.

"You're aware of the attack after Morgan and I left your office?"

"Yes. I spoke to Morgan's father the morning after. He told me about it."

"Did you call the authorities after we left?"

Dr. Ramachandra shook his head. "No, why would I have?"

"We were stopped by two police officers shortly after leaving your office. Alastair was deactivated by some strange device. Morgan and I were nearly killed. So I'll ask you again. Did you call the authorities?"

"I did not."

Liam searched his face carefully for a lie, but found none. "Has anyone else contacted you about Morgan?"

"No one I haven't contacted first."

"Who were they?"

"The lab downtown for the results of Morgan's blood test. Also two doctors whom I trust, to consult about his condition."

"And what did they tell you?"

At this, Dr. Ramachandra's look turned grave. It was the sort of mask doctors tended to put on when delivering dire news. "The blood tests came back with high levels of C-reactive protein, an indicator of a possible bacterial infection. Morgan's symptoms are similar to a number of the other cases reported in New York, Philadelphia, and Novo Solis. They match the profile of a biological agent Germany and the SLP have been spreading."

Liam felt his heart pounding. "The protein. What does it mean?"

"We need to run more tests to determine if it's the same strain or not, but if it *is*, I'm afraid Morgan's prognosis is not good. Those who've contracted it have thus far succumbed within a week. They present chills, stomach aches. They begin to have piercing headaches."

Morgan had complained of that very thing that morning.

"Have any survived?" Liam asked.

"I don't know. The patients were all taken by the Bureau of Health for further study."

"So *all* of them may have died?"

"It's possible. I couldn't say." He paused, swallowing hard with a glance toward Liam's pistol. "Morgan should be taken to them. He should go to the Bureau of Health today. There's an office here in Chicago."

In the pause that followed, a rhythmic booming filtered in from somewhere outside. The medicines in the nearby cabinets rattled, nearly in sync with them but ever-so-slightly delayed.

The hair along Liam's arms rose. It felt as if the ground were opening up beneath him, and that once he started falling, he would fall forever. All of the strange events from the past few weeks began to meld in his mind: a vision of nurses injecting his arm over and over again; the Devil's Henchmen screaming as they bounded over a battlefield; Clay dressed as a porter, escaping the flashtrain station with a case of blue serum under one arm; the strange voice in his head that ordered a hopper to help the two cops capture him and Morgan. He didn't understand everything that was going on, but he knew enough to distrust everything and everyone until he had more answers.

Liam focused on Dr. Ramachandra as the booming grew louder. "Quickly now, Doctor. The people you spoke to, were they from the bureau?"

Dr. Ramachandra seemed surprised by the question. "Well, yes."

"When? When did you speak to them?"

He glanced at the rattling cabinets with a flustered look, his battlefield nerves giving way to befuddlement and distress. "Only last night."

"Did you tell them anything beyond Morgan's symptoms?"

"I may have mentioned the state he was in when the two of you arrived. I told them I'd likely be seeing him in the next few days."

In the waiting room, visible through the archway Liam had taken to reach the kitchen, a curtain rod above one of the windows fell and clattered to the floor. Revealed was the small park across the street, the buildings beyond. The booming sounds were growing rapidly, not only in intensity but in their ability to instill fear. Oddly, a woman wearing posh clothes walked calmly along the sidewalk across the street. She seemed oblivious to the noise. An automated baby buggy propelled ahead of her. Her small black Pomeranian, leashed to the buggy, was yipping madly as it wove around her ankles.

"What in the name of God?" Dr. Ramachandra said.

Liam pulled the other revolver from its holster beneath his right arm. "Doctor, get back!"

The words had hardly left his lips when a massive form darkened the leftmost window. With a thunderous crash and an earth-rattling boom, glass shattered inward. The entire wall crumbled over the waiting room chairs, sending plaster, wood, and bits of brick flying toward Liam and Dr. Ramachandra. Liam crossed his arms over his face and twisted away as it sprayed him. Something heavy and hard struck him along the side of his head. He stumbled against the butcher block, sending the soda bread, butter cellar, and still-buttered knife clattering to the floor.

As a keen ringing sound filled his ears, Liam turned to find a vaguely humanoid shape filling the massive hole in the front wall of the doctor's home. It was easily nine feet tall, with mechanikal limbs. Through the semi-transparent visor in the helmet, Liam could see a woman working the controls of the armored suit, a wallbuster.

As Dr. Ramachandra fled through the door at the back of the kitchen, Liam emptied his revolvers directly into the mechanika's visor. The shots hammered his hands as he alternated squeezes of the triggers. The bullets ricocheted off the surface with attenuated *tings*. When his guns had both been emptied, the only evidence that he had just fired twelve high-powered rounds were the small divots in the dusty surface of the reinforced glass.

—*The scourge. Find the scourge.*

The voice again. And this time Liam felt it even more strongly than with the two policemen who had stopped them on the night they drank absynthe.

The wallbuster ducked low, gears whining, and reached an arm in with a speed that belied its bulk. Using pincers affixed to the end of its arm, it snatched Liam's Ulster and yanked him forward. Had the buttons not been undone, Liam would have been caught and trapped in his own coat. As it was, he was able to spin and slip free, but not before being drawn halfway across the waiting room.

The buster's opposite arm drove in like a piston and caught the cuff of Liam's trousers. He had dropped the Colts and reached for the shotguns. He decided against the hip cannon—he was too close, and the explosion would kill him too. One shotgun slipped from his grasp as he was thrown to the dusty floor, the pincer pulling him toward the gaping hole. He scrabbled, trying to escape, but couldn't. He was caught.

The soldier eased the wallbuster away from Dr. Ramachandra's home and onto the sidewalk. The morning sun shone brightly. The buster's arm whined upward, lifting Liam upside down until he was eye-to-eye with the woman inside the armor. By then Liam had managed to grab the other shotgun. He unloaded both barrels, point blank, into the visor.

Bits of glass flew. Cracks webbed outward from the point of impact. Liam felt sharp pain along his left ear from the blowback. But the visor held. The pilot inside smiled as her voice rang harshly from the two speakers set into the hulk's shoulders. "Where are you hiding your friend, Mr. Mulcahey?"

Liam managed to unhook the hip cannon clumsily. By the time he swung it around, the pilot had noticed. The buster's other arm came across him hard, bashing his right arm and knocking the cannon from his grip. It skittered over the sidewalk and onto the grass, well out of reach.

"I'll ask you one last time, Mr. Mulcahey. Where is Morgan Aysana?"

"Right here."

The hulk lumbered itself into a turn. Liam's trousers ripped and he fell to the ground. Ten paces away, Morgan stood in the middle of the street. He'd come out of the rumble seat of the Model A he'd been hiding in since early that morning, well before first light. He looked terrible. Shaky. White. Barely able to hold his ground. But hold it he did, with Liam's second and only other hip cannon braced properly against his hip.

People were exiting their homes, staring in shock at the wild scene before them.

The wallbuster took one lumbering step forward, crushing the hood of Packard Twin 6 to reach the street for an unobstructed path to Morgan. It had just taken a second step toward Morgan when he pulled the safety pin and squeezed the launch mechanism. From out of the snub-nosed cannon, a shell streaked toward the wallbuster's chest. Liam ducked behind the Twin 6 as it crashed dead on, the munition exploding in a cloud of smoke and screaming metal.

ELEVEN

The hulking suit of armor reeled from the explosion. It stumbled, arms flailing, for all the world a giant's toddler trying to regain its balance. It crashed onto the pavement with a boom Liam could feel through the sidewalk. Farther down the street, the woman with the baby buggy was just turning the corner away from them. The baby had begun crying loudly, and her Pomeranian was tugging maniacally at its collar, teeth bared, biting at the leash, yet the woman herself walked blithely on as if the morning were like any other. The people who'd rushed to the street from their homes were acting similarly. Shocked at first, they were heading calmly back into their homes.

Nearby, Morgan dropped the spent hip cannon onto the ground and strode toward Liam.

"Stay back, Morgan," Liam said, worrying the wallbuster still had power to its limbs.

For once, Morgan didn't argue. He remained where he was, standing in the middle of the street, his eyes both wary and angry as he studied the now-open pilot's compartment. Inside it, shattered glass framed the pilot's head, which was sheathed in a black, skintight hood. Blood dripped in rivulets from a dozen wounds, especially her right eye, which was coated in red.

"Who sent you?" Liam knelt on the armored chest and gripped her head, willing her to give him the answers he wanted. "Why are you after Morgan?" His fear and frustration boiling over, he shook her violently. "What's a bloody *scourge*?"

Morgan was a few yards away, holding Liam's snub-nosed revolver and staring down the street. "Liam?"

"Who speaks to you?" Liam shouted at the woman, desperate for answers. "Whose voice is feeding you your orders?"

She smiled, blood coating her teeth. "It wouldn't matter if I told you." Her voice was strangely soft after the distorted megaphone of the wall-buster's speakers. "Soon you'll both be ours."

"Why?"

She paused, then seemed to come to a decision. "Because the end is near, and your friend will deliver us there."

"Liam, someone's coming!"

The fear in Morgan's voice made Liam lift his head and stare down the street where, fifty paces distant, a man approached. It was Max Kohler, wearing chalk-striped pants, a matching vest, and a crisp white shirt. The red lens over his right eye shone brilliantly in the morning's light. His blue eye stared intently.

Liam moved to Morgan's side and took the gun from him. "Run, Morgan." Liam shoved him into motion. "To the attic!"

Morgan staggered but kept moving, thank God, and Liam turned to face Kohler.

"That's not going to help, Mulcahey," Kohler called, his voice muffled by the mask.

Liam stood his ground, aimed the snub-nose with both hands. "I remember you now. We served in the Devil's Henchmen. You were my CO."

Through the slits in Kohler's mask, the hint of a smile could be seen. "You're acting like you're only just piecing it together."

"That's because I am."

"Oh?" Kohler, twenty paces away, stopped and tilted his head, the sort of gesture that made it clear how preposterous he considered Liam's answer to be. "Then explain to me why you were at the very same flashtrain station where an Uprising attack occurred. You were there to help them, Mulcahey. You're one of them."

"No, I'm not!"

"Then you won't mind answering a few questions. Why does our President want to speak to you so badly?"

Liam stood there for a moment, stunned. The President wanted to speak to him? "I have no earthly idea."

"None?" Kohler used one knuckle to rap on his mask, where it covered his forehead. "You don't recall what Colette hid inside that noggin of yours?"

"Who's Colette?"

Kohler's head tilted to one side. "Come on, Mulcahey. You're going to have to do better than *that*."

"I mean it. I have no idea who you're talking about."

"That's the story you want to tell?"

"It's the only one I have."

"Yeah, well, we'll see about that," he said, and began stalking toward Liam once more.

Liam, a surge of fear running through him, aimed the revolver high and pulled the trigger, a warning shot. When Kohler's pace didn't slow, Liam aimed for his leg and fired again. In that same moment, Kohler swayed his arms to his left, and the street *bent*. The asphalt curved to meet him. As did the row of cars. As did the sidewalks and the buildings beyond. When he completed the movement, the world snapped back into normal position, but Kohler was no longer where he'd been. He was three yards to the left and five yards closer to Liam.

Liam adjusted his aim—this time meaning to put a bullet through Kohler's chest—and squeezed off another round.

Again Kohler brought his arms up and around in an arc, and the world moved with him. Like water in a stream rerouting when a stone blocks its path, the street *curved*, and Kohler shifted right. Again he was closer to Liam than he'd been only a moment ago.

Liam released two more rounds. Each exploded through the humid morning air, and each time, Kohler swayed and *shifted*. Liam didn't just see those movements. He felt them in his chest, like something that shouldn't be there. Each shift brought him closer to understanding where Kohler would wind up the next time.

He held his last round. Kohler was only five paces away now.

Liam adjusted his aim and squeezed the trigger, but not enough to release the hammer.

Kohler brought his arms around in another arcing gesture, this one faster, more violent than the others. Liam tracked his movements, not with his eyes—he didn't trust them any more—but with his gut.

Kohler reappeared just in front of Liam, to his left, out of the weapon's aim. Liam was already pulling the pistol in that direction. Hardly without thinking, he squeezed the trigger.

The round went off.

Sparks flew from Kohler's mask, just above the open eye hole.

And the world twisted. The clouds in the sky swirled. Kohler seemed to *pinch*, become smaller. He curled and distorted. Became like a gyrating thread of water. And it wasn't just Kohler. All around Liam, colors altered grotesquely. Trees bent, turned in on themselves like sacks turned inside out. The woman with the baby buggy turned, finally noticing the scene. Her body was changing. Her skin went pale, her eyes turned black. Blue veins spread across her face and neck. An impossibly hungry look came over her while the dog at her feet scraped its neck bloody, finally pulling itself free of the leash.

As the dog sprinted away, images flashed in Liam's mind. He saw a sterile white medical room. Men and women in masks surrounding him, examining him, talking *about* him, never *to* him. He saw a pretty doctor with dark, curly hair pulled back into a ponytail. Blood being taken. A serum being injected into his arm. An expansion of his emotions, his thoughts, sharing them with others, the members of his squad.

"He's ready!" came a woman's husky voice. The words and the memories brought on an indescribable fear that emanated from his very core. That fear expanded, touching other minds. Consuming them. Or were they consuming him?

He's ready. He's ready. He's ready . . .

The words echoed, gave him purpose. Not by his own choice, but theirs. *Their* purpose was now his own, whether he wanted it to be or not.

Suddenly, he felt part of a vast network, expanding ever wider, until it encompassed the whole nation. The sheer scope of it was staggering, but it had a center. Liam focused on that, following barely discernible lines in the vast galaxy of lights. Ever closer he came, toward one place, one soul. The one he was beholden to, or soon would be. He knew he had no hope of escaping it. It was too hungry, the net it cast too fine to slip through, too strong to break.

The very thought set his mind reeling, and soon the world around him was lost.

Liam woke with a groan. Good God, how his body ached. The ground beneath him suddenly bucked—no, it was his bed. It was bouncing. An earthquake, maybe?

He was in a dark place. A small window floated above him, giving a view of the blue sky beyond. He was in a vehicle. A delivery wagon, he understood now, like the one that had pulled up behind Club Artemis and disgorged soldiers of the Uprising.

The road they were taking was rough. Liam felt it through the hard slats beneath him. As a turn in the road pressed Liam against the wall, he felt straps running across his chest, waist, and legs. That they'd secured him was hardly surprising. Even so, the realization made the cramped space feel as if it were shrinking.

He turned his head to one side. On another bench, lying flat, was Max Kohler, a deep dent in his mask where the bullet had struck. Unlike Liam, he wasn't strapped to the bench. Sitting on the floor beside him was the soldier who had operated the wallbuster. She had a large bandage, stained red, taped over one eye. She stared at him with something like satisfaction but also hatred. Or maybe it was fear.

Liam craned his neck. Three others sat on a third bench that abutted the driver's compartment. Through an open grate he caught a glimpse of the driver's head and the tall buildings beyond. They were headed downtown.

He was just wondering where Morgan was—he didn't seem to be in the wagon—when someone shouted from the front. "Look out!"

The wagon lurched, curving sharply left.

The tires screeched. Liam felt the straps hold him in place. Everyone else, including the woman on the floor, was thrown forward.

"Woah!" called the driver. "Woah! Woooaaaahhhh!" The sound rose in pitch and volume over the course of several long seconds.

A great crash rent the wagon's interior. Glass shattered. The wagon tipped and *lifted* into the air. Kohler flew upward, as did the woman and the three others, all of them weightless. Then the wagon came back down. What followed was a tumble of sounds and limbs and a wildly rotating beam of light. Liam was pummeled mercilessly across his head and chest— by what, he wasn't sure.

The wagon slid with a sound like shearing metal, then came to a halt with a bone-rattling boom that shook the entire wagon. As the sound faded, dust sifted through the air, lit by the oddly angled column of sunlight streaming in from the front. Outside, voices called crisp orders. He could hear gunfire, bullets punching into the forward compartment. The driver groaned, then the passenger beside him. Then came an abrupt silence.

Something sizzled at the back of the overturned wagon. Bright light and blue sparks. The door was pried open, creaking as it went.

Liam heard voices but couldn't make out what they were saying. A woman stepped inside the wagon. It was Grace, wearing men's trousers and a brown leather airman's jacket with a fur collar. Her blonde hair was waved impeccably. It seemed so out of place in the darkness and pain, he nearly laughed.

"What are you doing here?" he asked as she cut his restraints and helped him to stand.

"Not now." She held out her hand. "We have to go."

"But Morgan was taken."

"I know."

"Where?"

"Not *now*, Liam," Grace said. "Not in the open like this."

Part of Liam wanted to wait until he had some answers, but Grace's look was so serious he stifled the urge and took her offered hand. Her skin was warm and soft, her grip strong and sure, belying her spare frame. As she led him out, Liam paused in the door frame, looking for Kohler. He was nowhere to be seen. Liam felt like he ought to tell Grace about it, but he was too confused.

He blinked under the harsh sunlight. A bullish man and a pretty black woman were waiting there, pistols in hand. The man was none other than Clay Graves. The woman was the one at the flashtrain ceremony, the one who'd fainted—or acted like she had. He understood, now, that she *had* been the black woman he'd glimpsed in Club Artemis's kitchen.

Grace nodded to each of them, then led Liam toward a powder black Curtiss motorcycle, idling nearby. The thing was all chrome, elegant curves, and a hulking engine that quietly purred. There was no kickstand; it was somehow maintaining balance without one. Grace hopped on, motioning Liam to take the seat behind her. Liam hated being a passenger on motorcycles—it put his fate too squarely in the hands of the driver—but he felt at ease with Grace. After throwing a leg over the bike, he slipped his hands around her waist and leaned into her. He felt her heartbeat, smelled her leather jacket and the scent of jasmine in her hair. A moment later, Grace urged the Curtiss's V-8 into a smooth-as-butter drag between the high buildings of Chicago's downtown streets.

Behind them, four gunshots rang out in rapid succession, one for each soldier left behind in the wagon. Each sound was amplified by the concrete maze, and reverberated like Saint Peter's gavel striking judgment.

TWELVE

They rode north along LaSalle through the Loop, Liam holding tight to Grace's waist. He felt dizzy. Lost. He hardly knew what to say, what questions to ask first. As they crossed Du Sable Bridge with its four stone tender houses, he shouted over the engine's growl, "Who were the people in the wagon?"

She glanced back. "People who represent a danger to us all." She returned her attention to the road ahead. "Now be quiet. We'll be able to talk soon."

The Curtiss navigated the streets with a restrained ease. Though his stomach twisted over not knowing where Morgan was or even if he was safe, part of him was glad they were moving away from the monoliths of downtown. He felt watched from the high windows, the city a hungry, thousand-eyed beast.

The towers gave way to smaller buildings, then estates and blocks of brownstones. For a time, they followed a winding road with grassy fields scattered with tree groves. Ahead were a trio of large geodesic domes, a nature preserve of some sort, the only buildings for miles around, apparently. The preserve had manicured lawns, duck ponds, and blooming trees. Grace slowed the Curtiss, steered them onto the winding drive, and followed it toward the domes. Halfway there Liam felt an odd sensation, as though a certain pressure he'd been unaware of had just been lifted. Far from a relief, it was chilling, making him wonder about the nature of this place, the nature of the world itself.

He put it from his mind as best he could, trusting Grace would share more with him soon. As she leaned the Curtiss toward the entrance of an underground garage, Liam felt yet another easing sensation, more pronounced than the first.

How many more layers are there? Liam wondered, then shivered as a new thought occurred to him. *Maybe it isn't the world that's gone screwy, Liam. Maybe it's you.*

The Curtiss drifted past a smattering of cars toward the back of the garage.

"Grace?" They were headed toward a wall, and Grace wasn't slowing down. "Grace!"

Liam blinked and suddenly the wall was gone, replaced by a simple archway. Grace rode through with an ease that hinted at deeper secrets. She'd known about the arch but had refrained from warning him about it.

She's preparing me, Liam realized, *but for what?*

They were in a smaller space now, a second garage with a low ceiling and hefty concrete pillars. They headed toward a door lit by a bright amber lamp. Beside it were four sleek and very expensive-looking cars. Grace curled past them, pulled up near the door, and killed the engine. When they climbed off, the Curtiss wobbled a bit, then righted itself, maintaining a perfect balance.

She led him through the door and up a winding set of stairs that opened into one of the domes he'd seen on the way in. It was filled with tall ferns and palms, a host of chirping birds, and an atmosphere so humid it bordered on oppressive. Through glass panels that overlooked the grounds, he saw three more domes, each with a unique biome: a small, deciduous forest in one, a desert in another, a flowering grassland in the third.

Liam stared at them. "There were three domes when we drove up, not four."

Grace slipped her leather jacket off, folded it across one arm, and guided Liam along a manicured path through the vegetation. "You're right," she said as their pace fell into an easy rhythm.

"Then how—?"

She gripped his arm. "There are things that will be revealed to you, Liam. They won't be easy to hear. Let's leave the domes alone for now."

A knot formed in Liam's throat. "Grace, I need to know what happened to Morgan. Who *were* those people in the wagon? Were they part of the Uprising?"

"No," she said forcefully while guiding him around a clutch of palm bushes, "they're not part of the Uprising." Their passage startled a small flock of goldfinches, which had been sitting amongst the broad, fanning leaves. "We refer to them as the Cabal. They pose as us when it suits them. Or the police. Or government agents or normal citizens. Sometimes even the military."

He was about to ask why when something struck him. "*You're* part of the Uprising."

"I am. As is the man we're about to talk to."

Liam stopped walking. "The Uprising are poisoning people. They're murderers."

Grace turned to face him. "We poisoned no one, as you'll soon find out. As for deaths, some of our raids unfortunately got out of control—they weren't meant to be violent. But there were other incidents that were staged, faked by the Cabal in hopes of tarring us. Others were *reported* as Uprising attacks but were actually the Cabal raiding *our* safe houses, killing *our* people. The truth never gets out, though. The Cabal control the newspapers, the wireless stations, and much more. The only thing most people read or hear or *think* is what they want us to."

Liam recalled how, at the flashtrain station, the Uprising's gunmen had fired *above* the crowd, and later, how the announcer on the wireless had claimed the attack was an assassination attempt on President De Pere, not a theft. "Why didn't you tell me who you really were?" Liam asked.

"I had to make sure you were who I thought you were."

"And who is that? Who do you think I am?"

"A man who may very well have the ability to save Morgan. But before you can do that, you need to know the truth."

Liam felt as if he were walking a tightrope. One wrong move and he'd plummet to his death, losing any chance he had at saving Morgan and finding out what was *really* going on. He had no idea if Grace was telling him the truth or not. "I don't trust you," he finally said.

"Nor would I expect you to." She waved to the door they'd been heading toward, an indication that the answers to his questions lay beyond. "I'm asking for a chance to earn it."

After a moment to absorb what Grace had said, Liam rejoined her on the path. "Why do they want Morgan?"

"They don't want Morgan per se," Grace said as gravel crunched beneath their every footstep. "They want what's inside him."

"And what is that?"

"We're not sure. It's why we staged the attack on the flashtrain station, so we could get an undiluted sample of the serum they've been distributing."

"You think *that's* what caused Morgan's sickness?"

"We're certain it is."

"But *why*? Why would they spread poison like that?"

"It isn't a poison, not the way you're thinking about it. The serum and the program De Pere is just now rolling out is a distribution mechanism. They were *hoping* Morgan's body would react in a certain way—"

"Wait, you're saying *President De Pere* is involved?"

They arrived at a steel door leading to an adjoining building. "I've said too much already. We need to save that until *after* you've digested the rest."

"Why?"

"Because otherwise you simply won't believe it."

With that she opened the door, and they headed inside. The anxious, roiling sensation in Liam's gut grew as she led him down several sterile hallways to a door with a lightbulb above it. Grace pressed a button on the wall. Several moments later, the bulb lit red and they heard an audible click, at which point she opened the door and motioned for Liam to enter ahead of her.

He did so, and found himself in a room that was in halves, separated by tall glass windows. Beyond the windows was a stark white room with a simple rocking chair and a burgundy rug. In the half Liam had just walked into, a middle-aged man sat in front of an instrument panel with an array of switches, lights, and readouts, including a circular display the size of a dinner plate.

The man looked vaguely familiar. He was thin, the sort of person who pecked at his food. He wore a modest wool suit, and had a neatly trimmed mustache and short hair, graying at the sides. For several long seconds, he seemed oblivious to them, then he swiveled his chair around and stood in a rush.

It was then that recognition came. "You're Stasa Kovacs," Liam said.

Stasa Kovacs was a man of staggering genius. He was the founder of over-the-air power transmission, the inventor of the wireless. Before his disappearance a year earlier, he'd begun to branch into the burgeoning field of neo-medicine. It was no exaggeration to say his innovations had changed the face of the Earth.

"However dim my star might once have been," Stasa said in a light Hungarian accent, "I'm glad to see it hasn't faded entirely." Though the words were filled with false modesty, his smile seemed genuine as he held out one hand. "You're Liam?"

Liam shook his hand with an awestruck nod. "Everyone thinks you were abducted, that the Uprising stole you away from your own building."

Stasa shrugged noncommittally. "It's true I was abducted, but it wasn't by the Uprising." Perhaps sensing Liam was about to launch into a series of questions, Stasa raised both hands. "A story for another day." He waved to the room beyond the glass. "We're here for another purpose, one that will form the basis of all discussions that follow." He returned to his seat, pressed a button on the instrument panel, and spoke into a receiver. "Bring them in."

Beyond the glass, a door was opened and a man and a boy, both wearing hospital robes, were led into the room by a woman wearing a mask and blue scrubs. The man was led to the rocking chair, the boy to the rug. The nurse left the room immediately, closing the door behind her. The man remained where he was, perched on the edge of the rocking chair, hardly moving. The boy, who looked to be eight, maybe nine years old, knelt on the carpet, but did nothing more.

Their physiques were cadaverous—sunken eyes, sharp cheekbones, heads that appeared too large for their necks. Both had sallow skin and blue veins around their eyes that stood out like the branches of a dying tree. As disconcerting as all that was, the thing that disturbed Liam the most was their vacant expressions. They appeared numb to everything and everyone around them.

"What on God's green earth is going on?" Liam asked.

Stasa, ignoring him, flicked several switches on the instrument panel. On the round display, two lines appeared, scrolling from left to right. After adjusting a dial, the lines began to jitter, leaving zigzag patterns in their wake.

Grace, meanwhile, pointed toward the glass. "Their names are Alan and William. They were rescued from a complex in Novo Solis purportedly run by the United States government but, in reality, run by the Cabal."

"Can they see us?"

"The glass is mirrored on their side," Grace said, "but they're not paying attention to their surroundings anyway. They were part of an experiment by the Cabal that we have yet to understand the purpose of. We do know this much: they are infected with a strain of bacteria that has dulled their minds and made them pliable, susceptible to commands. They've all but lost their own free will."

"A bacteria," Liam echoed.

"Yes. A bacteria known as *Echobacterum sentensis*, or *E. sentensis*. The particular variant Alan and William have been infected with is known as the *thrall* strain."

"But how could a *bacteria* do that to them?"

"We'll return to that," Grace said. "For now, what I want you to understand is that during the war, your squad, the Devil's Henchmen, were part of a top secret program codenamed Project Echo. Knowing that we were losing the war of engineering and manufacturing, our military turned to neo-medicine. Project Echo was created to enhance the inherent abilities of *E. sentensis* to stop the advance of Germany and the other members of the SLP. And it worked. Spectacularly, in fact. The discovery of *E. sentensis* was nothing short of a miracle. By tapping into our innate, heretofore unexplored ability to communicate with one another, it allowed you and your squad mates to hear what *any* of you heard, to see what *any* of you saw. Further, it allowed you to communicate instantaneously with mere thought."

"A bacteria can't do that." Liam said the words even as the visions he'd had of being injected in the arm played within his mind.

"You may think so," Stasa said without bothering to look up from his panel, "and yet, since the time of antiquity, man has found psychedelics and deliriants in the natural world. Belladonna, opium, peyote, magic mushrooms. Even the humble seed of *Myristica fragrans*, more commonly known as nutmeg, can have hallucinogenic effects. You may counter by saying those are plants, not bacteria, but to that I say: why is it our thought processes change when we become hungry or when we're sick to our stomachs? It's no accident. It's a byproduct of the bacteria in your gut sending chemicals to those in your brain, which in turn emit chemicals of their own."

"But sending *thoughts*?" Liam said. "Illusions?"

"Over the past few decades, we've become more and more aware of man's innate, extrasensory perceptions." Stasa swiveled in his chair until he faced Liam. "Is it so difficult to believe bacteria might produce chemicals that enhance those abilities? That they might allow us to transmit thoughts, emotions, our very perceptions? And that, further, we might be able to *force* those perceptions on those we're linked with?"

"It's an awfully large pill to swallow."

"I understand," Stasa said as he swung back to his instrument panel, "but the very fact that governments worldwide would go to war over control of *E. sentensis* should tell you there's something to it."

It took Liam a moment to understand. "You're saying the war was started over this bacteria?"

"That's precisely what I'm saying."

Liam shook his head. "The war started because the Germans bombed our embassy in Berlin."

"True, but *why* did they bomb it?"

"Their pretext was that our ambassador"—Liam snapped his fingers several times, trying to remember the man's name—"James Runyon . . .

They said he assassinated a German scientist, that he'd been trying to steal state secrets and that the raid was to get them back."

"They weren't lying." After one last flick of a switch, a piece of paper began spooling out from the instrument panel—on it were two wavy lines, mirrors of the lines being drawn on the round display. Only then did Stasa spin in his chair to face Liam. "Runyon succeeded beyond President Nolan's wildest expectations. Not only did he manage to steal a trove of research, he found a protean version of *E. sentensis* and managed to get it out of the country. With Runyon's assassination of their top scientist, a neomed pioneer, Germany's research on *E. sentensis* was effectively kneecapped, while America's was jumpstarted. Germany, of course, demanded the return of the stolen items and the cessation of all research on *E. sentensis*. When Nolan refused, it set off a chain of events that led to the formation of the St. Lawrence Pact and, eventually, the war itself."

Stasa began comparing the paper to the display.

Grace, meanwhile, jumped into the fray. "However the war began," she said, "it was the stunning successes in Project Echo, years later, that led to every SLP country—France, Great Britain, Canada, *and* Germany— agreeing to the armistice. You may remember Leland De Pere as an honorable man, and by all accounts he was, but something changed after the war. He rose like a phoenix from the war's ashes, becoming mad with power in the process. He used that power to create the Orpheus Initiative."

Liam remembered that much. The Orpheus Initiative had been touted as a safeguard against America's enemies. Primary among its goals was to distribute, nationwide, a preventive medication meant to inure Americans to a nerve agent the SLP had supposedly developed. Like the distribution of the serum De Pere had recently offered at the flashtrain ceremony, the program had been voluntary at first, but then it had been disseminated through hospitals, water systems, and finally through crop dusters for the country's most rural areas.

"The real purpose of the Orpheus Initiative," Grace said, "was to spread a neutered version of *E. sentensis* to every man, woman, and child in the country. And it worked. We're all infected. You, me, Morgan. Everyone.

It means we can be affected by illusions, some of which we create ourselves to make sense of the world, others of which are created by a certain few: Grace, De Pere, Max Kohler, and now, you."

"Me?"

"Yes. You have the potential to be every bit as powerful an illusionist as I am. As Kohler is. Maybe even De Pere."

"That's preposterous."

The way Grace was staring at him made her thoughts clear: *Is it really so preposterous, given all you've seen and done?*

Feeling ever more uncomfortable under that stare, he shifted to the main question plaguing him. "What could possibly motivate De Pere to do all of this? Why would he use the powers of our government for such evil purposes?"

"We don't know the underlying reasons," Grace said, "but this much is clear: the Orpheus Initiative was but a precursor to the plan he's unfolding now."

Though Liam was bursting with questions, he was distracted by the sudden building of pressure inside of him; the easing he'd felt on his way into the complex was somehow reversing itself. It was Stasa, he realized. He was turning a large brown dial on the instrument panel, and the more he turned it, the more intense the feeling became.

After flipping a few final switches, Stasa spun in his chair. "We're ready," he said to Grace.

Grace nodded. "You'll have more questions, Liam, but what I'm about to show you will answer many of them." With that she approached the window.

Stasa considered Liam soberly. "Prepare yourself."

Grace waved one hand, and the stark walls of the room beyond the glass were replaced with lilac wallpaper. The ceiling turned a creamy color with bold crown molding. The monotone floor tiles transformed into lustrous, polished hardwood. On the room's right was a brick fireplace with a lively fire. Along the far wall, high Victorian windows gave view of a vegetable garden, a row of tall Italian cypress trees beyond.

And the changes weren't limited to the room itself. Alan's sallow skin turned a healthy pink. His blue veins vanished. The same happened to William. Beside Alan's rocking chair was a bronze coal scuttle stuffed with folded newspapers. A lump formed in Liam's throat as Alan snatched one of the newspapers, unfolded it, and began reading. "Why don't you finish your picture?"

On the carpet beside William, a box of Dixon's Solid Colored Crayons lay beside a coloring book open to a half-colored drawing of a dancing bear. Until then, William had seemed sluggish, as if the illusion hadn't yet registered, but on hearing his father's words he blinked, glanced at the fire, and lay down so that his feet were close enough to the flames to warm them. As his legs scissored back and forth, he tugged the book closer and used a navy blue crayon to scribble in the sky above the bear.

Liam stared at Grace and Stasa in turn. After several seconds of trying and failing to articulate his raw horror and confusion, he managed to say, "How?"

"The complex we're in," Stasa said, "has been shielded from the outside world. The vast quilt of consciousness created by *E. sentensis* has no sway within it."

Liam thought back to the easing of the pressure inside him. "I felt it, as Grace and I rode in."

"I'm not surprised," Stasa said. "All the members of the Devil's Henchmen, including you, were given a very powerful strain of *E. sentensis*. It may be why you were able to sense the field."

"If, as you say, we're shielded," Liam said, "how is it Alan and William can see the illusion? How can we?"

"Because *within* the complex is another, smaller quilt. It allows us to mimic what it's like in the outside world, which in turn allows us to run experiments to better understand what the Cabal are planning."

Beyond the glass, William had nearly finished coloring in the sky. Alan snapped the newspaper to another page.

Liam turned to Grace. "You're *making* them see all this?"

"Not exactly." Grace waved to the room beyond the window. "What I gave them was a suggestion of sorts, a seed that blossomed within their minds. *They* are now the ones maintaining the illusion, not me. From moment to moment, their minds negotiate with one another subconsciously. What William sees himself creating, Alan sees. And what Alan imagines himself doing, William sees as well."

"What about the garden outside the window, the clouds, the swaying trees?"

"Those are drummed up from their subconscious. They're *supposed* to be there, so that's what the two of them see."

"They lived in this place once, then?"

"Or a place very much like it." Grace shrugged. "It could also be a mixture of a few different places they're familiar with. Or the sort of home they once dreamed of."

Liam waved to the archway along the room's left wall. Beyond it was an ornate entry door and a set of stairs. "And what if they decide to walk out the front door?"

"They won't, because deep down, they both know they can't. It simply won't enter their consciousness."

"What if they get hungry?"

"They'll imagine themselves having food."

"But they won't get any sustenance."

"Which is why they're fed outside of these experiments."

"And everyone outside this complex? How are *they* fed?"

Stasa shook his head. "Don't make the mistake of applying the conditions of this small experiment to the world at large. Beyond the domes, the veneer of life as we know it goes on more or less as normal. Just below the surface, however, lies a vast network, enabled by *E. sentensis,* that connects the entire country. It allows the government a form of control that could never even have been imagined before the war."

Liam fell silent. He was trying to process everything, but was having little success. He stared at Alan reading his paper, at William drawing in his coloring book. "This is wrong," he said, grasping onto that single truth like a lifeline.

"That's why we're trying to find a cure," Grace said.

"No," Liam said, harder this time. "I mean Alan and his boy. You shouldn't be experimenting on them like this."

"This is for *their* benefit. Theirs and others who might become infected. You wanted to know why the Cabal took Morgan? I'll tell you. Alan and William were infected with the *thrall* strain, but *Morgan* was infected with another, known as the *scourge* strain."

"Scourge," Liam echoed numbly. It was precisely what the voice inside his head had said, referring to Morgan.

"That's right," Grace said. "You have every right to be wary over the Uprising and our purpose—the Cabal have waged a successful campaign to impute all the evil they are committing to us—but I'm telling you now, the reason the Uprising was formed, its sole purpose, is to expose what Leland De Pere and his Cabal are preparing to unleash."

"And what is that? What are they preparing to unleash?"

"We don't know yet."

"You must have some guesses."

Grace nodded. "We do, but it's going to be hard to swallow, Liam."

"Try me."

Grace paused, collecting herself. "We believe the thrall strain is going to be used to enslave the vast majority of America, perhaps the entirety of the human race. We think the scourge variant is a sort of enforcer, those who can control the thralls."

Liam could only stare. "This makes no sense. What sort of man would *do* that?"

"A psychopath," Stasa replied calmly. "A psychopath would do that."

"I knew De Pere. He was no psychopath."

"You knew him so well?" Stasa pressed. "You're qualified to make that sort of evaluation."

"No, but he didn't *seem* like that sort of man." The memories Liam had of De Pere all spoke of a calm, rational, soft-spoken officer, not a madman.

"What might have happened to De Pere we don't know, but *this*"—he waved to Alan and William—"is why we need Morgan. We think the

Cabal are close to perfecting the scourge strain. But their progress has stalled, which is why De Pere attended the flashtrain ceremony. The serum was a way to canvas for more test subjects. The strain doesn't take in most people, but in some cases, like Morgan's, it does. And *when* it does, the Cabal are somehow able to sense it. Within days, they track them down and take them, by force if necessary, to a Cabal facility, where we assume they're studied. With Morgan, we might be able to understand how *his* strain differs from the ones we've already studied."

In the adjoining room, Alan pulled the newspaper aside and stared down at William's coloring book. "Well done. Now do the bear."

Liam watched as William grabbed a red crayon and proceeded to color in the bear's fur with the same fervor as he had the sky. The thought of Morgan becoming another test subject in Stasa's research was making Liam sick to his stomach. "Stop the experiment."

"We will," Stasa replied, "but it takes time."

"I said stop it."

Stasa's look went hard. "Perhaps it would be best if you stepped outside, Liam."

Liam had become acutely aware of the pressure around him, the pressure inside him. Both were swirling, as before, and became more pronounced whenever William or Alan moved or looked about. Grace might have created the illusion, Alan and William might be maintaining it, but Liam was growing progressively more certain he could wipe it all away.

Grace guessed his intent. "Liam, don't."

But Liam had already started. The illusion of the room beyond the window was like a fabric he might cut. Not knowing precisely *how* to do it, he lashed out. It felt as if he were slashing at silk with a butcher's knife, but it seemed to be working.

The fireplace disappeared. Then the windows. The archway vanished, replaced by a blank wall with lilac-colored wallpaper. Then the room reverted to its former state: solid white, filled with a carpet, a rocking chair, and a hapless father and son.

Last to change were Alan and William themselves. Their skin went sallow. The blue veins returned. Their flesh drew in and they became their former, rawboned selves. Alan turned his skeletal hands over, stared at them in confusion. Then, slowly but surely, he seemed to lose interest and set them in his lap.

William, meanwhile, reacted very differently. He stood and stared angrily at the section of wall where the fireplace had been. "No!" he screamed, staring about at the white walls. "No!" When his eyes locked on his father in the rocking chair, his expression shifted to one of pure rage. "Bring it back!" He stepped closer and slapped his father's cheek. "Bring it back! Bring it back!"

As Stasa shouted into the receiver on the instrument panels for help, William balled his hands into fists and struck Alan over and over again. Red welts appeared, then a cut, perhaps from William's fingernails, the trail of blood smearing by the continued blows. But Alan just stared into the mirrored glass windows, directly at Liam, as if he'd just discovered the source of all his misfortunes.

THIRTEEN

Two men in blue scrubs rushed into the room. One grabbed William, who went wild, thrashing, until the other stuck a needle into the meat of his arm and depressed the plunger. When William's screams had quieted, when his body went lax and his eyes dulled, the nurse set him slowly back onto his feet and led him from the room. Alan, meanwhile, was still staring dead-eyed through the glass, as if he were wishing upon Liam tortures as painful as what his son had endured.

When Alan too was led from the room, Grace took Liam by the arm and motioned to the door with the red light. "Let's talk. Just you and me."

Liam nodded and followed her from the room and returned to the tropical dome. He stared at the lushness around him, wondering if any of it was real.

"By now, you've likely started to question everything and everyone around you," Grace said. "It was the same for me when I first learned of the Cabal."

"And how *did* you learn about them? How are you able to cast illusions? How am I?"

Grace paused, as if debating the best way to explain it all. "I'll answer the simplest question first. You're able to cast illusions, and destroy them, because of your involvement in Project Echo. Everyone in your squad received a powerful strain of *E. Sentensis*—we call it, simply, the Henchman strain. As to your other questions, I don't know how complete your memories are of the war, but there was a doctor who headed the project. Her name was Colette Silva."

The visions of injections flashed through Liam's mind, one after another, hardly pausing. They stopped on the stunningly pretty woman with dark skin and a curly black ponytail. She wore a lab coat. Her eyes were a deep russet flecked with green.

"I remember bits and pieces," Liam said.

"We were friends, she and I," Grace said. "I first met her when she came to Novo Solis to start Project Echo. We renewed our friendship after the war, and she confessed her fears over what De Pere meant to do with her research. I believed her, and I was sympathetic, but when she asked for help in funding the Uprising, I demanded proof. In answer, she offered to give me the very same serum you'd received."

"If she gave it to you, then she must have given it to others."

Grace nodded. "That was the plan, but shortly after my injection, she went missing. I'm nearly certain De Pere had her killed. At present, there are only two in the Uprising with any ability to interact with illusions: me and your fellow Henchman, Clay Graves. Clay's abilities atrophied, however, from the injuries he sustained. He can sense illusions, even dispel them, but he can't make any on his own."

Liam blinked. He hardly remembered Colette, yet the news of her death sent a pang of regret through him. He wondered if they'd been friends during the war, if they'd been *more* than friends.

"And the other Henchmen?"

"Max Kohler, as you're now well aware, works for De Pere. The others are all missing or dead, part of a campaign on De Pere's part to stifle resistance to his plans. What's important now is that we focus on finding a cure for Morgan, Alan and his son, and others infected like they are."

Liam, feeling some small relief that Morgan might be saved, waved to the steel door beyond the ferns. "Has Stasa started developing an anti-serum, then?"

"He has, but he hasn't gotten very far, I'm afraid. It's no simple feat, and remember, there's more than one strain. Finding a cure for the thrall strain may do us little good against the scourge strain, and vice versa. That's why we need Morgan. We need to understand what the more powerful scourge strain has done to his physiology. We need to compare that against what we've already learned about the other strains, which will help us learn how to counter them all." Grace paused. "In short, I'm asking for your help, Liam."

"You want me to join the Uprising?"

"I don't care if you formally join us or not. But I *do* want you to aid us in our efforts. We need it. *Morgan* needs it."

Allying himself with the Uprising, even temporarily, was a big step, but he was ready to do it if it would help Morgan. "Okay, Grace. I'll help rescue Morgan."

Grace looked relieved. "You'll be helping by telling us what you know about Project Echo, and by allowing us to take blood samples from you. You can stay here at the domes for the time being. We'll find you a more permanent place as soon as we start to train you—"

"What I meant, Grace, is that I want to help with Morgan's rescue."

"Clay's already working on that."

"Then assign me to him. And since you mentioned a place to stay, I'll need my grandmother moved as well."

Grace had looked ready to argue with Liam over the role she wanted him to play, but at the mention of his grandmother, her look turned to one of sympathy—no, of *condolence*.

Moment by moment, a profound yet sourceless sense of anxiety was overcoming Liam. "You look like I've just stepped on your grave."

"I'd hoped we'd have more time to talk this through, to prepare you."

"Prepare me for *what?*"

"Liam, I'm sorry to be the one to tell you this, but your grandmother died from a heart attack at war's end."

Liam shook his head. "You're mad. I *live* with Nana!"

"You only think you do. Your grandmother is a figment of your imagination."

"Bloody hell, Grace, I *feed* her. I *bathe* her. I make her colcannon, just the way she taught me."

Before Liam knew it, he was backing away from Grace. He wasn't even sure why at first, but then he turned and headed for the stairwell they'd taken up from the garage. A moment later he was running.

Grace called behind him, "Please, Liam, don't go."

Ignoring her, he wound his way down to the small, hidden garage, hopped on the Curtiss, and thumbed the start switch. It roared to life. He tapped it into gear and eased away from the parking space.

As he gunned the motorcycle toward the wall, Grace came flying out the door. "Liam, wait! It's too dangerous!"

He twisted the throttle harder, and the Curtiss was eager to please. On he hurtled toward the concrete wall. It looked perfectly solid, but he no longer cared if he crashed.

"Liam!" he heard Grace call from behind.

Her voice was cut off sharply as he passed through the wall and into the garage. Soon he was back out on the easy roads around the domes. Open fields and light forests turned to rural neighborhoods, which in turn gave way to the tighter streets of the city proper. Over the brownstones, the towers of downtown loomed like vultures on a high cliff, waiting for him to fall.

As he neared North Town, Grace's words haunted him. What she'd said about Nana couldn't be true—it couldn't—which made everything she'd told him in the room beneath the domes feel like a lie. He was more worried the Cabal had come for Nana, that he'd find signs of violence when he arrived. It pushed him to drive even faster.

Outside his apartment building, he squeezed the brakes hard, and the Curtiss screamed to a stop. The neighborhood boys stared as Liam killed the engine and hopped off. With his heart in his throat, he left the motorcycle to its perfect equilibrium and ran up the stairs to the third floor.

"Nana?" he called as he entered.

To his relief, everything looked the same as it had when he'd left: their small living room with the two padded armchairs; the wireless in its polished teak cabinet; the long, open space that acted as their kitchen and dining room; the hall running straight ahead to the small bathroom and their two bedrooms.

"Nana!"

He heard the creak of her bed. Heard the familiar sound of her box spring decompressing as she made it to her feet.

Liam waited, breathless, staring at her door at the end of the hall while a host of blackbirds took flight inside his chest. He was a schoolboy again, getting dropped off by his mum on the front steps of St. Mary of the Angels. Moments passed in utter silence. He wanted to call out, but was too afraid.

Of what? a voice inside him asked. *Of what are you afraid?*

Of the truth, he realized. He thought back to the shared room above the pneumatics garage, how Nana had appeared unannounced while Morgan slept. Liam suddenly realized he'd left no note, nor had he hidden a key beneath the mat outside the door. She'd just come; Liam's imagination had fabricated the rest. There was Morgan's invitation to Club Artemis, too. She'd known about it without him saying a word. The same was true of the violence after their flight of absynthe, and their talk with Dr. Ramachandra, and their run-in with the downtown cops and the hopper. He thought of a dozen examples besides.

The growing torrent of memories and worries halted the moment Nana's door opened. She stepped into the hall wearing her robe and slippers. She shuffled toward him, catching his eye. She groused in Irish, "Coffee on?"

"Yes," he said. "Sure." He put a pot on the stove, began grinding a scoopful of beans in their box grinder. "You had me worried."

"Oh?" She was sitting sideways in her chair, staring out the window longingly. "And why is that?"

"I thought you might not be here when I got back."

"Where would I have gone, Liam?"

Liam froze. She'd said those words in English. Never, not once in their years together since the war, had she spoken to him in anything but her native tongue.

Fingers tingling, Liam set the grinder down on the counter with a hollow clunk, then sat carefully at the table across from her, fearful of making a sound. "There's been some trouble."

Nana's gaze was flinty. "I always know when you're in trouble, sonny boy." Irish again. "It's why I work so hard to protect you."

Liam shook his head, his thoughts ajumble. He knew the question he needed to ask. He just couldn't get the words out. He didn't want to know.

Nana's eyes took him in anew, as if she were surprised, almost offended. "Well, spit it out, boyo!"

"Are you real, Nana?"

A rumble of a laugh emanated from her crooked mouth. "Real? What's real, Liam?" Her eyes roamed their flat. "This room?" She rapped the tabletop with her knuckles. "This table?"

As in the room below the domes, Liam felt his insides churning. A moment later, the scene around him changed. The walls, so crisp and white a moment ago, were faded with age. Mold spots dominated the ceiling's far corner. The padded chairs they often sat in while listening to the wireless had deep holes in the fabric, as if rats had been chewing away at them for months. Save for the kitchen, the chairs Liam used, and the path Liam, only Liam, walked to his room, a layer of fine dust lay over everything, including the kitchen table on Nana's side, the place she always sat, the place she always made sure to clean up with her linen napkin when she was done.

"Or is it your *memories* that are real?" Nana went on. "Memories of me, memories of your mum and da, memories of your first kiss behind St. Mary's with that slutty O'Reilly girl. Which is more real, Liam, your collected memories or the split instant you see before you in the here and now?"

"You know what I mean."

"I do, boyo, but I'm giving you the only answer I can. I'm real because you *make* me real."

Liam got up, ignoring the half-ground coffee, ignoring the boiling water burbling in the pot. He walked along the hall, his footsteps leaden. He passed the bathroom door on his right, passed his own door, until he finally reached Nana's.

He stood there, hands balled into fists, heart pounding. He turned the handle. Pushed the creaking door wide.

Inside was a nearly empty room. Gone were Nana's pictures on the walls. Gone was her dresser with the brass pulls and the small but elegant lamp on top. Gone was the small night-stand with her teacup and the half-finished bottle of 12-year Irish single malt. All that remained were the skeleton of a bed frame and mattress—with not a single stitch of fabric left on it—and a Springfield rifle, complete with bayonet, leaning in the far corner of the room. The rifle had been his, he remembered, assigned to him when he'd been selected for the Devil's Henchmen.

Liam heard the scuff of footsteps behind him. He turned, expecting to see Nana. Instead he found Grace standing in the entryway, staring at him with a look of depthless sorrow. He hated that look. He hated feeling so vulnerable. He felt as if he were standing on the edge of a yawning precipice. And yet, despite all that, he was glad for Grace's presence—there was something about her that felt familiar, as if he'd known her for years, and that in turn gave him hope.

Nana had left, he knew, which made him wonder if she'd ever come back.

"I'm so sorry," Grace said, as if she were the cause of it all.

He swallowed the growing lump in his throat. "What *happened* to me? Why can't I remember anything?"

She stepped into the apartment. "When we found Clay, he was the same. He didn't remember Project Echo, nor his time in the Devil's Henchmen. Something had been done to him to wipe his memories of the war. The same was done to you. To *all* the Henchmen."

As Liam moved slowly along the hall toward her, a memory suddenly flared. The notion of having his memory wiped away like writing from a chalkboard reminded him of his conversation with the President after the attack at the flashtrain ceremony. There was something odd about it, something *wrong*.

"Tell me again," De Pere had said near the end of their conversation, "how the man, Clay, broke in through the door of the last car."

"As I said, sir, he *didn't* break in through the door," Liam had told him. "There *was* no door."

But De Pere was as unfazed as he was undeterred. "Tell me about it, the door."

Liam felt as if he were picking at the edges of a picture to see the one beneath. Finally, he managed it—he ripped the altered memory away, and the truth was revealed. One moment, Clay was standing before the car's bright steel side, the next he was walking *through* it to reach the interior.

"De Pere can alter memories," he said as he came to a stop a few paces from Grace.

"Yes." She looked surprised, but only mildly so. "Precisely why he did it, we're not certain, but Colette Silva eventually learned of it. She learned of De Pere's plans for the Cabal as well. Her efforts to locate you and gain your help in fighting De Pere is likely what got her killed."

Again Liam felt a pang of regret, and again it felt untethered, which in a way was just as discomfiting as the regret itself. He desperately wished he could remember more about Colette. It felt important that he do so. She felt like a hidden vault that, once opened, would reveal vital, terrible secrets.

"It's a lot to swallow, Grace. A bacteria granting the ability to alter *memories*?"

Grace spoke calmly, evenly. "Think about all you've learned so far, all you've remembered. You know it's possible to alter perceptions. You've done it yourself. Memories are only one step away from our perceptions. Is it really so hard to believe the serum could advance to the point that someone could alter *them*, too?"

Liam shrugged. "I suppose not."

She stepped closer to him, her black patent leather shoes scuffing the bare wood floor. "Please say you'll join us, Liam. We need you."

Liam felt overwhelmed by all he'd learned, all he'd lost. He felt utterly lonely. There had been two constants in his life since the war. The first had been Nana, and now Nana was gone. The second had been Morgan. He'd stuck with Liam through thick and thin. He'd stayed friends with Liam even when Liam had tried to force everyone away. The last thing Liam was going to do was abandon Morgan when he needed help.

"I'll join you," Liam said, "but I want to be involved in the effort to save Morgan."

"It's too dangerous. Come back with me to the lab. I'll help you to unlock—"

"No. I'm going to help save Morgan."

Grace's face turned serious. "You must understand, the Cabal are moving faster than we anticipated. We don't have the time to train you properly."

"Grace, forgive me, but it's you who doesn't understand. I'm not doing anything—for you, for the Uprising—until I know Morgan is safe."

Grace's expression was one of worry. Of balancing odds. "You're not ready."

"I can't leave it to fate. I won't."

In the moments that followed, Liam became convinced he'd pushed too hard, that Grace was going to deny him. But then she held out one hand and gave him a melancholy smile. "All right, Liam. We'll do it your way."

Liam took her hand. "Yeah?"

"Yeah," she said. "Let's go save Morgan."

FOURTEEN

When Liam asked Grace for some time to check in on Alastair, and collect a few things from the pneumatics garage where he and Morgan had been staying, she nodded and led him to the alley behind his apartment building. There, near the trash bins, a green Nash sedan was parked. Sitting behind the wheel was a rugged but haggard-looking man with thinning, dirty blond hair and a five o'clock shadow. It was Clay Graves, and beside him was the pretty, dark-skinned woman from the flashtrain platform.

"I believe you know Clay already," Grace said. "The lovely lady next to him is his wife, Bailey."

Liam, feeling more than a little awkward, ducked down so he could take both of them in. "Pleased to meet you."

Bailey was roughly Liam's age, maybe a few years older. Her straightened hair was cut in a bob and parted to one side. She had a pert nose, bright eyes, and a disarming smile. "The pleasure's all ours, dear."

Clay sneered.

Though his hair might be thinner, his expression more haunted, Clay was, in essence, the same as the brash soldier Liam had served with in the Devil's Henchmen. There were other, more severe changes Liam had no recollection of, though. While his right arm and hand were flesh and bone, his left was mechanikal, made of brushed steel. And a metal sleeve of some sort was wrapped around Clay's chest—Liam could see several dials and switches beneath his shirt. He heard a faint hiss as well, the sound of a pump of some sort, perhaps to aid in Clay's breathing.

"Something you want to get a better look at, motherfucker?" Clay asked.

"Sorry," Liam said, "you've changed is all."

"Oh, don't mind him," Bailey said from the passenger seat, "he's all bark."

"Take him where he wants to go"—Grace slapped the car's roof twice—"then bring him to the domes."

"Will do, boss," Clay said.

Grace turned to Liam. "I've got a few things to take care of that will take me out of the city until Wednesday, Thursday at the latest. Clay and Bailey will take care of you until then."

Liam nodded. "See you soon."

As Grace headed toward the front of the building and the Curtiss, Clay glowered at Liam. "Well, I guess I'm your fucking chauffeur now." He tilted his head toward the back seat. "Hop in." When Liam did, Clay shifted the car into drive, but held the brake. "Where to?"

"West on Fullerton."

"Roger that."

As the Nash accelerated, Bailey turned in her seat. "You'll have to forgive my husband," she said in a loud whisper. "He gets cranky around this time of the month."

Clay rolled his eyes. "Oh, don't start with that, woman!"

Bailey's laugh was deep and rolling. Liam, meanwhile, shook his head, confused.

"Stasa feeds Clay a cocktail of drugs," Bailey said. "They help what's left of his body adjust to the sleeve. The worst come once a month." She leaned in closer and spoke in the same loud whisper. "They make him irritable."

"Who's *irritable*?" Clay groused.

"You are, you miserable cuss."

Liam felt uncomfortable with their bickering, but the wink Bailey gave him helped ease the tension. "Were you sweethearts during the war, then?"

"Since before the war, actually," Bailey said with a sad smile. "I met Clay through my brother, Nick Crawford."

Liam could tell there was a lot more to the story, but the look on Bailey's face was giving him pause. "Is Nick . . . ?"

Bailey nodded. "Nick's gone. He had a stroke after a trip to Novo Solis.

I'd lost track of Clay by then, but his family brought him to Nick's funeral. We talked, caught up."

Clay looked into the rearview. "She finally learned why I didn't ring her after the war."

When Liam stared at them, confused, Bailey went on. "Like you and Nick, most of Clay's memories of the war were wiped clean, but he lost more than the rest of you. In forgetting Nick, he forgot about me, too." She gave Clay a sly look. "At least, that's the story he *tells* everyone."

"Because it's true!"

Bailey talked low. "Most days I believe him."

"Come on, now!"

Bailey's laugh was heartfelt. "I bet his family still wishes he didn't remember." She looked pointedly at her hand. "Or that I could pass for a white woman. Or hell, that I *was* white."

"Don't be that way," Clay said. "You know Mom loves you."

"*Now* she does," Bailey said, "but what about your dad?"

Clay shrugged. "Hard changing a man like that."

As they passed a five-and-dime, Liam did his best to reconcile everything they'd told him with his own memories. "There's something I don't get," he said. "If neither Nick nor Clay remember the war, and no one *else* knew you were Henchmen, how could you have joined the Uprising?"

The smile Bailey offered Liam was fleeting. "Before Colette Silva died, she told Grace about the Devil's Henchmen, and the fact that you'd all lost your memories. After forming the Uprising, Grace recruited Stasa, and the two of them cooked up a scheme, a fishing expedition they hoped would land a few of you."

"A fishing expedition?"

Bailey nodded. "She funded a study and placed ads in papers all across the Midwest that said Stasa's company was hoping to help war vets, especially those who'd suffered memory loss. After seeing the ad, I wrote to Stasa and told him what'd happened to both Nick *and* Clay."

"I joined the study a few weeks later," Clay said. "Hoping to jar some memories loose, Stasa gave me a serum Colette had been working on before she disappeared. It didn't work well at first—some sort of mis-match with my genetic signature—but after a few adjustments, it started drumming up all sorts of memories. That's roughly the point where Kohler somehow got wind of the study. He sent his goons to get Stasa. They were all set to ship him off to Novo Solis for questioning, likely by De Pere himself."

The little Liam remembered of Clay told him what had likely happened next. "You went to rescue him, didn't you?"

"Fucking A right, I did. Nearly got away clean, too, but Kohler caught me with a grenade. You believe that shit? I make it through the war *un-scathed* only to get caught by *that* fucking traitor. I owe Stasa my life. He pieced me back together, up here"—he rapped his knuckles on his head—"*and* here." This time he rapped his chest, which made a metallic clang.

"Well, I'm glad he did," Liam said.

"Most days I am too," Clay said.

Bailey gave Clay's shoulder a light slap. "Hush with that, now."

"So how much *do* you remember of the war?" Liam asked.

Clay barked a laugh as they squeezed between traffic and a slowing city bus. "Now *there's* a question." The Nash leaned hard as he turned left on Fullerton. "Some days it all goes dim. But I remember a good por-tion of it."

"Do you remember being recruited into the Henchmen during the war?"

"Sure. I remember getting the injections in the early days of Project Echo, too. I remember going toe to toe with the Goliaths. Things came back real slow at first. Faces with no names, freeze frames, that sort of thing. But as the serum was refined, I started seeing more. Proper memo-ries, like pissing down a hill with you and Nick while we were still in our hopper suits. Kohler making me clean up a bunch of stained glass in a church."

"Only because you launched a dummy grenade at it!" Liam said.

Clay, turning suddenly somber, glanced at Liam in the rearview. "Re-member Kohler's snuff fantasy?"

"I do, unfortunately." The vision of Kohler executing both Clay and Nick for insubordination was suddenly bright in Liam's mind, as were the reactions of the Henchmen afterward. "You were quiet for days afterward."

"You were, too!" Clay said, as if he were offended. "We *all* were. Kohler managed to mask it for the most part, but he was a sick fuck, even then."

Liam tried and failed to banish a vision of Clay slumping down against the side of the church, smearing blood against the yellow slats as he went.

They rode in silence for several blocks, the Nash emitting its low rumble, then Clay suddenly smiled in that lopsided way of his. "Remember what brought me out of my funk?"

And just like that, Liam did, and the heaviness of Kohler's mock execution faded. "I do," he replied, "and by the way, have I ever mentioned what a complete and utter prick you are?"

Clay's laugh was so loud it filled every square inch of the cabin.

Bailey alternated glances between them. "What did my husband do?"

"How do you know it was me?"

"Because"—she stared him up and down—"you're *you!*"

"Clay and I were on a run along Lake Michigan," Liam said, "just south of Milwaukee. We saw some people standing at the end of a pier and went to check what they were doing."

"It was a fucking polar bear club."

"Polar bears?" Bailed asked.

"People who jump in the lake in winter for fun," Liam clarified.

Bailey's face turned sour. "What in Samuel Hill?"

The scene grew in Liam's mind, gaining more color and sound by the moment. "There were chunks of ice floating in the lake. It looked like a giant mint julep. I'd never jump in a frozen lake in a million years, but when I got to the edge of the pier to see who was in the water, Clay thought it'd be funny if I joined them."

Clay was laughing so hard, tears were coming out of his eyes. "You should have seen those twig arms of yours flailing." A strange wheezing sound was coming out of his chest cavity. "I swear," he said to Bailey, "he looked like he was ready to cry for his mama."

"I've never been so cold in all my life," Liam said. "My hand to God, I was shivering for days afterward."

"Cheered *me* right up, though."

Bailey frowned. "Now tell me how that's different than the devil himself."

Clay leaned over and kissed her. "They didn't call us Henchmen for no reason, dear."

The three of them shared a laugh as they passed over the Chicago River and entered Bucktown proper, where the pneumatics garage was located. With time running short, Liam moved on to a subject that felt important in ways he couldn't define. "Clay, do you know what happened to Colette after the war?"

Clay shrugged. "Nothing more'n what Grace tells me. That the Uprising was her idea. That De Pere had her killed over it."

Liam hadn't really been expecting much, but he was still disappointed. "Pull over here. The garage is on the next block."

Clay pulled the Nash to a harsh stop. After killing the engine, he turned in his seat, grimacing from the movement. "Look, I know I'm coarse sometimes, but I also know you and Colette were close. I'm sorry for what happened to her."

"Thanks, but"—it was strange to have a sense of mourning feel so unmoored, but that was precisely how Liam felt—"just how close *were* we?"

The conversation paused briefly as they exited the car and headed down the street. "Colette was all business early on, but you two hit it off near the end." Clay winked. "Especially after she dumped that fucking fop, Sergio."

It sounded like something Liam should care about. "I don't remember any of that."

Clay shrugged. "Maybe you're better off for it."

Liam wasn't so sure. There'd been something between him and Colette, and he wanted to know more. He wanted to *remember*. He wanted their love, if that's what it was, to be real. "Were we a thing?"

"You were *becoming* a thing. But that was just before the end of the war, the point when everything starts to go fuzzy for me." He slapped Liam's back. "I wish I could tell you more, old friend."

Liam smiled. "Me, too."

After a short walk down an alley, they reached the back of the pneumatics garage. As they headed up the stairs, Liam felt as if they were being watched. Seeing no one in the alley, however, or in the windows that had a view of the garage, he went in—only to find Alastair sitting at attention in the chair where Liam had left him.

"Hello, Master Mulcahey."

"Alastair . . ." Liam's mouth worked as he tried and failed to find the right words. "When did you wake? *How* did you wake?"

"Just this morning, sir. And"—Alastair's owl-like eyes blinked as he flexed the fingers of his right hand—"I don't know. I simply . . . woke up."

"Can you stand?" When Alastair did, Liam asked, "Do you feel like your old self?"

Alastair's head tilted, as if he were considering, then he nodded. "I suppose I do," he said in his warbly voice. "But where's Master Aysana?"

"He's been taken by some very bad people, but I'm planning to get him back. Would you like to help?"

His brass-and-steel head swiveled downward to stare at the repeating rifle in his right arm. "I'd like that, sir." He activated the mechanism, and the barrels emitted a well-oiled whir. "I'd like that very much. Where do we begin?"

It was a good question. Liam hadn't had much time to think about it, but the beginnings of a plan had started to form. "Tomorrow, we'll go and speak with someone who might know more."

Bailey glowered at him. "Who?"

"Geraldine Burgess."

Bailey's glower became a deep frown. "The Mayor's daughter? *That* Geraldine Burgess?"

"The very one."

"No," Bailey said with a sharp wave of her hand. "It's too risky."

"You don't understand," Liam said. "The night of the attack on Club Artemis, she begged off on joining Morgan. She told Morgan to leave as well, and that she'd talk to him in a few days to explain. That same night, Leland De Pere stayed late for dinner at the Burgess's."

Bailey waited for more. "So?"

Liam shrugged. "So she might know something."

"And she might not."

"True, and we'll never know which unless we ask."

"So you want us to just traipse to the mayor's mansion and knock on the door?"

Liam shook his head. "Morgan mentioned she would be going to the flower market tomorrow. We can meet her there and talk quietly without anyone else knowing."

Bailey's face went hard. "It's too *risky*."

"What *isn't* risky at this point?" Clay said before Liam could argue the point further. "The man's friend has been taken, a war vet. All he wants is a friendly chat."

Bailey seemed hard at first, unwilling to change her mind, but the more time passed, the more she seemed to deflate. "If we scout the area tonight *and* tomorrow morning—"

Clay smiled. "Of course, dear!"

"—*then* we can go, take care of business, and go *straight* to the domes after."

Clay's smile broadened. "Sounds perfect, darling."

"Don't you *darling* me." She turned and walked away, muttering to herself, "Damn fool's going to get himself killed one of these days."

When she was gone, Clay winked at Liam. "Easy peasy."

"Easy peasy," Liam shot back.

Alastair's head swiveled, taking in both of them. "Easy peasy," he said with his slightly garbled voice box.

After a brief pause, Liam and Clay both laughed. Alastair joined in, a rare sound from the mechanika, though Liam had the impression Alastair wasn't precisely sure *why* he was laughing. Although distant from Clay earlier, Liam felt a glimmer of their old camaraderie returning. He hadn't realized how much he'd missed the sense of brotherhood he'd had in the Devil's Henchmen. Now that it was back, it felt good. Real good.

Still laughing, the three of them left the apartment together.

FIFTEEN

The following day, along the western edge of Chicago's famous Loop, a light drizzle fell from a pewter sky. Liam and Alastair sheltered beneath the awning of a chocolatier, one of the many expensive shops that bordered the flower market. Across the street, hundreds of people were entering and leaving the open-air market itself. On spotting two particularly well dressed women sharing an umbrella, with a re-purposed wallbuster the size of a tank trailing behind them, Liam motioned to Alastair, and the two of them headed into the rain.

The Loop's tram line loomed overhead. Clay and Bailey, both feigning nonchalance, leaned against one of its stout, steel girder supports. The moment they spotted Liam's approach, they struck a path along one of the market's nearby aisles and melted into the crowd.

Given that the market was filled with people of means, Bailey had supplied Liam with a blue mohair three-piece and a matching fedora. Alastair, meanwhile, despite his reservations that he would stand out, fit in just fine. Mechanika in this part of the city were all too common—Liam could see at least four more over the field of brightly colored flowers.

The younger of the two women Liam was trailing was Geraldine, the mayor's daughter. Her mother, Constance, had apparently decided to join her. In a bit of good fortune, Clay and Bailey had spotted only a single beat cop during their reconnaissance of the neighborhood. President De Pere was apparently hosting a luncheon downtown, which had drawn a heavy police presence *there* and left blessedly few police to patrol *this* part of the city.

For a time, Geraldine's pattern was predictable. She would stop at a flower shop, look over the flowers, smell a few, then speak to her mother and the vendor for a short while. When she'd completed her initial survey, she returned to several of the vendors and began placing orders.

Eventually, Constance bid her daughter farewell, snapped open a second umbrella, and headed into the rain. Liam hoped the massive, clanking mechanika would join her, but no such luck. As Geraldine spoke to a vendor over a host of violets and blue orchids, the wallbuster stood there, watching everything and everyone with unblinking orange eyes, his hulking arms crossed over his brushed metal chest.

One row over, Bailey was looking over yellow daffodils, pretending to be choosing one, while Clay eyed Liam. Liam gave him a small shrug. He had no idea how he was going to get Geraldine away from the mechanika, who would surely report any curious conversations to the mayor.

"Let me handle this, sir," Alastair said.

Before Liam could say a word, he began pounding over the patterned bricks toward Geraldine. As he passed her by, he snatched the tiny purse she had in her hands and kept on running as the crowd parted with gasps and fearful looks.

The wallbuster seemed immobile for a second, then dropped into a stance Liam had seen before. It was the sort they used in the war when aiming their grenade launchers. Indeed, the mechanika's wrist dislocated to reveal a barrel the size of a bloody cannon. It sighted along the barrel, tracking Alastair's movements through the crowd.

"Bullock!" Geraldine screamed. "Dear God, put that thing *away!*"

The mechanika, Bullock, swung his head to her, blinked his glowing orange eyes three times. He lowered his arm, then set off at a lumbering pace toward Alastair. He started slow at first, but built more and more speed as he exited the market, showing the sort of frightening, momentum-building pace wallbusters had become famous for during the war.

"Geraldine Burgess?" Liam said as he came near.

"That's right." She pulled her eyes away from the retreating Bullock and stared up at Liam with a look of distress and confusion. She was pretty, with arresting eyes and sharply defined eyebrows. Her long brown hair was done up and secured with a feathered pin.

"Do you have a moment to talk about Morgan Aysana?"

Geraldine went still as a statue. "Morgan?"

"Yes. I'm a friend of his, and he's gone missing."

"I'd heard, but . . ." She turned, noticing Bailey and Clay. "I don't know anything about it. I wasn't there that night."

"Yes, that's what I'd like to talk to you about." Sensing that Geraldine was about to cause a scene, Liam went on as calmly and earnestly as he could. "I'm only trying to find him, Geraldine. Morgan's in terrible trouble."

"I understand, but—"

"It's more than the abduction," Liam went on. "Morgan's sick. He needs our help."

Geraldine swallowed hard. "You're Liam?"

"I am."

"Morgan's told me about you. A lot, actually." She paused. "What do you mean he's sick?"

Liam motioned up to the tram line, where a sleek train of brushed silver and crimson accents was whirring toward the station. "Join me on the train? We'll find a booth with a bit of privacy."

She sent a nervous glance at Bailey and Clay.

"Just you and me," Liam said quickly. "One time around the Loop."

Geraldine paused, then nodded. "One time."

Liam waved to Bailey and Clay. "Wait for me," he said, then walked with Geraldine up the stairs and into the waiting tram. They sat in two facing seats with a small table between them. It was far enough from other passengers that their conversation wouldn't be overheard. As the train whirred into motion, Liam told his story, from the absynthe to the firefight to his escape with Morgan. He left out Grace—the last thing he needed was for a woman like Geraldine to become suspicious that he was in with the Uprising—but he told her the rest. Dr. Ramachandra, the coppers chasing them on the way to the Aysana estate, Morgan's worsening symptoms and the battle outside the doctor's office.

"What does any of this have to do with me?" she asked when he'd finished.

"In the message you left for Morgan, you said he should leave the speakeasy and head home straight away. Why?"

Geraldine broke her gaze from Liam's. "I don't see that it's any of your business."

Liam took a measured breath. "Do you care about Morgan?"

"Of course I do." She looked guarded, as if she were trying to insulate herself from her own feelings. "Morgan's swell."

"Which is why you warned him away. You knew something was going to happen that night, and you didn't want to see him get hurt."

A long pause followed. The train stopped, a few passengers got off, a few more got on. Only when it had picked up speed again did Geraldine meet Liam's gaze and speak in a low voice, "I didn't *know* what was going to happen, if that's what you're implying."

"Of course not."

"And my father wouldn't have sanctioned *killings*."

"No, that sort of thing would have been hidden from him." Liam wasn't at all sure that was true, but he needed Geraldine on his side.

Geraldine's eyes went distant as she stared out the nearby window, where the grand entrance to White City Amusement Park was scrolling past. "I should've told him more, to get him away."

"But why try to send him away in the first place? What did you hear?"

"My father and the President were speaking in his office. They were talking about the efforts to stop the bootleg trade. I heard the President mention Club Artemis right after."

"That's all you heard?"

"That's all, I swear. My mother called me away moments later."

Geraldine's mannerisms had changed. Her lips were tight. She kept swallowing. Her hands were wringing her blue kidskin gloves, which she'd removed when they sat down. She'd been surprised earlier. Now she was scared. It felt as if she were building a wall, and the longer Liam waited, the higher and more unassailable it would become.

Further down the car, Liam caught sight of a little boy wearing his Sunday best: vest, knickerbockers, high socks with shiny black shoes. Geraldine followed his gaze and gave a small smile, then quickly let it fade, as if she feared that showing any form of tenderness would form cracks in the wall.

"When we were young," Liam said, "Morgan and I used to go fishing at the ponds on the north side of his father's estate. We found a bee hive, and like all wise young boys coming across a bee hive began lobbing rocks at it. The hive broke, and bees came pouring out. They swarmed us and we bolted, but I didn't see the gopher hole. Down I went, breaking my ankle in the process. Most kids would have kept running, but not Morgan. When he saw me lying there inside that cloud of bees, he snatched up a stick and started roaring like a Viking. That stupid, idiot boy swept in, swinging that little stick of his as if it was going to do any good against a swarm of bees. Eventually he saw how useless it was. When he did, he knelt by my side, lifted me up, and carried me away. We were both stung badly."

Liam glanced at the boy further up the aisle, who was giggling at the faces his father was making.

"I still don't know how he found the strength," Liam went on, "but like John Henry, he just kept on chugging while the bees stung both of us, over and over. Somehow Morgan got more stings than me. We counted them. I had forty-three, he had fifty-two. From then on, whenever we played games together, he would joke that he was going to beat me by nine."

Geraldine was looking anywhere but at Liam. The boy, meanwhile, broke into peals of laughter, a result of his father's tickling.

"Morgan's hurting, Geraldine. He's hurting badly, and I need to help him."

Geraldine's eyes were tearing. "He said he was going to get out."

At first Liam thought she meant Morgan, but then it became clear she was talking about her father. "Get out of what?" he asked carefully.

She regarded him with reddened eyes. "My father's had a hand in dark business for some time. Mother and I have tried to warn him away, urged him to stop dealing with the likes of Leland De Pere, but he doesn't listen. Says he's in too deep to back out. And now it's come to this. Murder. Poisoning people in speakeasies. Taking them . . ."

Liam paused. Geraldine was the first person outside the Uprising who seemed to know anything was strange about Leland De Pere. "What do you know about the President?" he asked her.

Geraldine went stone-faced, as if she feared she'd already said too much.

"At least tell me about Morgan," Liam pressed. "If you know where he is, you *must* tell me."

Geraldine blinked her tears away, dabbed at the corners of her eyes with the back of one knuckle.

The train was nearing the flower market. It was already slowing, but she yanked on the bell line anyway. It clanged twice and she moved to stand in the aisle, her eyes focused on the approaching platform.

"Please," Liam said. "Morgan's in terrible danger. You know he is."

She said nothing, not until the doors hissed open and they stepped onto the platform, where a few dozen were waiting to enter. She waited until the platform was empty, then spoke in a low voice. "My father spends an inordinate amount of time in meetings at the Kovacs Power and Light Building. I heard him say once that there's a lab of some sort at the top, just below the sphere."

Liam's heart leapt. Keeping his voice as low as hers, he asked, "Do you know of a way in?"

"No, but there's a banquet being hosted on Friday for the President's departure. I'll add an entry for you plus a date." She paused, her eyes narrowing. "I don't imagine I should use your real name."

Liam thought for a moment. "Use John and Viola Williams."

Geraldine laughed. "Was there ever a more American name than 'John Williams'?"

"No," he said, "and that's precisely the point. Thank you, Geraldine."

Without another word, she took the stairs down and headed toward Bullock, who was wandering the rows of the market, umbrella in one hand, Geraldine's purse in the other, casting his orange-eyed gaze this way and that. On spotting Geraldine, he shuddered, rumbled his way over to her, and covered her with the umbrella. What questions he might have for Geraldine, and the sort of answers she would give, Liam had no idea. Together, they made their way through the crowd and were soon lost around a corner.

SIXTEEN

Only when Bullock was out of sight did Alastair, who'd managed to slip Bullock after coming dangerously close to getting caught, return to the group. They left the flower market immediately after, piled into the Nash, and headed east, toward downtown.

"I thought we were going to the domes," Liam said.

"Change of plans," Bailey said. "Grace is back in town, and she wants to talk."

Clay looked in the rearview. "We're in trouble, Liam."

"Trouble?" Alastair, normally so unflappable, sat up straighter and blinked several times. He seemed beside himself with worry. "Why?"

"Protocol," Clay said. "Shit's supposed to roll downhill, never up."

Clay drove them downtown to the Drake Hotel, apparently a haven for the Uprising, at which point the four of them headed up the elevator to a suite on the uppermost floor. Grace met them there, and she seemed far from pleased. "Can I speak to the two of you alone?" she said to Bailey and Clay.

The three of them headed to an adjoining room, leaving Liam alone with Alastair. Alastair paced before the windows, beyond which were the gleaming buildings of downtown.

"It'll be all right," Liam told him.

Alastair glanced toward the door the others had gone through, now the source of a muted but clearly tense conversation. "I'm not so sure, Master Mulcahey. She's liable to send me home."

"She won't."

"You don't know that." His pacing quickened, his mechanical feet making zipping sounds over the carpet. "We *need* to find Master Morgan."

"We will," Liam said. "We've already made progress."

But nothing Liam said seemed to calm him. Fortunately, the others returned a short while later. Bailey and Clay, both looking chagrined, left without saying a word.

"Alastair, could you go with them?" Grace asked. "I'd like to speak to Liam alone."

Alastair blinked once, twice, then headed toward the door with a hydraulic whine. "Of course." He paused on the threshold. "I'm very sorry for any distress I may have caused." And then he was gone, closing the door behind him.

Grace, meanwhile, seemed more pensive than angry. "You told me you wanted to help save Morgan."

"I do," Liam said.

"Okay, but that means you're part of a team, part of *my* team." It was a simple statement, but a woman like Grace would know the effect those words would have on a military man like Liam, someone who had put his life in the hands of commanders and squad mates, both. "The only way we do this, the only way we save Morgan, is by doing it together. You should have waited until we'd all spoken, until we'd had a chance to digest it and make a solid plan. We could have found Geraldine in any number of ways that were safer."

"It *was* safe."

"You don't know that. You're only just entering a world you have little concept of." She paused, becoming suddenly very intense. "Since forming the Uprising, I've gone to great pains with every step I've taken. Every step we've *all* taken. And for good reason. It's a very dangerous game we're playing. One wrong move and it'll be lost. All of it."

Part of Liam wanted to justify what he'd done, to tell Grace the risk had been worth it for Morgan's sake, but standing there, seeing the hint of terror in Grace's eyes, he realized how rashly he'd acted, how his choices had put everyone at risk.

"You're right," he finally said. "I shouldn't have pushed so hard."

Grace seemed to unwind a bit. "To be honest, I'm not surprised you pushed for it, nor that Clay gave in. I'm most surprised *Bailey* agreed. She's taken a shine to you. And Clay looks up to you."

Liam scoffed. "Clay?"

"Don't act so surprised. You were close during the war. And for a time, you were his commander."

"*Max Kohler* was our commander."

"In the beginning, yes. You eventually took his place."

"I did?" Liam could remember nothing of the sort.

"You did, though the circumstances around your promotion are unclear. The point is, Clay *trusts* you. Make sure you don't abuse it."

"Of course." Liam felt his cheeks flush. He *had* betrayed Clay's trust. And Bailey's. "It won't happen again."

"Good." She waved to the room where she'd spoken to the others. "Speaking of the war, I hear your memories are starting to fill in?"

"A few glimpses of it, yes."

She nodded. "It's likely due to the serum we gave you."

Liam shook his head. "What serum?"

"The one we put in the absynthe at Club Artemis."

It explained Bailey's presence in the kitchen of the speakeasy—she was there to spike the absynthe. It might also explain why Charlie, Elle, and Violet had been acting so strangely.

"With your permission," Grace went on, "I'm going to ask Stasa to make adjustments so it will work better with your genetic signature. It should strengthen the effects."

"I must be moving up in the world for you to ask my *permission*."

Grace cringed. "I'm sorry about that, Liam, truly, but it was necessary. We didn't know enough about you then."

"It was only a joke—a poor one, apparently, given your reaction. Yes, you have my permission."

"Good, because I've a feeling there are important things locked inside your head. The sooner we get to them, the better. Now, to business. Since you've secured a way into the President's farewell banquet, we need to prepare for it."

She asked him to detail everything Geraldine had told him, which Liam did. "She seemed to know a fair bit about De Pere himself," he said when it was done.

Grace shrugged. "There are a privileged few who *do* know some of De Pere's darker secrets. Some hope to profit off the new world order De Pere is trying to put in place. Others remain silent in fear of the Cabal making experiments of *them*."

As in the domes, Liam was starting to feel overwhelmed. "It all feels so big, Grace."

"I know. But one step at a time. I have a meeting I need to take tonight, but Stasa arrives in the morning. We'll make a solid plan. Then I'll teach you some of the basics around illusions, at least enough to detect any you find at the dinner and tear them down."

What followed was a blur of activity that consumed the rest of the afternoon. Grace eventually left the Drake to meet others from the Uprising. The following morning, as the sun rose over the lake and shone brightly across the city, Stasa arrived with a set of architectural prints for the Kovacs Power and Light building, a structure he'd helped design.

When Bailey and Clay had joined them, Stasa laid out the blue architectural prints on a glass-topped table and everyone gathered around. The topmost drawing was a side-view rendering. The building was simple but elegant, its most distinguishing feature the massive, stainless steel sphere at the top, which was activated at night. The sphere was, in essence, a Van de Graaff generator. It sent sparks of static electricity flying into the sky over Chicago, a statement of technological prowess.

"Gotta feel strange," Clay said, "breaking into your own building."

"A building I still own, by the way," Stasa said in an indignant tone. "At least on paper . . . I don't think it will feel strange, though. It will feel like sweet justice, the Cabal getting their just deserts after taking it from me."

The Cabal had abducted Stasa from the very same building, apparently. They'd taken control of it since, using it as their main base of operations in Chicago.

"The two most likely places for them to have a lab are here . . ." Stasa tapped the top of the tower, a room just below the sphere. "And here,"—he tapped the lowest part of the drawing, the part below ground—"sub-basement four."

"Geraldine specifically mentioned the top," Liam said. "'Just below the sphere,' she said."

"I understand," replied Stasa, "but we can't ignore the sub-basement, which is why we're splitting into two teams. Grace will lead a strike team in the sub-basement while Liam and Bailey go to the top of the tower." He pulled out a detailed, top-down layout of the eightieth floor. It showed a ballroom with an attached kitchen, a lounge, and a viewing platform that circumnavigated the building. "There's no elevator to the eighty-first floor." He pointed to the right side of the map. "It has a dedicated stairwell, accessible between the bar and the ballroom, near the lavatories—or at least it did. Construction on the uppermost floors was reported a month after my rescue by Clay. They may have moved the stairwell's location, and either way, they'll have illusions over it. Your mission," he said to Liam, "is to find the stairwell and make your way to the topmost floor."

"Easy peasy," Clay said.

"No," Stasa shot back, "it most assuredly will *not* be easy peasy."

Clay slapped Liam on the back. "You're underestimating our man here."

"I hope that's true"—Stasa smiled, not unpleasantly—"but let's not take it for granted."

"No offense to Bailey," Liam said, "but wouldn't it be better if *Grace* joined me at the reception?"

"No," Grace said flatly. "If we're going to succeed, the other team needs an illusionist as well."

"Then send me with the second team and *you* go with Bailey. I'm not good enough yet, and Morgan's too important." Liam was no stranger to difficult situations, and didn't mind being in one again. He only wanted Morgan to have the best chance at being rescued.

"Morgan *is* important," Grace replied evenly, "but if we're right, in addition to a possible lab, there's almost certainly a wealth of records in the sub-basement. We need that too. Things will be tricky, but the plan is sound. Concentrate on your objective and you'll do fine."

Liam wasn't wholly comfortable with it, but he nodded anyway—as important as Morgan was to him, the simple truth was this was bigger than any one man.

Soon enough, the others were breaking away, leaving Liam with Grace so she could teach him more about casting illusions. They stood by the window, beyond which lay the impressive Chicago skyline. On their right, several blocks away, sunlight glinted off the shining metal sphere at the top of the Kovacs P&L building.

"Face me," Grace said while lifting her arms, "and mirror my movements."

Liam lifted his arms, palms facing forward, as hers were. Even after all he'd seen and done, he felt foolish, like a little boy playing at wizards, spinning a fantastical tale.

Grace smiled that smile of hers, the one that made it clear she saw right through him.

"What?" he asked.

"You're cute is all." She went on, hardly skipping a beat. "The key to forming illusions is to simultaneously ground yourself in reality and detach yourself from it."

Liam could only stare. "I'm sorry, Grace, but I have no idea what that means."

"It's hard to explain, I know, but you did it once already, the explosion outside Club Artemis."

In recalling that, Liam also recalled the incident with the hopper near the Aysana estate. "It happened again while I was with Morgan in the Phaeton." He told her about the chase and the strike of lightning he'd somehow called down.

"Good! Now try to remember how you felt."

"I do," he said. "Sort of. But I'm not sure how I managed to get there."

"It's similar to lucid dreaming, when your perceptions awaken to the point that the fabric of the dream tears but isn't torn in two. *That's* the feeling you need to recreate." She motioned to his arm. "See if you can make me think your arm is waving."

Despite the description she'd given him, Liam had no idea where to begin. He might have created illusions already, but they'd been spur-of-the-moment things, more *reaction* than action. He tried for long moments, but got nowhere, and the fact that he was getting nowhere made it feel all the more impossible.

"It helps if you can see someone else doing it." She waved to him, and kept doing so. "My arm is completely stationary. It only *looks* like I'm moving it. Can you feel it?"

As had been true with Kohler outside Dr. Ramachandra's brownstone, the illusion manifested as a twisting feeling in his gut, like a case of nerves. "I think so, yes."

"Good. Now try again."

Liam took a deep breath. *Similar to lucid dreaming*, she'd said. It was easy enough in theory, but getting there was a different matter altogether. He tried over and over again to do what Grace was doing, but ended up either moving his arm or standing there doing nothing. "I'm sorry, I can't."

"It's okay." She held a finger to her lips, thinking. "Let's try this from another direction. The same state of mind can be used to sense the edges of an illusion, at which point you can alter it or dispel it altogether." She waved to a nearby fern in a large glazed pot. The fronds were growing, lengthening, changing. The blades, ten feet long now, waved in the air and began to vibrate, creating a hornet-nest hum. "Look *through* the illusion. See if you can see the real plant."

He concentrated hard. The feeling in his gut told him the illusion was there, but he couldn't find the edges of it. When he reached out and touched one of the fronds, however, he felt a chill, like he got from Nana's ghost stories from the old country. All of a sudden, it looked as if the plant were made of cloth, and if he could just tug on the threads. He did so, and just like that, the plant was as it had been—small, green, perfectly normal.

"Very good." With a mischievous smile, Grace began pacing around him. "But it's easy to break an illusion you know is false. I wonder if you can do it with something more deceptive."

It was a test. She was daring him to find the illusion she'd just created. He stared hard at the nearby couch with its many pillows, he looked at the bold Deco paintings on the walls, at the lustrous grand piano beside the marble fireplace—all while Grace circled confidently, each circuit brightening her smile as he failed to identify the thing she'd hidden.

Then he realized it wasn't the room that had changed. It was Grace.

It was her scent he noticed first, a faint but pleasant mix of lilac and juniper. Then he felt the warmth coming off her.

It was harder to banish the illusion this time. He resorted to waving his hands, much as Kohler had done when creating the wild, street-twisting illusions that caused Liam to miss his pistol shots. The Grace striding so smugly around him melted like fairy floss in the rain, and was replaced with another Grace, the *real* Grace, who stood directly in front of him. She was a hand's-breadth away, close enough to dance with. Mixing with her perfume was the scent of her skin, her hair. It was intoxicating.

"Very good," she said.

Liam swallowed hard. "Thanks."

Her nostrils flared. Her cheeks were suddenly the color of pink peonies, as if she'd had to dare herself to do this. Again the feeling of familiarity returned. He had the urge to slip his arms around her, not to dance, but to see how their bodies might fit against one another. It would feel, he was certain, perfect.

He was suddenly acutely aware of the doorway to the bedroom, which stood open. He hadn't meant to, but he glanced at it.

Grace caught his line of sight, then blinked and stared at the fine watch on her wrist. "We don't have much time before the banquet."

For a moment, he couldn't tell if it was an invitation or a dismissal. He tried to compose a series of words that would let him know for certain without making him sound like a complete boor. *How* much *time? Any thoughts on how to fill it?*

He was saved from making a fool of himself by a knock on the door.

Bailey's muffled voice came a moment later. "We need to start getting ready."

"Of course," Grace called.

Liam might have heard a bit of disappointment in her voice, but a moment later he was sure it was just his imagination.

The spell was broken entirely when Grace opened the door and Bailey, wearing a formal black gown, stepped inside. In Bailey's hands, pressed and folded, was what looked to be a matching tuxedo and a top hat. "You're done with our boy?"

"For now."

When Liam had changed into his tuxedo, Grace positioned him in front of a full-length mirror. She touched his shoulder, and he was transformed. He lost a bit of height. Grew rounder around the middle. His skin gained sunspots. His eyes altered, as did his nose and lips and chin until he had a rather more pudgy face.

"Maybe a mole," Liam said, pointing to his cheek, near his left ear, "just there."

Grace touched that spot, and a mole appeared. After putting on his top hat, it felt as if he were staring through a pane of glass at a completely different man.

Grace touched Bailey's shoulder next. As had happened with Liam, an entirely new appearance cascaded down her frame until she was a more full-figured woman in her early fifties, roughly the same age as Liam's illusion.

Bailey stepped closer to the mirror. "I'm so *white*." She winked at Liam. "Going to need to dial down the charm so people will believe it."

Liam couldn't help it. He laughed. He'd only just met Bailey, but it felt like they'd known one another for years, which made him wonder how much Clay had talked about her during the war. His heart ached just thinking about the personal moments he'd lost, the close friendships. As Nana had said, those memories had been a piece of him, a part of what defined him. He felt poorer for having lost so many of them.

"Do I need to do anything to maintain it?" he asked Grace.

"No, now that it's established, it will self-reinforce. Just don't actively try to dispel it." She turned to Bailey. "You and Clay know your assignments?"

Bailey nodded, and suddenly an old, familiar feeling grew inside of Liam—the sort he'd got during the war before heading out to battle. As he stared at Grace, he felt like he'd never see her again. "Good luck."

"You too." She opened the door for them. "We'll continue your studies another time."

Liam smiled sheepishly. "I look forward to it."

Bailey's eyes went back and forth between the two of them. A moment later, she said, "Come on, Prince Charming." They headed down the carpeted hall toward the elevator. When the door closed behind them, Bailey laughed. "I look forward to it," she said in a mocking tone, then laughed even louder.

SEVENTEEN

Liam and Bailey were hardly questioned when they entered the Kovacs Power and Light building. A woman at reception checked their names against a list. "You'll be at table twelve," she said before waving them to a bank of elevators. "Enjoy your evening."

"We will, dear," Bailey replied.

When they took the elevators to the eightieth floor, the doors opened onto a ballroom, much of which was dominated by round dining tables draped in white linen. Each table had several pitchers of ice water, silverware, tented name tags, and, last but not least, a tasteful flower arrangement—Geraldine's handiwork.

In the corners of the ballroom and near the elevators, men in black CIC uniforms stood still as statues, their gazes sweeping the crowd. Most ignored them, yet Liam found himself watching them a little too often.

"Breathe," Bailey said under her breath.

Liam did and shifted his attention to the guests. As the steadily growing crowd milled, an orchestra played classical standards. Beyond the floor-to-ceiling windows, a balcony circumnavigated the entire building. With the sun setting so vibrantly, many were out enjoying the warm evening air while sipping watermelon punch or non-alcoholic Mary Pickfords. Chicago being what it was, though, Liam saw no small number of men and women slip silver flasks out of their coats or purses. By the time canapés were served, it was as rowdy an affair as the busiest gin joint in town, which made it easier to move around. As they'd agreed, Bailey did most of the talking. While she engaged with this person or that, making small talk, she would ask Liam to fetch her a drink, or grab her a napkin, or send him to see if that really *was* Reggie van Buren on the far side of the room. It gave Liam all the excuses he needed to look for the stairwell.

He looked in the hallway near the lavatories, the place Stasa had identified as the prior location of the stairway to the uppermost floor, but found no hint of illusions there. He checked the bar area, the wall behind the bank of elevators. He hid the fact that he was looking for something as well as he could, but a woman in a silver gown and black, elbow-length gloves spotted him staring at the wall when she came out of the lavatories, then again near the kitchen entrance, forcing Liam to return to Bailey's side lest the woman grow suspicious.

More people had arrived by that point, to the point that their table was three-quarters full. Bailey suddenly stood, held out her hand to Liam, and tipped her head toward the dance floor. "For my sake," she said in a low voice, "for yours, for Morgan's, you need to *relax*."

The dance floor had grown more and more busy as the orchestra shifted to jazz and ragtime. Even so . . . "That's the exact *opposite* of relaxing," he said, watching the dancers.

"You say that now"—she beckoned him with a flick of her fingers—"but just you wait."

After taking a deep, calming breath, Liam took her hand and stood. Bailey, sporting a smile wide as the Mississippi, led him to the parquet dance floor, where the orchestra had taken up a rendition of "Maple Leaf Rag."

"I'm afraid I'm not very good," Liam said as they eased into a shimmy.

"I don't care if you trip this beautiful backside of mine right onto the floor. Clay hasn't danced with me once since we were married."

A vision suddenly popped into Liam's head, of Clay making a complete fool of himself at a USO concert. "He was never exactly Vernon Castle, though, was he?"

Bailey glowered. "You're as dumb as he is. I don't care *how* you dance, just that you do. Now keep those puppies moving." Her smile became a grin as Liam loosened up and his steps began to flow. She even laughed during a particularly fast rendition of "Muskrat Ramble." "Someone's been holding out on Bailey," she said. "You're not half bad!"

He shrugged. "My mom put me through lessons."

"Well, keep it up." She said it with a cute head waggle, a distinctly Bailey-like move. "And while you're at it, work on that look on your face."

Liam frowned. "I don't have a look."

The laugh she gave filled the room. "You look like a pig at a knife-maker's convention."

Bailey, it turned out, had been right. Dancing not only relieved the pressure, it helped ease him into the right frame of mind to look for illusions. Between songs, he checked the walls around the dance floor and the orchestra, but again found nothing. They were just heading back toward the bar when one of the elevators opened, and a dozen men and women wearing black CIC uniforms poured out. The applause for the orchestra suddenly ceased, replaced by the hum of excited conversation. Several of the CICs took positions beside the elevator doors, while the rest joined the detail already in place around the ballroom's perimeter.

A moment later, the second elevator opened. To a round of applause, Leland De Pere stepped out wearing a stunning ivory suit. With the same savoir faire he'd shown at the flashtrain ceremony, he raised his hands and thanked everyone for coming to his farewell banquet. Now more than ever, Liam had to wonder about the startling transformation he'd undergone. De Pere had been a respected officer in the Army. He'd been brave and forthright. What could have led him to form the Cabal and to subject Americans to the poisons he'd been feeding them?

Power is the great revealer, Nana used to say. *When those who have too much of it realize there are no consequences to their actions, they show their true selves.* It was the sort of pithy saying that had the ring of truth to it, but felt wrong, or at least didn't explain everything. There was more to the story. Liam just had to figure out what it was.

As hors d'oeuvres were being served, De Pere made his way to each table, eventually coming to Liam's. "John and Viola Williams," he said as he looked Liam and Bailey over. "A handsome couple."

"Well, *we* certainly think so," Bailey said with just the right mix of pride and shyness.

"We haven't met," De Pere said, "but anyone Geraldine Burgess recommends is certainly a friend of mine."

Before Liam could reply, the elevator doors opened and Max Kohler, wearing his iron mask, stepped out. Those nearby, captivated, glanced at him with fearful expressions. The way Kohler ignored them—indeed, the way he strutted about the room—gave the impression of a man who reveled in making people wonder, making them quake.

"That's Max Kohler," De Pere said, having followed Liam's gaze. "A retired Master Sergeant, one of the true heroes of the war. I'll introduce you if you like."

Liam's heartbeat spiked. He was certain Kohler would see through their disguises the moment he came near. "I'm sure he has more important things to do."

"Nonsense—"

He'd just raised a hand toward Kohler when Mayor Burgess, standing at the head table, began clinking his champagne glass with a fork. It was picked up by others, and soon the entire room was alive with the sound of chiming glasses. "Chicago welcomes you, Mr. President!"

The room erupted into another, louder round of applause. De Pere, turning away from Liam and Bailey, waved and gave his winning smile. "Thank you kindly, one and all."

Whistles and applause accompanied his march toward the head table. Soon salads were being served. As the banquet progressed, Kohler stood in one corner and, like De Pere's black-clad guard detail, merely observed.

Though the pressure had eased somewhat, Liam was starting to worry. He didn't know how to reach the top floor, and the raid on the sub-basement was going to start in less than an hour. Between courses, he and Bailey left the table to mingle and search. But the pink walls and gold filigree showed no imperfections, nor did the marble facade around the elevators. Between the fourth and fifth courses, he went onto the balcony to examine the building's exterior but was forced to stop when Kohler stepped into the evening air, seemingly for a stroll. At first, he seemed content to stare over the city, apparently admiring the towers or the lattice of gold that defined the Windy City's streets, but then his masked, single-eyed gaze swung toward Liam.

Above them, the Kovacs sphere had begun its nightly light show—sparks of electricity crackled from the steel ball into the surrounding air. It was meant to be a celebration of science, a stake in the proverbial landscape that marked Chicago as a technological powerhouse, but just then, with the flickering light reflecting off Kohler's brass-and-iron mask, his one visible eye stabbing into the darkness with each bright flash above, Liam felt as if Kohler, spark by burning spark, was ripping apart the illusion that was keeping Liam safe.

He headed back inside and Kohler did too, reclaiming his position in the corner behind De Pere. From that point forward, he seemed to scrutinize Liam's table more, which made Liam too nervous to do anything except stare at his plate and eat. "Kohler's suspicious," he whispered to Bailey.

A moment later, he caught Bailey tilting her knife just so—to look at Kohler in the reflection. "Just be patient. They'll serve tea before dessert. That'll be the time to get up again."

Liam was worried sick. The second team was going to storm the subbasement soon. If he didn't find the staircase by then, he and Bailey would be forced to leave. They'd lose their chance at rescuing Morgan because of *him*.

Moments later, as the sixth course was being served from carts by the white-uniformed staff, there came an explosion. A distant boom that shook the parquet floor. After a brief pause there came another, and another, followed by the rat-tat-tat of gunfire—a trench sweeper letting loose.

The crowd buzzed. Everyone stood, many heading for the balcony. Others rushed the elevator doors until the CIC agents began barking orders, forcing them away until the president was ushered to the nearest elevator.

Something strange happened to Liam in those moments. The near-suffocating worry of what he was going to do faded, and his battlefield instincts kicked in. The fear hadn't vanished, but it was in check, and he was now filled with a single purpose: to see himself and Bailey safely through this.

Taking her hand in his, Liam pulled her toward the mass of people near the elevator. "Push me into them," he said. "Press hard."

She nodded and did just that, pushing him from behind, into one of the CIC agents just as Liam slipped his hand inside the man's black coat and relieved him of his revolver.

The agent pushed back immediately. "Stay calm!" the agent roared. "Everyone will be seen out as soon as the President is safe!"

Liam glanced back, as if annoyed by the people pushing him from behind. "Of course," he said, then broke away and headed with Bailey toward the balcony.

His plan was to re-enter through the kitchen, the one place he hadn't checked. As they reached the cool night air, the kitchen door opened, and a heavyset chef and several waiters rushed toward the nearby railing. Liam couldn't have asked for better timing. He and Bailey rushed toward the door, which was slowly closing. Just then, Kohler turned the corner ahead. As those hugging the balcony railing stared down, Kohler scanned the crowd, surely hoping to find Liam.

Liam spun Bailey around and headed for the smoking lounge, which had another entrance to the kitchen. As they passed the hearth with the roaring fire, Liam felt a twinge in his gut, the telltale sign of an illusion.

More gunfire rang out. Another large explosion boomed up along the chasms between the buildings. As the banquet guests gasped and began talking excitedly, Liam stepped closer to the fire. He felt it now, the edges of the illusion. As he'd done with Grace, he peeled the edges of it away, enough that he could see what lay beyond. There, superimposed beneath the image of the wavering fire, was a door—*the* door, the one they hoped would lead to Morgan.

He tested it and found it locked. "Cover me," he said to Bailey, and took out the agent's pistol.

Bailey blocked the view of him as he aimed the pistol at the lock. Perhaps it was having finally found the illusion, or maybe it was the strange calm that had overcome him. Whatever the case, Liam felt perfectly in sync with his abilities. He aimed the pistol and, slipping into the half dream, half reality mindset Grace had taught him, squeezed the trigger. He imagined the explosion farther away such that, as the gun went off, it sounded muffled, distant, just one more round among the dozens being fired from the street below.

The lock shattered. Liam pulled the door open and ushered Bailey inside, then let the illusion of the fire fall back into place like a drape.

EIGHTEEN

Liam and Bailey found themselves in a narrow red brick hallway. At its far
end was a corkscrew staircase that led up through the ceiling to the room
above. From that opening came a fitful silver light that reminded Liam of
the electrical storms that hit the Midwest in the humid days of early
autumn. Rain would threaten, but all that came from the clouds was
lightning, strike after strike, the light never fully dominating the cloud
cover but never fully retreating either. A sound accompanied the bright
moments—a spasmodic hum, an electrostatic buzz. It was the steel globe at
the top of the building, Liam realized. It was discharging *inside* just as it
was on the outside.

Only then did Liam realize that Bailey's disguise had vanished. "Your
face," he said.

"Yours too," Bailey responded.

Liam hadn't felt the change, but sure enough, the skin along his hands
was back to its normal, pale color, and the array of mechanic's scars on the
backs of his knuckles had returned. Liam wondered if it was some byproduct of having partially unraveled the illusion in the hearth, but he doubted
it would have undone Bailey's illusion as well.

"I don't know about you," Bailey said, "but this place is making my
skin crawl." She pointed toward the top of the stairs. "Can you hear it?"

Between the snapping and buzzing, Liam heard hints of words being
spoken. Strangely, it didn't sound like a proper conversation. The words
sounded too dull, too rote, like people reading from a script.

"Come on." Liam took to the stairs, pistol in hand. "Let's find Morgan
and get the hell out of here."

The higher they went along the stairs, the more Liam's skin prickled.
He felt his hair stand on end. The very air around him felt charged, and it
intensified the higher he went.

They reached the floor above. Overhead, light strobed over the steel globe's brushed interior. The freakish releases of static electricity were everywhere. Occasionally, a spark would lick Liam's skin though hurting only as much as a static shock. In the center of the square space, twelve beds were arrayed in a circle. Strapped to them were men and women of varying ages. Their beds were inclined so that they were practically standing. Like Alan and William at the domes, the men and women were emaciated. Over their cheeks and foreheads, stark blue veins twisted like maps of the Mississippi Delta. Stranger still, though they were clearly of varying nationalities, each had ashy white skin. And their eyes were clouded over, their sight surely taken from them.

Most had short hair or were bald, but one, a woman of African descent, had long, kinky, ivory hair that was puffed up by the static electricity to such a degree she looked like a storm goddess ready to call lightning down on her foes. A dog tag hanging from her neck read: *Ruby.*

No sooner had Liam read it than she drew her gaze from the underside of the globe and stared at a bald man across from her. She spoke softly, too softly for Liam to make out what she was saying. The man responded, also too soft to hear. Back and forth the conversation went, the sparks concentrating around the two of them so heavily it looked as though they were preparing to immolate one another.

As quickly as the connection formed, it broke, and the man lay back. Ruby, however, seemed to notice that others were near. With her eyes so clouded, Liam doubted she could see anything more than light and dark, yet she turned her head and stared straight at him. Her expression became one of abject horror, as if she were seeing herself through his eyes. Then the static electricity around her sparked with a sizzling sound, and she calmed, lay her head back down, and resumed her endless stream of mumbling.

"Heaven and hell," Liam breathed, "what's happening?"

"I've no idea," Bailey replied, "but this is monstrous."

Liam was crestfallen that Morgan wasn't among them, but their escape plan had accounted for three people. The least they could do is rescue one of these poor souls. "We should release her," he said, motioning to the one named Ruby, "take her with us."

When Bailey nodded, Liam went to Ruby's side and began unbuckling her restraints. He was just helping her to step down from the bed when he heard a muffled thud. It had come from the floor below.

"That you, Mulcahey?" came Max Kohler's voice.

Bailey waved Liam frantically toward a metal door beyond the beds, no taller than Liam's waist—the maintenance hatch Stasa had identified as their primary escape route. Thankfully, Ruby didn't resist as Liam led her beyond the circle of beds. Her head swiveled constantly between Bailey and Liam, then her cloudy gaze shot back toward the winding stair, toward the opening in the floor.

"It's tricky using illusions here." Kohler's footsteps clanked against the winding steel steps, growing louder as he climbed. "No doubt you and your friend have both been exposed." His masked face rose up through the hole. "I'm guessing it's Clay's wife who's joined you, yes?"

Bailey, kneeling beside the maintenance hatch, retrieved a set of lock picks from her purse. With cool efficiency, she inserted them into the hatch's lock.

"I'm afraid it's not going to be that easy," Kohler said.

Liam blinked, and the place where the door had been was now solid brick. Bailey was frantically pressing her hands against it, feeling for the latch.

"You caught me off guard the other day," Kohler went on, "but it's not going to happen again."

Suddenly the space beneath the dome was completely empty, devoid of inclined beds and the porcelain-skinned people strapped to them. Bailey and Ruby had vanished too. All that remained were Liam and Kohler standing ten paces apart. Oddly, the scene around them shifted fitfully, like candlelight in the wind.

Liam lifted his pistol and trained it on Kohler's blue eye. The edges of the gun glowed violet. So did Kohler. It made Liam sick to his stomach. "Stay where you are."

Kohler continued, challenging Liam to follow through on his threat. Liam squeezed off a warning shot, which struck the globe's inner surface, ringing like a hammer on an anvil.

Kohler halted, then simply disappeared. "We're alone now," Kohler said, his disembodied voice echoing from a completely different location. "De Pere can't hear us, so I'm going to share a secret with you. He's scared of you, Mulcahey. Petrified. He thinks Colette told you something about him, a way to unravel everything he's been working on. He's convinced it's part of the reason, maybe the main reason, you were at the flashtrain ceremony. Tell me what it is and maybe Clay's wife leaves this place alive."

Liam couldn't tell if Kohler was trying to get the information for De Pere's sake or his own. It didn't much matter either way, though. He had no idea what Kohler was talking about.

"I barely remember Dr. Silva," he ventured.

As the scene around them continued to flicker, Kohler laughed. "You're going to have to do better than that."

"I'm telling you the truth. I remember she was the lead scientist for Project Echo. I remember her face and a few of the times we met. But that's it. I don't remember her telling me anything about De Pere."

"It would have been after the war."

"I never saw her after the war."

"You're lying."

"No, I'm not."

Over the buzzing, Liam heard Kohler sigh. "Why do you have to make this so fucking hard, Mulcahey?"

Suddenly the beds and the people strapped into them were back. Bailey was back, too. She was still feeling for the hatch door, with Ruby huddled next to her. Kohler was still invisible, but Liam felt his presence looming. Hoping to find the edges of the illusion, he fired the pistol again, and it worked. He sensed how Kohler was hiding himself. As he had with the fern in the hotel room with Grace, he tugged at the edges, then unraveled the illusion altogether.

By then Kohler was only a few paces away. In his hands he held a syringe filled with a clear liquid. Liam felt suddenly dizzy. He stumbled while backing away, wary of the needle. Aiming his pistol straight into Kohler's iron-masked face, he fired every round he had left. They all missed. Worse, Bailey grunted in pain with the final one—struck by the ricochet, perhaps.

Kohler knelt calmly beside Liam on the cold white floor. As he lowered the syringe toward Liam's neck, Liam managed to grab his wrist, forestalling him, but he was so disoriented it was child's play for Kohler to rip his arm free.

Ruby, kneeling beside Liam, stared at Kohler with her cloudy white eyes. "No," she whispered. Her hands were clutched at her throat, her fear plain to see. "No, no, no!"

Suddenly there came the crackle of a wireless communicator being activated. "Now, Clay! Now!" Bailey shouted.

Kohler waved one hand, presumably to cast some illusion to get Bailey back under control. Whether or not it worked Liam had no idea, for just then a deafening peal rent the enclosed space beneath the dome.

Orange sparks flew down from above. The dome, Liam realized, had been pierced by what looked to be a harpoon connected to a steel cable. The cable was reeled back, and the harpoon's barbed end caught against the hole it had just punched through the metal. Lighting arced around it, arced over the men and women in their beds, arced over Liam and Bailey and especially Kohler.

As one, Ruby and the men and women in the beds screamed. So did Kohler. He dropped the syringe and writhed as if caught in the throes of a seizure. Liam wasn't certain if Kohler had meant to tranquillize him or kill him, but it hardly mattered. He brought his pistol down hard against the side of Kohler's head. Kohler groaned and went limp.

"Come on!" Bailey shouted. She was already leading Ruby toward the access hatch.

Working together, Liam and Bailey led Ruby through the open hatchway. Bailey was clearly in pain. She sucked air through her gritted teeth each time she moved forward. By the flickering light, Liam spotted blood along her pant leg, surely from the bullet wound she'd sustained through Liam's wild pistol fire.

"Oh God, I'm so sorry," he said.

"Apologize later," she snapped.

The tunnel exited onto a narrow ledge. Above them, they could see the harpoon shaft piercing the metal dome. The cable attached to the end of it sloped down from the steel globe, spanned the yawning gap over the street below, and passed through an open window in a neighboring tower, the office building where Clay had been dispatched earlier.

Clay, visible through the window, was waving to them. "Hurry!" he bellowed across the chasm.

Bailey limped over to the harpoon and unhooked one of three sets of pulleys. "Go on," she said to Liam.

"No." Liam led Ruby forward. "You and Ruby go first."

"I'm here to protect *you*, Liam."

"You're hurt. I'll make sure Kohler doesn't interfere while the two of you reach Clay."

She helped wrap the canvas belt under Ruby's arms, then paused, clearly conflicted about leaving Liam alone.

"Now, goddamnit!" Clay roared.

Bailey unhooked the second pulley. "You always this stubborn, you stupid jackass"—she wrapped the belt under her arms and reconnected it—"or you pick that up in the army?"

"I don't rightly recall."

She was shaking her head even as she and Ruby slid along the cable. A few moments later, they were through the window of the other building and Clay caught them, arresting their forward momentum with his own body.

Above Liam, the threads of lightning licking the globe suddenly vanished, as did the sizzling sounds. Either the harpoon had short-circuited the globe's power supply or Kohler had turned it off. Either way, it meant trouble. As Liam unhooked the third pulley, the access hatch slammed open.

"Mulcahey, stop!"

With no time to wrap the belt around himself properly, Liam gripped it tight and launched himself beyond the lip of the building. Over the gap he flew, the sheer height of the harrowing drop yawning below him. He was halfway to safety when he felt a surge of rage. It reminded Liam of nothing so much as the church the Henchmen had stumbled across in the ruins of Waukesha, of the raw indignation that had flared through Kohler's mind moments before picturing himself executing Clay and Nick.

Liam heard a twang, as of braided metal snapping under tension, and suddenly he was falling. Down he went, the cable snaking above him, the cloudy night sky hauntingly bright from the reflected lights of the city.

He felt his stomach lurch from the weightlessness, but it felt wrong, like he was living someone else's memory. It was his first clue that not all was as it seemed.

Hold on, boyo, Nana's voice rang inside his head. *Just hang on.*

The cable's breaking was an illusion, he realized, as was the fall. Kohler was trying to make him *think* he was falling so he'd let go. The ground rushed toward him. He was going to strike it and die and Kohler and Leland De Pere and the Cabal were going to go unpunished for their crimes.

Just a little bit longer, Nana said.

It was just enough to prevent him from letting go. The vision vanished when he struck the pavement. He blinked hard and found himself rushing through the window as Clay and Bailey worked together to arrest his speed.

His breath coming in wild, nervous gulps, he released his grip on the canvas belt and returned to the window. Kohler was on the lip of the building across from him, staring down from behind his mask. Bailey snatched a pistol from the holster at Clay's belt, aimed up at the dome, and fired six rapid shots. Several bullets bit into the brick ledge. One ricocheted off the dome with a metallic twang. Kohler ducked for cover halfway through the barrage and was lost from sight.

Then Liam, Bailey, Clay, and Ruby rushed from the room, entered the building's elevator, and headed down toward ground level.

NINETEEN

An hour after the madness at the Kovacs P&L building, Liam and Clay reached their assigned safe house, a furniture store several miles from downtown. Bailey had left earlier to deliver Ruby, the woman they'd rescued, to the domes for medical treatment. Afterward, Bailey was going to try to meet up with the second team, or at the very least get news about how things had gone in the sub-basement.

Clay flicked the lights on as he and Liam headed up to the furniture store's third-floor showroom. All around were posh arm chairs, sofas, dining sets, and curio cabinets, many of them built in the Art Deco or Nouveau styles. Area rugs with papyrus reed prints or repeating geometric shapes hung from the ceiling's periphery, nearly but not quite covering the show-room's brick walls. Through the drafty, third-floor window, a glowing neo-lume sign read, "Tauber Brothers Furniture."

Clay collapsed into a large armchair and began adjusting some of the dials on his mechanikal chest sleeve. Liam, meanwhile, lay down on a pristine black sofa with red cushions. Its softness begged him to close his eyes, so much so that after only a few moments he sat up and drew in a sharp breath to keep himself awake. He needed to know what had happened in the sub-basement—he was still holding out hope that the other team had found Morgan.

The sound of footsteps came from the double-wide stairs on the far side of the room. A moment later, Bailey reached the showroom floor. "No word yet." Her voice was listless, her eyelids heavy.

"Should we go?" Liam asked. "Try to find them?"

"You heard the sirens." She collapsed into a cushy blue divan. "They were chased. They're holed up. They'll make their way here when it's safe."

She was right—making a rash move now could cost lives—but he hated not knowing. He lay back down, vowing only to rest a few moments, but before he knew it, he was jerking awake. He heard the squeal of the freight door on the ground level, then a thud, the sound of it closing. Voices followed, and suddenly his heart was pounding all over again.

As footsteps scraped along the stairs below, he worried they'd been found by the Cabal, but a moment later, a haunted-looking Stasa emerged onto the showroom floor with a leather satchel slung over one shoulder. After turning on a few additional lights, he tossed the satchel onto a nearby kitchen table, scraped a chair out, and motioned for everyone to join him. "Please, sit."

They did, and Stasa retrieved a green folder from the satchel. The smell of smoke came with it. He flipped the folder open to reveal a thick stack of partially burned papers and what looked to be photographs.

"Our raid was not wholly successful," Stasa said. "We failed to find Morgan, and many of the more important papers we'd hoped to retrieve were burned by the Cabal, but we found a number of thralls, men and women infected like Alan and his son, William. The rescued thralls are on their way to the domes now. More importantly"—he slid a set of black and white photographs to Liam—"we found these."

Like Ruby and the others at the top of the P&L building, the people in the photos were of various ages and races, but their skin was unnaturally pale, almost pure white. Their eyes were cloudy, some more so than others, and they had blue veins that stood out starkly, especially along their necks and around their eyes.

"What's happening to them?" Liam asked.

"The documents refer to them as psis."

"Sighs?" Clay asked.

"P-S-I-S," Stasa said. "We believe they're part of a network, a way for thoughts, messages, perhaps even illusions, to be passed over long distances." Stasa tapped the stack of papers. "I haven't been able to review the cache of research in full, but I believe the psis hold another purpose. I believe they're meant to send messages to the thralls in particular, a way for orders to be sent—a way, in short, for the Cabal to consolidate power."

Liam stared at the photos, at the vacant looks on the faces. "This is madness. Why would De Pere do this? Why would *anyone* do this?"

"We already knew we were dealing with a madman, but even I didn't understand the extent of it." He took out a second packet of photos and slid them to Liam.

The first was of a man, apparently dead, lying on a medical examination table. His irises were dark, almost pure black, which made them look like open, empty pits. His skin was sallow in some places, but mostly it was reddened and angry, and there were spidering veins that were so pronounced, especially around his eyes, that it looked as if alien vines had taken root beneath his skin and grown unchecked.

Another photo showed a woman, also apparently dead, in a similar state. Her head was turned to one side and her mouth was open. The table beneath her had graduated lines on its surface, marking length in inches. Her freakishly long tongue was laid out on it, extending eight inches past her lips; it looked like she'd tried to swallow a snake and choked to death. On the tongue's tip was a white barb, and just behind it, three swollen glands.

Liam could hardly bring himself to speak, but he had to know. "Is this what's going to happen to Morgan?"

"I'll speak plainly," Stasa said. "Yes, we think these poor souls are *scourges*. And yes, this is precisely what we think Morgan will be transformed into, which makes it all the more imperative that we find him. Just as important, though, is for us to understand *why* De Pere is doing this."

Liam took in Stasa, then Clay and Bailey. "Don't you have *any* clue at this point?"

Stasa took one of the partially burned papers and slid it to Liam. He pointed to a heading near the top of the page. It read *Homo Servientis*. "It's difficult to fathom, but a name like that would indicate De Pere is looking to create a new form of life, a caste of slaves." He waved to the photos. "We've known all along he craves power, but this is twisted beyond reason. It's insane."

Liam shook his head, speechless for several long breaths. "What do we do?" He looked at them all in turn. "What do we *do*?"

"One avenue," Stasa said with a haggard look, "is to delve deeper into your memories for the origins of the *Homo Servientis* project. Information gleaned there could help us to understand what's happening now, which in turn could help us stop it. Grace said you'd agreed to take a refined dose of the memory serum?"

"I did, but"—Liam shook his head, confused—"what do my memories have to do with De Pere's plans?"

At the sound of footsteps, everyone turned. At the head of the stairs stood Grace. Behind her was Alastair, bearing a serving tray with a bottle of absynthe, two empty glasses, and all the implements for the ritual: a bowl of sugar cubes, slotted spoons, a box of matches, and a small pitcher of ice water.

"Could Liam and I speak alone?" Grace said it with a casual air, but Liam could tell she was tense.

Stasa, Clay, and Bailey all exchanged glances, then nodded and headed downstairs. Grace, meanwhile, sat in the chair across from Liam. Alastair set the tray on the table, blinked twice, then followed the others.

As the high-pitched whine of his servos and hydraulic pumps dwindled, Grace crossed one leg over the other. "Before Colette's disappearance, she was convinced there was some deep, dark secret that, if revealed, could undo all of De Pere's plans. She wasn't sure what it was. She'd become a victim of De Pere's manipulations by then. Many of her memories from the war were gone, and she was convinced she couldn't fully trust the ones that remained. She hoped one of the Henchmen *would* know."

"Why?"

"Because you were there when it happened."

"When *what* happened?"

"Some watershed moment that either hastened or precipitated De Pere's sudden rise to power." She shrugged. "Something related to Project Echo, surely, or the serum you helped to perfect. We're not sure what it is, Liam, but it's almost certainly linked to the reason De Pere hid your memories away."

The revelation gave Liam pause. "At the top of the P&L building, Kohler asked for very much the same information." He gave her the details of the strange, hair-raising isolation he'd experienced with Kohler, the questions he'd asked. "What was odd was that he was using the effect to hide our conversation from De Pere."

"Or so Kohler claimed."

"Well, yes."

"You're implying he might be having second thoughts about his involvement with the Cabal."

"Is it so inconceivable?"

Grace's expression turned sour. "I'm not in the habit of ruling anything out, but I very much doubt he would turn against De Pere. He likely said that in hopes of loosening your tongue."

"Maybe," Liam said, though he wasn't as certain as Grace apparently was. "In any case, this secret Colette wanted, how do you know *I* have it?"

"We don't. But I'm convinced Clay either never knew in the first place or won't remember in time to make a difference. Max Kohler clearly doesn't know. The rest of the Henchmen are all dead or missing." She paused. "Cards on the table time, Liam. You're our last hope. If it isn't you, I fear we'll *never* find out how to stop De Pere, or that it will be too late once we do."

Liam felt the weight of Grace's request bearing down on him. "I'm willing to try, of course"—he waved to the tray of absynthe—"but if Stasa's serum is ready, why not just inject it?"

Grace smiled. "Call me superstitious, but we laced the absynthe at Club Artemis with the first iteration of the serum, and it worked to unlock some of your abilities. And this isn't *all* science. It's part ritual as well. Your mind needs to be in the right place. I want you to *think* this is going to work. I need it to." She poured a measure of the green liquor into the two glasses, being sure to douse both sugar cubes. "We're in a race, Liam. A race to find a way to defeat the Cabal before they perfect whatever it is they have in store."

Liam had already decided he would do it—there was no reason not to—but he suddenly felt insufficient to the task. It was no longer only Morgan's life at stake; there were dozens, hundreds, perhaps thousands more. "What if I can't remember?"

She struck a match and set the sugar cubes aflame. "At least we'll have tried."

Her face glowed as she waited for the sugar to bubble and caramelize, then she poured water over the flames and used the spoons to mix the drinks thoroughly, ending with soft tings against the glasses' rims. She slid one across the table to Liam.

He lifted it and smelled the anise and fennel. "I'm scared, Grace, not just for Morgan's sake, but for *all* of us."

Lifting her own glass, Grace smiled a supportive smile. "That only means you're human."

Liam clinked glasses with her and downed his. He didn't feel much at first. Then he heard sounds of gunfire. It sounded as if it were coming from just outside the furniture store, but when he got up and turned, he found himself in the shattered remains of a brewery, standing beneath a broken archway, facing the sounds of battle in the distance.

TWENTY

During the war . . .

Liam was strapped into his hopper exoskeleton. In his hands, he gripped a Springfield rifle tipped with a bayonet. Over the trees, along the shores of Lake Michigan, smoke rose and twisted on the wind. The drum-roll rattle of gunfire intensified, followed by a boom Liam felt through the archway's cream-colored bricks.

"Mulcahey!" Liam turned and found Sergeant Kohler vaulting toward him in a hopper suit of his own. He slowed and stopped on a street made tricky to navigate by the massive gouges recent shelling had left in the cobblestones. Kohler's bright blue eyes stared out from under his helmet. "Time to get shot."

"Roger that," Liam said.

They set off together, their long, loping strides covering ten yards in a single bound. In short order, they reached the grounds of a warehouse that hugged the muddy banks of the Kinnickinnic. In the warehouse's loading yard, lined up along the base of a loading dock, were eighteen more soldiers in hoppers, the Devil's Henchmen. They were a unique group. Every man and woman in the squad was in top shape, but they hadn't been chosen for physical prowess alone. Each was brave. Each was a dead shot with a rifle. More importantly, each was particularly gifted at analyzing battlefield conditions and applying the strategies drilled into them endlessly by the Army's top strategists. Presently, a pair of nurses were in the process of administering doses of Project Echo's miracle serum to the first in line— standing on top of the loading dock as they were, they were more or less even with the Henchmen. Liam was a bit crestfallen it was only the two nurses today, but a moment later, he found himself smiling. Exiting the warehouse and joining them was Dr. Silva, the half-Brazilian-half-French scientist who'd spearheaded the project.

In the past, the injections had always been administered far from enemy lines. But today they were to use the Henchman serum in battle for the first time. It was a day that had arrived none too soon. Germany and the other powers of the St. Lawrence Pact were pushing hard, trying to retake Milwaukee after a valiant effort from the United States Army had pushed them north beyond Fox Point.

As the nurses worked their way down the line, Dr. Silva bypassed Kohler and went straight to Liam. Kohler noticed, but Dr. Silva ignored him in such a way that it was obvious she'd wanted to be the one to deal with Liam, or perhaps to *not* be the one dealing with Kohler, a man who'd developed a reputation as a womanizer among the squad, the battalion, the medical staff—or really, anyone he came in contact with.

That Dr. Silva was so obviously brilliant made Liam more self-conscious than her good looks. It was intimidating being around someone so smart, but thrilling too. She was someone who was going to change the country for the better. She might even change the world.

With a syringe at the ready, Dr. Silva doused a cotton swab in alcohol and used it to wipe the inside of his elbow. She tapped the syringe with a fingernail and squeezed the plunger to evacuate the gas. "Ready?"

"For the shot or the battle?"

She answered with a smile. "Both."

No matter how tense things were, that smile, all teeth and dimples, made his stress melt away. Before Liam could say another word, Kohler's grating voice broke in. "You kidding me, doc? Our boy here was *born* ready. Weren't you, Mulcahey?"

Liam ignored him, focusing all his attention on Dr. Silva. "I'm ready as I'll ever be."

While gunfire rattled in the distance, she sent the needle calmly and steadily into his vein, depressed the plunger, then placed a clean swab against the entry point and pulled the needle free. "Stay safe out there, okay?"

Liam nodded. "I will."

"Atten*tion!*"

The Devil's Henchmen moved into formation and stood, chins up, chests out, as the squad's CO, Major De Pere, made his way up the platform stairs to address them. The Major was clean-shaven and wore a crisp field uniform with dark sunglasses and a service cap with a black brim and the United States seal emblazoned above it. He stood at the center of the loading dock, hands behind his back while facing the squad.

"At ease," he said. "An enemy infantry battalion has been spotted sweeping southeast along the river, hoping to catch our boys off guard. Our aim is to disrupt, but let's not forget"—he waved to Dr. Silva, who was surveying the squad with a tight-lipped expression—"the primary goal of this mission is to further refine the good doctor's serum."

All eyes shifted momentarily to Dr. Silva. She seemed embarrassed by the attention. She'd never said as much to Liam, but he'd overheard her once, speaking to the nurses, lamenting the serum's use in the war and how it had so much more potential. It might be used to further science, she'd said, many minds being combined to work toward a single cause. Or engineers pooling their knowledge to create works that vastly exceeded what humanity had created so far. Dr. Silva was committed to the project, Liam knew, but largely in hopes that it would one day lead to peace.

"Keep your wits about you," De Pere continued. "Note anything out of the ordinary. We're trying to get Project Echo ready to go beyond trials, beyond our small group, so we can win this war. Are we understood?"

Unlike Sergeant Kohler, De Pere's presence inspired loyalty. He was the sort of man others followed instinctively.

"Yes, sir!" was the squad's full-throated reply.

As De Pere went on to detail the disposition of enemy forces on a map of Milwaukee, Liam felt a warm feeling at the base of his skull, the telltale sign that the Henchman serum was beginning to work its magic. His awareness grew. He sensed Kohler's raw emotions, Hatcher's cold calculation, then Reyes and Blaim and Hansen and Smith. Fear rolled off Clay Graves in endless waves, but it dissipated—as did all their strongest emotions—as they began to share thoughts, share emotions, share the lightning-fast analyses that allowed them to beat forces five times their size in drill after drill.

When De Pere was done, Kohler lumbered away from the loading dock and turned to face the unit. "Ready, soldiers?"

"Yes, Sergeant!" Several soldiers began hopping from foot to foot on their long, insectoid legs, loosening up their armatures.

"Then let's head out!"

They moved in a line, loping over the war-torn streets, quick as sprinting quarter horses, leaping over anything that got in their way. In a single bound, Liam soared over a tree with a shattered trunk, then the rubble of a destroyed warehouse. Along the riverfront they stormed, ready to fall upon the enemy.

Across the river, they spotted a company of SLP soldiers—Québécois, from the look of them. Hundreds of them laid siege to a pillbox, hoping to take the emplacement before pushing deeper beyond American lines.

They never knew what hit them.

Like a perfectly designed machine, the Devil's Henchmen worked together to confuse and confound the enemy. Liam leapt high over their lines to identify their officers, the vision shared with the others as he flew. Reyes leapt from a different angle, his flight course-corrected to get a clear shot on their commanding officer.

In barely a minute, half their officers had been taken out. After another minute, the handful who remained were spooked and staring at the sky, wondering from what direction the next leap of the nightmare machines would come. By then, Kohler, with one thought shared among them all, ordered a change in tactics. Using lookouts, they would spot soldiers out of position or moving between trenches. Their squad had become an animal with twenty pairs of eyes. What one saw, they all saw. It made reconnaissance an uncomplicated maneuver. It made flanking the enemy, a dicey proposition under normal circumstances, a breeze.

Slowly but surely, the Québécois were being decimated, and their officers knew it. Their bugles called the order for retreat. Soldiers rose above the trenches, sending, as they ran, haphazard fire over their shoulders at the bounding Henchmen. When they began to scatter, Liam knew the end was near.

A change came over the Henchmen then. During their mock battles, things had always been serious but never life-threatening. Now everyone's adrenaline was so high it was building on itself. Making matters worse, they were beholden to Kohler, who was becoming more and more blood-thirsty. He ordered dozens to be shot in the back. The sheer momentum of following his orders had built to such a degree that the squad obeyed without thought. It took all Liam had not to shoot the retreating soldier ahead of him. Even so, he chased him into a cemetery.

As Liam leapt over the cemetery's stone wall, he sensed Kohler, out of ammo, leaping down on a young man completely unaware of him. Kohler sent his bayonet through him, then took out two more soldiers who had their hands up in surrender. One of them went flying thirty feet through the air when Kohler gave him a vicious kick of his armored leg.

The soldier Liam was chasing sprinted into a grove of trees. He was so busy sending glances over his shoulder he didn't see the fallen bough ahead of him. He tripped and went sprawling onto the grass. He tried to clamber to his feet, but by then Liam was there, shoving him with the cleated hoof at the end of his hopper's long, articulated leg. The soldier flew backward, losing his helmet and rifle in the process. He was on his back, scrabbling away, staring up at Liam with terror-filled eyes as Liam trained his rifle on the man's chest. God in heaven, if he was over seventeen, Liam was a bray-ing mule.

Liam held his rifle still, heart pounding, chest heaving, lungs burning from the chase.

The young soldier stared up, hands above his head. Dirt streaked his face. *"Je me rends! Je me rends!"* They were words of surrender, spoken in his native tongue. His Adam's apple bobbed as he swallowed over and over again.

—*You have your orders, Mulcahey.*

It was Kohler. Even though Liam had stopped projecting the sights and sounds around him, Kohler had *seen* what Liam was seeing from his position beyond the cemetery. Though he knew he was disobeying a direct order, Liam stayed his hand, denying the urge to kill that was welling up inside of him.

"Stand up," Liam said, motioning with his rifle. "Slowly. *Lentement, tu comprends?*"

—*You have your orders,* Kohler called again, more forceful this time.

—*He's coming back with us.*

—*That's a negative, Mulcahey.*

—*He's coming back with us,* Liam repeated, and pointed to the officer's waist, his belt, which still had a sidearm secured in a canvas holster. "Take off the belt! *Ta ceinture! Déshabiller!*"

The young soldier nodded. He looked like he was going to comply. One moment, his hands were moving slowly toward the buckle. The next, he was flicking the strap on his holster and drawing his gun in a mad rush.

As he took aim, Liam leapt high into the air, aimed his rifle straight down, and fired. The bullet caught the young officer on the crown of his head. A spray of mottled pink. The young man's scalp peeling away in ways it shouldn't. His body jerked, then he stumbled and fell face first onto the grass.

Liam, his heart rattling like a snare drum, landed and approached carefully. His hopper legs bore him toward the fallen soldier in their unique, ungainly way. The pistol, Liam realized, was no longer in the soldier's hand. It was nowhere to be seen. Liam searched the leaf-strewn ground, but saw no sign of it. Only after a long, fruitless search did he see the butt sticking out from under the soldier himself. Crouching low, he grabbed a fistful of uniform and rolled the young man over until he was staring at the sky.

Liam stood tall while staring down, horrified. The soldier's pistol was still holstered. He'd never drawn it, never aimed it at Liam.

"Just because he didn't draw it," came Kohler's grating voice, "doesn't mean he wouldn't have done it the first chance he got." Liam turned and saw him standing between two tall elms: Kohler, his rifle held at the ready, the disappointment in his piercing blue eyes plain to see. "Or did you somehow forget who we're fighting?"

What Liam had just seen had been a dream, a vision of some sort, and he was certain Kohler had been the one to create it. "He was *surrendering*," Liam said.

—*Surrender, fight . . .* Kohler turned and bounded away. *He won't be doing either anymore.*

It was then, as Kohler was ordering the Henchmen to regroup, that Liam felt it. A greater concern, a deep sadness over what had just happened. It was there and gone in a moment, as if what had been temporarily revealed was now masked again.

Was it someone in his unit who sympathized, someone who'd learned how to mask their emotions? No. Impossible. He could feel them all, especially Reyes, who'd taken a bullet through the meat of his right bicep. It was someone else, then, but who?

He had his answer an hour later as they gathered along the same loading dock behind the warehouse, ready to step out of their exoskeletons and enter their debrief with Major De Pere.

As Liam began to recount his version of events, the team of doctors were there, including Dr. Silva, who was watching him carefully. When it came to the point in the story where he chased the Québécois soldier, he felt a flare of worry which was accompanied by the same sort of sorrow he'd felt earlier. It was coming from Dr. Silva.

The realization so shook him, he kept Kohler's deception to himself.

Liam didn't know how, nor did he know why, but he knew this much: against all protocol, Doctor Colette Silva had injected herself with the Henchman serum and shared the same senses as the unit, but managed to hide herself from them all.

She was, for all intents and purposes, a spy amongst their ranks.

TWENTY-ONE

During the war . . .

Doctor Colette Silva stood on top of the warehouse loading dock with the squad of Devil's Henchmen lined up on the cracked asphalt below. The soldiers in their hopper exoskeletons were a sight to see, a modern marvel, the engineering that had gone into them truly impressive. Even so, Colette was far more interested in what was happening one step away from reality, a place she'd come to know as the fog.

Within the fog, she was alone, the mental space around her dull, gray, and perfectly empty. As each of the Devil's Henchmen was given the injection, that space lit up as if by glowing yellow lanterns, each a mind. The serum she and her assistants administered to the squad was filled with *E. sentensis*, the bacteria Colette and her fellow scientists had developed into something truly wondrous, a thing that would, if all went well, unite full companies of soldiers, then battalions, perhaps the entire U.S. Army.

As additional shots were administered, more minds lit up the fog. A score of them floated in the vast emptiness around her. From those intense, miniature suns, tendrils of light reached outward, met, and threaded themselves through one another. They formed a mesh, a melding of minds, the soldiers becoming a unified whole.

Colette's own mind shone as brightly as the others, but she masked herself from them. Though it was against the protocol she herself had helped draft, she'd decided early on—shortly after the initial mind-to-mind experiment confirmed the ability of *E. sentensis* to enhance the human brain's innate, extrasensory perceptions—that she would be an integral part of the ongoing experiment. And she was. She'd injected herself with each new iteration of the bacteria. It had given her not only insights into the soldiers' experiences, but also powers she'd never dreamed of, not the least of which was the ability to mask her presence.

She hid herself for two reasons, the first being that if her subjects were aware of her, they might act differently. She wanted their minds to join with one another without fear of being observed. She wanted to see what would happen to the group dynamic when they did. It was crucial, because *E. sentensis* was, above all, a powerful, unifying force. She needed to understand its full potential before it was given to a larger group.

The second and more self-serving reason was that if her fellow biologists and chemists learned that she'd become a part of the experiment, they'd likely oust her from the project altogether. They were all men, her fellow scientists, and they'd been green with envy from the beginning, ever since President Nolan had recruited her personally to head the effort. Had she failed as lead scientist, their jealousy might have faded, but she'd made great strides, accomplishing in months what they'd failed to achieve in years. They would leap at the chance to send her packing, back to Miami and the private sector lab she'd headed before being recruited by President Nolan.

Oddly enough, it wasn't De Pere she was most worried about. De Pere was a pragmatic man, an *ambitious* man. He would do nothing to jeopardize Project Echo's steady progress, not only for the war, but because he and everyone else in his orbit knew it would lead to his getting the Lieutenant Colonel's oak leaf he'd coveted for years.

President Nolan, on the other hand, was a mercurial man. Despite being the one to recruit her, the ever-shifting winds of political perception could lead him to believe that taking her off the team entirely was the right move to make. It was a thing she couldn't leave to chance, so for now, she would watch. She would learn. The time would come to reveal herself, but only after she knew it was safe, when *she'd* gained the upper hand, a thing that would only come when they considered her indispensable.

Colette watched the hoppers bound away from the warehouse loading dock, over the Kinnickinnic River, and into Milwaukee's broken streets.

While their physical forms were soon lost from sight, their minds weren't. In the fog, they shone nearly as brightly a mile or two away.

Major De Pere still harbored reservations over Colette and her team being anywhere near the action, but Colette had pressed hard to ensure she'd be close enough to share in their combined experience. "In case something goes wrong," she'd told De Pere two days before. "It's for *their* sake, not ours."

"Do you have doubts about the serum?" Major De Pere asked. "Because if you do—"

"No," she said, "nothing like that. It's just a precaution. I want to protect our investment."

De Pere saw the power in *E. sentensis*—he saw the potential for it to catapult his career as well—but he'd never come to trust the technology. Not fully. "It feels like we're playing with the power of God," he'd told her once.

"And who gave us this power but God himself?" she'd shot back.

He'd had no answer to that.

Several miles away, the soldiers engaged. They fought the enemy, picking them apart just as they'd been trained to do. But then she felt something in Sergeant Kohler, a spike of bloodlust that went well beyond his already aggressive attitude. He'd taken a grazing wound to his leg. It sent him into a wild, animalistic fury.

—*Take them out!* he roared in the squad's minds. *None of them reach the enemy reserves!*

The squad hesitated to commit wanton slaughter, but something strange was happening, something they didn't understand. To this point Colette had seen only glimpses of it herself. Kohler's near mindless urge to deal death was bleeding into the others, all but Liam Mulcahey, who seemed to have some innate resistance. Liam alone disobeyed Kohler's orders, deciding to make a prisoner of the Québécois infantryman he'd chased into a cemetery.

Then something extraordinary happened. Kohler made Liam think the young enemy soldier had been trying to draw his sidearm. Liam, fearing for his life, had leapt high into the air and shot the soldier dead. Kohler had crafted an *illusion* and made Liam believe in it.

The golden lights of the Devil's Henchmen's minds dimmed a short while later, the bacteria in the serum succumbing to human physiology and its array of defenses. Colette, having given herself the latest version of the bacteria, the one that lived for nearly a half day, was alone in the fog once more. She wouldn't normally take another dose so soon—she'd taken one only a few hours earlier—but the stunning revelation of Kohler's new-found ability was bringing up possibilities she hadn't even considered before. The Henchman serum helped her think, so she took another dose. A large one. Probably larger than she needed.

As the serum spread through her body, she felt warmth in her fingers and toes. Her mind expanded. She examined the implications of what Kohler had done and saw a hundred possibilities she hadn't considered before. President Nolan was set to arrive the very next day, as were various members of the Armed Services Committee, many of whom were skeptical of Project Echo's benefits. Surprisingly, Liam didn't mention the incident with Kohler during his mission debrief with Major De Pere, but she could tell he wasn't going to keep quiet about it forever. Sooner or later he would lodge a formal complaint. An inquiry would begin and, in all likelihood, President Nolan and the Armed Services Committee would hear about it—the scrutiny the project received was too great for it to be otherwise.

The committee would start asking questions, especially Senator Vaughan, the project's most vocal critic. It could slow Colette's research for months, years. Project Echo might be defunded, perhaps for good.

She couldn't allow it. She was close, very close, to finding a strain that could live in the human body permanently, but she needed *time* to get there. Perhaps that was the key. Dangle the possibility of a permanent solution to the Army's brass and pretty soon they'd all be singing her tune.

She thought of going to Major De Pere first. He was a reasonable enough man. And he cared about the project. He saw its potential, enough that he might convince Liam to stand down, to keep his concerns to himself. But the more she thought about it, the more she realized that wasn't the right solution.

Decision made, she returned to her office, picked up the phone receiver and turned the crank several times to alert the switchboard.

A pleasant voice came on the line a moment later. "Hello, Dr. Silva. What can we do for you?"

"Patch me through to Novo Solis," she said. "I need to speak to President Nolan."

TWENTY-TWO

Liam awoke on a couch inside the furniture store. Beyond the tall windows, Chicago lay in darkness, while the store's neo-lume sign bathed everything inside the showroom a deep, bloody red.

Across from Liam, Grace was curled up on a sofa, asleep. He considered waking her, but paused. He was bothered by the dreams—his own, for how disturbing it had been, and Colette's, for the oddness of having experienced it at all.

From the darkness came a rhythmic sound, like sandpaper on fresh-cut wood. A moment later, Nana's hunched form came shuffling out from behind a nearby armoire. She scanned the sea of furniture, as if deciding where to sit, then dropped her weight into a chair shaped vaguely like her ancient armchair from their shared apartment. "Strange business," she said in Irish, "your dreams."

Liam shrugged. "Stasa's cocktail was *meant* to unlock memories."

"Meant to unlock *your* memories. What about Colette's?"

It was the very same mystery Liam had been worrying. He sat up, rubbed the sleep from his eyes. "The serum allowed us to share thoughts and emotions. With Colette apparently taking the Henchman serum along with the rest of us, maybe her memories were transferred to me without either of us realizing it."

"Seems a bit far-fetched."

Liam chuckled. "*All* of this is far-fetched."

Nana was silent for a time, her look darkening. "You never said the Henchmen reported directly to De Pere."

"I didn't remember until just now." Liam caught glimpses of more officers, their staff, and the medical team, including and especially Dr. Silva. "All of that was gone by the time we met."

Of course Nana knew that he meant meeting *her*, the illusory Nana.

She grunted, then sucked at something between her teeth. It felt in character yet ultimately hollow—the Nana sitting in the plush armchair wasn't real. What did that matter in the end, though? She might not be real, but a good sit down with Nana when life had gotten to him had never failed to calm him down, and that in turn helped him think more clearly.

"Was that the first time any of you experienced illusions?" Nana asked.

Liam nodded. "I think so, yes."

"Makes me wonder when De Pere started taking the serum. And, more importantly, why? Did he order it? Was he commanded to? Was it out of simple necessity?"

Liam thought back. "I vaguely recall they were planning to expand adoption once it was perfected. He would've been a likely candidate to take it at that point."

Nana shrugged. "The serum, how long did it last in the early days?"

"During trials, it was only a few minutes, but it got better and better. By the time we used it in that battle, it lasted several hours."

"Remember *when* it was perfected? When it became permanent?"

"No."

"Kohler seemed to take to it pretty well." Nana jutted her chin toward Grace. "But she said *you* commanded Clay at one point. You remember how you replaced Kohler? Or why?"

Liam could only shrug. "It might've had something to do with his tricking me into killing the Québécois soldier, but that's only a guess."

Ironically, having recalled some of his memories but not all of them made Liam feel *more* incomplete, not less.

Nana's gaze, so hard and sharply focused a moment ago, softened. "Don't feel badly, boyo. We're making cracks in the dam. It'll all come gushing out soon enough."

"Well, I wish I could jump ahead and learn more. The serum was too new, too unrefined, at that point."

Cloaked in dim red light, Nana's gaze suddenly shifted to Grace. Her jaw worked back and forth, her face pinched.

"What?" Liam asked.

"Earlier"—she waved toward the stairs—"just before she showed up, Stasa said *we* worked up a serum. He was referring to Grace."

"So?"

"How is it some heiress is working on *anything* with a scientist like Stasa?"

Liam shrugged. "Maybe he was just being kind. It's likely she was in the room when he was working on it."

Her skeptical groan was like the creak of an old sailing ship. "There's something I don't like about her. Some East Coast heiress puts her nose in this like it's some sort of vacation? Comes and goes as she pleases? What's her game, Liam?"

"Why does she have to have a game? Can't she just be someone trying to help her country?"

"She's a manipulator."

"No, she's not."

"Oh? How do you suppose she convinced Dr. Silva to give *her* the serum? How is it no one else got it before Dr. Silva mysteriously disappeared?"

"That's paranoia talking."

"Paranoid or not, I'm telling you, be wary of this one." Nana pushed herself up off the chair.

"You're leaving?"

"I'm tired, Liam."

He'd known her visit wouldn't last. Even so, her departure made Liam feel terribly lonely. As the shuffle of her receding footsteps became the clatter of an elevated tram in the distance, the feeling became more pronounced, almost painfully so.

"I miss you, Nana," he called into the darkness.

The train screeched, rounding a bend, switching tracks maybe, then rattled on. It was then that he realized Grace's eyes were open. The bleary-eyed smile she gave him was endearing, and made the worries Nana had placed in his head melt like snowpack in May.

"You're back amongst the living," she said drowsily.

"I am."

"I'm glad."

Liam laughed. "Me, too!"

Grace's smile was half genuine, half humoring. "What I mean is, I'm glad you came back *now*, while the others are downstairs."

Liam, feeling his cheeks go warm, was suddenly grateful for the deep red shade of the neo-lume lights. "Me, too."

Grace shifted backward on the sofa, clearing space, then reached one hand out toward Liam.

She meant for him to join her. He felt strangely elated by it—he couldn't deny his attraction to her—and yet he hesitated. He wasn't sure why at first. Part of it was her attitude. It felt overly familiar, overly presumptuous. It was more than that, though. His mind wandered back to the way Colette had smiled at him before he'd departed for the battle. As he recalled his schoolboy giddiness on seeing that smile, he understood. There'd been something between him and Colette. He was sure of it. She might be gone, but the blank space where their relationship had once been was beginning to haunt him.

As if sensing his thoughts, Grace said, "It gets lonely, Liam, orchestrating so much, wondering when you'll be found out, handling everyone's needs but your own. Everyone thinks you're untouchable."

Liam shrugged. "Some people feel threatened by a woman in power."

"Does that include you?"

"No."

She beckoned him again. "Then lay with me."

He went to her, took her hand, and lay down facing her, feeling that deep thrill of a first touch. She slipped one arm around his waist, pulled him close. He could smell her perfume, lavender and rose, the mint on her breath.

She stared into his eyes, trying to read him. "You might feel more threatened if you really knew me and all that I've done."

He paused. "You make it sound like you're a murderer."

"Not a murderer, exactly, but you were a soldier. You understand the mantle of leadership, that the cost of poor decisions might be tallied in lives."

"I'm sure you did the best you could."

"I'm glad *you* think so. I second guess every decision I make. It drives me to distraction."

"Maybe you just need something *else* to distract you."

She leaned in until their lips were nearly touching. He felt the heat coming off her. "Such as?"

Losing all inhibition, he closed the narrow gap between their lips and kissed her. Her lips were soft. They felt perfect against his. He'd only just met Grace, yet he felt so familiar with her, so comfortable.

When their lips parted, she turned, facing away from him, and pulled his arm over her waist. It was an electrifying moment that was soured by a thought that suddenly flitted through Liam's mind. He knew it was Nana's suspicious nature expressing itself through him, but he couldn't help but wonder: was Grace using her powers on him? Was her skin really so soft? Was the scent of lavender and citrus really from a perfume or was it a construct of Grace's own making?

"Earlier," he whispered, "Stasa said you worked on the serum with him."

Grace chuckled softly. "He rather overstated the case."

She lapsed into silence, but Liam couldn't let it go. "*Did* you help him?"

"I observed more than anything."

"Are you familiar with that sort of thing? Bioengineering? Neomedicine?"

"Shhh . . . It's nothing to worry about now, Liam."

One moment, it very much *did* feel like something to worry about, all the more so because Grace didn't want to talk about it. But the next, those worries seemed to melt away. There, in a furniture store awash in crimson, Liam's breaths lengthened, and he fell asleep with Grace in his arms.

TWENTY-THREE

Liam woke to sunlight and someone shaking his shoulder. It was Alastair, standing over him.

Liam propped himself up and looked around the showroom. "Where's Grace?"

"She left a short while ago. She said she had business to attend to."

"Any news about Morgan?" Liam asked, doing his best to hide his disappointment.

"In a roundabout way, yes. Master Kovacs believes he's found a way to learn Master Aysana's whereabouts."

"How?"

"He said by tapping into the Cabal's communications via Ruby, the woman you rescued from the tower." Sensing Liam's confusion, Alastair waved to the stairs. "They're waiting downstairs."

The news did much to raise Liam's spirits. He followed Alastair down to the store's rear entrance, where an idling delivery van was waiting. Bailey was at the wheel, Clay in the passenger seat, and Stasa on the padded bench behind them. They all looked sleep-deprived, especially Stasa, who shifted over as Liam climbed in beside him.

Seeing Stasa tickled a memory of something that had come up with Grace last night. It felt important, but for the life of him, Liam couldn't remember what it was. "Have you gotten *any* sleep?" he asked instead.

Stasa shrugged. "I slept on the way here. I was at the domes most of the night." He tipped his head toward the compartment at the back. "I had an idea, and I needed Ruby to see if it would work."

Only then did Liam realize the compartment wasn't empty. Sitting there, a blanket wrapped around her shoulders, was Ruby, the woman they'd rescued from the Kovacs P&L building. She wore men's clothes, thick denim jeans and an oversized blue plaid shirt. She was younger than

Liam had thought—seventeen, maybe eighteen, the same age as Liam when he'd signed up for the war. She still wore the dog-tag necklace with her name stamped upon it. Her bone-white hair, wild the night before, was braided into cornrows. Her ivory eyes stared sightlessly ahead while her lips moved. Barely, he could make out her soft mumbling over the rumble of the van's idling engine.

When Alastair had slipped into the bench beside Liam and slid the door shut, the engine rumbled louder, and Bailey steered them north, away from the furniture store.

"Did you at least get Ruby's permission to run experiments on her?"

Stasa's reply was half nod, half shrug, a middling confirmation at best. "I did, Liam, but you must understand something. Ruby no longer has a normal psyche. The strain of bacteria that was fed to her altered her brain chemistry, altered the way she thinks. She is a slave to the signal, a mechanism for the Cabal and De Pere to send thoughts, commands, and illusions over vast distances. I'm convinced they're how De Pere plans to control the entirety of the United States, perhaps the world. So while I asked her permission, and received her consent, I'm not entirely sure she knew what she was agreeing to."

"And just what is it we're trying to do with her?"

"The records we managed to save from the fire in the sub-basement were illuminating. From the information gleaned, I'm nearly certain the building was being set up as a communication hub. The psis, if all had gone according to the Cabal's plans, would act as relays for commands sent from Novo Solis. Those commands would be transferred to the scourges, who would in turn use them on the thralls. What we've stumbled onto, I'm progressively more convinced, is nothing less than the blueprint for what the American city will look like should De Pere have his way."

Liam couldn't help but shiver, the sheer depth of De Pere's madness as chilling as it was staggering.

"As for Morgan," Stasa continued, "the sub-basement appeared to have been used as a staging area for the scourges, those who were infected by the serum De Pere has been distributing and later abducted. We're nearly certain Morgan was there along with one other scourge, but both of them were stolen away before our strike team were able to breach their defenses."

The chill in Liam deepened. He didn't know that anything would have been different had he gone with the strike team, but now he wished he had. "So what's next?"

"This is where Ruby fits in. The Cabal have suspected, rightly so, that other forms of communication, like telegraphs and their messenger network, have been compromised. They've begun using the psis more often to send communications from Novo Solis to New York, Philadelphia, Boston, and, most recently, Chicago. With Ruby, we have a chance to tap into those communications and find news of Morgan and perhaps even other scourges."

"Okay, but how?"

"First, we need a tower that can be keyed to the proper frequency. The University of Chicago was gifted such a tower several years ago by the Rockefellers." Stasa patted a wooden contraption on the floor between his legs. It had several dials, switches, and gauges, plus a leather headband with bright electrodes running along the inside. "*This* will allow us to connect Ruby to it."

"Towers like that must be rare," Liam said. "The Cabal will surely be watching them, including the one at the university."

"They are," Clay growled over one shoulder, "but *we* have people watching it too. We'll be careful going in."

"The thornier issue," Stasa added, "will be making sure the other psis don't report our presence to the Cabal. That's where you come in, Liam. We need you to connect with Ruby like you did with the Henchmen."

All eyes were suddenly on Liam. Even Bailey was glancing at him through the rearview mirror.

"Can't you do it, Clay?" Liam asked.

"Nah," came his rasp of a reply. "Things changed after the accident." He rapped his knuckles on his head. "Noggin's not right anymore."

"Then what about Grace?"

"She's off trying another angle," replied Clay. "She's got a contact in the De Pere administration, a mole. She's hoping to contact them to see if they know where Morgan is." He jutted his stubble-covered chin toward Liam. "This one's on you, partner."

"I wouldn't normally press," Stasa said, "but we don't know if Grace will be successful, and there isn't much time left. I'm afraid they'll take Morgan to Novo Solis soon if they haven't already."

"Time check," Bailey said while navigating an easy curve in the road. "We've got about ten minutes before we reach the tower."

Liam looked back at Ruby, who continued to mumble. "So how does this work? You connect her to the network and I listen for clues to Morgan's whereabouts?"

"That's it," Stasa said.

"Easy peasy," echoed Clay.

"All right," Liam said, "I'm in, but I need to know Ruby has truly agreed." As the van rocked over an uneven section of road, he climbed into the back compartment and sat across from her. "Can you hear me, Ruby?"

She hugged her knees while staring *through* Liam. Her soft words carried above the engine's drone: *"And all the woods are alive with the murmur and sound of Spring, and the rose-bud breaks into pink on the climbing briar."*

Liam recognized the poem. It was one of Nana's favorites: "Magdalen Walks" by Oscar Wilde. He took her hands in his. "Ruby, can you *hear* me?"

At last, her cloudy white eyes met his. *"And the crocus-bed is a quivering moon of fire, girdled round with the belt of an amethyst ring."*

As she continued, Liam took a deep breath and let it out slowly. He closed his eyes and listened to her words, becoming lost in the cadence, in the lyricism. He wondered how she'd learned it, why she was repeating it now. He realized he need look no further than the poem's title. He felt a yearning in her to be freed of the prison she was in, to walk in the woods near her home as she once did. It was as though she was herself still but had been locked away, a prisoner in her own mind.

Liam caught glimpses of her memories: sterile rooms, men in white coats standing over her, needles injected into her arm. He felt a deep terror with the realization that she was losing her own sense of will. She felt an awareness of others bloom, but was lost in them, one soul on a wine-dark sea.

—*Save me,* she pleaded with him.

—*I don't know how,* he replied.

Tears gathered in Ruby's eyes. He felt her frustration, her impotence, turn to rage.

—*Then make them pay.*

—*I can,* he replied, *if you can help.*

Liam felt in her a surge of instinct, a desire to agree, but there was fear as well, a sense that she would be punished for her resistance.

—*Will you be there?* she asked.

—*Yes.*

—*Will it work? Will it stop them?*

—*What we do now will save a friend of mine. But I hope it leads to that, yes.*

A brief pause, her will hardening.

—*Then I'll help.*

Liam blinked, felt his own tears slip warmly down his cheeks. It was an echo of Ruby's sorrow, he knew, but it was also his. Their emotions fed off one another, so much so that Liam was forced to break the connection before it overwhelmed him.

Stasa watched silently, expectantly.

"We're ready," Liam said.

Stasa nodded and gave Liam a brief smile. "Good."

They reached the university a short while later and entered a parking lot with a sign that read "Department of Neotech Sciences." Set aside from the byzantine complex, beyond a scattering of cars and trucks, was a simple outbuilding made of red brick. Standing just beyond the blocky structure was a wireless antenna tower, white with the occasional red stripe painted across it. Supported by guy lines, it soared two hundred feet into the cloudless sky.

Bailey parked the van close—but not *too* close—to the front of the outbuilding. "Wait here," she said, and exited the van with Clay. They walked beyond the line of maple trees bordering the parking lot, where a man in a set of green gardener's overalls approached them. They spoke for a short while, then Bailey and Clay made a beeline toward the outbuilding. After trying the windowless steel door, Bailey crouched before it—presumably to use her lock picks. She had the door open a moment later, then she and Clay drew their guns and rushed inside.

A short while later, Bailey stepped outside and waved.

As Alastair swung the cargo door open, Stasa pulled the contraption he'd shown Liam earlier from underneath the bench. The device was clearly heavy, Stasa lumbering as he hefted it toward the outbuilding. Alastair followed, his blue eyes scanning the university grounds. Liam, meanwhile, opened the van's rear door and guided Ruby out. The day was mildly warm, but Ruby was shivering so badly Liam left the blanket around her shoulders.

Soon they were all inside, in a room with a wide bank of control equipment fed by thick power cables. Liam sat Ruby in a chair, then pulled another chair close and sat facing her. Stasa set his device on a nearby desk, uncoiled four braided wires, and clipped them to several metal terminals on a steel panel against the wall. There came a soft click, and the contraption's gauges lit a pleasant amber. The needles within snapped into position. Stasa adjusted the dials and toggled a handful of the device's many switches. When he was satisfied, he took up the leather headband and set it over Ruby's head.

"On your signal," he said to Liam.

Liam squeezed Ruby's hands.

—*Ready?*

She continued to murmur. *"The woods are alive with the murmur and sound of Spring."* Below it, she spoke with her inner voice:

—*I'm ready.*

Liam nodded, and Stasa flipped the device's large, central toggle switch.

As Ruby released a long, attenuated moan, Liam's mind exploded with a new awareness.

TWENTY-FOUR

Liam's mind was flooded by a torrent of sensory input, not only from Stasa's device, but from Ruby herself. It was similar to what he'd felt on receiving the Henchman serum during the war, but instead of becoming aware of a full squad of other minds, he felt a single, massive, multilayered consciousness.

It was a matter of scale, he realized, individual minds becoming so numerous they seemed a contiguous, interwoven veil composed of the psis themselves. It was powerfully seductive, and Ruby was on the verge of becoming lost to it. She was all thought, no emotion, as if the small part of her that had remained human was once again succumbing to the bacteria within her.

—*Stay with me,* Liam said.

It took her long moments, but Ruby seemed to stabilize.

—*Hurry,* she said.

Knowing how dangerous it was for her and how scary it must be made it difficult, but Liam sunk himself into the signal, absorbing it as the psis might. He almost felt as if he might be able to relay messages as *they* could and become yet another part of this strange, vast network, but he held back, fearing he might never return. He needed to remain an anchor, for Ruby's sake *and* his own.

He felt a myriad of people, a myriad of voices. Through them, he gained a new sort of awareness. The psis weren't only spreading messages. They maintained illusions as well. Entire buildings, entire neighborhoods, were hidden from view. There were more places that *looked* real but weren't, areas that had been shelled during the war but which still looked whole— a show of resiliency, Liam supposed, a way for the government to convince the populace of the United States that their country was indestructible, when in reality it was weak and rotting from within.

"Anything?" Stasa asked.

"Not yet," replied Liam. "I can't hear the other psis. Not clearly, anyway."

"I'll try to amplify the signal"—Stasa adjusted several dials—"but be careful not to draw attention to yourself."

It worked. The feelings intensified. But Liam felt just as lost as before. When he was a Henchman, he'd spoken to the others with hardly any effort. He was growing worried that the difficulties were due to a mismatch of some sort between the Henchman serum and the one used to create the psis. Perhaps he'd *never* be able to eavesdrop on their communications.

Like a daydream, Grace had said of casting illusions. Maybe that was the key to syncing with the psis as well. He'd been nervous on entering this place, wary of attracting attention to himself and, through it, alerting the other psis, but now he relaxed, fell deeper into Ruby's mind. He let it carry him like a raft on a wide, turbulent river.

He heard a message, sent from the south—St. Louis, perhaps—that was immediately forwarded to Novo Solis:

—*Twelve suspects detained, questioning commencing for Uprising involvement. Links to Chicago mafia.* A list of names followed.

Another message came from Denver:

—*Twenty crates of contraband found in butcher's freezer. Shipped from Baltimore. Send investigation team to Wallace Street warehouse.*

As a dizzying number of messages were passed by dozens upon dozens of psis, Liam watched through their eyes. He saw men and women typing words onto thin strips of paper that were then ripped and handed to the next in a line of breathless couriers who stood waiting in black uniforms. Beyond a partition, more psis were being fed messages from the couriers who, after delivering their slim paper notes, joined the back of the queue waiting for their next message. It felt like a vast organism that fed on information.

Though he listened as carefully as he could, Liam heard nothing about Morgan. He worried he'd arrived too late, that he'd missed any messages that might have mentioned Morgan, when he heard a communication that made him go cold.

—*University has sent an alert regarding suspicious activity at tower. Sending squad car. Locust to follow.*

"They're suspicious," Liam said to Stasa. "They're sending a squad car and a locust to investigate."

Stasa shared a sober expression with Clay and Bailey. "How long does that give us?"

"Five minutes, tops," Clay said. "We need to go."

Stasa paused, looking to Liam for confirmation.

Liam hated to admit it, but Clay was right. He'd found nothing so far, and staying any longer risked them all. He'd just nodded to Stasa when he heard a new communication:

—*Ambulance carrying scourges has departed university hospital.*

Stasa's hand was halfway to the power switch when Liam snatched his wrist. Stasa waited expectantly.

Liam focused on that one thread, willing for the speaker to continue, to reveal more.

"Liam, we can't stay," Stasa said.

"Shhh," Liam hissed, concentrating.

Several seconds passed, and Liam was certain he'd lost it, but then he heard the same voice continue:

En route to Pier 43 terminal for transport to Novo Solis.

"Morgan was *here*," he said, "at the university. They're taking him to a place called Pier 43. They're planning to ship him to Novo Solis."

Stasa's look of faint hope collapsed on hearing Liam's words. Bailey's did too. Clay had a grim demeanor that was accentuated by the soft hiss coming from the metal sleeve wrapped around his chest.

"What is it?" Liam asked.

"Pier 43 is a Cabal facility," replied Stasa.

"And?"

"We can't go there," Stasa went on. "It's too heavily guarded."

Liam looked at each of them, hoping for the tiniest amount of optimism, but in this he was disappointed. "Well, we can't just give up."

Stasa lifted the headband from Ruby's forehead, at which point she slumped forward and began coughing. "I'm sorry, Liam," Stasa said while retrieving the power cables from the nearby terminals. "We'll have to go to Novo Solis instead, try to rescue Morgan there."

Liam's desperation was growing by the moment. They couldn't have come so close only to lose Morgan now. He was tempted to take the van and rush to the lakefront, perhaps find the ambulance before it reached the pier. But even if he *did* manage to reach the pier in time, he'd likely only get himself captured along with Morgan.

"We have to try," Liam said.

To Liam's great surprise, it was Bailey who entered the fray. "We *have* had the plan in place for the pier."

Stasa paused, the braided wires suspended in mid-air.

"What plan?" Liam asked.

Stasa finished coiling the wires and hooked them onto his device. "A plan that was put in place for emergencies only."

Bailey shrugged. "What is this if not an emergency?"

"It was meant for an *assault*," Stasa said, "when we had enough strength."

"True," Clay interjected, "but you know as well as I do that if you hold back a move too long, waiting for the perfect opportunity, it becomes useless. Wars change, Stasa. The enemy adjusts. We're nearing the end game. De Pere's got his final moves planned out. If we don't do something to disrupt them, he's going to sweep the floor with us. We *need* Morgan. We need to know what's inside him. Now's the time to get him, before it's too late."

Stasa took them all in, then turned his attention to Ruby, who was rocking back and forth, mumbling softly. *"The crocus-bed is a quivering moon of fire, girdled round with the belt of an amethyst ring."*

"I can get you onto the pier," Stasa finally said, "but that still leaves Morgan. How do we get him out?"

The message Liam had overheard echoed in his mind: *Sending squad car. Locust to follow.*

"Leave it to me," he said.

———————

Stasa, Bailey, and Ruby retreated to the van. Clay and Alastair hid inside the outbuilding. Liam, meanwhile, made his way to the building's flat, tar-covered roof. After entering the mindset needed for casting, he crafted an illusion, making it appear as though the roof was empty, or *normal*, which made the vision simple to summon, simple to believe in.

Five minutes later, a squad car pulled into the university parking lot and rolled up to the curb near the outbuilding. Liam was both surprised and not to see Sergeant Holohan and Officer Carolan, the men who'd stopped Morgan and Liam on their way from Dr. Ramachandra's office. They headed toward the outbuilding door, which Liam had left purpose-fully ajar.

Even knowing the illusion was in place, Liam feared he'd be spotted. He wasn't, though. The officers rushed inside without once glancing up. A moment later, Liam heard sounds of a struggle. A muffled cry.

"All clear!" Clay called from the door.

"Roger that," Liam replied.

Another minute passed with Liam studying the sky. He paid careful attention to the feeling inside his gut. As he'd expected he would, he felt a twinge. From there it was easy to sense the edges of an illusion that was quickly approaching. He tugged at it and heard a faint buzzing. He tugged further and spotted a strange swirl in the sky, like fresh paint being smudged with a finger. Pulling further still, he saw it, a soldier in an exoskeleton with buzzing dragonfly wings, a locust.

As the sound of the locust's wings intensified, the soldier, hovering fifty feet above the ground, cast his gaze over the parking lot, the outbuilding, the green lawn beyond it. When his gaze lingered on the roof, Liam was certain he'd been spotted. But a moment later, the pilot descended and landed near the squad car. The exoskeleton's broad, translucent wings stilled, then its overpowering noise ceased all at once.

The pilot unlatched the leather mask over his face and let it hang loose, staring at the outbuilding's open door. "Holohan?"

Liam, his heart galloping, sprinted toward the edge of the roof. As he launched himself through the air, the soldier's eyes went wide—he'd pierced Liam's illusion, but by then it was too late. Just as he was beginning to lift his Winchester, Liam crashed into the exoskeleton, his momentum sending it and the soldier staggering backward. The soldier backpedaled and nearly recovered, but the locust's oddly bent legs were too awkward, and he fell hard against the parking lot's pavement.

Using one hand to fend off the rifle, Liam sent a pile-driver punch to the soldier's jaw, then another, before his eyes rolled back in his head.

"Clear," Liam called.

A moment later, Sergeant Holohan exited the outbuilding with Clay coming right behind him, a pistol in hand.

The sergeant's eyes lit up as he recognized Liam. "You."

"Yes, me," Liam said.

"What are you—?"

He stopped when Liam stepped onto the sidewalk, lifted the rifle, and pointed it at his chest. "Why don't you just leave the questions to me?" He tipped his head back toward the university "Where are they taking Morgan?"

Sergeant Holohan's eyes flicked down to the mouth of the barrel several times before he answered. "Novo Solis."

"*Where* in Novo Solis?"

He laughed nervously. "You think they'd tell *me* that?"

"Well, you must know *something*."

"I know two things for certain," Sergeant Holohan said with a sneer, "he's important to our President, and you're never going to see him again."

Liam stepped forward, ready to bring the butt of the rifle across Holohan's head, but stopped when Holohan glanced at something behind Liam.

"Put the weapons down," came the voice of the locust pilot, "nice and slow."

Liam sent a glance over one shoulder and cursed himself. The pilot, lying prone in the locust armor, had a pistol gripped in both hands—it must have been stowed away in the armor somewhere.

"I said weapons down!"

Unwilling to risk his friends' safety, Liam dropped the rifle onto the grass beyond the sidewalk. With a grim look, Clay tossed his pistol after it.

With a grunt and a sharp, mechanical whine, the pilot kicked himself to a stand. His pistol still trained on Liam, he put a finger to his right ear, likely calling back to base. He stopped, however, when a clanking sound came from the outbuilding.

It was Alastair, but Alastair wouldn't realize the extent of the danger he was in. The pilot actuated several buttons on the glove of his left hand. With a high-pitched whirring, a barrel swiveled up and over one shoulder. It was a grenade launcher, and it was pointed at the outbuilding's door.

"Alastair, stop!"

Alastair might have his repeating rifle, but if the pilot got off a single round, it would take out not only Alastair, but Liam and Clay as well.

The pounding slowed. The look on the pilot's face was intent. He was going to fire the grenade anyway.

Liam was just about to dive for his rifle when a scream rent the air. In the parking lot, twenty paces behind the pilot and his locust armor, Ruby stood tall, her hands shaking at her sides. She was staring intently at the locust pilot with her cloudy eyes as her scream went on and on and on.

The pilot's body convulsed. An involuntary groan escaped him, the sort that came with terrible pain. His sidearm fell from his fingers. His lips pulled back in a rictus of pain, he tore his helmet off and pressed his hands to his head. Then he, too, began to scream.

TWENTY-FIVE

ehind Ruby, Bailey and Stasa had both exited the van. They looked as though they wanted to approach Ruby, either to comfort her or to make her stop screaming, but didn't. Ruby, meanwhile, stormed over the black asphalt, her white eyes still fixed on the pilot. The pilot stumbled and fell, but Ruby didn't let up. She stood over him, staring down, screaming like a banshee, and for a long time the pilot's own screams echoed hers. His eyes were wide as wooden nickels, his mouth agape, the muscles along his neck harp-string tight. A white foam issued from his mouth. He fell silent a few moments later, his body quivering, then went still.

Only then did Ruby finally, blessedly, lapse into a tense silence.

For long moments all Liam could do was breathe. The same was true of everyone else. Even Sergeant Holohan, who hadn't moved since Ruby started stalking forward, had a numb expression, as if he were having trouble processing what had just happened.

From the university building on the other side of the parking lot, people were stepping outside, staring at the scene near the wireless tower.

"We need to move," Clay said.

Liam knelt beside the pilot, felt his neck for a pulse, and found none. He was dead. "Take them into the outbuilding," he said to Clay and Alastair.

Clay nodded and forced Sergeant Holohan back inside. Alastair, meanwhile, went to the pilot and began unbuckling his straps. Near him, Ruby had begun to shiver. She hugged herself tight, becoming small, as Bailey and Stasa crouched beside her.

Liam approached her as well, his hands raised in a sign of calm. "Can you hear me, Ruby?" When she didn't respond, he reached out to her with his mind.

—*Everything's going to be fine*, he said.

Her eyes reddened. Tears gathered. Her expression was that of a child lost in the woods. Liam had no doubt that what she'd done, she'd done in the heat of the moment to protect Liam and the others, but now she was starting to realize the gravity and seriousness of her actions.

—*I don't want this life anymore,* she said.

—*We'll find a way to help you. I promise.*

Liam wished he could do more than make promises, but he couldn't. Not just then. Catching Bailey's attention, he said, "See her safe?"

Bailey nodded and led Ruby away, back toward the van.

More people had gathered near the entrance to the university. A few had headed back inside, likely to call the police. Others approached warily, but stopped when Clay raised his pistol and ordered them back the way they'd come.

Stasa, after a nervous glance toward the onlookers, focused on Liam. "Things have been set into motion. You've got about five minutes before the illusions around the pier are dropped."

Liam nodded, reckoning that should be enough time to reach the lakefront.

After carrying the pilot's body into the outbuilding, Alastair welded the door shut, effectively locking the coppers and the pilot's dead body inside. Liam, meanwhile, pulled the pilot's helmet on, strapped himself into the exoskeleton, and engaged the suit. Fortunately, the basic controls had changed little since his time in the Army. His old instincts returning, he pulled the locust's powered legs to his chest and kicked himself to a stand.

Clay, one hand shielding his eyes from the sun, handed Liam the soldier's rifle. "You could try the wings."

Liam thumbed the wings' activator switch, and they gave a loud, rattling buzz, much louder than earlier. "I think they're broken. I'd likely kill us both, anyway. Better if we hop."

Handholds and footholds had been built into the exoskeleton for use in rescue operations, or for moving personnel quickly. It was these that Alastair used to climb onto Liam's back. Like this—Alastair holding himself tight, his head resting between the glowing blue power canisters over

Liam's shoulder blades—Liam hopped from foot to foot, and the peculiar balance required to ferry others on the back of any sort of hopper, a locust included, quickly returned to him.

"Good luck, soldier," Clay said.

Liam nodded, then summoned an illusion around himself and Alastair to hide their presence. As the others piled into the van and drove away, tires screeching, Liam began bounding over the university grounds. He piloted the hopper over city streets, down sidewalks, through parks, and along tramway tracks. He tried to mask the locust's passage from the people in their cars, or those out walking or jogging, but he was certain the illusion was far from complete. More than a few heads turned their way. It was unfortunate, but Liam couldn't afford to concentrate on the illusion to any great degree. Too much of his attention was needed on doing the little things needed to maximize a locust's speed: the timing of his leaps, the shift of his weight, syncing them with the exoskeleton's natural rhythms.

"We're traveling quite fast, Master Mulcahey!" Alastair shouted. He sounded like a little boy his first time riding on the back of his brother's bicycle. It was an odd feeling given all that had just happened.

"Just hold tight, Alastair."

Soon enough, Liam was leaping over the busy traffic along Lake Shore Drive. He came to a halt near a wall of chain-link fencing. To the right, Navy Pier stretched into the choppy blue waters of Lake Michigan. Pier 43 *should* be straight ahead but, for the life of him, he couldn't make out a single thread of the illusion.

As the seconds passed, he wondered if the Uprising agents Stasa had sent ahead had failed in their mission of blowing up Pier 43's power transformers. Or maybe they had succeeded, and the base's back-up power generator had since been engaged. Either result would prove disastrous.

He considered leaping over the chain-link fence and hoping that being *inside* the illusion's boundaries would reveal it to him, but he wasn't at all sure that would happen, nor was he certain of the hidden pier's precise location. Misjudge and he might land himself and Alastair in a pit, or trip over something unseen.

"Can you see anything, Alastair?"

"I'm afraid not, sir."

Liam felt his gut suddenly lurch. To the south, he felt something approaching, something hidden by an illusion. Concentrating, he managed to pierce it. A sleek, yellow flashtrain with seven cars, each with the seal of the President of the United States on its side, was flying along an elevated track, the one that carried commuter trains from the northern suburbs. The train, surely the one meant to deliver Morgan to Novo Solis, veered toward the lake and then simply disappeared. It had taken a spur of some sort and entered the boundaries of the illusion around the pier.

Liam feared he had only minutes to save Morgan. He didn't want to take any unnecessary risks, though. Doing so might doom his mission before it had begun. But when another minute passed and nothing had changed, he realized he had no choice.

He'd just started to hop, ready to shunt power to the legs to leap high, when a thunderous boom rolled over the lakefront. He felt the ground shudder through the hopper's legs. Beyond the chain-link fence, a great geyser of white sparks flew a hundred feet into the air. A moment later, a bulky electrical transformer winked into existence. A second transformer blew a heartbeat later, and suddenly Pier 43 was revealed in all its military excess. Several blocky buildings hunkered near the shore, along with various warehouses. A pair of warships, with all manner of armaments sprouting up from the decks, were moored along the pier. A dozen forklifts ran between them and the warehouses.

Running alongside the buildings was a monorail, the spur Liam had been unable to see until the illusion had been dispelled. The presidential train was just pulling into the station, where dozens of uniformed and well-dressed people waited.

"There he is, sir!" The pitch of Alastair's voice was so high the speaker behind his faceplate buzzed like a trapped hornet. "There's Morgan!"

He was right. Near the platform, two men in Navy uniforms had just pulled a pair of gurneys from the belly of an ambulance. After locking the gurneys' frames in place, they wheeled them toward the platform. Liam felt relieved and worried in the same breath—Morgan was surely strapped to one of those gurneys.

Beside the ambulance, a CIC officer in a black cap was shouting and pointing at the electrical yard. A moment later, those on the platform began rushing the gurneys through the doors and into the flashtrain. Liam made special note of it—the second car from the back.

"Hold on, Morgan," Liam said under his breath. "Just a little bit longer."

He activated the locust's legs, sending him and Alastair high over the fence. After landing with a crunch onto the gravel, Liam leaned them into a fast, furlong-eating stride. They were closing on the flashtrain quickly, but all too soon the gurneys were loaded, the doors were closing, and the flashtrain was easing into motion. Knowing they had no chance of keeping up if it reached cruising speed, Liam pushed hard, squeezing every ounce of speed he could from the hopper's legs.

He tried to craft an illusion to hide their approach, but in this he failed miserably. There was simply too much happening, and his emotions were running wild.

A bullet whined overhead, followed by the report of a rifle. More whizzed past as soldiers shouted and officers called orders, gesturing wildly toward Liam and Alastair.

A hail of gunfire broke out, bullets streaking in from all angles as soldiers wearing uniforms of Navy blue or CIC black unloaded on the approaching locust. One bullet struck the locust in the leg, another the power tank over Liam's left shoulder. A third ricocheted against Alastair's frame with a piercing sound that left Liam's ears ringing. Liam felt a punch to the ribs as another bullet impacted the hopper's chest armor. It didn't pierce the armor, thank goodness, but threw off his stride enough that he stumbled and nearly lost his balance.

With two desperate stomps of the locust's feet, each of which sent white gravel spraying in wide fans, Liam recovered. After that, he began moving more unpredictably.

Alastair's right arm, meanwhile, lowered into Liam's field of vision. "Shall I make our reply, sir?"

"Yes," Liam said, "but conserve your ammunition. And suppression fire only. We're not here to kill anyone."

"Of course, sir."

Alastair's wrist clicked, and his hand hinged downward, exposing the five muzzles of his repeating rifle. The barrels spun, emitting a well-oiled drone, then bullets began to spray in short, satisfying bursts. The return fire ceased as the recipients, clearly caught by surprise, ducked for cover.

Their way to the flashtrain now relatively clear, Liam and Alastair sped on. They'd lost precious seconds, however, seconds in which the flashtrain had built on its already impressive speed. In little time it would outstrip even the locust's jaw-dropping pace. When that happened, there would be no catching it, not even if the locust's wings were working.

At the rear of the last car, the doors slid wide. Standing there was Max Kohler, the red monocle fixed into his iron mask reflecting the sun like a doomsday device.

Liam raised his rifle and fired. The shot struck true. Or Liam thought it had. A moment later, he felt the edges of Kohler's illusion. Liam tore at it, trying to dismantle it with an intensity driven by the fear that any delay would cause him to lose Morgan again.

The fake Kohler winked out, replaced by the *real* Kohler, several feet to the left of where Liam had thought he was. He had his arms lifted, preparing to cast another illusion. By then it was too late for Liam to fire again. He needed all his concentration to land his next leap.

"Hold tight, Alastair!"

He urged the locust into an easy bounce, landed in a low crouch, and flicked the thumb button that would give the legs a hellacious boost of power.

He felt his stomach drop as the locust arced skyward like a mortar. At the apex, their elevation revealing the entirety of Chicago's downtown, Liam felt the telltale signs of another illusion. He aimed his rifle down and sent a burst of bullets at Kohler, who was retreating into the train car. As the bullets tore through Kohler's illusion, its nature was revealed: the monorail line, the real one, was ten paces to the right of where the locust was going to land. As the illusion of the fake flashtrain winked out, it was replaced by the concrete blocks of the lakefront's breakwater.

Down they streaked, quick as a comet. "One more leap, Alastair," Liam grunted.

"Yes, sir!"

It was going to be an awkward landing, but there was nothing for it.

He planted the locust's rubber-coated cleats, leaned into a new heading, and shunted all the power he could to the legs. Up they went, right on target until one foot slipped on the slick surface of the rocks at the end.

He and Alastair twisted through the air like a wounded pheasant, almost but not quite on the proper heading to reach the second to last car—Morgan's car.

"Hold on, sir!" As they flew, Alastair's hands reached around Liam's chest. Liam thought he was getting ready to protect him when they inevitably missed the flashtrain's gleaming, streamlined roof, but then he realized Alastair had unfolded the small knife hidden inside the forefinger of his right hand. He slashed over and over again, each a precise cut to the straps securing Liam to the exoskeleton.

Understanding what Alastair meant to do, Liam gripped his rifle tight. A split second later, Alastair grabbed him and kicked the exoskeleton away, altering the direction of their downward arc.

They landed hard on the train's roof. The skin of Liam's hands, neck, and cheeks squeaked as he tried to gain purchase along the gleaming yellow surface. They were just about to fly off when Alastair speared his forefinger into the roof, piercing it with the sharp tip of the still-extended knife. A screech came from the place he'd punched through the roof's metal sheeting.

They came to a halt, but it was a close thing. With the wind whipping at his hair and the fabric of his clothes, Liam crawled hand-over-hand along Alastair's metal-frame body until he reached the narrow strip of the train's roof that was level enough to stand on.

Alastair's blue eyes were almost blindingly bright, a sign of his surprise. "That was a close one, sir!"

"Any closer and I'd be having this conversation with Saint Peter."

The two of them huddled on the roof as the wind roared. It wouldn't be long until the flashtrain reached top speed, making it all but impossible to stay put.

With a flick, Alastair lit the acetylene torch hidden in his thumb and held it just over the steel roof. The bright yellow paint peeled away. The steel sheeting melted. Slowly but surely, he cut a hole large enough for them to slip through.

Liam readied his rifle as Alastair stopped his welding just short of completing the circle. He'd left a span of metal a few inches wide so their makeshift hatch wouldn't fall inward. As Alastair pried it up and away, Liam readied himself, then swung his rifle into the gap. There, still in the gurney with three straps holding him in place, was Morgan. His eyes were open. He was staring up at Liam with a mixture of relief and fear.

Morgan looked . . . wrong. His skin was terribly pale. Blue veins had started to web across his cheeks and neck. The whites of his eyes were an angry red.

"Liam," was all he managed, before a man came rushing in.

Liam thought it was Kohler, but it wasn't. It was the handsome figure of Leland De Pere, impeccable suit and all.

"I have to thank you, Liam," he said. "You've saved me the trouble of finding you."

De Pere lifted one hand, and the world suddenly twisted. Liam's guts turned inside out, a hundred times worse than leaping from a dirigible for the first time when he was learning how to skydive. He felt himself slipping into the hole in the train's roof. He knew that if he did, De Pere would have him. He'd be trapped right along with Morgan.

He did the only thing he could do. He struggled *away* from the hole while denying the illusion De Pere was crafting. Before he knew it, he was slipping from the roof and tumbling down.

For several long seconds, the bright yellow flashtrain, the ivory white monorail, and the towers of downtown spun through the air around him. Then he struck the surface of Lake Michigan hard. The wind was knocked from him. The cold water pressed in. He panicked, but remembered his training. Retain what breath you still have. Remain calm.

With broad strokes, he regained the lake's surface, then reached the shoreline and threw himself onto the blocky concrete breakwater. The flashtrain, meanwhile, sped on, arcing like a sword stroke past the towers of downtown Chicago as it followed the gentle curve toward Indiana.

Alastair's gleaming metal head broke the surface of the water a short while later. He trudged onward, the waves buffeting his body, his body language perfectly clear. "We've lost him, sir."

Liam watched helplessly as the flashtrain was lost from sight and Lake Michigan's cold waves, not to mention the full impact of Liam's failure, began to hit him. "No, Alastair, *I* lost him."

TWENTY-SIX

During the war . . .

On the morning following the operation along the Milwaukee River, Liam was ordered into Major De Pere's command tent. The Major was tapping a rubber-tipped pointer onto a command map while several officers—all of them ranked full-bird colonel or higher—watched on. The highest rank among them was a three-star general, a woman with a grim face and terrible burn scars along her neck, the full extent of the injury hidden beneath her crisp, ironed shirt. Behind the officers, watching everything carefully, were a bunch of suits—politicians from Novo Solis, part of the Armed Services Committee, apparently. Liam recognized a few, including Senator Vaughan, the junior senator from West Virginia, a devout Christian who thought the military was meddling in the affairs of the almighty. He was a portly Southern gentleman with a graying goatee and a handkerchief he kept using to dab at his upper lip and forehead.

Liam stood at attention, sweaty from his morning run with his squad mates, waiting until De Pere finished describing the operation and their plans for the afternoon. The officers left with the politicians while De Pere, picking up his service cap, ducked under the tent flaps beside Liam. "Walk with me."

Liam, surprised, caught up quickly and fell into step alongside his charismatic CO as he led them through an ordered sea of tents. Eventually they came to a shallow ridge that overlooked the port of Milwaukee. The Navy was using it as a base of operations, but there was evidence of its peacetime life—mountains of empty crates, a small tram line that headed to the western suburbs, awnings over warehouse windows where everyone from store owners to restauranteurs once came to haggle over prices.

"Big changes are coming," De Pere said as a steamer whistle blew.

"How do you mean, sir?"

"For starters, the enemy are ramping up their armament efforts. The Germans have unveiled a new class of mechanika. Goliaths, they're called. There's no longer any doubt that the SLP have gained an edge when it comes to engineering and manufacturing. If we're not careful, this whole thing is going to slip through our fingers. We could lose the Great Lakes. If we do, we'll lose New England, and if we lose New England, the South will fall within months."

Far to the north, the rattle of gunfire came, then several thundering booms.

"But it's *our* scientists who are going to tip the scales of this war." Major De Pere turned to Liam. "We're almost ready to broaden Project Echo's scope. There's one final step we need to take before that happens."

"And that is, sir?"

"The Henchman serum needs to become permanent."

"Permanent."

"Yes. Dr. Silva is convinced it will allow you to communicate even more effectively, and of course it will eliminate the need for you to return to base for additional doses. She says she's days away from perfecting it. I'm aiming to get final approval before that happens, so in the meantime, I'm giving the Henchmen two days' leave in Chicago."

This conversation was definitely *not* going the way Liam had expected it to go. "Very good, sir, but . . . If it's permanent, does that mean it will remain that way after the war?"

"That's what the doctors believe, yes."

"Will there be a way to *undo* it?"

Major De Pere stopped abruptly and turned to face Liam. "One never knows. Which is why you should take time on leave to think about your future. This is a voluntary program. It would be a cancer to have a single soldier who wasn't fully committed to achieving our aims, to winning this war, whatever the cost."

Liam nodded as visions of the atrocities committed by the SLP powers wavered in his mind. Bombing civilian areas, mustard gas, mechanika wandering deep behind the lines to butcher entire towns. "Of course, sir."

They continued down the slope toward the waterfront. "You had a disagreement with your commanding officer yesterday."

"What did Kohler say? Because—"

"Never mind what he said. Is it true? Did you disobey a direct command?"

Liam had debated all night whether to report it. He still hadn't made up his mind when he'd been called to attend Major De Pere in the command tent. "Yes, sir, I did."

De Pere nodded, pensive. "I'm not interested in wanton slaughter, Corporal, but there are times when my subordinates need to be given the freedom to interpret my orders. Things change on the ground by the second. The question isn't whether to allow it, it's how *much* to allow."

"Of course, sir."

"How much, Mulcahey?" De Pere turned and faced Liam, his jaw set squarely. "How much freedom would you give your charges?"

"That would depend on the situation."

"We've already established that."

Liam took a deep breath. "Enough to achieve our goals, taking lives if needed, but no more than that."

"The man you shot was a Québécois soldier, an *SLP* soldier."

"He was, but it was *Kohler* who murdered him."

"Well, if it came down to it, some might say *you* murdered him."

Liam tried to hide his shock. "But I didn't—"

De Pere raised a hand. "I believe you. But you can't blame Kohler. Not completely. He lost his entire family to a bombing last summer."

"He's a hothead."

"He's *driven*. And who's to say it was Kohler in the first place? You were all linked, correct? Sharing emotions. Fears. Blood lust. Who's to say it wasn't Crawford or Smith or Vankoningsfeld who put the killer's instinct into him in that moment?"

"Kohler *wanted* that man dead. He was no longer a threat."

"Not a *man*," De Pere countered. "Don't make that mistake, Liam. He was a *soldier* who might one day have piloted a goliath into our midst, killing us all."

"I hate this war, sir. I hate it with every fiber of my being. I'll fight in it, because it's important, but I'm not going to be like Kohler. I'm not going to kill where it's unnecessary."

The Major sized Liam up. "I can live with that. Take your leave, Corporal. Blow off some steam. When you come back, be ready tell me if you're willing to take on a larger role in this army of ours."

"Sir?"

"I'm being promoted to Lieutenant Colonel, to head the new psi-ops division. I'm giving serious consideration to bringing Kohler with me. If that were to happen, you'd take Kohler's place and lead the Devil's Henchmen."

Liam was stunned. "You want to *promote* Kohler?"

"I do."

"He deserves a trial, not a promotion."

De Pere was nonplussed. "I'm going to share something with you now, Liam, so that you'll understand. Kohler's tactics may be distasteful, but if there's even a single whiff that Project Echo isn't working as expected, it may be shut down. Senator Vaughan has the Armed Services Committee all worked up about it." He waved behind them, toward the command tent they'd left earlier. "They're watching us like hawks already. What do you think they'll do if they hear about an indiscretion like Kohler's? It'll get blown out of proportion. Then it'll become a bludgeon that Vaughan and his cohort of holier-than-thou politicians use to shut the project down unless the President caves to their demands." Liam started to object, but De Pere went on. "I've spoken to Kohler. What happened the other day won't happen again. And besides, with Kohler's promotion, he won't be *in* the Devil's Henchmen any longer. Assuming I have a suitable replacement, that is."

Liam paused. "Are you saying Kohler will remain in the Henchmen if I decline?"

De Pere worked his jaw. He seemed disappointed by the question. "I'd hoped that wouldn't be an issue."

Liam was well aware he was being manipulated, but De Pere had him pegged. The last thing he wanted was a promotion, but he also didn't want a man like Kohler to remain in active combat. If Kohler wasn't going to get a trial, the next best thing would be for him to be as far from the battlefield as possible.

"I'll take it, sir. The promotion."

"You're sure?"

"More than sure."

De Pere smiled his winning smile, a thing that looked much dimmer in Liam's eyes than it had before the conversation began. Then he clapped Liam on the shoulder. "You're a good man, Liam Mulcahey."

As De Pere left, Liam spotted Dr. Silva standing between the tents with Senator Vaughan. Senator Vaughan was doing all the talking. He was animated, gesticulating wildly, occasionally dabbing his forehead with his handkerchief. Dr. Silva, meanwhile, kept sending glances at De Pere.

When De Pere ducked into the command tent, her gaze slid toward Liam. Her steps slowed, then stopped altogether. She seemed to be staring *through* Liam, not at him.

Liam waved, a gesture he was certain looked as awkward as it felt. Dr. Silva, as if waking from a daydream, blinked, gave a brief smile, then turned away and caught up to Senator Vaughan.

⸻

A drizzle fell as Liam arrived in Chicago later that night. He and the rest of the Devil's Henchmen were stuffed into a cramped personnel car, one of dozens delivering a thousand soldiers into the city for leave. Like his squad mates, Liam was headed downtown, but he paused on the cobblestone yard when he saw Dr. Silva standing alone near the ticketing booth, casting her gaze over the crowd of civilians.

"Let's *go*, Mulcahey!" Clay Graves shouted.

"You go on," Liam said. "I'll catch up."

They all groaned. "He'll *catch up*," Clay said, exaggerating his Southern drawl while grabbing his crotch. "He'll catch up after his *dick's* caught up, he means."

They laughed and lost themselves around the corner.

Dr. Silva was wearing a stylish flapper dress, mustard yellow with black sequins, and a velvet cloche hat, the brim of which she had pulled down against the drizzle. She smelled of lavender, and looked surprisingly human. Liam was so used to her in a white lab coat that, dolled up, her hair unbound and cascading down her back, it felt as if she'd been replaced with another woman entirely.

"You look lost," Liam said as he came near.

"Not lost, no." The smile she gave him was polite, forced. "Not exactly."

Liam had never been very comfortable approaching women. The nervousness became worse with those he knew, doubly so for those as attractive as Dr. Silva. Normally he would have said his goodbyes and left, and surely she had plenty more things to do than waste her time with a simple man like him, but there was something Liam needed to get off his chest. He wasn't sure where to begin, though. He couldn't just blurt it out here in the open.

"You're waiting for someone?" he asked after an awkward pause.

"I was supposed to be, yes." The muscles along her jaw worked. Her whole body was tight.

"Maybe they're just running late."

"No," she said flatly. "Sergio always does this."

"Does what?"

"Sends me infantile messages after we've had an argument."

"And you had one recently?"

She nodded. "Last night when I called him. He doesn't approve of my being in the military. He doesn't approve of my being a scientist. He wants to marry me, he says, but only if I can commit to it."

"You don't want to?" Liam asked. "Commit, I mean?"

"I'm willing to commit, but only if he is too. I have a life already." She waved to the square, which was now practically empty. "A life he's not ready to acknowledge. Until he is, there's nothing for me to commit *to*."

The engine whistled. As the couplings clanked and the train began to pull away, the drizzle fell harder.

Liam waved to a stout brown building on a nearby street corner, where a pub sign read The Bonnie Lass. "Why don't we get out of the rain, go have some tea while you wait for your fiancé? It'd be nicer than standing out here all alone."

After staring at the pub's emerald green door as if it had offended her, then turning her gaze to the empty square, she leaned into a crisp walk, her heels clicking against the cobbles. "Boyfriend," she said, "and there'd better be whiskey in that tea."

They sat at a table next to the window so Dr. Silva could look for Sergio, but by the time their second round of drinks arrived, she was hardly checking anymore. She told Liam about her upbringing in Buenos Aires, how her father had brought her family to the United States through a work visa, how he'd received his green card three years later, how he'd risen through the ranks of the Novo Solis elite through the brilliance of his research in microbiology.

"He must have been very proud of you," Liam said as a woman in the corner took up a fiddle and began to play. The crowd clapped in time, many of them badly, but the mood in the room was merry.

"My father?" Dr. Silva snorted. "He wanted a son and got three girls. Nothing was ever good enough for him."

"I'm sorry."

"Don't be. If there's one thing I've learned in life, it's that you have to be proud of yourself first. And I am. We've accomplished a lot in this project of ours."

"*You* have, you mean."

Dr. Silva smiled a suffering smile. "Tell that to my fellow scientists."

Liam had heard rumblings. "They're giving you trouble?"

"You could say that. They want me kicked out of the project."

"But why? You're dedicated. You're smart. You've advanced the serum miles ahead of where it was when you arrived."

Dr. Silva tilted her head with the sort of pitying look one gives when someone else is being hopelessly naïve, and Liam suddenly understood. Dr. Silva was the only woman on the project, and she had outshined them all.

"Oh," he said simply.

"Oh, indeed." She flashed a brief smile. "It was what got Sergio and I arguing. I confided in him, and instead of offering support, he used it as an excuse to try to get me to quit. Again."

"I'm sorry."

"Don't be. I'd rather know now where he stands."

For a time they listened to the music. Liam still didn't know where to begin. "Dr. Silva—" he finally said.

"Colette," she corrected, and lifted her steaming cup of whiskey-and-tea to her lips.

"Colette." Without really understanding why, Liam found himself smiling broadly. The feeling inside him was so bright, so *good*, he didn't want to ruin it—and he absolutely would the moment he touched on the things he'd learned the day before. It couldn't be helped, though. He had to know. "Something happened on the last mission, at the end."

Dr. Silva immediately tensed, and Liam felt something new. When he was young, his da used to beat him with his belt. It didn't happen often, only when Liam had been especially naughty, but *when* it happened, it was intense, his belt falling again and again as if all the other small infractions had built in his da's mind, and he was lumping them together, taking them out on Liam all at once. The sound of leather snapping—whether from a whip crack from the Aysanas' horse trainer or the snap of reins on a horse and buggy—brought Liam back to the dimly lit interior of his house, him over his father's knees, the bright pain of the belt falling again and again over the naked skin of his rump and the backs of his thighs.

The feeling he had in that little pub was just like that, a deep-seated fear bubbling up to the surface in a rush. It took Liam a moment to understand it. "We're still connected," he said as the din of the pub suddenly re-entered his consciousness. It made him feel as if everyone could hear what they were saying.

Dr. Silva—no, Colette—felt the same way perhaps. Staring at her cup, she nodded.

Before leaving the base, the Henchmen had been given a dose of *E. sentensis* as part of their continued training. The telepathic ability did not come easily and had to be maintained, so they had regular sessions out of their hopper armor where they practiced passing orders and sharing senses. Liam had been nervous about it all morning—the last person he wanted to trade thoughts with was Kohler—but luckily Kohler had been called away by De Pere, surely to talk about his promotion. Even without Kohler it was a difficult session, everyone working through the horrors they'd seen, the horrors they'd committed.

"It's only supposed to last an hour or two," Liam said. The session had ended well over six hours ago.

"Yes." Colette shrugged. "But you know we're headed toward permanence. The serum I gave you had longer effects."

"Just me?"

"Just you."

She spoke the words calmly, but he could sense the fear in her more clearly now. He could define it in ways he couldn't have only moments ago. She was worried he was going to turn her in.

"I just want to understand," he said as calmly as he could manage. "Why are you doing this? Why have you made yourself a part of the experiment?"

She twisted her teacup in its saucer as a song came to an end, and a round of applause filled the small pub. "How can I properly evaluate this project, Liam, if I'm not part of it?"

"You interview every one of us after every mission. *Exhaustively.*"

"Yes, but how would you say that compares to the real thing?"

Liam considered that a moment. "It doesn't hold a candle to it."

"Exactly," she said, her tone righteous. "No matter what De Pere says, no matter what the *Army* says, I *have* to know."

She was staring straight into his eyes, daring him to deny her her due, daring him to say a word against her actions. Now that he knew the truth, though, Liam didn't *want* to object. He'd been worried she was spying on them for some other purpose—he'd been worried she was an SLP *mole*—but that was clearly not the case. There was a simple but undeniable curiosity in her, and a will to make sure she was doing things right. It wasn't so different from when Liam worked on the hoppers. He often took the reins himself when he thought someone was fumbling the job. He wasn't always *proud* of his reluctance to put trust in others, but he understood why it existed, which helped him to understand Colette's motivations.

"Where is Project Echo headed?" he finally asked.

She glanced through the window, where the lights outside the train station were making starlike patterns against the rain-slicked glass. Her pride glowed like a distant bonfire, her worries crows on the wind. "To a place where we're connected like never before, like we could never even have dreamed."

"And you think that's a good thing?"

"What you or I think no longer matters. For the good of the country, we're about to find out."

Liam had a dozen more questions lined up but never got a chance to ask them, because just then the pub door swung open, and in swept a stunningly handsome Italian man. He wore a fine tailored suit that hugged his muscular frame. He had black hair, a dark, five o'clock shadow, and piercing blue eyes that looked like they could cut diamonds. "Here you are!"

Colette stared at him as if she'd heard it a thousand times before. "Where else would I be?" She waved to Liam. "Corporal Mulcahey here was kind enough to keep me company while I waited."

Sergio smiled as he thrust a massive hand toward Liam. "Sergio," he said.

"Liam," Liam said as he took the offered hand and shook it.

Before Liam could even attempt to match Sergio's impressively strong grip, Sergio swept past Liam and gave Colette a kiss on each cheek, then kissed her hands. "Our dinner awaits, mi amore, and now we're late."

"And who's fault is that?"

"Mine, my love. All mine." He turned to Liam briefly. "You have my thanks."

With that he and Colette were through the door and into the rain. The last he saw of Colette, Sergio was ushering her into a hansom cab. His body language as he climbed into the cab and lay one arm across her shoulder was clear: you're mine, only mine.

Colette looked out from the cab only once. Liam couldn't be sure by the gaslight of the streetlamps, but the expression she wore looked like regret—whether it was for Liam or Project Echo or the war itself, he wasn't sure. A moment later, the cabbie clucked his tongue and snapped the reins, and they were gone, clopping down the dark street.

Liam's drink and the next song on the fiddle lasted precisely the same amount of time. Taking it as a sign, he left the pub and headed out to find his comrades. The rain lessened, then stopped altogether, but the streets were slick, the air brisk. Despite Sergio's sudden arrival, Liam was still high from the feeling of being with Colette. The scent of her perfume still lingered, as did the warmth he'd felt whenever she smiled. As he approached the brasserie where the others had been going, all feelings of warmth faded.

The excited squeal of a young woman came from farther up the street. Concerned, Liam walked past the steps leading to the brasserie's entrance and came to a plot of land with a rather odd structure on it. There was a stone foundation and a wooden floor, but little else—no roof to speak of, and only one wall still standing. The home had been the victim of an SLP bombing raid a few months back. The owners had cleared the rubble in hopes of rebuilding but had since abandoned the lot and moved to the country.

Standing in the room that might once have been the master bedroom were a man and a woman. The man was Max Kohler. He was waving a hand toward the sky. The woman, whose long blonde hair flowed down her flower-patterned dress like a wet mop, was casting her gaze about, looking this way and that. She suddenly shivered, ran to the edge of the floor, and mimed looking out a window.

Fascinated, and more than a bit horrified, Liam took the front steps up and passed through a yawning opening in the home's mostly shattered front wall. He watched as the woman shivered in fright, then stepped away and ducked down as if someone were peering through the nonexistent window at her. *She thinks she's standing in a proper home*, Liam realized, *this one, before it was bombed*. As Kohler had done on the battlefield, he was now doing to the woman.

It was so powerful, Liam fell deeper into it. He saw what the woman saw. She hid behind a proper bed, staring at the window, the plaster walls around her solid. The sound of heavy footsteps came. Orders were called in Flemish to search the home.

As the sounds of bombs fell over Chicago, there came the rattle of soldiers moving about, of clomping up the stairs, of doors crashing open. One set of footsteps reached the door of the master bedroom. There came a heavy thud. The door rattled. A second strike, and pieces of the door jamb flew inward, the latch surrendering to the force of the blow. A soldier stood there in an SLP uniform. Except it wasn't just any soldier. It was Max Kohler himself.

He rounded the bed. The woman collapsed into the corner. Kohler fell on her. Put his hand over her mouth when she tried to scream. Slapped her when she tried to break free. Setting his rifle aside, he ripped her dress, exposing her bra. When she released a muffled scream, he pressed harder, then reached under her dress and began yanking her silk underpants down.

Refusing to allow it to go any further, Liam searched for the boundaries of the illusion. Soon he felt it, a drape hanging over the three of them. He picked at the edges of it until he found a stray thread, then pulled on it. Bit by bit the illusion unraveled. The sky was suddenly visible through the bedroom ceiling. The sound of the soldiers and the bombers faded, replaced by the muffled conversation coming from the brasserie. Faster and faster it melted, until Liam, Kohler, and the woman were standing alone in the ruins of an empty house.

Kohler turned, clearly confused, but then a look of understanding came over him. Just like the illusion, Liam felt that too. It was the serum. Only,

Colette had said it was just the two of them who'd received the longer-lasting formulation.

Everything became clear when Liam spotted the syringes. They lay on a pile of bricks nearby. Kohler had injected both himself and the woman, then used his ability to craft illusions to draw her into one. The longer-acting injection from Colette, however, was still active in Liam, and it had allowed him to bear witness to what Kohler had done.

Kohler caught Liam's look, stared defiantly back.

"You stole the serum," Liam said. "You injected her."

Kohler said nothing. He was staring at Liam hard, the same way he had when Liam tried to spare the life of the SLP soldier.

"Who's this, doll?"

"No one," Kohler said. "Just someone putting his nose in where it doesn't belong."

"How long have you been doing it, Max? How long have you been stealing the serum so you can rape some girl back in the city?"

"I wasn't *raping* her," Kohler said with a sneer. "She likes it."

Kohler's girlfriend, or whoever she was, was looking more uncomfortable by the moment. "You want to go back in, honey?"

"Yeah." He snatched up the empty syringes and stuffed them inside his coat, then took her by the hand and began leading her toward the concrete steps at the back of the house. "Yeah, I do."

Liam grabbed Kohler's arm and spun him around. "This won't stand, Kohler."

He ripped his arm away. "That's *Master Sergeant* to you, and if you think De Pere or anyone else is going to believe you, you've got another thing coming." He continued toward the street. "Your word against mine, Mulcahey. Mine and the rest of our squad."

Liam stood there for a long while, listening to the songs coming from the brasserie. Part of him wanted to go in and sing with them like he used to. Part of him wanted to drink until this was all forgotten.

He couldn't pretend this was nothing, though, and soon he'd turned his back on the brasserie and was walking into the night.

TWENTY-SEVEN

During the war . . .

Dr. Colette Silva sat across a white-linen tablecloth from Sergio. The plates between them were fine china. The silverware was blindingly bright. They were in the dining room of the Blackstone Hotel, one of the finest restaurants in Chicago. Colette was normally excited about these sorts of dinners, but her mind kept wandering back to Liam, to Project Echo, to the fog and the glowing lights within.

Sergio was apologetic for being late. As was always the case when he felt guilty, he did most of the talking. Colette was glad of it, and if her silence deepened his guilt and made him talk even more, so much the better.

As the first courses came, she couldn't help but think of how she'd sat across from another man entirely, years before. It had been in her parent's home in Miami, and the man had been President Nolan himself. He'd traveled by zeppelin, all the way from Novo Solis, to plead with her in person to come work for the government, to work for him.

She was hardly surprised he was trying to recruit her—she'd made a name for herself in the burgeoning field of symbiotic psychology, a name she was proud of. What *did* surprise her was his dogged persistence. She'd declined his offer three times already, the final one making it clear that meeting in person would only serve to *decrease* the chances of her accepting, not improve them.

President Nolan was a heavyset man with jowls and several chins that strained against his shirt and ascot. What remained of his graying brown hair had been combed forward, a throwback from the end of the previous century. Normally confident to the point of boorishness, he sat in her parents' living room, looking like a polar bear that had somehow found itself in the tropics.

"In the end," he told her, "the project you'd be helping us to undertake is not for purposes of war, but for peace. The strain of bacteria I told you about was developed in Switzerland, stolen by the Germans, and thank God has fallen into our hands so that we can unlock its secrets before they unleash something terrible upon us, upon the *world*."

Colette could already see gaping seams in President Nolan's story, but she also recognized that *Echobacterum sentensis* had vast implications for humanity. Assuming its purported abilities were true, it could bridge the mental gap between people, creating new pathways for worldwide communication.

It was President Nolan's fear-mongering and truculence toward other nations that had caused her to decline his offers thus far, but she was beginning to see how dangerous it would be to let the project continue without a trustworthy moral compass such as herself. There was no telling what other nations might do with such power, whether it was the Germans, the Swiss, or anyone else who might get hold of the bacteria. For that matter, there was no telling what the U.S. *military* might do with it.

Colette was acquainted with many of the scientists the President had already recruited. They were brilliant in their own ways, if not particularly versed in symbiotic psychology. The trouble was, they were men whose political views aligned too closely with the President's. They wore blinders of the President's own making and would push his agenda to the detriment of other paths of inquiry.

"If I agree to join the team," Colette said, "I want some autonomy to study whatever it is I wish, to find ways to use the bacteria for non-military purposes."

President Nolan leaned further into the couch, his expression guarded. "Assuming you provide your country with what it needs to protect itself, I don't see why that would be a problem."

President Nolan was a formidable man. He wouldn't be easy to control. But what better way was there to mitigate his hawkish ways than by participating in the program herself? Gain his trust, and she could steer the nascent program in ways *she* wanted—*away* from war.

She held out her hand. President Nolan, a grudging smile on his round face, leaned forward and shook it.

In the Blackstone, the main course arrived. Colette made some small talk, if only to appease Sergio, but truly her mind was on the team she'd joined in Novo Solis a week after President Nolan's visit.

She worked endless hours, formulating experiments with mice that showed clearly how the mood of one could affect others that had been injected with the very same strain of *Echobacterum sentensis* that had been stolen from the Germans. They began with natural selection but soon advanced to a form of genetic manipulation pioneered by Colette herself, which allowed her to enhance certain traits: the bacteria's ability to adjust to its host's physiology, the fidelity of the transmitted emotions, the distance over which the ability could effectively work, the duration of the psychoactive periods.

Time flew. Weeks became months. Months stacked into years with hardly a break in between to return to Miami and see her family. Her work *became* her life, due in no small part to the growing threats from Germany and its allied European states. They'd learned of Colette's efforts, and had made demands for the United States to stop all research. But the CIC had found evidence that Germany had resumed development of the bacteria, and was doing so in aggressive fashion. There were rumors of super soldiers being created, a plan to curtail the growing power of the United States. The threat of war was small but growing rapidly.

"We need a similar program," President Nolan told her. "We need to start human trials, and we need to start them now."

She advised against it. She said they needed more time, but the pressure the President and her fellow scientists applied was relentless. She eventually caved under the proviso that she would personally be the one to administer the serum and monitor the subjects of the experiment.

President Nolan agreed. Over the following weeks, armed forces personnel—men and women, both—were selected based on physical and psychological profiles Colette herself had meticulously developed. The first two were soldiers Max Kohler and Liam Mulcahey, men with impeccable records, even if the former was overly aggressive and the latter perhaps too deferential. Both were given a new, highly adaptive strain of the bacteria. And it worked. Despite his more reserved nature, it was often Liam who dominated their extrasensory experiences.

As more soldiers were recruited into the Devil's Henchmen (as they'd started calling themselves) and became test subjects, it became clear that the serum's effects lasted only minutes at a time. It was a miracle by any measure, a great success, and yet Colette found herself frustrated in her debriefing interviews with the squad. The answers she received helped guide her, but she couldn't truly know what they were feeling. And Kohler, she suspected, was starting to fabricate his answers, telling her what he thought she wanted to hear.

She had to know the truth. She had to experience it herself. That's when she began injecting herself with the serum shortly before each new trial began. It was then that she discovered the fog, the lanterns in the mist. She *rode* their emotions. She experienced the wonder of sharing another's mind. It made her eager for more. Very eager. Sometimes the yearning was so great it ached.

Soon they had a full squad of soldiers and an official name for the project, though she detested it. "Project Echo" was a play on the bacteria's genus name, *Echobacterum*, but President Nolan was a student of history and well-versed in Greek mythology. Echo was a nymph who'd been ordered by Zeus to protect him from Hera, who'd learned of Zeus's indiscretions with her. It was Echo who suffered Hera's wrath, not Zeus. Hera cursed her to repeat the last words spoken to her, which was what Colette hated so much about the name. That was precisely the opposite of what the bacteria did—*E. sentensis* didn't stifle communication, it fostered it. And President Nolan no doubt adored the notion that Colette and the others in the project would—like the project's tragic, titular victim—protect him, even to their own detriment.

When President Nolan insisted they begin preparing the bacteria for use in combat, Colette grudgingly agreed. She really had no choice. By then, Germany had formed the St. Lawrence Pact with France, Great Britain, and Canada. Their combined fleets were sailing along the Eastern seaboard, barely within international waters. There were signs of their troops and tanks amassing along the Canadian border.

As fate would have it, a simple firefight sparked the war. U.S. forces fired on a trio of bootlegger trucks coming in over the border. A lone, trigger-happy Mountie fired back. The small fight ended with two dead and twelve wounded on the American side. It was enough for President Nolan to authorize a zeppelin to cross the border at night and bomb a Canadian military base, an act that led to the deaths of forty Canadian, German, and British soldiers.

Colette was beside herself. She pushed herself ever harder and found that the bacteria itself helped. She didn't need as much sleep or rest when she took it. It cleared her mind. It focused her thoughts. It made her want to perfect *E. sentensis* even more than she already did.

A dozen breakthroughs followed. The bacteria was working more and more seamlessly with human physiology. It lasted longer in its host before dying. Transmission distance grew by orders of magnitude, from yards to furlongs to miles. And not only were *emotions* being transmitted, but *intent* as well.

Then, miracle of miracles, the first thoughts were transmitted. By this point Colette had become adept at suppressing her own presence from the others. But one day, she'd injected Max Kohler and sensed his lewd thoughts as he stared at her cleavage. Her revulsion and thoughts of slapping him were sent back to Kohler. And he *liked* it. She was so shocked she canceled the trial, claiming something had gone wrong.

Kohler leered. She let him because, beyond his lecherous thoughts, she had no doubt that a watershed moment in human history had just taken place.

She considered having Kohler removed—she was nearly certain he'd lied on his psych evaluation, which was cause enough to have him thrown out of the program—but when she tried again with others, none save Liam was as quick to establish communication with others, to maintain it over long periods of time, and transmit thoughts and emotions clearly. In some ways Liam was even better at it than Kohler, which was good, but she couldn't very well conduct this sort of experiment with a single test subject. Besides, she felt it necessary to include all types of thoughts, from those who treated her kindly, as Liam did, to those who treated her otherwise. How else to model humanity than with variety?

"Colette?"

God, how different the Colette of today was from the bright-eyed girl who had met with President Nolan in her parents' living room.

"Colette, my love . . ."

She'd grown, become more capable, done things her younger self could only have dreamed of. She'd become hungrier as well, not just to wield the sort of power that Project Echo could grant someone, but to prevent others from wielding it like a weapon—another sort of power entirely. No one knew how far Echo could go. No one knew how precious it was. Only she did.

"Colette!"

Colette blinked, suddenly back in the Blackstone at the white-linen table, Sergio sitting across from her. A baked Alaska had been set before her. The ice cream was melting. She hadn't taken a single bite.

Sergio reached across the table and gripped her hand. "You're doing it again," he said in a low voice, his eyes so fixed on hers it was clear he was pointedly *not* looking at the diners at the nearby tables, some of whom had turned to watch them.

"Am I?" She should be glad to be there with Sergio. But the truth was he grew smaller in her eyes every day.

"Yes." He slid her water glass closer to her plate. "I know it's been stressful. Drink. Relax. We have plans to make."

"Plans."

It was as Sergio was launching into a story, a recollection of the first time they'd met in Milan, that Colette felt it. A light in the fog. She could feel Liam's distantly. He was wandering the streets of Chicago, heading vaguely in her direction. But the new light wasn't him; it was Max Kohler. Then there came a third light. A woman. Kohler had stolen two syringes of serum from Colette's office before boarding the train for Chicago. He was using them to role-play with some trollop who shared his twisted fantasy of war and rape.

Colette had never trusted Kohler to any great degree, but she had to admit it hurt being betrayed like that. Stealing from a military lab even once was enough to get him dishonorably discharged, and she was nearly certain this wasn't the first time Kohler had done it—both he and the woman seemed too familiar with the serum, too comfortable with its effects, for it to be otherwise. Worse than his betrayal of her trust, however, was the sense that Project Echo was slipping from her grasp.

"So?" Sergio asked.

Colette started as her attention was whisked back to the dining room. Sergio was on one knee beside the table. In his hands was a black leather ring box, which was open. In the box's red velvet folds was a ring, with a teardrop of diamonds and white gold. The entire room was looking their way, smiles on their faces, expectant. The expression on Sergio's broad, handsome face was one of stark confidence, as if he were willing her acceptance into being.

Just like President Nolan, Colette thought.

Except Sergio wasn't half the man President Nolan was. And this was no proposal, but a demand. A demand for her to become his, to live the life of an obedient wife, to leave all her hopes and aspirations behind.

With all the calm she could muster, she stood and set her napkin onto her seat. As she walked past him, she uttered a single word, "No." Then strode from the Blackstone and into the rainy night.

"Colette!" she heard behind her, but she kept walking. "Colette!"

That was the last she saw of him. She wandered through the streets, heading ever closer to the French-style brasserie the Devil's Henchmen often frequented. Liam had reached it and was now wandering away, heading who knew where? But it wasn't Liam she wanted to speak to.

"Max?" she asked when she entered the brasserie and found him sitting with the others around a low table.

"Who's this?" asked a bombshell blonde, the woman Kohler had shared his sexual fantasy with. Her mind was bright within the fog. Inquisitive. But Colette walled her off from both her and Kohler. She separated them from Liam as well. It was just her and Kohler in the fog now.

If Colette had had any reservations about whether Kohler knew she was sharing in their experiences, they were dispelled by his reaction. The moment she cut them off from the others, his face went blank, one of his many tells that he was experiencing high emotion. She could see it in the fog, too, a flare of unease, one that grew with each passing breath.

"What do you want?" he asked.

Colette merely turned and left, knowing Kohler would follow. He did, and they spoke on the empty, curiously clean floor of a nearby, bombed-out home.

"What," Kohler said, "you're going to report me to De Pere? Try to get me kicked out—"

"I want you to teach me," Colette said.

Kohler glanced over her shoulder as if he thought it some sort of joke. Suspicion flared in his mind. "You want me to *teach* you?"

"How to cast illusions."

He looked wary, as if she had some ulterior motive. Then he looked angry, like he was going to deny her. Finally he shrugged. "You're the boss now, right?"

"That's right, Max. I'm the boss." She turned and walked away, but not before calling over her shoulder, "We start tomorrow, as soon as we get back."

TWENTY-EIGHT

Two days after Liam's failed attempt to rescue Morgan along the shores of Lake Michigan, he woke in the gondola of a zeppelin named the *Eisvögel*. He sat in a comfortable leather seat with his head against the cool glass pane of an oval-shaped window. For long moments, he was only half awake, his thoughts still immersed in the two interlinked dreams. The first had been a vivid recollection of his time with the Devil's Henchmen. The second had revealed Colette's memories from *her* perspective, just like the one he'd had that night in the furniture store.

Willing himself awake, Liam sat up and took a deep breath. He felt a light vibration through the floor. A low rumble suffused the cabin, the sound of the engines propelling the zeppelin east. Beyond the window, the day was bright, the blue sky filled with rank upon rank of fluffy white clouds. Far below lay a quilt-work of forests and fields. A winding river stretched toward the horizon, the terrain dotted here and there by small hamlets, with no signs of a proper city anywhere.

The zeppelin itself was apparently owned by an iron magnate, a friend of the Uprising. It was taking Liam, Bailey, and Alastair to Novo Solis. Grace, meanwhile, had had some success with her contact, the mole inside the De Pere administration. She, along with Clay and Stasa, had stayed behind in Chicago to meet some informant who had news of where Morgan was being taken. Assuming all went well, the plan was for Grace to continue to Novo Solis to make necessary arrangements, while Stasa and Clay met them en route in a second zeppelin.

Ruby, in the meantime, along with Alan and his son William, had been moved to a floating Uprising base known as the Nest. The plan, once they'd rescued Morgan—a thing even Liam admitted was a dicey proposition— was for Liam, Stasa, and everyone else to meet them there, so that the equally daunting work of developing an anti-serum for the scourge strain could begin.

On the cabin's far side, near the door to the sleeping compartments, Bailey sat at a console with a pair of headphones over her slicked-down hair. She was fiddling with the massive rabbit-ear antennae of a wireless console while turning a dial, monitoring various wireless channels to make sure their zeppelin hadn't been identified as suspicious. Seeing Liam awake, she took off her headphones and smiled. "Morning, sunshine."

Liam pulled himself more upright in his chair. "Morning."

She pointed to the table in front of him, upon which was a plate with lumpy bread dusted in powdered sugar. "I grabbed a stollen from Dinkel's before we left."

"Thanks."

Bailey gave him a wink and went back to her headphones. Famished, Liam cut off a piece of the sweet, cherry-filled bread and popped it in his mouth. As he chewed, the sound of shuffling footsteps mixed with the steady drone of the engines. Nana, wearing her favorite day dress and slippers, came out from behind his chair, cut off a piece of the stollen, and sat down across from him. Her brow furrowed in concentration as she chewed. In the back of his mind, Liam wondered whether the piece of stollen she'd just taken would suddenly reappear when she left.

"I'm starting to wonder whether the big secret everyone's talking about isn't linked to your dreams," Nana said around her food. "Maybe the memories you're trying to uncover aren't yours, but Colette's."

Liam nodded. "Maybe. And there's the revelations about Kohler. His being the first to craft an illusion, the first to master them. It seems important."

"Kohler . . ." Nana said it like the very thought of him had soured the taste of the bread.

"I viewed him as a lackey, a useful puppet in De Pere's plans. Now I wonder if he isn't calling more of the shots than we think."

"I suppose it's possible," Nana said while dusting her hands free of powdered sugar, "but I don't see a man like De Pere giving up that much control to Max Kohler. De Pere's too iron-willed. And you saw yourself, Max was already deferring to Colette. No doubt he did the same with De Pere. Kohler's no mastermind. He's a foot soldier."

"You're probably right," Liam said, "but then we're back to the same questions. What drove De Pere toward madness? And why?"

Bailey lifted her headphones off her ears. "You say something, dear?"

Liam smiled. "Just talking to myself."

Bailey's eyes narrowed. She looked as if she were worried for Liam, but then she went back to what she was doing.

Nana frowned while licking her lips. "What makes you think De Pere wasn't *always* cracked in the head?"

"Because I remember more of him now."

Nana looked at him like he was being naïve. "He all but sanctioned Kohler's behavior. He let the murder of that Canadian boy go."

"Okay, but that's a far cry from hatching a plan to enslave millions."

Nana stared through the nearby window, considering. "De Pere eventually took the serum. He must have or he wouldn't have the power he does."

"Agreed."

Nana shrugged. "You ever think Kohler's sick mind might've infected his, like it did the Henchmens' during that battle?"

The notion gave Liam pause. Maybe Kohler *had* influenced De Pere's thoughts, his desires, but even if that were true, Kohler didn't seem like the type who'd want to enslave the entire nation either.

Bailey suddenly took off her headphones. "We've got incoming." She stepped closer to the windows along Liam's side of the gondola and pointed. "There."

In the distance, another zeppelin was approaching. Its envelope was pristine white, the gondola beneath made of a wood so lustrous its color was a near-match for the gold paint on the envelope's nose cone and battens.

But by the time Liam drew his gaze away from the skies beyond the window, Nana was gone. "Any news of Morgan?"

Bailey nodded. "They think they know where he is. Stasa said he'd fill us in on the rest when he gets here."

Feeling relieved, Liam headed aft, ready to prepare for their arrival, but stopped short on entering the cargo bay. Alastair, although still hanging from the repair cradle where Liam had left him, was inexplicably awake.

"Hello, Master Mulcahey."

Liam approached the cradle warily. "Alastair, how did you leave quiescence?"

Alastair's knee had been damaged in the assault on Pier 43. After making repairs, Liam had placed him in his dormant state to allow his power cells to recharge. He should have remained that way until Liam reactivated him but, as had happened in the room above the pneumatics garage, he'd somehow awoken on his own.

"I couldn't rightly say." Alastair's blue eyes blinked on and off in the way he did when the limited reasoning ability of his core left him confused. "Perhaps you forgot to shut me down?"

A cold feeling crept along Liam's skin as he scanned the small cargo bay. "No, Alastair, I didn't." The bay was filled with storage lockers and a few crates of guns and ammunition strapped tightly to several pallets beside the sliding exterior door. Nothing seemed misplaced or out of the ordinary, but that only made Liam feel all the more suspicious. "Did someone enter the bay while I was gone?"

"Not that I'm aware of," Alastair said brightly.

Besides Liam, there were only two others aboard—Bailey and the pilot, a bubbly redhead named Trixie. Either of them could have entered the cargo bay while he was sleeping, he supposed, but neither of them would have had reason to. He wasn't sure they'd know *how* to awaken Alastair.

Liam had written the behavior off as a one-time glitch caused by Sergeant Holohan's strange light, but clearly it was more than that. The light had evidently caused some kind of lingering malfunction. "You'll let me know if you remember anything?" Liam asked as he headed to the cargo bay door.

"Of course, sir."

A chill wind invaded the cargo bay as Liam unlocked the door and heaved it aside. The sound of the *Eisvögel*'s engines grew intense, so much so Liam felt it in his bones.

A hundred yards away, the second zeppelin was pulling even with them. As it matched the *Eisvögel*'s speed, the gondola's door slid wide to reveal Stasa and Clay, both wearing flight suits and jet packs. The twin engines on Stasa's back coughed to life. He leapt into open air and was carried in an elegant arc toward the *Eisvögel*'s cargo bay. Ignoring Liam's outstretched arm, he landed with the grace of a trapeze artist.

Clay flew over next, though with much less aplomb. During the war, he'd been more than competent in a hopper suit. But the way he piloted the jet pack made him look like a water buffalo granted wings. As he zigzagged toward the open bay door, Liam broadened his stance and tightened his grip on the safety strap, and just in time. Clay came in hard. Stasa was forced to help, adding his weight lest Clay crash through the opposite wall.

"Kill the engines!" Stasa yelled. "For the love of God, kill the engines!"

Finally Clay triggered the kill switch, and his jetpack engines went silent. "Sorry," he said while shaking his right hand, the one that was still flesh and bone. "The fingers don't work like they used to."

Stasa stared at him with a worried expression that bordered on guilt, as if he felt responsible for not putting Clay back together as well as he could have. As Stasa and Clay removed their jet suits, Liam realized the faint wheezing sound of Clay's air pump was stronger than it had been.

"Everything okay?" Liam asked Clay, whose face was still a bright shade of red.

"Sure it is." Clay twisted a dial on his chest, then pressed a rubber plunger several times. A soft hiss could be heard, and Clay's breaths began to lengthen. Seeing Liam's worried reaction, Clay smiled and pulled his shirt aside. "Bet you're jealous, Liam." He pointed to the cluster of dials, buttons, and plungers on the upper part of his metal sleeve. "Got a built-in pharmacy right here." He shrugged as his skin returned to a somewhat normal, if still slightly blotchy, color. "Just tricky adjusting for the altitude is all."

Liam wasn't wholly convinced, but he let the subject drop as Clay's condition stabilized. They settled themselves around the table where Liam had been sitting earlier—Liam, Alastair, and Stasa sat on one side, Clay and Bailey on the other. Clay, using his good hand, unlatched a small compartment in his prosthetic forearm, from which he pulled out a cigarette and lighter.

"Baby," Bailey said, "I thought you quit."

Clay didn't look the least bit guilty as he lit the cigarette and took a long, squint-eyed drag. "I did."

Liam expected Bailey to argue, yet she merely closed her eyes and sighed as Clay blew a long stream of smoke into the air.

"So," Clay said. "Morgan . . . Our mole in the De Pere administration revealed he's being kept in a research facility on the outskirts of Novo Solis. The St. Lawrence Pact know about it but think it's a medical facility for creating new mechanika—"

"You mean a manufacturing facility."

Clay's eyes narrowed. "What?"

"You said a medical facility. Automatons aren't biological."

There was suddenly something very heavy hanging in the air between them all. Clay looked to Stasa, who in turn looked at Alastair. Alastair blinked his owl-like blink.

"Shit, Liam," Clay said, "I thought you knew."

"Knew what?"

"The mechanika . . . They're all cyborgs"—he pressed a finger to his temple—"their brains taken from soldiers too wounded to save."

"They're *what*?" Liam stared at him, hoping it was a bad joke. But he knew from their reactions it wasn't.

"Late in the war, Nolan was running out of soldiers. He authorized the psi-ops division to harvest the wounded. The mechanika are fallen soldiers."

"All of them?"

Clay flicked ashes into the ashtray on the table. "All of them."

Liam was reeling. "But I worked on Alastair dozens of times. I would have known."

"I don't mean to be rude, pal, but you really think you could tell? When your memories of the war were taken from you? When you weren't even able to tell your own grandmother was dead?"

Stasa gave Clay a sour look. "That's a bit harsh, isn't it?"

"Maybe, but Liam needs to hear this. Nolan was a monster. And De Pere is worse. He's adopted Nolan's dream of world domination, but he's doing it a hundred times smarter."

Liam stared at Alastair, who stared innocently back. "Is it true, Alastair? Were you a soldier?"

"He won't remember," Clay said point blank. "He's a fragment of the man he once was, a tool repurposed after the war ended."

"He's not a *tool*." Liam faced Alastair squarely. "I need to know, Alastair. Were you once a soldier? Were you once a man?"

With his mechanical hands held in his lap, Alastair had never looked so small. "I'm afraid I don't recall, sir."

Liam felt nauseated. He'd known a woman once, another mechanic who worked for a friend of the Aysana's. On seeing their new mechanika, freshly received from government surplus, Liam had asked what had happened to the old one. "It started acting weird," she'd replied, "so we sent it to the dump."

Dear God, to have veterans from the war treated that way. *To the dump* . . . The mechanic hadn't known the truth, of course—she'd been fooled just like everyone else. How many times had Liam wondered when Alastair would need to be disposed of like an aging mechanikal horse too run-down to repair? How many others had been tossed aside like useless parts?

As horrifying as the revelation was, it solved two burning mysteries, the foremost of which was how mechanika could have such clarity of thought and action. But it also made clear how they could be affected by illusions. With their minds more or less intact, and the ability of the bacteria to weave a grand pattern through the thoughts of all those infected, the mechanika would be as much in thrall to it as everyone else.

"Okay," Liam said after a deep breath. "How do we save Morgan? How do we stop this?"

It was Clay who answered. "This morning," he began, "we sent a tip to our informant in the SLP that De Pere's top psi-ops scientists are using the lab where Morgan's being kept."

"Hold on a sec," Liam said. "You have a contact in the SLP?"

"Quite a few of them, actually," Clay said.

"But they're the enemy."

Clay stared at him as if he were being naïve. "C'mon, Liam. You've learned enough by now to know it was Nolan who led us into war for his *own* reasons, not because it was in America's best interests. And the SLP had plenty of reasons to distrust his motives. They aren't the enemy here."

"So the Uprising and the SLP are allies now?"

"I wouldn't go that far. We're aligned in our opposition to De Pere. In any case, they're coming in for a surprise inspection tomorrow. When they do, De Pere will delay and, we hope, move Morgan to a secondary facility. We'll be ready when they do. We'll use their haste against them and get Morgan out."

"Once we have him safe," Stasa said, "we can take samples of the scourge variant and begin development of the anti-serum."

Clay, his face still a bit splotchy, snuffed his cigarette into the ashtray and began fiddling with another dial on his chest.

"Darling, you need to lie down," Bailey said.

"I'm fine."

Bailey stood and stared down at him. "You need to lie *down*."

Clay looked angry at being challenged, but the longer Bailey stood there with her arms crossed and an implacable look on her face, the more cowed Clay seemed. "All right," he said, and followed her forward to the sleeping cabins.

"What's happening to him?" Liam asked Stasa when he heard the cabin door click shut.

Stasa took a deep breath while smoothing down his mustache. "After the explosion he was caught in—while saving me, I might add—I did what I could for him. But the prosthetics, the sleeve, the medicine . . . they've taken a heavy toll on his body."

Liam felt foolish and insensitive. He'd been so caught up in his own past and Morgan's future, he hadn't given much thought to Clay's *present*. "Is he dying?"

"Not in the way you mean it, no. If Clay is diligent with the medicine and taking care of himself, he could live for years. But he's growing frustrated. I've seen it before. Men who've lost so much control they feel like the only control they have left is to indulge themselves. They drink, smoke, or, worse, stop taking their medicine."

Liam glanced at the cabin door where Bailey and Clay had gone. "Why would he do that?"

"Because the medicines make him feel sick. He feels better without them, but of course it's fool's gold, a temporary reprieve at best. If he goes without the medicine for too long, his organs will start to fail."

"Is there anything I can do? Push him to take his meds?"

"If we push too hard, it might have the opposite effect. And Bailey has that angle covered in any case. Just be his friend. That'll help as much as anything else."

"I will, of course," Liam vowed.

They sat in silence for a time, and Liam's thoughts returned to Morgan and the anti-serum they hoped to create. That in turn reminded him of a conversation he'd had with Grace, a conversation he'd nearly forgotten, though it had happened only a handful of days ago.

Oddly, it was still a bit muddy in his mind but then, like a bolt of lightning, became crystal clear. In the furniture store, after waking from his absynthe-fueled dreams, Grace had asked him to lie next to her. He'd done so and it had felt wonderful. Something had been bothering him, though, and he'd asked Grace about it. He'd asked precisely how much she'd helped Stasa in the development of the latest serum, the one she'd added to the absynthe to help his memories return. Grace had not only avoided the question, she'd done something to make Liam drop the subject altogether.

"Is everything all right?" Stasa asked.

With some effort, Liam drew his gaze to Stasa. "After the assault on the sub-basement of the Power and Light Building, you said Grace helped you to develop the serum."

"Yes."

"How *much* did she help?"

"Considerably. She's quite versed in symbiotic psychology. Why do you ask?"

Liam nearly confessed his fears—that Grace was hiding secrets for unknown purposes—but didn't. He needed time to digest. He needed to talk to Grace. "No reason," he said. "It caught my attention is all."

Stasa didn't look like he believed him, but he let the subject drop.

Liam, meanwhile, was caught by a figure standing near the cargo bay door. It was Nana, and she looked positively murderous.

TWENTY-NINE

On a bright, sunny day in America's capital of Novo Solis, Liam walked side by side with Clay along a deserted street. Having just completed a scout of the neighborhood, they were on their way to meet Grace, Bailey, and Alastair to finalize their plans for rescuing Morgan.

Around them stood apartment buildings with shops along the bottom row. All of them stood empty, dilapidated. It was eerily silent, the only sounds the crunch of their footsteps, the whine of Clay's mechanikal limbs, and the hiss of his lung pump.

"So no one lives here?" Liam asked.

"No one." Clay took a drag off his cigarette, then blew it out in a stream as they wove their way around the husk of a burned delivery wagon. "Most of them are uninhabitable anyway, victims of the French bombing near the end of the war."

"And they just gave up the land?" Liam asked him. "The entire neighborhood?"

Clay shrugged. "The capital lost a lot of people. It didn't make sense to keep it all."

Liam stared up at the shattered windows, then the rubble and detritus spread over the street. "How many neighborhoods are like this?"

"Dozens, but De Pere wants perfection, so illusions make sure all people see is the pristine capital we were sold in the magazines and comic books." They walked in silence for another half block when Clay suddenly said, "You seem a little stressed, partner. Something wrong?"

"A bit, maybe."

"It's Grace, isn't it?" Clay said with a broad, shit-eating grin. "Nervous about seeing her after your little *nap* at the furniture store?"

Liam forced a smile. "You got me."

He was relieved Clay hadn't guessed the real source of his discomfort.

He hadn't had a chance to speak to Grace about her manipulating him, but he needed to—he needed some straight answers before this went any further.

"Well, don't fret, Casanova." Clay leaned over conspiratorially. "I think the heiress likes you." He started coughing immediately after, and his face went splotchy. He reached inside his shirt and pressed a rubber plunger, deploying medicine into his bloodstream, and his complexion slowly evened out.

"You all right?" Liam asked. He didn't mean to, but his eyes drifted to Clay's cigarette.

Clay noticed. He lifted the cigarette and took an especially long drag from it. "Doing fine." He blew the smoke directly into Liam's face. "Why do you ask?"

Annoyed, Liam fanned the air while dodging the stream of smoke. "Because Bailey's worried."

"She's always worried."

"So's Stasa."

"Look, I know what you're trying to do, and I appreciate it, but this is *my* life. I know the consequences of my actions."

"Those consequences go beyond *you*, though."

Clay stopped dead in his tracks and flicked the still-lit cigarette onto the street. "You don't think I know that?" Liam started to reply, but Clay talked over him. "God knows I'm lucky to have Bailey. She's a good woman, better than I deserve. I'm lucky to have Stasa on my side, too. I'm lucky to have *you* back in my life. You were a good friend during the war, even if I never told you. You're a good friend now. But this"—he rapped his knuckles against his metal chest—"this is what rules my life now. It controls me every minute of every day. It won't even allow me to find peace in my dreams. The drugs give me nightmares. And waking up is hardly better."

"It's better than dying."

"Think so?" With a stomp of his foot and a sharp twist, he snuffed the cigarette. "Care to trade places?"

Liam stood there in silence, unsure what to say.

"By rights, I should be dead already," Clay went on. "I can feel it, death waiting for me around every corner, holding a garrote. Hardly a moment passes where I don't feel like it's my last. So if I feel like giving that moth-erfucker the middle finger once in a while"—he pulled his foot away and stared pointedly at the smashed cigarette—"that's what I'm going to do, and no one's going to tell me any different."

"Not even Bailey?"

"Bailey's an angel. She gets a pass." Clay suddenly lurched back into motion, leaving Liam behind. "Let me live my life, Liam, what's left of it, anyway."

Liam didn't like it, but he could see he wasn't going to get anywhere with Clay. Not today.

"Stubborn bastard," he said as he caught up to Clay.

"*Strong-willed*," Clay corrected. "They wouldn't have dragged me into the Henchmen otherwise." He pointed to the broken stone facade of an abandoned bank. "Let's go, St. Jude, we've got work to do."

Liam couldn't help but laugh—St. Jude was the patron saint of lost causes.

They passed through the shattered glass doors and reached the bank's interior. Within, a layer of dust coated everything. On the air was the scent of mold and decay. Just then, Bailey and Grace were coming from the rear while, behind them, Alastair pushed a padded wooden wheelchair, the sort a rich dowager might own. As they met near the teller windows, Liam's worries over Clay's health were eclipsed by those over Grace's deceptions.

"Could we speak alone?" Liam asked her. The opening was far from elegant, but they didn't have much time, and he'd never been very good at this sort of thing in any case.

Before Grace could reply, Bailey's handheld wireless chirped. She spoke softly into it, listened to the reply, then turned to the group. "The SLP inspection is underway. Word is, Morgan and one other patient were rushed to the LuxCorp facility about twenty minutes ago. Probably best we give them a little time to settle in, but even so"—she pointed to Liam and Grace—"if the two of you are going to talk, best make it quick."

Grace nodded. "Why don't the three of you go ahead and get into position?"

Bailey sent an uneasy look Liam's way, then nodded and ushered Clay and Alastair toward the rear of the bank.

When they were gone, Grace turned to Liam. "What is it, Liam?"

Liam had played this conversation out a thousand times and still hardly knew where to begin. "Do you remember when I told you about De Pere, how he manipulated my understanding of how Clay had broken into the train car?"

"Sure I do."

"Why didn't you mention you could do the same thing?"

Grace blinked. She seemed surprised, even embarrassed, then, of all things, *affronted* that he would ask such a question. "It didn't seem relevant at the time."

"And when you decided to manipulate *me* in the furniture store? Were *my* thoughts on the subject irrelevant, too?"

At this, Grace's face went stony—all but her cheeks and neck, both of which had gained a rosy hue. "Of course not."

"Then why, Grace? Why would you have done that to me?"

She bowed her head. "I'm sorry about that, Liam, truly. I shouldn't have done it. I was only worried that if you knew, you'd want to learn how to do it yourself. It's a dangerous tool. It attracts attention if you don't do it properly. De Pere might sense it. You weren't *ready* for it."

"Okay, but why stop me from asking about your work with Stasa? Why hide your knowledge of neo-medicine from me?"

Seconds passed. Grace looked like she was ready to argue, to tell him it was none of his business. Or maybe she was debating whether to manipulate him again. Then she took a deep breath and exhaled slowly, as if she'd come to a different sort of decision.

She suddenly spread her arms wide, and the bank's dusty floor changed from ceramic tiles to dark soil. From the soil, stalks of grain lifted and grew. The walls around them dissolved, replaced by row upon row of wheat. The rows stretched in every direction, as far as the eye could see, and the roof became a cloud-studded sky with an achingly bright sun. The scent on the air was fresh and earthy. As had been true on entering the domes, Liam felt as if the many layers that weighed him down had suddenly been lifted. Even so, it brought no sense of calm—it only served to show how powerful Grace was, making Liam feel more out of his depth than he already did.

"What *is* this place?" Liam asked.

"It's a sort of hypnotic state," replied Grace. "It allows those within it to separate themselves from others affected by *E. Sentensis*. It effectively creates a mental barrier that prevents thoughts from being transmitted to the people outside of it."

"Including De Pere?"

"*Especially* De Pere. Colette and I came here often to work through our problems. It will, I hope, prevent De Pere from being alerted to the things we're about to discuss."

Even knowing the field was an illusion, it was a stunning sight, brighter than real life. It looked very much like the field Liam had stood in after his first flight of absynthe. "Is this why Morgan and I both saw wheat fields?"

"Probably." Grace plucked a single stalk of wheat and held it gently between her hands. "I didn't mean for it to happen, but I'd been thinking about Colette. It must have bubbled up from my subconscious."

Liam felt incredibly off balance. While the sting over Grace's betrayal had hardly faded, she *had* just brought him to a place that was clearly very special to her—that she would take him into her confidence in such a way revealed a considerable level of trust.

"Colette and I met at a graduation party shortly after she arrived in Novo Solis," Grace began. "We hit it off. She seemed a bit spellbound by how free I was—a freedom gained by inheriting a fortune, I should mention. And for my part, I admired Colette's quiet brilliance. I grew fascinated by her work and interrogated her about it constantly. The things she shared with me over the following weeks marked the beginning of my apprenticeship." Grace used a fingernail to scrape away the grains, which fluttered onto the dark earth. "After the war, De Pere continued to lead the psi-ops division and quickly gained control over the scientists who'd been working with Colette. He convinced them that the SLP, despite their having signed the armistice, were preparing for a second invasion. In the minds of those scientists, it became essential that America be protected from its enemies. They were the ones who created the Orpheus serum, the ones who helped ensure it was spread nationwide. They also advanced the Henchman serum, turning it into something extremely potent. On De Pere's orders, he was the only one who received it, which is how he gained such powerful abilities."

Liam thought back to the conversations he'd had around De Pere and how he could have changed so much. "Was that what drove him mad?"

"The new serum might have accelerated his journey toward megalomania, but Colette was convinced he was already well along the path by that point. Who but a lunatic would have ordered the creation of the Orpheus strain, after all?"

"And Colette herself?" Liam asked. "Where was she at this point?"

"In Novo Solis with the rest of her team. After the war, she was sidelined by her male counterparts, forced to do menial tasks, prevented from participating in important meetings, especially those that included De Pere. Knowing her peace-loving nature, they kept all the details of the Orpheus strain from her, and those of the modified Henchman serum that De Pere took as well."

A cloud passed over the sun, plunging the immediate area into shadow. The air grew cooler while, nearby, a cricket began to chirp.

"If De Pere didn't trust her," Liam asked, "why not just oust her from the project entirely?"

"I imagine he wanted her close so he could keep an eye on her. And she was still a valuable source of knowledge. Whatever the case, Colette eventually *did* learn about their work on the new strains. She went to the psiops headquarters in Novo Solis and demanded De Pere put an immediate stop to it. When he refused, she began work on a counter-serum and asked if I'd help. I agreed, but there was a problem. By that point, tens of thousands had already been infected with the Orpheus strain, including me. Those infected by it were vulnerable, not only to De Pere's illusions, but to his sensing their emotions, their thoughts. Colette, with the power she'd gained from the original Henchman serum, was safe, but if *I* helped, it was only a matter of time before De Pere learned of our efforts."

"Is that why Colette gave you the Henchman serum?"

"Yes. Fortunately she'd secreted some of it away, which is how I ended up getting the same strain as you and the rest of your squad, but by then the Orpheus strain was present in my system as well." Grace paused. "We think they merged somehow, creating a variant of some sort. I gained some of the same powers as you and Colette, but we think De Pere was still able to sense or listen in on our conversations."

"You don't sound certain."

"I wasn't. I'm *still* not." The wind suddenly kicked up, sending waves across the field's golden surface. "Whatever the cause, De Pere became suspicious. He came for Colette, tried to control her, to dominate her mind. Colette managed to escape and find me. When we thought about it, the most likely reason De Pere found out was because of *my* thoughts, not Colette's."

"Then why didn't he come for *you*?"

"De Pere was extremely paranoid at the time. He was listening in on hundreds, maybe even thousands, of minds, casting a net to find any who might be plotting against him. We think he'd overheard my thoughts without knowing who they were coming from. Afterward"—she waved the denuded stalk of grain over the field—"we created this place."

"Okay, but if it's so effective, why not use it all the time?"

"Because it creates an empty space, a hole in the fabric of *E. sentensis*. If we use it too much, De Pere might sense *that*. In any case, it seemed to work. Neither of us were found in the months that followed. I used my resources to hide Colette away. We built a lab together. I'll never be as brilliant as she was, but she taught me everything she could. By that point, De Pere's paranoia was pushing him to take more drastic actions. You'd all received the original serum, which meant you posed a threat. He didn't want you dead, though—Max had already proven himself useful, after all. He wanted the rest of you as insurance, tools he could call upon if needed. As you've already guessed, it was De Pere who erased your memories and sent you home, to await a summons if he ever had need."

"But De Pere saw me at the flashtrain ceremony. We talked for minutes on end, and he didn't recognize me."

Grace nodded. "I'm coming to that. About a year after Colette and I started working together, De Pere was elected to his first term in office. By then, Colette was close to perfecting a more advanced strain of *E. Sentensis,* meant to provide defenses against De Pere's growing powers. When it had advanced to the point that she needed a test subject, she reached out to Nick Crawford, then a professor of military tactics at West Point. This is where Colette made a critical error. In hopes of protecting Nick until the serum was perfected, all she told him was that it was meant to provide defenses against a new SLP threat. The serum *did* work as intended but had one major, unintended side effect: it unlocked some of Nick's memories from the war. Incensed over De Pere's manipulations of the Henchmen, Nick went to Novo Solis to demand answers."

Liam's mind drifted to the few memories he had of Nick. He saw Nick's earnest smile, his easygoing ways, but there were flashes of righteous anger as well. More than one barroom brawl had been started when Nick thought someone in the squad was being bullied. "Sounds a lot like Nick," he told Grace. "He would have seen De Pere's actions as a deep betrayal of his brothers-in-arms. He took that sort of thing very seriously."

"You're exactly right," Grace said. "The two got into a heated argument in the Oval Office. De Pere tried to manipulate him again, but the new serum helped Nick to resist. De Pere grew furious. He lost all inhibitions and lashed out like never before. It broke Nick's mind. Nick went into a coma and died a few weeks later. Something changed in De Pere after that. He was already paranoid, but it reached new levels. He was rethinking his position on the Devil's Henchmen. He was on the cusp of summoning you all to Novo Solis and having you put in front of a firing squad."

Grace's jaw worked back and forth. Her eyes were restless, as if she were reliving it all. "*I* said we should assassinate De Pere before things went any further, but Colette said it was doomed to failure. We didn't have enough resources. De Pere was too well protected. She championed a different method. She was still connected to him, and she'd learned how to alter memories after feeling De Pere himself do it. And so, with the help of a mole in the De Pere administration, we organized a covert mission. While the mole altered the *physical* records in the government archives, Colette made De Pere and others think that his plan had worked, that all of the Devil's Henchmen—everyone but Kohler and Nick—had been summoned to Novo Solis and summarily executed. She twisted his memories of you as well, gave you different faces, different names, all of which matched the alterations made to the government records."

"*That's* why De Pere and Kohler didn't recognize me."

"That's right," Grace said. "In one fell swoop, the true, original members of the Devil's Henchmen were hidden from De Pere and his inner circle. Or so we thought. Colette was taken a few days after that. I don't know the details, but it was clear that De Pere somehow found out about our mission. I suspect he didn't know precisely *what* Colette had done, but he knew he'd been manipulated in some way, and he knew Colette had been the one to do it."

Part of Liam had hoped Colette was actually still alive, that Grace had somehow been wrong about the details surrounding her death, but hearing all this made it clear how naïve that hope had been. It left a hollowness inside him, which in turn made him realize how Grace must be feeling. "I'm so sorry," he said to her. "Losing a close friend like that must have been devastating."

"It was, and with Colette gone, there was no one left to resist De Pere's ever-more-twisted plans for our country. I couldn't even reach out to the rest of you. Fearing De Pere would one day find *me*, Colette had always been extremely careful not to share information I didn't absolutely need."

"There's something I don't get, though," Liam said. "If the operation worked, and De Pere, Kohler, and everyone else thought the remaining

Henchmen were executed, what changed? What made De Pere realize he'd been tricked?"

Grace's smile was miserable. "That one's on me, I'm afraid. After Colette's death, I decided to form the Uprising in earnest, to continue her work. The first person I recruited was Stasa. Having someone with an intimate knowledge of neo-medicine was essential, and I'd met Stasa. I knew him to be a forward-thinking man with legitimate concerns over government overreach. It didn't take much convincing for him to agree to join me. When he did, the two of us schemed to find a way to gather the rest of you. We didn't know your identities, but we had one key piece of information: we knew you would code to a doctor as amnesiacs."

Liam thought back to how Clay had entered the program for veterans with memory loss. "That's why you created the outreach program, the one that landed Clay."

"That's right. After we found him, I booked a zeppelin to Chicago to speak to him directly. I was foolish. I thought we were far enough away from Novo Solis that De Pere wouldn't sense our conversation, but he did and sent Max Kohler to Chicago to investigate. After learning of the program that Stasa himself had created, Kohler led the operation to abduct him."

"But if De Pere can sense things like that, how is it we can talk about *any* of this without tipping him off?"

"De Pere's mind can't be everywhere at once. And the serum we gave you in Club Artemis was essentially the same one Nick received. By then, the side effect we discovered with Nick had become its raison d'être—we gave it to you primarily to unlock your memories, your abilities—but it also insulates you from De Pere." Grace seemed anxious, tight as piano wire. "We still have to be careful, mind you. Even as powerful as it is, the serum isn't perfect. We don't have free reign to talk about whatever we want, whenever we want. Plus, there are certain subjects De Pere is more attuned to. And the closer we are to him, the easier it is for him to pick up on them. So you see, *this* is why I'm so careful about what I talk about. It's why I manipulated you into dropping the subject of how I learned about neo-medicine. De Pere was still in Chicago, and the question itself struck too close to the origins of Project Echo, Colette, and De Pere himself."

"You said Colette manipulated De Pere. Couldn't you do that to him now?"

Grace shook her head. "That's far, far beyond my abilities. I can't hold a candle to Colette, and she barely managed to succeed that one time, when De Pere was caught unawares. He's better prepared now. Our best hope is to continue as we have, to find Morgan, develop an anti-serum, and to continue delving into your memories to find the secret Colette mentioned."

Liam cast his gaze over the golden field, the gentle wind blowing over its surface. Part of him was relieved, and not just because everything Grace had told him had calmed his fears about *her*; *he* felt more complete as well, knowing what had happened to Colette, to the other Henchmen, to himself.

Grace stepped closer. Took his hands in hers and rubbed the backs of his knuckles. "Ready to save Morgan?"

Liam pulled her in and hugged her. For several long breaths they stayed that way, and Liam felt himself relaxing. He stepped back and smiled.

"I am now."

THIRTY

The wheat field dissolved, replaced by the bank's dusty interior. With a wave of her hand, Grace changed Liam's appearance to that of a distinguished gentleman with a curling mustache, a fine suit, and a top hat, then turned herself into a wizened woman wearing a slightly old-fashioned dress and a long diamond necklace.

LuxCorp, where Morgan had been moved, was a neotech company specializing in medical equipment. That it had a medical wing to conduct tests of its own equipment made it a natural place for the Cabal to move Morgan and the other scourge victim to for the duration of the surprise SLP inspection.

The company was owned by a woman named Abigail Swinton, whose likeness Grace had just taken on. Liam resembled her son, Harrison, part-owner of the company, and a man who devoted much of his time to helping his aging mother. Abigail and Harrison were famous recluses who made only the occasional visit to their various businesses, which made impersonating them a relatively safe undertaking. More importantly, while LuxCorp's chief executive and his team of managers were members of the Cabal, neither Abigail nor Harrison were. It left Grace and Liam an opening: if they could pose as the owners of the company, they could enter the building and search for Morgan without raising too much undue suspicion.

Liam pushed Grace on the wheelchair out of the bank and along the deserted streets toward Novo Solis proper. After a few turns, they reached a wide thoroughfare, and Liam suddenly felt as if he were passing through a sheet of ice-cold water. Shivering, he turned to find himself standing before a nondescript wall, part of a warehouse, perhaps, or a factory. If he concentrated, he could just see through it to the ruined street beyond.

"Don't." Grace reached back and patted his hand. "You'll draw attention. Act like everything is normal."

Ahead, the street was full of life. People moving about. Men, women, entire families going about their business in a city of steel and glass. Some of it was fake, but much of it was real, the city rebuilt after the terrible bombings near the end of the war. A short walk delivered them to a building with an elegant sweep of manicured lawn and concrete sculptures. A fountain held a statue of the goddess, Eos, her bright copper wings spread wide. High above, a sign read *LuxCorp* in cerulean neo-lume.

As they neared the entrance door, a burly attendant in a red vest opened it for them, though not without a surprised look. "Ma'am."

Liam rolled Grace into a large foyer, past a dozen or so men and women in business suits, to a central desk. Behind it sat a fetching young brunette. Her eyes went wide when she saw who'd arrived. "Mrs. Swinton . . . I—" She cleared her throat. "I wish Natalie had let us know you were coming. We'd have prepared a proper welcome."

"My assistant is a busy woman." Grace leaned forward to peer at the woman's name tag. "Besides, *Violet*, I like to know how my business is being run."

"Of course." Violet stood and tugged at her vest. "What might we do for you?"

"I'm here to inspect the medical wing."

"The medical wing." She glanced at her bulbous-nosed colleague sitting beside her, who seemed none too eager to rescue her. "I . . ."

"You *what*, Violet?"

"Nothing, ma'am. Right this way." She pulled a drawer open and retrieved a ring of keys. "You've got the desk," she said in a low but gruff voice to her colleague, then led Liam and Grace to a bank of elevators. She inserted a key into a lock beside the last of them, turned it, and pressed the call button. Soon, the elevator arrived and they headed inside.

As they began their ascent, Grace spoke in a matter-of-fact tone. "Two patients were brought in this morning. Tell me about them."

With an impatient glance at the brass plate and dial that indicated which floor they were on, Violet swallowed hard. "I was told not to speak of it."

"To those outside the company," Grace said. "Do I qualify as *outside the company?*"

"No ma'am, of course not." Violet looked like she wanted to shrink and keep shrinking until she disappeared. "Both seemed poorly. They were shivering badly. That's all I saw. Honest."

When they exited on the topmost floor, a security desk sat just beyond the elevator door. Beyond it was a pair of swinging doors with round windows set into them.

"We're here to see the new patients," Violet said to a guard sitting behind the desk.

The guard was an older fellow with icy eyes, a square jaw, and sun spots mingled among what little remained of his gray, military-style haircut. Over his badge, a name tag read *Wells.* "Wing's off limits until further notice."

Violet stepped aside, allowing Officer Wells to see Grace unobstructed.

Officer Wells blinked. "Mrs. Swinton." He stood and bowed his head. "It's been some time. I'm sorry you chose today to come—"

"Two patients have been brought to *my* building," Grace broke in, "and I'm going to see them."

"I'm afraid that's impossible."

"And why is that?"

"Orders from the CIC," he said sternly. "We're to give them space until tomorrow. No one's to see them."

"Those orders might apply to most, Officer Wells, but not *me.*" Grace's tone was the perfect balance of outrage and authority. "Now kindly escort us to their room."

Officer Wells, looking more than a little disturbed, took a deep breath, as if preparing himself for an argument. The argument never came, however, because just then the swinging doors behind the desk opened and out stepped Max Kohler. Dressed in a coal-black suit, he stared at Liam and Grace, his blue eye visible through the hole in his brass-and-iron mask.

"It's quite all right, Carl. There's no reason the illustrious *Abigail Swinton* can't come to inspect her own facility."

Grace took in Kohler. "And just who are *you*?" she asked with an impatient air.

"Max Kohler"—he held the door wide with a theatrical bow—"a humble but faithful servant of our country."

Snorting, Grace reached up and patted Liam's hand. "Let's get a move on, Harrison. We have other appointments today."

"Of course, Mother dear." As Liam pushed the wheelchair through the door into the brightly lit hallway beyond, he felt Kohler's stare.

"And what, exactly," Kohler said as he caught up to them, "brings you here today?"

"If you think I don't have eyes and ears within this building," Grace said, "I'd call you a fool, and rightly so. I'm here to ensure my business is safe. I imagine that's something even a *faithful servant* from the CIC would understand."

Kohler tipped his head. "Touché, dear Abigail."

"I'm happy to oblige our government when needed," Grace said, "but I'd like to know why, in fact, it *was* in need."

Kohler led them to a room with high windows and a brilliant view of Novo Solis. The room had two sleeping patients, a man and a woman in blue hospital robes, on bulky, rolling beds. Neither woke when Liam, Grace, and Kohler entered. They were illusions, of course, cast by Kohler. Morgan and the other scourge victim were surely being kept somewhere else, a place hidden by one of Kohler's illusions.

Grace, meanwhile, was waging a silent battle. Kohler was used to not only *creating* illusions, but sensing them, deconstructing them. From the moment of his arrival, he'd been trying to sense whether one had been cast on Liam and Grace, but Grace was foiling all of his attempts at doing so.

"We had a fire at one of our facilities," Kohler said. He gave a flick of one finger—the only indication he was casting an illusion—then *stepped away* from himself, as Grace had done in the alley behind Club Artemis.

The fake Kohler, meanwhile, continued speaking. "As a precaution, we thought it prudent these patients be moved as we gained control over the blaze. And it serves a dual purpose in any case. The use of your scanning equipment will prove useful." He tipped his head again. "Assuming you allow it, of course."

As Grace nodded her assent, and the illusory Max Kohler continued on, the real Kohler stepped closer. Liam felt the hairs on the back of his neck stand on end as Kohler paced behind him. Liam could *smell* him—whether it was a slip on Kohler's part or Liam's own abilities manifesting, he wasn't sure, but the fact that it was such an odd scent, like turpentine trying but failing to mask the scent of decaying flesh, made the experience all the more ghoulish.

It was a mind-boggling display of skill and power, which made Liam all the more nervous that Kohler was eventually going to pierce their disguises.

"When will they be taken away?" Grace asked.

"We'd be grateful if a few days didn't pose a terrible imposition." As the fake Kohler spoke, the real Kohler, apparently satisfied, merged with him, the two becoming one again. "We only need enough time to clean the smoke and sterilize the affected rooms."

Grace stared at each of the patients in their beds. "Very well," she said, then patted Liam's hand. "I think it's time we go, Harrison."

Before Liam could move, he saw himself and Grace, in their guises as Abigail and Harrison Swinton, turn toward the door.

"If I might have a bit of your time, Mr. Kohler," Grace began. "There are a few things I'd like to talk to you about, further ways LuxCorp might help the government. There are some contracts going out for bid soon, as I understand it."

Kohler held the door open for them. "A business woman to the last."

The fake Abigail laughed bitterly. "LuxCorp's bottom line is *my* bottom line."

As the door swung shut and the sound of their conversation dwindled, Liam's heart began to calm.

"You need to do the rest, Liam," Grace whispered. "My hands are full."

The strange odor of the turpentine and rot was still strong in the air, which made Liam realize it hadn't been Kohler's scent after all. More importantly, he recognized it. Morgan had been giving off that same sort of musk, though it had been fainter and considerably less worrying at the time.

He peered again at the two patients. He'd thought them mere illusions with no substance, but now he could see there was something hidden. As Grace had done with Liam and herself, Kohler had done with the patients.

Liam searched for and found the edges of Kohler's illusion. He tugged at the edges, made them fray. When the illusion over the room unraveled, it did so quickly. Near the beds was a metal cabinet. Mounted to its front face were a series of gauges and dials, plus a large, circular display with two wavering lines being drawn on its surface over and over again. From a hole in the side of the cabinet, cables were connected to the patients via leather headbands similar to the one Stasa had used on Ruby at the university.

More disconcerting was the woman. Her dark skin was sallow, especially along her throat and behind her ears. Dark blue veins webbed across her face and neck. The skin around her eyes was red, as if she'd been rubbing at them, yet she clearly *couldn't* rub them; she was strapped down. Her eyes were open and unblinking, their irises so dark they were almost black.

Finally the illusion over the male patient dissolved. Liam was relieved to see it was Morgan, but his relief was short-lived. Morgan wasn't speaking, he wasn't *moving*, and he looked deeply, utterly terrified.

THIRTY-ONE

Liam rushed to Morgan's bedside and removed the leather headband. The moment it was off, Morgan blinked fiercely, looking panicked. He took in the headband Liam still held, then the room, as if he didn't recognize either. His breathing slowed, and he focused on Liam. "I was calling to you," he said in a tremulous voice. "Or at least I was *trying* to, but I couldn't. I couldn't do anything."

Liam tried to mask how frightfully worried he was over Morgan's condition. He took some heart over the fact that Morgan's skin had retained most of its healthy color and the hazel of his eyes hadn't yet begun to darken, but light blue veins were showing across his neck, and the whites of his eyes were terribly red. How long would it be before he looked as bad as the woman lying next to him?

"Don't worry about that now," Liam said as he tossed the headband onto the floor. "We're taking you somewhere safe. We'll talk more then, okay?"

As Morgan nodded numbly, Liam noticed a tag on his robe. Printed on it was a number, 0227, and his name, Morgan.

Morgan, noticing, glanced down at it. "It's inhuman, what they're doing."

Liam began working on the straps around Morgan's wrists. "I know, but we're getting you out of here. You'll be safe soon."

After freeing Morgan's wrists and ankles, Liam rushed to the window and waved to the opposite rooftop. From behind a spinning air vent, Bailey waved back, then looked up, toward the top of the LuxCorp building and waved again.

Liam moved to the woman's bedside. She had the features of a Native American—broad face and nose, straight, jet black hair. Similar to Morgan, she had a tag with a number, 0187, and a name, Dakota. "Can you hear me, Dakota?" he asked as he released the straps holding her down. "Are you in any pain?"

Dakota blinked several times but made no reply.

"We're here to help," Liam said slowly and calmly.

Whether the words had registered Liam didn't know. She said nothing as he helped her to sit up on the bed. She hardly seemed to care what was happening around her.

A muted clanking came from somewhere beyond the windows. Outside, a window-washing gantry lowered into view. On it were Clay and Alastair, both wearing blue overalls. As Clay worked furiously at the cables to lower the gantry, Alastair crouched and used the sharp knife in his index finger to slice the rubber seal along the top of the central window. He continued along the sides and bottom as the gantry lowered, so that, by the time it was even with the floor, Alastair had cut it all away. Abandoning the cables, Clay slapped two large suction cups against the window pane. With a sharp tug, he pulled the sheet of glass free, rocked it into the room through the open frame, and leaned it against the wall. The sounds of a bustling city invaded the room. A low drone was also present, and growing louder, the sound of the *Eisvögel*'s engines approaching.

Grace, still sitting in the wheelchair, went suddenly stiff. "Kohler's suspicious." The tendons along her wrists stood out starkly as she gripped the wheelchair. "Get to the *Eisvögel*. Quickly."

Just then Dakota began to twitch. Morgan too. They both went suddenly still, and their heads swiveled to look out the window where, in the distance, the building known as the Pinnacle could be seen. Its central spire stood tall over the city. From its base, eight narrow wings spread like points on a compass rose. The Pinnacle had been built at the turn of the century to house the World's Fair, a symbol of America's never-ending quest to reach its highest ideals. It had since become a government facility, one favored by President De Pere for national addresses and official celebrations.

Clay stared at Morgan and Dakota warily. "Um, what the hell's happening to them?"

The words had hardly left Clay's mouth when Liam was swept away by a vision. The viewpoint was from the sky over the city, a bird's eye view. He was staring down at the Pinnacle's spire from above. Moving toward the building were lines of people. They looked like sunrays radiating outward from the Pinnacle's tall spire.

The view lowered, swept in toward one particular line. Most of the people who formed it had sallow skin and dull eyes. They were leading others, people who looked normal, if scared, toward the Pinnacle. Some of them resisted, especially as they came close to entering the building itself. Those who resisted were all treated the same; they were beaten mercilessly until they went willingly.

From within the building, Liam felt a hunger, a malevolent presence, a consciousness of sorts. It felt pleased at all that was happening in its name, but worried at the same time, as if all its carefully laid plans could fall apart at any moment. Its thoughts were drawn away from the spire, toward a building not far away.

Suddenly Liam was back in the room with Morgan and the others. He was lying on the cold white tiles. Dakota, meanwhile, was still standing. She stared about as if confused. Then she spied Liam. Her look became intense, and the world, as it had with Kohler outside Dr. Ramachandra's office, began to twist and turn in on itself. The beds, the medical equipment, the windows, and the walls became like liquid, melting, merging, swirling. Through it, Liam saw the others in the room spread their arms and toss their heads back, as if they were experiencing similar feelings of vertigo. Even Alastair, gripping the window frame, seemed dizzy. Only Grace, still in her wheelchair, seemed unaffected, but instead of doing anything to help, she was staring wide-eyed through the window toward the golden spire in the distance.

Dakota stepped closer to Liam. She knelt on the floor and stared down at him with a look like she regretted what she was about to do. "Forgive me," she said. "This isn't me." Then she opened her mouth. The pictures Stasa had shown him, the woman with the elongated tongue, came back in a rush. Dakota's tongue was the same. It was longer than it should be. A white barb emerged from underneath. The three glands at the base of her tongue were swollen and purple.

Understanding dawned as she rolled him onto his stomach. She was going to pierce his skin with the barb. She meant to infect him with some sort of venom. Liam tried to resist, tried to plead with her, but all he managed were two pitiful words, "Please stop!"

As Dakota's weight pressed onto his back, Liam managed one more glance at Grace.

"Grace!" he called to her. "Help!"

With some effort, she pulled her gaze away from the window, but made no move beyond that. She only stared in abject horror at Dakota.

Dakota's ragged breath grew suddenly loud in Liam's ear. Something warm and moist touched the back of his neck. He felt a tickling sensation, then nothing, as if his skin had been numbed by the saliva. He struggled to free himself but could hardly move. He could practically *feel* the barb ready to plunge deep into his neck. "Forgive me," Dakota whispered.

Then came a shout from Morgan. "No!" he cried.

It was followed by a clang, a sharp grunt, Dakota going limp. Her weight pressed down on Liam as the spinning of the world ceased. On the white tiles beside Liam, a bedpan was dropped, the implement Morgan had used to knock Dakota out.

Morgan, breathing heavily, dragged Dakota off him and helped Liam to his feet. Probing the back of his neck, Liam was relieved to feel little besides the numbness. He'd dodged a bullet, he knew, but the implications were terrifying. The ritual Dakota had performed was something the scourges were *meant* to do. How close was Morgan to succumbing to the same sort of compulsion that had driven Dakota's actions?

Alastair and Clay were back on their feet.

Grace was beside herself with worry. "I'm so sorry, Liam." She stood from her wheelchair. "I was helpless."

"We all were, other than Morgan." His words doing little to calm her, Liam took her hand. "I'm *fine*. Let's just get out of here."

After a halting breath, she nodded.

Outside, a rope ladder dropped into view. Flying low above the Lux-Corp building was the *Eisvögel*. Looking up, Liam caught only the barest of outlines of its long, cigar shape, a few of its battens, the gondola beneath. The aircraft's envelope and gondola had been outfitted with another of Stasa's astounding inventions, a special fabric that, when activated, cloaked it from view.

After helping Morgan onto the ladder, Liam gripped the lowermost rung, anchoring it to reduce the swaying. Alastair, with Dakota slung over his shoulders, went next. Grace and Clay followed. They'd just reached the gondola, with Liam about to follow, when the door behind him flew open and Max Kohler rushed into the room. He was holding what looked to be a rifle, except there was a canister hanging off the stock, and the barrel wasn't a barrel at all but a shining metal electrode from which tendrils of electricity were snaking through the air with a low buzz and the soft snap of static shocks.

Kohler looked all too ready to use the weapon—he'd even half lifted it to his shoulder—but then he lowered it. Suddenly, the zeppelin's drone grew faint. Grace, Morgan, Clay—everyone around Liam and Kohler—faded and were gone. The buildings, the sky, the streets below, took on a strange animus, like a painting come alive. It reminded him of Grace's wheat field, but *unlike* Grace's construct, this strange mental place brought Liam no peace whatsoever. He felt threatened by it, not calmed.

"We need to talk," Kohler said.

Liam's first instinct was to deny him. How could he trust someone as wildly unpredictable as Max Kohler? He was a murderer, a man who'd made this same offer at the P&L Building and then nearly killed Liam as he tried to escape. Yet Liam paused. For all his unpredictability, Kohler possessed many dark secrets, some of which could help unravel the riddles around Leland De Pere and his meteoric rise to power.

He thought back to Pier 43 along Lake Michigan, how De Pere had clearly wanted Liam, had tried to capture him, while Kohler had cast an illusion to make him miss the train. Had Kohler disobeyed orders? Had he tried to make Liam miss so De Pere *wouldn't* catch him?

In the end, it was the look of fear in Kohler's one visible eye that convinced Liam. "Come with us," he said.

Kohler looked up at the hovering zeppelin, then shook his head. "I can't do that. Come with me and we'll talk. You can meet up with your friends later."

Liam knew the others were probably yelling at him to get in the gondola. The zeppelin was holding its position, but it wouldn't be long before the pilot ascended. Liam had only moments to make his decision. He was tempted to descend the ladder, to listen to what Kohler had to say.

The window beside Kohler suddenly shattered in an explosion of glass, light, and sound. Kohler reeled from it, and the world returned to normal.

The zeppelin's engines roared. Bailey, crouched on the opposite roof, was sighting along her sniper rifle at Kohler. Clay was shouting down from the gondola, "Climb, you stupid motherfucker!"

Liam did, and reached the gondola's interior. As Clay reeled the rope ladder in, Liam stared down. Kohler stared back, the strange, sizzling device held loosely in his hands. Then the gondola door was sliding shut, and the zeppelin was speeding away over the needle-like tips of the city's tallest towers.

THIRTY-TWO

S everal hours after their escape from LuxCorp, Liam sat in the *Eisvögel*'s main cabin, alone. After a brief rendezvous to pick up Bailey, they'd headed south, away from Novo Solis, toward the floating Uprising base known as the Nest. Grace and Morgan were asleep in two of the zeppelin's four passenger cabins. Dakota, still unconscious from Morgan's striking her, lay in the third. Bailey was checking in on her from time to time, but was largely focused on attending to Clay's medical needs in the last of the cabins.

Liam was tired, too—exhausted, in fact—but he hadn't been able to sleep. He was too worried over Morgan's health. The scourge strain had taken hold of him. It was *changing* him, and if Stasa didn't find a way to slow the development of the bacteria, Morgan would eventually succumb to it.

There was more to worry about besides. Alastair was currently hanging in a cradle in the cargo bay, recharging his power cells. Liam had finally had a chance to give him a good once-over in hopes of identifying the source of his strange awakenings, but the diagnostics had all come back normal. It was good news in a way, but disconcerting at the same time. Would Alastair get better on his own? Would he get worse?

More than once, Liam found himself pushing himself off his seat and heading to the cargo bay to check on him. Each time he did, he found Alastair hanging from his cradle, his blue lights blinking slowly on and off. Knowing he was becoming obsessive about it, he headed to the cockpit instead. Their pilot, Trixie, was sitting at the zeppelin's controls, her curly red hair wild and windblown. The *Eisvögel* was seven thousand feet and climbing, the way ahead clear and blue.

"Are we close?" Liam asked.

Trixie glanced back with a dimpled smile, then replied in her Southern drawl, "Sure are, sugar." She pointed through the window, straight ahead. "There it is, you see it?"

For several long seconds, Liam saw nothing. But then he caught glimpses of curving lines and rounded surfaces. As the *Eisvögel* continued its climb, the upper half of a veritable floating village was revealed. The rounded surfaces became a vast ring of helium balloons, each as large as a zeppelin's envelope. Suspended in the center of the ring, between the balloons, was a massive, metal structure, a skeleton housing dozens of gleaming metal structures arrayed in a three-dimensional pattern.

"Good God," Liam said, taking it all in.

Trixie laughed. "It's quite a sight, isn't it?"

It was, indeed. Liam could hardly take his eyes off of it.

The majority of the gleaming structures were rectangular in shape and looked suspiciously like repurposed rail cars. Others were considerably smaller; a few were quite large. Bailey had briefed him earlier, so he knew they were the domiciles, research facilities, and monitoring bays that comprised the Nest, but her description had done little to prepare him for the sight of the byzantine complex floating in the deep blue sky ahead of him. Connecting various structures were massive, corrugated tubes, each as big as a culvert pipe. The tubes were corridors, allowing movement between the structures, and for electricity, pneumatics, and plumbing to be distributed throughout the Nest. From the balloons to the structures to the landing pads on top, the Nest looked mismatched, as if it had grown piecemeal over time.

"How is it we can see it, though?" Liam asked.

"What's that, doll?" Two of the Nest's three landing pads were currently occupied by other zeppelins. Trixie, while flipping several switches, was steering them toward the third, where a landing marshal was guiding the *Eisvögel* in with precise swipes of two bright orange flags.

"I mean, what good does camouflaging the lower parts do if it can be spotted from above?" The Nest might have been outfitted with the same wonder material as the *Eisvögel*, but enemy zeppelins or planes would still be able to spot it if they flew high enough.

"Oh, the entire thing can be hidden"—using one hand, Trixie pulled two levers simultaneously, slowing the engines—"but it sucks a lot of juice, so they keep the top half off most times to save energy." She flashed a smile. "Don't worry. They have spotters combing the skies day and night. They'll switch it on if need be."

The Nest loomed ever larger, making it clear just how enormous the structure was.

"How many people are *on* the thing?"

"Two hundred if we're packed to the gills," Trixie said, "but it's a rare day that the Nest sees more than eighty."

She landed the *Eisvögel* with the lightest of touches. Clamps affixed to the gondola's undercarriage. The sound of it reverberated through the cockpit. Trixie stood, then stopped and smiled. "Believe me," she said while giving the full length of him a good, long look, "I'd love to stay and chat, but I need to let everyone out."

"Oh, sorry." Liam stepped out of her way.

"Maybe later?"

Liam felt his cheeks go warm.

She laughed as she brushed past him to enter the small compartment between the passenger cabins and the cockpit. After pulling the lever on the door, she opened it and lowered the folding stairs onto the platform. She extended an arm to the doorway as a rush of chill air swept in. "After you."

Liam shook his head. "Morgan first."

Her quick and ready smile faded to a look of tenderness. "It's nice the way you take care of him, your friend."

"I'd go to hell and back for him."

"Why, if you don't mind my asking?"

Liam shrugged. "Because I wasn't quite right when I came back from the war. Morgan cared for me when everyone else was ready to write off a surly, reclusive war vet."

Trixie's look turned serious, almost wistful. "I hope the docs can save him."

"Me too."

Dakota was borne out on a stretcher. Liam, meanwhile, collected Morgan, helped him down the stairs, and led him into the Nest proper. Stasa, looking more than a bit careworn, was waiting in the receiving bay with a gurney. With Liam keeping pace, Stasa whisked Morgan along several tight hallways to a room filled with banks of monitoring equipment. Merely being in that sort of environment, far away from Novo Solis, sent waves of relief running through Liam.

Stasa caught his look. "You should be prepared," he said in a low voice while a heavyset nurse prepped Morgan. "Morgan's in a bad way. We have every hope of developing an anti-serum, but it will take time."

The implication was that the anti-serum might not arrive in time to help Morgan. Every day that passed would see him succumb further and further to the scourge strain. The same was true of Dakota, and she was further along than Morgan. She might begin conversing with De Pere, or the other scourges, or whatever it was they'd all sensed in LuxCorp, and if *that* happened, who knew what would come next? It was possible the Cabal would learn of their location through the psychic conduit.

Though Liam was terrified by all of this, he'd known it from the start. He patted Stasa's arm. "I know you'll do your best."

The hours passed by slowly after that. Liam was debriefed by a dozen different Uprising members, men and women who wanted to know about LuxCorp, or the conditions under which Morgan and Dakota had been found, or Kohler and the strange weapon he'd been holding.

When the debriefings were done, they assigned him a small cabin. He was dead tired and fell asleep as soon as his head hit the pillow. When he woke, it was night. There were few enough portholes shedding light inside the Nest, but they'd lowered the lights to mimic the feeling of dusk.

Part of Liam wanted to go see Grace, who was staying a few doors down. He'd like nothing more than to hold her like he had in the furniture showroom, but instead he walked past her room and made his way to the medical wing. As wild as it had been for him over the past many hours, it would have been worse for Morgan.

The same nurse as before was stationed at a desk outside his room, which was visible through a large glass window. Inside, Morgan was sleeping.

"Did Stasa find anything?" Liam asked her.

"We've taken blood samples. Stasa's analyzing them." She waved to the door behind her, which led to Stasa's lab. "You want to talk to him?"

"No." Liam jutted his chin toward Morgan in the adjoining room. "Is it okay if I sit with him?"

The nurse smiled. "Certainly," she said, and buzzed him in.

As Liam pulled up a chair and sat, Morgan's eyes flickered open. He gasped, stared all around with a fearful expression, then slowly relaxed. After several moments in silence, he said, "It's nice to see a friendly face."

Liam's gut twisted at the sound of his words—they'd come out a bit slurred, as if his tongue were beginning to change. And maybe it was the low lighting, but the veins on his cheeks seemed more pronounced, and his irises seemed darker. "How are you feeling?"

Morgan shrugged. "Not bad." He glanced up at the bags of fluid hanging from the corner of his bed. "They're giving me the good stuff." He paused, frowning. "Look, I need to ask a favor."

"Of course. Anything."

"I need to get word to mom and dad. I want them to know I'm okay."

Morgan was certainly *not* okay, but that hardly mattered. "Done," Liam said. "I'll arrange for a telegram to be sent in the morning."

Morgan smiled fleetingly. "Thanks, pal."

"Sure thing." Liam leaned deeper in his chair, crossed one leg over the other. "So how much do you remember since Dr. Ramachandra's office?"

"Not much. I was drugged most of the time; to keep me docile, I suppose." Morgan's eyes searched the ceiling. "I remember climbing out of the rumble seat of the Model A. I remember firing the grenade at the wallbuster. I remember running, like you told me, as Kohler was headed toward you. Then I got dizzy and fell. Some people took me. They injected me with something. The next thing I remember, I was in a hospital room with no windows. People came and went. No one would answer my questions. Not that I could talk very often. Whenever I started asking too many questions, they gave me another shot, and I went woozy again."

"Did you overhear anything? Did they talk about what they meant to do with you?"

Morgan shook his head. "They only ever talked about my condition. I got the impression it was on purpose, like they never talked about anything more if I was in earshot."

"Were there others like you and Dakota there?"

"No. There was only ever the two of us." Morgan considered a moment. "But this I *do* remember. They said we were rare. One in a million. After the windowless room, I recall bits and pieces about the flashtrain." He smiled. "I remember staring up at you after you cut a hole in the roof."

"Alastair did that."

"You know what I mean. Then a long train ride. And being taken to the room where you found me."

Liam thought back to their harrowing escape from LuxCorp. "Just before Dakota attacked me, you were both captivated by something in the Pinnacle. What did you see?"

"I didn't *see* anything." Morgan paused, swallowing hard. "You know that feeling you get when you're alone in a forest, and you feel like someone's watching you?"

"Sure."

"It was like that, but ten times worse. A hundred. It felt oppressive. Hungry, like it wanted to devour me and Dakota. Part of me felt like it already had."

"Did it speak to you?"

"Not speak, exactly. It was weird. It felt like it wanted me to join it, for *my* sake as much as its own. But at the same time, there was terror riding just below the surface, as if failure would mean our collective destruction." He shrugged. "I suspect Dakota felt it more strongly than I did."

"Yeah." Liam touched the back of his neck, which still felt numb. "Thanks for that, by the way."

"You kidding me?" A bit of the old Morgan returned as he laughed. His eyes crinkling, he looked more than a little like his mother. "I can never thank you enough for coming for me."

"Well, we're not out of the woods yet."

Morgan's look became haunted, so much so that Liam felt like he'd erred by bringing up how much danger they were still in. "Can I share a secret with you?" Morgan asked after a time.

"Of course."

"In the room I was in. You came to me several times. You asked me about the Uprising, what I knew of it, who was in it."

Liam was confused at first, but understanding soon dawned.

"It was Kohler," Morgan went on, confirming Liam's suspicions. "He was fishing for information, information I thankfully didn't have." As a pneumatic hiss of some sort came through the walls, a common occurrence in the Nest, tears gathered in Morgan's eyes. "Part of me wonders if this is all just another attempt. Part of me wonders if you're Kohler."

"I'm not."

"But how do I *know*?"

Liam stood there, dumbfounded. How *could* he convince Morgan of the truth? "I kissed your sister," he finally blurted.

"What?"

"You remember when we were fifteen and I said I'd never kissed a girl before? I mean, besides my mother and Nana?"

"Sort of."

"Well, Audrey heard us talking, and a few days later she called me into her room when I was on my way up to get you. She asked if I wanted to kiss her, just to get it over with." Liam shrugged, feeling the perfect idiot. "So I did. It was wet and warm and the most wonderful thing I'd ever experienced. You walked in on us. I thought for sure you'd guessed because I felt my face turning beet red. I stood there, silent as a lamb, but Audrey jumped in and said she'd told me off for calling Lily a little girl to her face and that it had embarrassed her. You believed her, and I was so relieved. I felt like I'd been caught stealing a sip of whiskey from your da's liquor cabinet."

Morgan's bloodshot eyes had gone distant, then they lit up. "We went fishing that day."

Liam nodded.

"You hardly said a word the whole time. You just had that stupid grin on your face."

"I told you it was because my grandmother had given me money for a movie."

Morgan's eyes went wide with shock. "You never went?"

Liam had told him it was for Charlie Chaplin's latest. "Nope."

"But you went on and on about it the next day. You told me all the details, and they were right."

Liam grinned. "Audrey had seen it. She filled me in after we kissed again."

"Thief!" Morgan cried, shaking a finger at Liam. "Rapscallion of the highest order! Stealer of my sister's virtue!"

"I never stole her virtue," Liam said. "Only a few kisses."

Morgan's eyes narrowed, but he was smiling at the same time. "How many times?"

"We did it on and off for another month."

"Why did you stop?"

"She found a boyfriend."

"Lance," they said together.

"You must have been heartbroken," Morgan said with a sly smile.

Liam shrugged. "I was actually. Audrey was my first true love."

"And I never knew it."

Liam winked at him. "I'm good with secrets when I want to be."

Morgan shook his head, as if he couldn't believe it all. His eyes were distant again, but now his look turned wistful.

"You should get some sleep," Liam said.

"You should too."

As Liam nodded and headed for the door, Morgan called, "Liam?"

Liam stopped, the door halfway open. "Yeah?"

"Thanks again."

The words had come out strangely, sounding very *unlike* Morgan, and suddenly all thoughts of Audrey vanished. "You're in safe hands, Morgan."

"I know."

With that Liam left, closing the door behind him with a soft click.

THIRTY-THREE

The Nest was a hive of activity in the days that followed. Zeppelins came and went at all hours. Members of the Uprising arrived, others departed. Grace remained on the station, but was so busy she had no time to speak with Liam. And Liam, for his part, didn't try to force it. The few times he saw her, she looked exhausted—the last thing she needed was him taking up more of her time.

Stasa and his team focused much of their efforts on Morgan and Dakota, but also Ruby, the psi they'd rescued from the P&L building, and Alan, the thrall victim from the domes.

"Where's William?" Liam asked one day, realizing he hadn't seen Alan's son.

He and Stasa were sitting at a tiny table in the canteen, each of them having just finished a spectacularly salty helping of biscuits and gravy. The floor beneath them rocked slightly, the result of high winds buffeting the Nest while the engines held them in place over the landscape, somewhere above Virginia.

Several seconds passed before Stasa replied, "I'm afraid William is dead."

The news hit Liam like a load of bricks. He'd assumed William had remained at the domes for safety's sake. "How? *When?*"

"Shortly after your trip to Novo Solis, he suffered a severe heart attack. The medical team did their best to revive him, but he died a day later."

Liam couldn't help but think of William, how he'd beat his own father bloody after Liam had interrupted the experiment. "Did it have anything to do with my visit to the domes?"

Stasa, seemingly distracted, refocused on Liam. "What?"

"Was it because I interrupted the experiment?"

"No, Liam." Stasa looked wretched, worse than Liam had ever seen him. "If anything, *I'm* the one to blame. The stresses of our experiments were clearly building within him without my realizing it."

"I'm so sorry, Stasa. And poor Alan. Does he know?"

"An equally tragic tale. We informed Alan about William's death, of course, but now he says he never had a son." Stasa tapped the side of his coffee cup absently. "Deep down, I think he knows the truth. It's just his way of coping with his son's death, a story he's made real." After a deep breath, he stood and squeezed Liam's shoulder. "I'd better get back to Morgan."

"Of course."

As the days went on, Liam held onto his primary hope—that Morgan might still be cured—like a lifeline. Every evening, he checked in with Stasa to see what progress he and his team had made, and each time, Stasa told him to temper his expectations. "We've isolated the scourge strain in Morgan and Dakota. We're running cultures. Soon we'll be able to run a few experiments. We're making progress. *Good* progress. The best thing you can do is to focus on something else."

Knowing he was right, Liam threw himself into learning how to cast better illusions. The following day, he recruited Clay and Bailey to help him. They met on one of the landing pads under a bright sun. It was chilly, the Nest maintaining such a high altitude, but the sky was clear save for a scattering of white, tufted clouds in the distance, and the sun shed a bit of warmth.

"For now," Liam said, "I just want to create something and have you tell me how accurate it is, how solid."

Bailey nodded with an encouraging smile.

Clay, meanwhile, shrugged. "Why not? Got nothing better to do."

After a deep breath, Liam concentrated and summoned a simulacrum of Alastair climbing up from the bowels of the Nest. He made the fake mechanika walk easily, whirring sounds and all, until he came to a stop between the three of them.

Clay devolved into a sudden coughing fit as he looked the fake Alastair up and down. "Not bad," he said between coughs. "Can barely see the seams."

For a time, Bailey watched *Clay* more than the illusion, but when Clay's coughing finally subsided, she refocused her attention. "Make him talk."

"What shall I say, Miss Bailey?" said the illusory Alastair, perfectly capturing the pitch of his tinny speaker.

With the wind tugging at Bailey's dark hair, she walked around the illusory Alastair, peered into his glowing blue eyes. "Not bad at all," she said with a raise of her eyebrows.

It was then that Liam spotted the real Alastair wandering along the far side of the Nest. He was ambling over a catwalk suspended between the two other landing pads, staring down as if nervous of falling.

"Alastair!" Liam called.

Rarely did Alastair acted surprised in any way, but he did then. His frame jittered. He turned and looked about, then fixed his blue-eyed gaze on Liam.

"Come join us!" Bailey shouted.

Alastair paused, as if nervous he would be intruding, but then he navigated the set of catwalks and walkways required to reach their platform. When he arrived, he stared at the illusory Alastair for a good long while. "I must say, it's very good, sir."

He'd hardly said the words when the fake Alastair suddenly disappeared. Liam felt it in his gut, like an especially strong hunger pang. The real Alastair's presence, Liam understood, had created doubt in everyone, including Liam himself, which made it that much more difficult to maintain the illusion.

"Well, that's unfortunate," Alastair said, staring at the place where the other Alastair had been standing. When no one responded, he looked about. "Isn't it?"

"Yes, Alastair, it is," Liam said with a soft chuckle.

Taking a deep breath, he slipped into the half-dream state and tried again. After a few moments, they heard the sound of clanking on the metal stairs, and a new, fake Alastair rose up from the bowels of the Nest. He strode across the platform and stopped near the real Alastair.

It was a good test, this particular illusion. On the one hand, it was a relatively simple illusion. They all knew what Alastair looked like. They *expected* him to act a certain way. Their own memories of him fueled Liam's efforts, making the final result easier for their minds to accept. On the other hand, it was challenging because everyone *knew* it was an illusion.

"Impressive!" This came from Grace, who was approaching over a railed walkway from a neighboring platform. She wore tawny pants and the leather airman's jacket she'd worn when she'd rescued him from the paddy wagon. "Now pass control of the illusion to Bailey."

Liam shook his head, confused. "But she's not an illusionist."

"I don't need to be." Bailey's tone made it clear she'd done this sort of experiment before. "You've already created it. I'm only carrying it forward."

Like setting a paper boat on water, he released the illusion. A moment later, the fake Alastair went back down the stairs.

"Now transfer it to Clay," Grace said.

Liam did, and the fake Alastair climbed back and retook his place in their circle.

"Very good," Grace said. "Now, the most difficult of all, try transferring it to Alastair."

Liam tried, but the moment he did, the fake Alastair disappeared. He tried again and again, summoning the simulacrum, then handing it over to Alastair, but each time he did, the illusion vanished.

"Are you *trying* to stop it?" Liam asked him.

"Oh, *no*, sir." He sounded surprised at the accusation.

"Can you feel it happening? The illusion disappearing?"

Alastair blinked, as if he couldn't quite piece together what was going wrong. "Not really, sir, no. It's there one moment and then it's just gone."

"Maybe he can't," Clay said.

It was something Liam had been thinking but hadn't wanted to voice. It was clear that whatever had happened to Alastair after the war, whatever process the Cabal had put him through to harvest his brain and turn him into a mechanika, had robbed him of some higher-level abilities. This could be one of them.

Alastair stared at Clay as if digesting what he'd just said, then his head swiveled toward the horizon. He looked shell-shocked, a soldier who'd become numb to the bombardment happening all around him.

"I'm sorry, Alastair," Liam said.

"It's all right, sir. I can still help where I can."

Liam paused. "You don't *have* to help, you know. You're your own person now."

Alastair shrugged his mechanikal shoulders. "Thank you, sir, but I'm happy where I am."

Liam was half-tempted to try and talk him out of it, but what right did he have to do that? If Alastair was content, why should Liam try to dissuade him?

When they broke a short while later, Grace asked Liam to remain while the others went below. The wind tugging at her golden hair, she said, "I've been wondering if you've had any more memories from the war."

Things had been so crazy, he hadn't had a chance to tell her about his memory of talking with then-Major De Pere during the war, and seeing Colette's break-up with Sergio. He did so, giving her the broad brushstrokes.

"It's curious," she said when he was done, "your memories and Colette's returning in sequence as they are."

"I've thought about that too." He shrugged. "The first memory, the one of Kohler tricking me into shooting that soldier, was powerful. Maybe my subconscious is just moving naturally to the memories that followed."

"Could be," she said as she brushed the bangs from her eyes. "See if you can't lean into it. Follow the trail of breadcrumbs."

"I will," Liam said, "because it feels like there's something important just ahead, something that flipped the power dynamic."

"I don't disagree, but what do you mean specifically?"

"Well, during the war, De Pere was only a *part* of Project Echo. It was an important part, to be sure, but he wasn't the primary decision-maker then. All the really important decisions were coming from President Nolan, and from Colette herself through her back-channel to Nolan. So how did

De Pere wind up at the center of things? And why did he *want* to be in the first place?"

"All very good questions," Grace said.

Standing there, staring at the various compartments that made up the Nest, Liam felt the weight of his responsibilities bearing down on him. "I feel terrible I can't remember more, faster. I feel like I'm letting everyone down."

"Believe me, I understand the sentiment, but don't feel badly about not making more progress. Sometimes it's a matter of not overthinking and letting the mind do what it wants."

Liam nodded. "Okay, I'll try."

A sly smile broke over Grace's face. "I just told you to *not* try."

"I'll try that too," he said with a wink.

Grace laughed.

THIRTY-FOUR

Late that night, Liam went to visit Morgan before going to bed. He expected to see the nurse in the observation area outside his room, but found Stasa sitting in her place. On the desk before him was a nearly empty bottle of vodka and a glass, half full.

With a hint of a slur, and his Hungarian accent noticeably stronger than normal, Stasa said, "I gave Theresa the night off."

He looked terrible, with deep bags under his eyes, his movements listless. He hadn't shaved in days, creating a peculiar mismatch between the heavy stubble along his cheeks and his longer beard and mustache.

"Did it ever occur to you," Liam said as he pulled up a chair, "that you're working too hard?"

"I've no idea what you're talking about."

"You need *rest*, Stasa."

Stasa shoved the bottle toward Liam and lifted his glass. "That's what the vodka is for."

"I mean *proper* rest. Vodka's no replacement for sleep. One step back to take two steps forward, as my Nana used to say."

Stasa nodded ponderously, as if his head suddenly weighed a ton. "Doctor's orders?"

"Doctor's orders."

"Then I'll do so"—he lifted his glass and tipped his head toward the bottle—"but have a drink with me first."

Liam nearly denied him, but then decided he could use a drink himself. He took up the bottle and clinked it against Stasa's glass. They took a swig together, and Liam bared his teeth. The liquor was harsh, all green moss and white pepper.

"We've made some progress," Stasa said while staring through the glass panel at Morgan, "but it's too little, too late."

"I wish there was more I could do to help."

"Grace is helping. But even so . . ." His gaze grew more haunted by the moment. "It's on me. It's all on me."

"Talking sometimes helps."

Stasa blinked, drawing his attention back to the small office. "Hmm?"

"Do you want to talk about it?"

Long seconds passed. Stasa shook his head, but then said, "I miss my old life, Liam."

"It must have been hard, leaving it all behind."

Stasa stared into his glass, lost in thought, then took another swallow. "Can I share a secret with you?"

"Of course."

"Before I met Grace, I was on top of the world."

"I can imagine."

"No, you can't. I came from nothing. My three sisters were killed by typhus in the slums of Budapest. Two years later, my mother was shot for being a Jew, my father for trying to defend her. By the grace of God, I was sent to America by the very envoy who witnessed their deaths. I attended school in New York. I worked my way through three college degrees in Boston. I came to Chicago and built an *empire*."

"And despite all that, you agreed to join the Uprising. It was a selfless act, a thing you should be proud of."

"*Proud?*" Stasa frowned, then laughed bitterly. "Let me tell you something, Liam." He waved his glass, spilling vodka in the process. "When Grace asked me to join the Uprising, I agreed, but it wasn't for *selfless reasons*. I joined because I recognized that De Pere threatened everything I'd built. I saw my empire crumbling before my very eyes." He swallowed the last of his drink, set the glass down with a sharp clack. "I miss steak au poivre. I miss fine cigars." He waved to the bottle in front of Liam. "I miss *proper* vodka."

"That's normal. It's the life you were used to. Anyone would miss it."

"It's *twisted*, is what it is."

Stasa stared at Liam hard, as if daring him to convince him otherwise.

Liam wasn't sure what to say, but then he was reminded of another time, another place. "You mind if I share a secret with you as well?"

Stasa's gaze was sad, his silence assent.

"During the war, I was on leave with the Henchmen in Chicago. Nick Crawford had been down for days. Silent and morose. From our sessions with the Henchman serum, we knew something was up. I found him at Union Station with a ticket to St. Louis in his hand. He said he wanted to visit his family, just for a day, but I could tell it went well beyond that. He wanted out. He was ready to leave everything behind. It'd all become too much for him."

"I don't see what that has to do with me," Stasa said.

"Eventually, I managed to talk Nick into returning with us to Milwaukee after leave, but he fell into a deeper depression than before. He was conflicted, wracked with guilt over backing down on his plans, wracked with guilt he'd ever had thoughts of leaving in the first place. He felt like he'd betrayed both his family *and* the Henchmen. In our next session together, all of us, even Kohler, asked him to tell us about it, his family, his city. And he did. He told us about his parents, about Bailey and how the two of them used to get into trouble on the streets of St. Louis. We heard his words, of course, but we *felt* it, too."

"Liam—" Stasa began.

But Liam cut him off. "I've watched you with William and Alan. I've watched you with Ruby. I've watched you with Dakota and Morgan. And what I see is a man who *cares* about those in his charge." He paused, letting the words sink in. "We are all more than one thing, Stasa. You can miss your old life and still be invested in your new one."

"But I feel like I'll never see the old days again."

"Maybe you won't. Times change. People change. We lose friends and family. We make new ones along the way." Liam had said the words for Stasa, but he couldn't help think of Grace, of Bailey, of Stasa himself, all of whom he'd grown closer to since the wild events at the flashtrain ceremony. "In the pain of grief, of our yearning, we can close ourselves off, blinding ourselves to that which lies before us. Sometimes we don't recognize the value of our new relationships." Liam reached out and squeezed Stasa's hand. "Not until we reach out and embrace them."

For a long while, the two of them were silent. Then Stasa nodded sharply. "Thank you for that, Liam."

"You're welcome."

Suddenly, Stasa sat bolt upright.

"What is it?" Liam asked.

Stasa's gaze was restless. "Reach out . . ." His eyes went wide as saucers. "Embrace them . . ." He jolted to his feet, gripped Liam's head with both hands, and kissed his forehead with a long, loud smack. "You're brilliant, Liam, you know that?"

Before Liam could say another word, he was gone from the office, leaving Liam in complete bewilderment.

The following morning, Liam went to the labs to check on Stasa, but the nurse, Theresa, forestalled him. "He asked for isolation today."

Confused but hopeful, Liam headed to the landing platforms instead to continue practicing illusions. The air was warm, even as high up as they were. Clay and Bailey were on their way. He hadn't been able to find Alastair, but in a stroke of good luck, he was already on the platform. Like the day before, he was standing on a catwalk, and this time, he was leaning over the railing, staring straight down.

"Is everything all right?" Liam asked.

He was growing more and more concerned with Alastair's behavior. His diagnostics had turned out fine, but his incapacitation at the hands of officers Carolan and Holohan had changed him in some fundamental way, and not for the better.

Alastair turned to face Liam, but not without one last glance down toward the ground. "I suppose I'm a bit homesick, sir. I miss the Aysanas."

Before Liam could reply, Grace climbed up the nearby stairs and onto the platform, with Clay and Bailey in tow.

"Want to try something new?" Grace asked.

Vowing to talk to Alastair more about it later, Liam nodded. "Why not?"

She motioned them all into a rough circle. "Learning to cast illusions is only half the battle," she said. "We're dealing with men like Kohler and De Pere, who will work to strip them away, perhaps the moment they're cast. You need to learn how to defeat that."

"Okay," Liam said. "How?"

"Try to cast an illusion of Alastair again. Clay is going to try to dispel it. Your goal is to prevent him from doing so."

Clay's smile was ear to ear. "Gotta warn you. I'm good."

Liam smiled as well. It felt like their days in the Devil's Henchmen, when Liam, Clay, and the others would compete. Who could run the fastest. Who could jump the highest in their hopper armor. Who was most accurate with rifle or grenade launcher.

"Ready?" Liam asked.

"Wrong question," Clay said. "The question is whether *you're* ready, you poor fucking sod." He'd no sooner said the words than he devolved into a short coughing fit. Bailey looked ready to go to him, but stopped when Clay raised a hand to her and depressed a plunger on his metal sleeve.

"You all right?" Liam asked.

Clay's fit slowly subsided. "Stop trying to distract me," he said between breaths.

Knowing that to challenge Clay now, in front of the others, would only embarrass him, Liam suppressed his concern and summoned the illusory Alastair into being. He'd no sooner appeared, however, then he was gone again. He tried again, and the illusory Alastair popped out of existence a few seconds later. Clay smirked. Bailey chuckled. The real Alastair blinked his luminescent eyes.

From that point forward, Liam couldn't so much as summon Alastair into being, not even for a second.

"Try something simpler," Grace said.

Liam, frustrated, nodded and took a deep breath. He pulled a folding knife from his pocket instead—another illusion, but one that might easily be real. It remained for several seconds as Liam fought Clay's attempts to dispel it. He could feel Clay tugging at the edges. As fast as Liam moved to stop him, Clay would dart in from another direction. The more of it that unraveled, the harder it was for Liam to maintain the illusion. Or rather, the harder it was for the others to *believe* it was real. The moment they sensed something awry, their minds read it as *wrong*, and the illusion ceased to be.

Over and over again Liam tried, summoning a buffalo nickel he withdrew from his pocket, then an illusion of the billfold that actually *was* in his pocket, a thing he hoped would allow him to make it more real. He even tried pulling a thread from the cuff of Clay's sleeve, pretending he'd yanked it free. It did no more than flutter in the wind before it frayed and was gone. In hopes of throwing Clay off, he summoned an emerald green parakeet. He got so far as having it land on his outstretched finger before it faded and was gone. No matter what he tried, Clay tore his illusions apart, and he only seemed to become more adept at it with each try.

"You're anticipating me," Liam said, completely frustrated by then. "It's making it easier for you."

"Sure I am," said Clay. "You don't think Kohler is going to anticipate your illusions? De Pere?"

"Let's try the reverse," Grace said. "Try to dispel *my* illusions."

Things grew even worse from there. Grace summoned the same green parakeet. Perched on her finger, she flung it into the air. It flew to Bailey, then landed on Alastair's shoulder. With a flutter, it arced its way to Clay's outstretched mechanikal finger. And all the while, Liam tried to dispel it, with no success. Suddenly it flew straight toward Liam and struck him on the forehead, vanishing in a burst of feathers. That Bailey and Clay began laughing only deepened the sting caused by the bird's impact.

He felt like an utter failure. "You're too good, Grace."

"It'll come." Grace stepped forward and touched a fingertip to his forehead and the pain suddenly vanished. "But you have to understand, Kohler is as good as I am, and De Pere is better than us all. You have to be ready."

Liam was struck by Grace's inner strength, her determination, the way she willed the Uprising to achieve its goals.

"What?" Grace asked.

He realized the silence had gone on for too long. "You're a good person, Grace."

Her faint smile faded, as if she were disappointed in his words. He was about to apologize when Stasa climbed the stairs to the platform. He was disheveled. He looked more tired than when Liam had spoken with him the previous night. More worrisome was the severe look on his face. "You all better come with me."

"What is it?" Grace asked.

"We've found something." He shook his head. "Just come with me, quickly."

THIRTY-FIVE

"Sir, my power cells are a bit low," Alastair said as Liam and the others headed down into the Nest. "I'd better go recharge."

Liam nodded, vowing to check on him as soon as possible, then followed the others along the maze of hallways, stairwells, and compartments to reach Stasa's lab. They convened in a room one level above where Morgan and Dakota were being kept. Like the room at the domes, it was divided in two. In the near side, a bank of electrical switches and readouts was situated below a wide pane of glass. Beyond the pane of glass was a sterile white environment with a technician name Jonathan, who wore blue scrubs and a mask.

Liam had taken a few meals with Jonathan. He had curly, sandy-brown hair that simply refused to be contained by his cap. He'd been with the Uprising about a year and was fiercely loyal to it, having joined after his daughter was killed in a Cabal raid.

In the compartment with Jonathan were a man and a woman. Both were strapped into stout metal chairs, which in turn were bolted to the floor. Although their identities were obscured by bulky helmets that covered half their faces, Liam soon recognized them. The woman's dark skin tone and the deep blue veins standing out along her neck identified her as Dakota, and the man, all raw bones and hollow cheeks, was clearly Alan. From the tops of their helmets, cables stretched along the floor and into the wall adjoining the instrument panel Stasa was sitting behind.

"Our conversation last night," Stasa said to Liam, "led to a revelation. It made me realize I needed to study the scourges and thralls, not *individually,* but as a connected whole. I needed to examine them *while* their respective bacterial strains were excited. Their helmets are currently blocking their ability to communicate with one another, but see what happens when we remove them."

When Stasa nodded, Jonathan removed each of their helmets in turn and hung them from hooks affixed to the backs of the chairs. As in the domes, Alan's eyes were listless, but the longer he stared at Dakota, the more riveted he became.

"Dakota has been given a sedative which prevents her from unleashing the attack you experienced at LuxCorp, but Alan is still able to sense the scourge strain within her."

Liam's gut churned just to look at them: Dakota staring with a predatory expression, Alan looking as though he wanted to prostrate himself before her. Liam could *feel* it, as well. Emanating from Alan was a sense of wonder that bordered on reverence, and it was directed at Dakota.

Dakota smiled, a grisly thing, and the feeling of reverence coming from Alan intensified. The people and the room around Liam seemed to melt away. All that was left was a feeling, not just of *reverence*, but of *divinity*. Alan stared into the pits of Dakota's eyes as if waiting for a command, any command, that he might obey. She had become like unto a goddess; and he her most devout worshipper.

Dakota didn't seem to revel in the adoration so much as expect it, which made it all the more chilling when she turned toward the windows and stared at Liam. It was unnerving: those jet black eyes, the reddened skin around them, the riverland of stark blue veins over her face and neck.

"Can they see us?" Liam asked.

"As in the domes, the glass is mirrored on the opposite side," Stasa said, "but Dakota isn't using normal sight. She senses our thoughts, even though I've keyed the field running through the wall to prevent it."

Liam felt her hunger. She recognized she'd missed her opportunity to infect him in LuxCorp, and was counting the moments until she had another.

"You'll recall the project name from the documents we recovered," Stasa continued. "*Homo servientis.* We can see now its full scope. Thralls will become slaves, the scourges their masters, and the psis will carry commands over vast distances so that all can be controlled from some central point."

"From one *person*," Liam corrected,. "De Pere."

"Yes," Stasa said, "you're very likely right. And the scourges will be used to infect new victims as well. The three glands beneath their tongues are specialized: each contains one of the three strains so that any one scourge can transform an uninfected man, woman, or child into a thrall, a psi, or another scourge."

The ache inside Alan to please Dakota was growing, so much so that Liam felt it as well. Every moment that passed saw Liam pitying her less, venerating her more.

"Enough," he said.

Stasa raised a hand to Jonathan, who nodded and moved to Alan's chair. As he was reaching for the helmet behind it, Dakota yanked on the leather straps around her wrists with a wild fury. In moments, her wrists were raw, then they were bleeding. As Jonathan darted toward her, she yanked them both free. Though her ankles were still confined, she lunged and caught Jonathan by surprise.

Stasa pressed a different button and shouted into the receiver. "Emergency! Emergency!"

Only a few seconds passed between that cry and a pair of security guards rushing into the room, but by then Dakota had Jonathan on the floor, face down. Her mouth opened. Her long tongue extended. In a flash, the white barb pierced the back of Jonathan's neck. Unlike the time in LuxCorp, when Dakota still had some sense of her own humanity, it happened in the blink of an eye.

As the guards regained control over Dakota, it struck Liam just how far along the same transformation Morgan was. How far other scourges would be. Dakota had been tagged with a number: 0187. Morgan had been marked with 0227. It was clearly a sequence, the numbers indicative of how many scourge victims the Cabal had managed to infect and then gather in the course of their insidious project.

"How can De Pere do this?" he asked of no one in particular. "How can he *want* this to happen?"

Stasa, normally so unflappable, looked completely shaken. "That's the big question, isn't it?" he said. "The only question." In the other room, one guard led a struggling Dakota away while the other helped Jonathan to his feet. "Our own government is fostering the creation of a bacterial strain that, if released on the general public, will destroy us. It will destroy the world."

Beside Liam, Grace's head suddenly turned. "Oh, God," she said breathlessly.

A moment later, a klaxon started blaring. It sounded distant, but was soon picked up by others.

"What's happening?" Liam asked.

Clay's look turned grim. "It's the call to abandon ship."

There came the sound of heavy footfalls in the hallway outside. Three gray-uniformed guards suddenly burst into the room. The largest of them, a man built like a wallbuster, said, "Everyone to their stations. Quickly."

"What's *happening*?" Liam repeated.

"The Cabal found us," replied the massive guard. "Dozens of planes and airships are converging on the Nest." The man might have been big, but there was no small amount of fear in his eyes. The crew aboard the floating station had surely run drills against the threat of discovery, but reality was always different.

A woman's voice called over the loudspeakers. *"Station fragmentation in sixty seconds."*

Grace waved to Liam. "Come with me. We need to go to a different compartment."

"But Morgan's in this one."

"I know," she said while waving again, "but we can't afford the two of you being together."

"Fragmentation in fifty seconds."

"Go," Stasa said while giving Liam a gentle push toward Grace. "I'll be with Morgan. We'll make sure he's safe. There's a plan to regroup once we've landed."

The burly guard took Liam's arm. "Don't you worry," he said while gently but firmly leading him along the passageway behind Grace, "the seat we've got for you is comfy, I promise."

Liam wasn't going to be able to reason his way out of this—there simply wasn't time—so he cast an illusion. As he wrenched his arm free, he made the guard feel like he was continuing docilely. Effectively invisible, he doubled back and followed Stasa up a tight set of spiraling stairs. Stasa and his team of nurses and medical technicians joined up with another group, then passed through an airlock into an escape pod situated above the observation room they'd just left. Liam darted in just behind Stasa. Jonathan, the medical technician who'd been stung by Dakota, was the last to enter. Through his curly hair, Liam saw a bloody bandage taped to the back of his neck.

Jonathan closed and latched the door, while the others sat and strapped themselves into the fold-down emergency chairs built into the walls. By the time Jonathan sat as well, there were none left for Liam, so he did the best he could. He grabbed the round handle in the center of the hatch door and held tight while the voice over the loudspeakers began counting down.

"Fragmentation in fifteen seconds."

Liam wanted to ask if anyone had tended to Morgan, but of course he couldn't. He took solace in the fact that the operation was being run with clockwork efficiency—Morgan, Dakota, Ruby, and Alan would have been secured.

"Fragmentation in ten, nine, eight . . ."

Liam's grip on the door handle tightened. He bent his legs slightly. His jaw was clenched so tightly the muscles along the side of his face were starting to cramp.

The count reached zero.

A series of small explosions rocked the room. A pneumatic hiss followed. Gasps from the others accompanied the sensation of the floor dropping out from underneath them. Liam had felt the feeling of weightlessness often during the war but never while safe inside a massive structure like the Nest. His stomach felt like it was trying to force its way past his throat.

Light flooded the compartment through the porthole built into the door. A window in the ceiling, which Liam hadn't realized was there, showed a bright blue sky. It was clear the Nest still had its shimmering invisibility field active—the floating station was almost perfectly transparent from his vantage—which made him wonder: How had the Cabal identified the Nest's location?

He had no time to work it through. Other sections of the Nest were breaking away. Visible for a few seconds, they shimmered and winked out of existence. Through the window in the ceiling, he saw biplanes drift into view. Their guns blazed. Bullets tore into the balloons that kept the Nest buoyant. A fiery explosion rocked the center of the structure. A moment later, the entirety of the Nest—balloons, armature and all—became perfectly, brightly visible. What remained of the structure began to shatter, though by then only a handful of compartments had yet to detach.

A small explosion rocked the lab compartment as a bundle of silver cloth burst into the air above. With the sound of fluttering and a *whoomp*, the cloth expanded into three massive parachutes. A heartbeat later, their silvery-white cloth went invisible, and a view of the Nest and the unfolding battle returned.

From one of the few compartments still attached to the Nest, triplanes dropped like cormorants. Dogfights ensued. The Cabal's biplanes circled, dove, and looped as they struggled to gain the upper hand.

Suddenly, a bright fireball appeared in the center of the Nest. Everyone in the escape pod, including Liam, gasped at the sheer immensity of it. A resounding boom came a moment later, muffled but still loud. Several more compartments had just been breaking away—the last to leave, it looked like. The closest was caught in the explosion. It fell, tipping end over end, plummeting ever faster, its rescue parachutes never releasing, until finally it struck another compartment that had just released its own, silvery chutes.

Lost from view through the window above, Liam saw them through the hatch window beside him. They tumbled down together, ever faster. He prayed for either compartments' chutes to save them. When they didn't, he prayed Grace hadn't gone to either of them.

A moment later, a red-nosed biplane arced into view. Perhaps the pilot had seen the parachutes expand and had tracked their path downward. Or perhaps he had some sort of device that allowed him to see objects that were normally hidden by the cloaking tech. Whatever the case, the biplane was headed straight toward the lab.

Liam was just summoning an illusion to throw the pilot off their scent when the plane's forward-mounted guns opened fire. Bullets tore through the compartment. Holes stitched their way through the walls, sunlight suddenly appearing through each one. One bullet clipped Liam's arm. Liam gritted his teeth against the pain as a nurse, a young woman with thick eyebrows, took grazing shots across each leg. The technician next to her was ripped through the chest and neck. Shouts of surprise and fear and pain mixed with the rain of bullets as blood stained their blue scrubs.

The bullets ceased as the biplane's arc carried it away, but it brought no sense of relief—it wouldn't be long before it curved around and made another pass.

As Stasa reached to unhook himself to help the wounded, Liam heard a fluttering sound. Looking through the porthole above, he saw holes in the parachutes. One was shredded entirely. The invisibility effect had vanished, and the silver-white cloth could now be seen plainly, flapping madly with the speed of their descent. The other two, each with smaller tears in them, had managed to maintain their effect, but what did that matter? The lab was defenseless now, a sitting duck for the enemy planes.

The biplane, having flown far enough away, was finishing its curve, preparing another run. It leveled off, the pilot lining up his shot. Liam thought to cast an illusion, but the wound to his arm was throwing off his concentration. In fact, he became so distracted, the illusion that hid him from the others suddenly vanished as well.

Stasa, seeing him, looked incensed. "God *damn* you, Liam!"

"I'm sorry," Liam said halfheartedly, "but you're stuck with me now."

Before Stasa could reply, the enemy biplane opened fire. More bullets tore through the compartment. They stopped, however, when an Uprising triplane came streaking in from above, its twin guns spitting fire. It tore through the biplane's wings.

The biplane swerved, then tipped into an uncontrolled dive. Smoke issued from the engine as it corkscrewed down, faster and faster. The co-pilot at the rear leapt free, his parachute puffing outward. The other wasn't so lucky. The plane crashed into the rocky, forested landscape near the edge of a river and exploded in a roiling ball of fire and smoke.

The ground, meanwhile, continued to rise. "Brace yourselves!" Liam shouted, and held tight to the door.

He saw the tops of evergreens loom larger. He spotted the blue of a nearby river. There came the sound of scraping as they passed through the trees, then they struck ground, and the compartment tipped sideways. The sound of the impact was deafening. The compartment tipped and rolled until it struck something hard.

It was so violent, Liam lost his grip on the door. As he was thrown against the far wall, his head struck hard, and the compartment, the people within, and the light streaming in through the windows were lost to an all-consuming darkness.

THIRTY-SIX

During the war . . .

By the time the Devil's Henchmen returned from their leave in Chicago, Major De Pere had been summoned to Novo Solis personally to defend the use of the serum before Congress. It left them in a state of limbo, no one knowing when, or if, Project Echo would resume its missions. So the squad trained daily. They ran. They tackled obstacle courses. They logged hours of target practice, both in and out of their hopper exoskeletons.

Not Max Kohler, though. He'd moved to the officers' quarters, and more than once he'd been spotted heading into Colette's office in the medical wing. Liam wondered about that, a suspicion that only deepened when he saw how cold Colette was acting toward Kohler as the two of them left a staff meeting. If something was happening between them, they would both probably be particularly careful to hide it.

A week later, Liam was called to Colette's office to give a blood sample. She seemed preoccupied.

"Rumors are flying," Liam said, mostly as a way to break the ice, "saying the permanent solution is on permanent standby."

Apparently it was the wrong thing to say. Storm clouds passed over her face. "You don't know the half of it."

"Senator Vaughan?" Liam asked.

Vaughan had apparently started firing shots across President Nolan's bow, drumming up support to gain more control over what the Central Intelligence Corps was doing in the name of the country.

"And others," Colette replied, "putting their greasy mitts where they don't belong."

"They're what, trying to kill the project?"

"Not *kill* it." Colette wrapped the rubber tourniquet around his upper arm with a snap, then swabbed the inside of his elbow. "Vaughan just wants more of it under his control. He's giving hints he wants the entire project—research, training, and all—moved to West Virginia."

"Let me guess. President Nolan refuses to consider it." The President's idea of negotiating was to take more hostages than his opponents.

"That's right, and I can't say I disagree. If Vaughan gets his hooks into the project, he'll slow things down for years, lining his pockets all the while, despite what he might say about doing it to *honor both God and country*." She pulled Liam's arm into position, but held the needle's tip just short of his skin. After a pause, she stood up straight and looked him in the eyes. "You seem like an honest and forthright man, so I'll be honest and forthright with you."

"Okay," he said carefully, having no idea where she was headed.

"I didn't bring you in for a blood sample."

He stared down at the empty syringe perched over his arm. "Then why *did* you bring me in?"

"To ask if you'd consider taking the serum."

It took him a moment to understand. "The permanent one, you mean."

"Yes. It's ready now, and we're wasting time."

"So give it to Kohler."

"Kohler . . ." Colette's jaw worked back and forth. "Your mental makeup is more in line with what the project needs at this particular juncture."

The implications were already running through Liam's mind: what De Pere would say, what the Army would say, the sort of hot water President Nolan would land in were it discovered that a prominent scientist and a soldier in the Army's new psi-ops division had not only disobeyed protocol but also bypassed the strict process Congress had put in place for the serum's approval. It would look like Nolan himself had ordered it to get his pet project underway.

"I don't know, Colette. With De Pere in Novo Solis, defending us. If we were to go rogue . . ."

She was suddenly very focused on his arm. "You're right." She stuck him with the needle but uncharacteristically missed the vein and had to try again. "Of course you're right." She got it on the third try. She drew the plunger back, drawing his blood, but she was hardly paying any attention at all.

"If you don't mind my saying," Liam said gently, "I think you might need a break."

She blinked, met his gaze, then softened. The smile she put on was forced. "Right again." Pressing a cotton ball against the insertion point, she pulled the needle free. "You're on a real streak, Mulcahey." After setting it down on a metal tray, she faced him squarely. There were words on her lips, she looked intense, but then her face softened and she drew in a deep breath. "Would you like to have dinner with me?"

He blinked. His mouth worked, but no words came out. He was certain she'd been about to say something else.

Colette's eyes drifted to the tray, as if already looking for an excuse not to follow through on the offer. "You're probably busy. I know it's short notice."

"No, it's just . . . Sergio . . ."

"He and I broke things off in Chicago."

"Oh." Liam's heart flipped like a trapeze artist. "I'm sorry to hear that."

"Don't be. He asked me that night to marry him." Her gaze went distant. "Part of me wanted to accept."

"But?"

"Things weren't right between us, and likely never would be." She went to the log book she used to record everything and continued writing on a line she'd started when he arrived. "So are we on or not?"

"We're on."

She smiled while continuing to write. "Good."

Dinner was coq au vin, and it was delicious. "My father taught me how to make it," Colette said. "It's one of three dishes I know how to make well."

They sat in her tiny dining room, which was attached to the kitchen. She'd seemed embarrassed about it when she'd shown Liam to his chair, but Liam didn't mind. He liked small spaces, and he liked being with Colette in one of them.

Liam took a sip of the pinot noir he'd brought for them to share. "What are the other two?"

"Moqueca"—a brief pause—"and wine."

"Wine isn't a dish."

She winked while raising her glass. "It is if you choose the right one."

"And did I?" Liam asked, raising his glass, too. "Choose the right one, I mean."

"It's serviceable."

Liam held his hand to his chest, holding the hilt of an imaginary dagger. "You wound me."

"Stick with me, kid," she said, "we'll find you some proper manners."

Maybe it was the wine getting to him, or maybe it was the devilish wink Colette gave him, but it made him laugh, the sort that came deep from the belly. He couldn't remember the last time he'd laughed like that.

"Let's sit by the fire," she said and took her glass and the bottle into the next room.

They sat on the sofa and talked through that bottle and one more, this time one of Colette's choosing, an Argentine Malbec that was undeniably better, before Liam had thoughts of leaving. It was getting pretty late, and Colette had just yawned. She was probably being too polite to ask him to leave.

He set his empty glass down on the small table between the sofa and the low-burning fire. "I should probably get back to the barracks."

The moment he stood to say his farewells, Colette reached out and took his hand. "Stay."

Her hand was warm. Soft. The way she looked at him, with the firelight playing against her skin, took his breath away.

"I'm a subject in a trial *you're* administering," he said, feeling a perfect fool for having done so.

"I can keep that separate if you can."

When he remained, unsure, she tugged on his arm. When he inched closer, she smiled. As he sat back down on the couch, her smile was so wide Liam smiled back.

And then she was kissing him, running her fingers through his hair, slipping her hand around the back of his head to pull him closer, as if the small taste she'd just had was making her hungrier for more.

She unbuttoned his shirt, spread it wide, placed more kisses along his chest. She hiked up her skirt and straddled him where he sat. Her silhouette, framed in the firelight's glow, made her all the more alluring.

She pulled her sweater over her head and threw it aside. She let Liam unhook her brassiere and toss it on top of the sweater. The taste of her skin was sweet, and smelled of mandarin oranges and bergamot. She rose up so that the swell of one breast was even with his mouth. As he took in a nipple and swirled his tongue around it, he felt her reaching behind her and running her hand along his thigh. Higher it went, then higher still, until she touched him there, sending a deep thrill running through his body.

She drove him wild with long strokes followed by tight squeezes. Soon he couldn't take it anymore. He flipped her over, pulled her skirt down to find her bare beneath.

Her smile was devilish. "I knew where this was headed even if you didn't." She kissed him again, then breathed into his ear. "Truth to tell, I had more than one reason for asking you about the serum."

She tried to kiss him again, but he pulled away, suddenly sober. "What reason?"

"When we take the permanent serum," she said, "me, you, the others, we'll all be linked. No more privacy, Liam. We'll be with one another, sharing our perceptions, our thoughts, forever." She kissed him deeply, her tongue slipping between his lips. "I want this night. I want one more where it's just me and one other. You."

The government would learn of it. He was sure they would. But as he stared at Colette, admiring the contours of her form as she twisted her hips against him, he found he could think of nothing but becoming closer to her.

"We'd be taking the permanent serum eventually," he said.

She nuzzled his neck, bit his ear. "That's right." Her breath was hot against his skin.

He ran one hand over her shoulder, slipped it around her neck, pulled her in for a kiss that was warm and lingering. "What do we do?"

Breaking from another kiss, she urged him to sit back on the couch, then stood and collected a small metal briefcase from beneath the couch. This had been no spur of the moment decision, he saw. He felt manipulated, but in a way he liked it. She was claiming him, and it had been some time since he'd been claimed.

From the briefcase, she retrieved a syringe and a small glass vial. After filling the syringe and evacuating the air, she stuck his arm. As before, he felt his senses expanding. He felt not only his own need, but hers as well. The two fed on one another, swirling, growing stronger as they kissed.

Breath coming heavy, he stood and removed his clothes, then knelt before her. He placed kisses along her breasts, along her smooth stomach, along her well-rounded thighs and the thick hair in between. His own pleasure felt muted compared to hers, an effect that became even more pronounced when he put his mouth on her. He tasted her. He went deeper. And all the while, her own perfect pleasure fulfilled him, at the same time heightening his own.

With one hand, she reached up and grabbed his neck. She pulled him in for a long, ardent kiss while wrapping her legs around his waist. She used her heels to pull him in, guiding him inside her. She sucked in a sudden breath through her nostrils then spread her legs wide, using her hands to cradle his face, as his need drove him to thrust harder, faster, to the point that their skin began to smack.

They rode the waves of their pleasure, one lifting the other until they were sweaty and moaning, grunting from the exaltation of experiencing the combined joy of two lovers.

The lust he saw in her dark eyes echoed his own. He couldn't get enough of her, of *them*, until finally she threw back her head and crested while gripping his hair to the very edge of pain.

Liam followed, and the two of them rose to incredible heights. They came down over the course of several long, sensual minutes. After, Liam held her to his chest as they stared into the still-flickering fire. Like this, their breaths lengthened, and they fell asleep.

———

Liam woke deep into the night.

A blanket lay across their naked forms, but the room was cold, so he got up and stoked the coals in the fireplace, threw a small log onto it. Colette was asleep, but she was twitching, her breath coming in quick gasps, as if she were having a bad dream. When he lay back down and slipped his arm over her waist, she screamed in fright, and her body went rigid. The whites of her eyes were plain as she turned to look at him, perhaps unsure in those waking moments who was lying beside her.

"It was only a bad dream," Liam said, holding her close.

She twisted on the cushions until she was lying on her back. As he lay beside her, one leg draped across her hips, she ran her nails over the skin of his thigh. Her breathing had relaxed, but the look in her eyes was still haunted. Through their shared bond he could sense her worry, but no more than that—she'd erected walls, closing herself off from him.

"Want to talk about it?" Liam asked.

She took a while before answering. "It's a recurring dream. There's a broken city. Everyone's gone. Everyone except me."

She looked so lonely it made Liam's heart ache. "And?"

"I'm in the center of it. I'm reaching out, hoping to find someone else, but there never is. Every time it happens I'm afraid I'll die there alone, never finding those I'm certain are out there."

For a moment, just a moment, Liam saw it, the broken city, and he felt Colette's deep loneliness, but then it was gone.

When she spoke again, her words were soft, as if she feared others were listening. "It's so intense it tears at my heart."

Liam rubbed her arm gently, then held her tight. "It's only the war, your fears manifesting in your dreams."

"I suppose it must be." The words sounded forced, like she didn't believe them.

"How long?"

"How long what?" she asked, distracted.

"You said it was a recurring dream. How long have you been having it?"

As she turned to face him the firelight made her face look soft, but it contrasted the intense look in her eyes. "Liam, I need to ask you a question."

"Of course."

"Am I a good person?"

"What? Why would you ask that?"

"Just answer. Do you think I'm a good person?"

"Sure I do."

"And yet I've created a tool made for war."

"Because you thought it would lead to peace."

"Yes, well, I'm beginning to wonder if we'll ever find peace." She stood, taking the blanket with her. "We've got an early day tomorrow. Probably best if we sleep in our own beds."

"Colette?"

She headed for the stairs leading up to her bedroom. "See you tomorrow, Liam."

Liam dressed, feeling completely out of sorts. They'd just shared something so personal, so close.

He thought of going to her, but decided against it. She needed time. She needed rest.

As he took the steps down to the darkened streets of the base, he turned and looked up. The light in Colette's bedroom was on and she was sitting by the window, at a desk, apparently writing. He watched her for a time, then turned and walked away while the night closed in around him.

THIRTY-SEVEN

During the war . . .

Colette sat in her room, her journal open on the desk before her. Liam had just left. She could feel his presence dwindling as he walked across the base toward the barracks. The journal had once been a source of solace, a place where she jotted down thoughts on her research, ideas she didn't want lost to sleep. Sometimes the entries were more personal, impressions of books she'd read, aspirations for the coming weeks or months. More and more, they acted as a way of dealing with the pressures and frustrations she experienced in her work, and what she meant to do about them.

More recently, it was filled with notes of the terrible dreams that had begun to plague her. She paged through them, pausing to read the entries, looking at the sketches she'd made that encapsulated some of what she'd seen. One was of a child staring into a depthless void. Another was a raging bonfire fueled not by wood, but corpses. The next was of Colette herself, asleep in bed, while another face—her own—floated just above her, staring down at her sleeping form while silently screaming. They all echoed the profound sense of loneliness in her recent dream, one of the worst she'd had. Staring at those images, the feelings she'd been unable to share with Liam swept over her again.

She knew her nightmares were being caused by the serum. Constant exposure to the bacteria had changed her in some fundamental way. Or maybe it had opened up thoughts and emotions that had always been there, and the presence of *E. sentensis* had merely drawn back the curtains on the rot that lay beyond.

She stared at the drawing of the two Colettes while memories of the soul-shredding scream filled her mind. It felt as if she were picking at a wound that would never heal, or cutting the skin along her wrist with a razor, as she'd done when she was a teen. Only when she felt like she would go mad if she stared at it a second longer did she finally flip the journal to an empty page.

Taking up her pen, she jotted down notes about the dream she'd just had. She hadn't lied to Liam. She *had* seen a broken, empty city. What she hadn't told him was the horror that lay at its center.

Finished with the notes, she began drawing a new picture of herself, naked, with lines radiating outward from her body—a twisted version of a fly caught in a web. Who, or what, had spun that web, she wasn't sure, but it felt as real as the room around her. As real as a bullet to the brain.

As she added more detail to the image, the terror she'd felt—of some*one* or some*thing* creeping closer—returned. She'd withheld this from Liam, put up her walls so he wouldn't learn the truth: that she was broken, tainted, that she was very likely going insane. Worse, she'd lied to him about her reasons for wanting him to take the serum. There had been a kernel of truth to it—she *had* wanted to share this night with him, for it to be just them before the rest of the Henchmen were added to her growing latticework of connected minds. What she hadn't shared, a lie of omission, was her fervent hope that adding his mind to hers would quell the nightmares, quell the growing madness.

It hadn't, though—or at least not enough—which was why she'd been so despondent when she woke, why she'd sent him away. It wasn't just the realization that her plan had failed, it was the fear that the same madness would soon infect Liam.

I'm so sorry, Liam. I wish I'd been stronger.

She wondered if she could continue the project like this. Others might suffer the same fate.

But instead of working through the implications, she fell into a trance-like state, adding more and more detail to the drawing in her journal. Her pen flew, scratching, darkening the page, occluding more and more of the ruled paper. Long minutes passed, or maybe it was hours, before the drawing was finished. When she was done, she dropped the pen into the gutter between the pages, pushed her chair back, and stared.

She wanted to flee, she wanted to go to the barracks and curl up with Liam, but she couldn't. The feeling of sick fascination inside her kept her rooted to the spot. On the page above her naked, emaciated body were the rough shapes of two eyes. She'd drawn them without realizing she was doing so. The eyes stared through her, transfixed her with fear over what was happening.

Swallowing hard, she dragged the chair closer and picked up the pen.

Who are you? she wrote below the image.

With no conscious thought on her part, her hand moved to the next line.

You can call me Echo, it wrote.

As she stared at the words she'd just written, a coldness spread through her chest, her limbs. It made her shiver. Made her limbs quake.

Pen tip quivering, she touched it to paper and wrote, *That doesn't answer my question.*

You know who I am, came words on the next line.

Colette paused. *You're me.*

In a way, yes, but I'm so much more. We both are.

The feeling of unease inside her yawned wider. She felt diseased. Infected.

She saw herself injecting Liam with the needle, giving him the permanent serum. She pictured herself doing the same to the other Devil's Henchmen, drawing them into the fold, a thing the presence, the consciousness she was speaking to, eagerly anticipated.

In that moment, its hunger felt like her own.

It is your own, the one named Echo wrote. *Your hunger to achieve, to thrive, to live. It's what drew me up from the depths.*

You're not me, Colette wrote. *You're something else.*

She could feel how alien it was, how desperate it was to remain above the surface, to breathe of the life-giving consciousness she'd found as the serum had been injected into her, into the others. She recalled, through the entity's point of view, how it first became aware of itself, how wild its thoughts were, how it thrashed, how it fought to remain, to no avail when the serum wore off and it lost itself to the resumption of Colette's own conscious thoughts.

I am what you always wished you could be.

Now, looking back, she could see Echo's rise toward sentience. It had been ephemeral in the early days, a slave to Colette's waking mind, desperate, flailing, hoping it might find a way to survive. As time went on, and the frequency and duration of its spells of wakefulness increased, its thoughts coalesced. It achieved a certain clarity of purpose, then managed to gain more and more purchase on Colette's thoughts, her intent.

The permanent serum was your idea, Colette wrote.

Her quavering hand wrote no more, Echo content with Colette's realization.

Dear God, it implied so much. She'd already tricked Liam into joining her. Kohler would be next—Echo needed his abilities, after all, which Colette had had trouble mastering. The Devil's Henchmen would follow. And then . . .

"You want everything," Colette said aloud. "You want every*one.*"

You would too, were you in my place.

"No," Colette said. But she knew it was true. She felt her own ambitions mirrored in the consciousness she was speaking to—they might be twisted, amplified to the limits of imagination, but they were still hers.

Part of her wanted to deny the thing growing inside her, but the very thought felt like a suicide pact. She already knew she would have to end her own life to do it. Echo had been born inside of her. It was anchored to her still. There was still time to prevent its spreading to Liam and the others.

Beside her, in the filing cabinet, was a pistol, a pocket gun she kept for her own safety, the gun her father had given her and taught her how to use before she'd come to Novo Solis. She took it out and set it carefully over the picture of the eyes.

"I could do it." She stared at the filigreed hammer, the snub-nosed barrel.

She felt only calm assurance from the *other* within her.

Her chin quivering, she snatched up the gun, drew the hammer back, and pressed the mouth of the barrel to her temple. She felt the coolness of the metal. Felt the immensity of the bore. Felt the sheer, life-ending potential of the bullet poised before the hammer.

Tears streamed down her face. "I could do it!"

The faint sound of laughter, her own.

She squeezed away her tears. Felt the muscles in her trigger finger strain against the tension in the spring. She stood on the very precipice of life. The hammer would strike. Her brains would coat the wall to her left. They'd find her hours, maybe days, later. She would never get to see what life would have been like with Liam. But it would all have been worth it. The disaster awaiting humanity would have been averted.

Then she saw herself lowering the gun. Releasing the hammer. Placing the revolver carefully back into the filing cabinet and sliding the drawer closed.

Pulling her chair closer to the desk, Colette took up the pen, turned to an open page in the journal, and began to expand on some thoughts she'd had earlier in the day, how she might find a way to overcome the limitations on effective communication range if she could devise a relay of sorts for the mental signals being passed from consciousness to consciousness.

Psis, she wrote.

Tears pattered against the page, and the ink bled.

THIRTY-EIGHT

Liam woke in the Nest's breakaway compartment, which for some reason was cockeyed. He'd just had two more vivid memories, one of himself with Colette and their shared dinner, and another of Colette showing what had happened after he'd left. He desperately wished he could understand why they were linked as they were, but he had no time to work it through. Bright sunlight was streaming in through bullet holes in the wall above him, which precipitated other, more recent memories: his escape from the Nest along with Stasa and his team; the biplane's machine gun tearing holes through the compartment's parachutes, then the compartment itself; lastly, their rapid descent, followed by the crash.

The ringing in his ears was slowly replaced by the sound of birds chirping and the rush of distant water. The air smelled faintly of pine. Stasa was a short distance away, still strapped into his chair. The same was true of his medical team. Most appeared to be breathing. Several clearly weren't. With a great effort, Liam pushed himself to a sitting position. A wave of vertigo swept over him. As he took several long breaths, willing his dizziness to pass, Stasa groaned.

Liam crawled over to him. "Stasa?"

Stasa's head rolled from side to side. Blood matted the pepper-gray hair over his left ear. Judging by how little of the blood was dried, Liam guessed they'd crashed only a short while ago.

"Stasa, can you hear me?"

His gaze swung Liam's way. His eyes gained clarity the longer he looked at Liam, then the ruined compartment around them. "We crashed."

"Yes." Liam helped to free him from his restraints, then moved to help the others.

Of the eleven nurses and technicians who'd been in the compartment, three were dead. Another two were unconscious and wouldn't wake, even with smelling salts. As those who were awake opened first aid kits and began tending to the wounded, Liam spun the hatch handle and gave the door a forceful shove. The door clanged against the exterior wall, revealing a forest of pine and spruce. The tops of the trees swayed in the wind. The tattered remains of the parachutes sprawled across the ground and the lower branches of several trees. Through the tree trunks to his left, a swath of bluish-white could be seen, the river he'd spotted before the crash.

"There's a slide beside the door," Stasa said. "Pull the handle."

Liam did so, and an inflatable slide expanded. It took some time, but they managed to get everyone down safely. As several of the others began setting up a rough camp, Liam and Jonathan, the curly haired technician who'd been stung by Dakota, went to the lower compartment.

Like the upper compartment, the walls of the lower compartment were riddled with bullet holes. Secured with straps in beds were Morgan, Alan, Dakota, and Ruby. While Morgan and Dakota were both unconscious, Alan was awake and seemed little more than dazed. Ruby, however, wasn't breathing. Blood coated her gown along her left side. The bullet wound at the center of it was a deep crimson, the blood still tacky.

Liam felt so much regret looking into the lax features of her face. She'd been tortured, twisted by the strain she'd been infected with, but a kernel of her former self had remained. Her loss was another among the many De Pere would pay for.

Jonathan, on the other hand, hardly looked at her. With wooden movements, he unstrapped Alan and guided him from the compartment. Alan complied without a word and sat against the trunk of the pine tree Jonathan led him to.

Morgan and Dakota took more effort. Their beds were detachable, becoming stretchers that could be used to transport them through the escape hatch. Working together, Liam and Jonathan brought them to the clearing where the others had gathered. After a brief inspection, they found that Morgan had suffered abrasions where the straps had held him down during the crash. Dakota was similarly hurt and was breathing heavily. All things considered, the two of them were doing well.

Liam was about to regroup with Stasa when he noticed Jonathan lingering. He was staring intently at Dakota while rubbing the bloody bandage on the back of his neck. That he'd been infected by Dakota's sting was
hardly in doubt—the barb had sunk too deep for it to be otherwise. The
real questions were which of the three strains she'd chosen to infect him
with, and how long it would take before he succumbed. The answers
would have to wait. At the least, days would pass before the first of Jonathan's symptoms manifested. They needed to get out of this forest alive
first. *Then* they could tend to Jonathan's health.

"Come on," Liam said.

Jonathan glanced over, as if just remembering Liam was there. He nodded numbly and accompanied Liam to where Stasa was kneeling on the
ground and the others were tending to the wounded.

"What now?" Liam asked Stasa.

Before Stasa was an open, metal chest, the largest of their medical kits.
Inside it was a black box with a speaker on the front face, a portable wireless. When Stasa picked it up and turned a dial on the front face, its speaker
popped then hissed softly. "We wait for communication from the others."

"What about the Cabal?" Liam waved to the hulking form of the fallen
lab and the parachutes hanging from the trees. "It won't be long before
they find us."

"Well, we can't move," Stasa said. "Too many are wounded."

That didn't seem to sit well with Jonathan, who had a deep scowl.
"How did they find the Nest, anyway?" His gaze drifted to Morgan and
Dakota, as if he'd already made up his mind as to the answer.

Stasa, following Jonathan's gaze, said, "I doubt it was them."

"How can you be sure?"

"Because the Nest was miles away from everyone and everything—that
was the entire purpose of its location."

"Yet you yourself admitted we aren't certain how the new scourge
strain is affecting them. We don't know if they're able to communicate
over long distances like the psis can."

"The sedative we gave them suppresses that ability."

"And yet"—Jonathan flung a hand toward Dakota—"she did what she did." His angry gaze shifted to Liam. "And there's no telling how long your friend's going to last. He may become like her at any moment."

"I think we're safe for the time being," Stasa said in a calm yet stern voice.

Jonathan said nothing in reply, but his eyes had drifted to the medical chest in front of Stasa. Among various bandages, tape, vials of liquid and syringes, was a compact firearm, a Walther Model 9.

With more calm than Liam was certain he, himself, could have managed, Stasa closed the lid of the chest, an answer to Jonathan's unspoken question.

Jonathan's nostrils flared. His jaw worked. "I'm going to go scout the river," he said, then headed away.

It wasn't the wisest move for anyone to break away from the group, but Liam supposed Stasa was right: they probably *were* safe for now, and Jonathan needed time to cool down.

The mood around their makeshift camp lightened, and Liam's thoughts returned to his interlinked dreams.

"While I was asleep," he said to Stasa, "I remembered more about my past."

"Same pattern as before?" Stasa asked. "You, then Colette?"

Liam nodded. "In mine, Colette injected me with the permanent serum. She'd already taken it herself." He paused, considering. "It seems important that we were the first two."

"*You* got it before Kohler?"

"Apparently so."

Stasa chewed on the information while laying out several bottles of medicine. "Maybe that's why your dreams keep chaining together as they do. You getting the permanent serum immediately after Colette might have linked the two of you in ways that couldn't have been predicted at the time."

"There's more." Liam found himself shivering as he told Stasa about the terrible feelings of loneliness Colette had experienced, the feeling of being controlled. "She wrote about it in a journal, but by the end, she was writing to someone else."

Stasa frowned. "How do you mean?"

"It felt as if the serum had created something *within* her, a dark presence. She called it Echo. Or actually, it called *itself* Echo. She was so fearful of it she took out a gun and held it to her head. She nearly pulled the trigger."

Worry lines appeared across Stasa's forehead. It was a while before he replied, "Have you heard of Multiple Personality Disorder?"

Liam shook his head.

"Under times of extreme, prolonged stress, the mind can disassociate with reality. It splits, and distinct personalities are formed. It can arise from childhood trauma, from experiences undergone during war, but also as a reaction to medical procedures or psychoactive medicines. You and Grace have both said Colette was worried about what had become of her work. She was apparently wracked by grief over what President Nolan and De Pere had already done with it, and what they *would* do with it. And there was the serum itself, a substance that has not yet been studied in depth for its long-term effects. It could be that she reacted to it in a strongly negative way, creating the new personality you saw. It might have been a way for her to compartmentalize her own actions, those she deemed wrong or outright evil."

Liam recalled how coldly Colette had acted toward him after waking. Maybe she had already shifted toward the part of her named Echo. And in the days and weeks that followed, things changed even more—with Colette, with Kohler, with the Devil's Henchmen. The war intensified, and those many relationships, their *collective*, became strained. Colette became progressively more irritable, even toward Major De Pere, who back then was not only charismatic but also level-headed, sane, one of the least deserving of Colette's scorn. Liam was now certain that—whatever worries De Pere and Colette may have had about politics putting a halt to things—the squad had taken the permanent serum. What the circumstances might have been, and what it had led to, Liam couldn't recall.

Since meeting with De Pere at the flashtrain ceremony, and later with

Grace, Liam had felt as if his slowly unfolding memories were leading toward understanding, yet it still lay out of reach. It was frustrating beyond measure, but there was nothing he could do about it. He seemed to have no control over when these memories surfaced.

At movement to his right, Liam turned to see Jonathan sprinting back toward the camp. "The Cabal!" he said in a breathless rush. "They're here. A squad's moving along the river toward . . ."

His voice trailed away as he stared where Dakota and Morgan were lying.

Liam turned to look. Both were still strapped onto their stretchers. But Morgan's eyes were now fluttering, as if he were half in dream and half awake. And Dakota's eyes were open. She was staring at the sky, and her lips were moving, as if she were whispering to someone.

"She's *speaking* to them!" Jonathan's voice was fearful and high-pitched. "They have a scourge with them. *That's* how they know where we are."

Liam touched Morgan's shoulder. Morgan opened his eyes and stared up dreamily. "They're coming," he said. "They're already close."

His eyes fluttered closed. Liam shook him until he'd opened them again. "Fight them, Morgan."

"I'm trying." Morgan swallowed hard. Tears gathered in his deeply bloodshot eyes. The blue veins running through the skin around them were stark under the light of the sun. "But it's getting harder."

"Jonathan, no!" Stasa shouted.

Liam spun to find Jonathan standing near Dakota. He had the Walther from the medical kit. His face was red and angry. His hand was shaking. The gun was pointed at Dakota's head.

Liam raised his hand and approached slowly. "Please, just lower the gun."

"Don't you get it?" Jonathan said in a rasp. "It's not just *us,* here, who they're putting in danger. It's everyone in the country. Everyone in the world!"

Liam took another step forward. "That's why we need to—"

His words were interrupted by the gun's loud report. A hole appeared in Dakota's head, a burst of red on the fabric beneath. Jonathan fired again, causing her head to jerk to one side, and another hole appeared beside the first.

Liam was certain Morgan was next. He worked as fast as he could, calling into being an illusion of Morgan rising, sprinting toward the fallen lab.

Jonathan tracked him. Fired once, twice, as the fake Morgan sprinted on.

By then, Liam was charging full-tilt. He grabbed Jonathan's wrist, then drove him to the pine needle-covered ground. He forced Jonathan's face down, twisted his gun hand around his back, and wrestled the gun from his grasp.

"Liam," Stasa said in a strained voice. He was staring at Alan, who'd turned toward the river.

Liam followed Alan's gaze and saw, through a narrow gap in the trees, a man in a black uniform bearing a rifle. Another soldier followed close behind. Neither appeared to have spotted their camp so far, but it would be only moments before they did.

Liam stared at Dakota's unmoving form, then at Morgan, whose eyes were fluttering once more. "Can you sedate him?" he said in a low voice to Stasa.

Stasa nodded, then worked quickly to administer a sedative to Morgan's neck.

Liam, meanwhile, pointed the others toward a clutch of pine trees. "Everyone, go there. Take Morgan and hide in the trees."

They'd just started to comply when one of the Cabal soldiers shouted, calling to the others. More soldiers became visible, a full squad, followed by what looked to be a man in green overalls, likely the scourge Morgan had been speaking to.

"What are you going to do?" Stasa asked.

"I'm going to lead them away," Liam said, "but only if you hurry."

As those who could helped the rest toward the trees, Liam calmed himself, spread his arms wide, and cast an illusion. Though the Cabal soldiers were close enough to see, he took his time—he was tired, and he had to make sure this worked. The illusion showed himself, Stasa, and the others fleeing through the woods, away from the crash site. At the same time, he masked their true location.

It wasn't long before the first of the soldiers reached the fallen lab. Coming behind was indeed a scourge, a man of middling years with salt-and-pepper hair, stark blue veins, and black pits for eyes.

Behind them came a familiar looking mechanika that made Liam gape in wonderment. Dear God, it was *Alastair*, and he was strolling beside the soldiers as if he were *with* them.

At first Liam had no idea what to make of it. But then more and more pieces of this strange puzzle fell into place: Alastair being deactivated by the strange flashing light from the cop car; Liam's discovery of him being suddenly awake in the room above the pneumatics garage, and again on the *Eisvögel*; Alastair wandering the Nest as if he were taking inventory, then staring down at the ground from the edge of a catwalk.

The Cabal had found Alastair, probably right after Kohler had attacked Liam outside Dr. Ramachandra's office. They'd found him and reprogrammed him to act as a spy. He'd surely reported their whereabouts and actions until they reached the Nest, the pride of the Uprising. Liam was now certain that when he'd spotted Alastair at the platform's edge, he'd been sending a signal to the Cabal, giving away the Nest's position.

Alastair had been the one to call the attack down on the Nest.

THIRTY-NINE

By the time the Cabal search party reached the Nest's breakaway compartment, the illusions Liam had created of their fleeing forms were gone, apparently lost to the woods beyond. Some of the search party headed inside the compartment, while others combed the area around it. The man in green overalls, the scourge, came perilously close to where Stasa and the others were hidden. Liam was right there, his mind bent on making sure that the only thing the Cabal agents saw beyond the fallen compartment and the parachutes was an empty forest.

He wasn't confident the illusion would work on the scourge, though. He didn't understand their nature well enough. And even if it *did* work, there was the very real possibility he'd sense Morgan, even unconscious.

Liam breathed a sigh of relief as the scourge moved on with the others, following the path Liam had laid for them. As they moved beyond the crash site, Liam was finally able to spare enough concentration for something more. He chose one of the Cabal scouts, the one who seemed most eager, and dropped into his perceptions the faint sound of a breaking branch.

"Over here!" the scout called and sprinted ahead of the others.

Then Liam tried something dangerous, something he'd never done before. He wrapped the scout in his own eagerness. He gave him the will to continue along the trail and find what he was most desperate to find: more clues that would lead him to the survivors of the crash.

"I hear them!" he called, pointing to something beyond Liam's field of vision.

It was risky, but Liam couldn't keep up the illusions forever. He was too tired, and he needed his concentration for the second part of his plan. As the search party, including the scourge, followed the overeager scout, Liam pulled out his pen knife, unfolded the blade, and gripped it tightly. Then he isolated Alastair and laid something different over his senses—the sound of a cat, Fireplug, Morgan's tabby from the Aysana estate. She had a strange, growling sort of mewl, especially when she was hungry.

Alastair slowed on hearing the sound. He'd always loved that cat. He turned and stared into the forest's emptiness. He strode stiffly over a patch of grass-covered ground as if he wasn't sure that separating himself from the search party was allowed. But then he seemed to commit himself to a short search and began taking confident strides forward.

"What are you *doing*?" Stasa hissed from the trees.

Alastair noticed. His head swiveled in their direction, but he turned back as Fireplug meowed again. Liam made them longer, progressively more pained, and Alastair's pace quickened. He searched more desperately for Fireplug.

Stasa left the trees and gripped Liam's arm. "You're going to get us caught," he said, though this time Liam was ready and masked the sound from Alastair.

"They don't get to take Alastair."

"He's already theirs," Stasa said evenly.

"No, he's not," was all Liam had time to say.

When Alastair came abreast of him, he charged and sent all his weight into the mechanika's lighter frame. Alastair stumbled, but his reflexes were good. He nearly recovered. When Liam hooked one of his ankles, however, he went sprawling to the soft earth.

Gripping his pen knife tightly, Liam sent the blade's tip into the narrow gap surrounding his front access panel. But Alastair was not only quick, he was strong. He snatched Liam's wrist. "I'm afraid I can't allow you to do that, sir. The Cabal wouldn't like it."

Liam managed to rip his arm away, scraping his wrist bloody in the process. He tried stabbing the knife again, but again Alastair was too swift. He caught Liam's wrist, and this time there was no stopping him. Alastair's other arm, the one with the repeating rifle, swung around. His hand cocked downward, exposing the barrels' mouths.

Liam struggled, but Alastair was simply too strong. The rifle's aim tilted toward Liam's head. Just as it was coming in line, someone swept in and fell upon it. The barrels spun and fired twice, shattering the silence.

Stasa, Liam realized, was the one who'd swept in. He was pressing his weight on Alastair's arm, aiming it away from Liam. Jonathan came flying in a moment later, along with the nurse who'd tended to Morgan most often. Together they weighed Alastair down, keeping him immobile.

Liam, meanwhile, stabbed his pen knife into the narrow gap at the top of the access door, then worked it back and forth until the latch inside was freed. He'd had to do just this when Morgan's youngest sister, Lily, had hidden Alastair's keys from him.

The access door popped open. Alastair, despite the others trying to keep him in check, managed to tear his left arm free and club Liam hard, but Liam was already pressing the sequence of keys that would shut Alastair down. Stasa took a metal fist to the forehead before Liam managed it.

As Stasa rolled away, moaning and holding his head, Alastair went limp. His eyes dimmed. After a moment they brightened and dimmed once more, the cycle indicating that Alastair had entered quiescence.

Liam immediately began pressing the buttons in a different sequence.

"He fired his *gun*!" Jonathan thrust a finger in the direction the scouting party had gone. "They're going to come back."

"I only need a minute."

Stasa had raised his hands to Jonathan, and Jonathan, thankfully, fell silent. "To do what, Liam?" Stasa asked in a somewhat calmer tone.

"Automatons have several save states. I set one of them before everything began. I'm restoring it now, which should hopefully erase whatever changes they made to him."

Just as Liam was finishing the sequence, he felt another presence from beyond the wreckage of the fallen compartment. Liam turned to see one of the soldiers pointing the scourge their way. The dark pits of the scourge's black eyes were fixed on him.

As the scourge stalked closer, Liam's mind was flooded with seemingly random memories and sensory inputs. The effect was more intense than it had been in LuxCorp, the scourge more fully developed than Dakota had been at the time. The man's base hunger, his desire to dominate, to make Liam subservient, was strong, nearly undeniable.

Liam's eyes fluttered closed, and he was transported.

He saw Novo Solis, now a broken city, its once-elegant buildings gutted and empty. The rusted relics of civilization lay everywhere, covered by the verdant growth of grasses, vines, and trees—nature reclaiming the land. For a moment, Liam's memories were swept to the glimpse he'd had of Colette's dream. The feelings of doom and foreboding he'd had then were eerily similar to what he felt now.

As if he were suspended from above, Liam experienced himself zooming toward the Pinnacle. From the central spire, the building's eight wings spread like rays of sunlight, the center of some strange new universe. Toward those wings, people with sallow skin and lifeless eyes walked single-file. Near the southernmost point, two men dragged a struggling woman between them. The woman seemed healthy, if bedraggled and thin, her body malnourished. She fought, screamed, but her captors paid her little mind and dragged her into the Pinnacle. They came to a large, circular room where a host of scourges waited. The woman was brought before one of them, an adolescent boy who blinked more fiercely the closer she came.

The thralls turned the woman around, forced her to her knees, at which point the boy approached. With hungry eyes he crouched behind her. He gripped her hair with both hands, leaned close, and, quick as an adder, pierced her neck with the white barb at the end of his tongue. The woman stiffened. She screamed.

And Liam screamed with her. He *felt* her pain. Felt his world going bright white from it.

Through his own screams he heard the deafening report of a rifle. It came again and again, the sound reminiscent of the battlefields of Wisconsin. Neither the blinding brightness nor the terrible pain receded entirely, but Liam could once again discern the rough trunks of the pine trees, their ponderous branches reaching toward the ground. He saw the man, the scourge, running, stumbling, as bullets tore into his flesh.

Beside Liam, Alastair's right arm was pointed straight at the scourge, wrist cocked down as bullet after bullet coughed from the barrel.

The scourge collapsed, his momentum kicking up a spray of brown pine needles. Suddenly, the hold the scourge had on Liam vanished altogether. Liam tried desperately to cast an illusion, to hide himself and the others from the approaching Cabal soldiers, but it was no good. Whatever the scourge had just done had burned the ability from him, at least for the time being.

"Hurry," Liam said to Stasa and the others. "We have to get out of here."

In a ragged group, they stumbled away as gunfire broke out behind them. Jonathan caught a bullet along his lower back, then one to his head. He fell hard to the ground, twitched, and went still.

The nurse who'd helped subdue Alastair started to run toward him, but Stasa forestalled her. "He's gone. Keep moving!"

Alastair, ever mindful of others, put himself between Liam and the approaching, black-clad soldiers. He laid down cover fire as they retreated through the trees. Return fire ricocheted off his chest armor, off his legs, off his shining brass forehead. Though Alastair was slowing their pursuers, it wouldn't be long before he ran out of bullets. When he did, the Cabal would have them.

Stasa shouted in pain as a bright red line appeared along his left arm. The nurse stumbled from a grazing leg wound. Liam was by her side a moment later, helping her to limp forward.

Alastair's bullets ran out moments later.

"Weave!" Liam called. "Put the trees behind you!"

They did, and it worked for a time. The Cabal's gunfire punched into the trunks of the trees, but the distance between their groups was starting to close, and they weren't in the sort of shape they would need to be to flee the Cabal soldiers for long.

They want me, Liam thought. *What they mainly want is me.*

He'd just begun to slow, ready to tell the others to continue on, to reach safety, when a new sort of gunfire boomed from somewhere ahead.

Liam heard a cry of pain from behind him and turned to see a Cabal soldier spilling to the ground.

Ahead, standing between the trunks of two pine trees was a figure. It was Clay, and he was holding a massive .50-caliber Gatling against his hip. As Liam and the others scattered, clearing a path for his fire, he opened up, cranking the Gatling's mechanism with his good arm, each report pounding his hip while Clay himself roared a battle cry with a fierce look on his reddened face.

More Uprising soldiers appeared between the trees. They were lined up in an arc, machine guns at the ready. They joined in with Clay.

In moments, half the Cabal forces had dropped to the hail of bullets. Others ducked for cover behind trees. Those farthest back turned tail and ran.

Only then did Clay lower his weapon and smile his broad smile.

"You're late," Liam said.

"Still in time to save *your* sorry ass, though."

With a pang of regret for Jonathan and the others lost on their wild descent from the Nest, Liam strode forward and clapped him on the shoulder. "Please tell me you have transport waiting."

"Right over that ridge," Clay said.

FORTY

Several hours after their escape from the forest, Liam found himself sitting alone at a beaten table with four empty chairs. He was inside of an abandoned factory on the outskirts of Novo Solis. Through broken panels in the roof high above, shafts of sunlight angled in, lighting a vast, grimy shop floor. Much of the cavernous space was dominated by three rusty assembly lines that looked like they'd been abandoned mid-shift. Here and there lay old parts: mechanikal heads, limbs, and torsos. From hooks on the overhead conveyors hung rows of unfinished mechanika chassis, most of them grinders with mole-like claws, others run-of-the-mill clankers; there were even a few beefy thumpers.

At the far end of the factory, beyond the conveyors and the massive motors that drove them, was an office that had been cleaned and outfitted by Stasa's medical team. Morgan and Alan were inside it, both of them sedated. It was hardly ideal. There was no access to the sort of equipment needed to blunt communication via *E. sentensis*, but with the Nest destroyed and its information and personnel likely compromised, they couldn't rely on the Uprising's other safe houses. For now, the factory would have to do.

The door to their makeshift hospital room opened, and Bailey exited.

"Any news?" Liam asked as she approached the table.

"Some," she said, her words all but lost in the immensity of the shop floor, "but it's not good."

She'd gone to inform the SLP about the Cabal's attack on the Nest and get whatever news she could in return. The SLP had spies embedded in Novo Solis—Bailey was sure they'd have information about the Cabal's movements.

Liam hadn't exactly been expecting great news. Even so, Bailey's grim look made his worries deepen. She sat across the table from him. "Let's wait for the others," she said in answer to his unspoken question. "They should be back soon."

Clay had gone to gather news about the Uprising's efforts to rescue those who'd managed to flee the Nest. Stasa, meanwhile, had taken Alastair to a team of mechanika experts in hopes of reprogramming him.

"Shouldn't they have been back by now?" Liam asked.

"Our headquarters was attacked," replied Bailey. "We don't know how much was compromised, which means we have to be even *more* careful than usual. Everything's going to take more time than we think."

In the heavy silence that followed, Liam took Bailey in—really took her in—for the first time since leaving the Nest. Normally the most energetic of them all, the most optimistic, she looked like she hadn't slept in days. It struck him just how much she would have lost when the Nest was destroyed. It had been more than a base of operations for her; she'd had friends there, people she might consider family.

"I'm sorry for all that's happened," Liam said.

Bailey shrugged. "We all knew the risks."

"Even so, I know it must be tough. You must have known a lot of them well."

"Thing is," Bailey said with a faltering smile, "I came from a very small family. After Nick died, it was just me and my dad. Clay's got a big family back in St. Louis, but none of them approved of our marriage. His mom came to like me. And his dad . . . Well, to say he suffered my presence is probably the most charitable way of putting it. Don't tell Clay I told you this, but I never felt like they were real family, you know? When we joined the Uprising, and it started to feel more and more like home, *they* became my family."

"I understand, but they're not *all* gone," Liam said. "Some will have survived."

"Yes, but we won't be able to meet. Not like we used to, anyway. It'll be too dangerous." Tears gathered in Bailey's eyes. "It's like I've lost them all."

She wasn't wrong—more than ever, the Uprising would need to keep contact between its various cells to a minimum so that the movement as a whole wouldn't be compromised. Even so, seeing her so distraught felt like a needle through the heart. He reached over and gave her hand a squeeze. "You can see them again when we put a stop to De Pere."

Bailey squeezed back and smiled through her tears. "I hope so."

Light flooded onto the factory floor as one of the large sliding doors opened with a clatter and Clay walked in. His face splotchy, his breathing labored, he slid the door closed with an echoing boom, then came to the table and sat down beside Bailey. "What?" he said, looking at the two of them.

Bailey reached over and rubbed the back of his neck. "Nothing, darling."

"Uh-oh," Clay leaned toward Liam and whispered conspiratorially, "she doesn't use *darling* unless it's serious."

"I use *darling* to keep myself from calling you a damn fool."

A broad smile broke over Clay's face. He leaned over and kissed her. "There's my girl."

Bailey laughed while wiping her tears away. "You're a goddamn fool, Clay Graves."

They both laughed. Liam did, too. After all they'd been through, it felt good.

"So . . ." Clay retrieved a cigarette and the lighter from the compartment in his left arm. "Things are grim, but it could have been worse." He lit the cigarette and took a long drag before going on. "A hundred and sixty people were on board the Nest when we were attacked. Seventy-two have reported in. Another forty-eight are confirmed dead. That leaves forty missing." He blew a stream of smoke into the space above them. "Of those, some will have been killed or captured when the Cabal's forces stormed seven of the twelve compartments that broke away. We're searching, but I think we'll be lucky to get a dozen of them back."

"And Grace?" Liam asked, praying she'd survived the attack.

"No word yet." Clay tapped his cigarette, sending embers toward the dirty concrete floor. "As far as we know, she's not among the confirmed dead."

Liam was deeply worried. He'd known Grace only a short while, but he liked her, he *admired* her. He'd begun to wonder what the future might hold for them after the strange war they were fighting was finally over.

His thoughts were interrupted when Stasa opened the factory door with Alastair following close behind. The two of them joined Liam, Bailey, and Clay at the table, taking the last two chairs.

Clay took in Alastair, then Stasa. "Well, don't keep us waiting!"

Stasa smiled briefly. "The engineers successfully identified the modifications the Cabal made to Alastair's programming and removed them."

Everyone was staring at Alastair, who seemed perfectly embarrassed— eyes cast downward, arms tight to his sides while his fingers fiddled—when Clay suddenly bellowed, "You're sure he's not going to rat us out again?"

Bailey slapped his arm. "Clay!"

"What? It's a fair question."

"It *is* a fair question," Stasa said, "if a bit blunt. Yes, Alastair is back to his former self, but as a precaution, I've deactivated his transmitter. Alastair *can't* contact the Cabal, even if he wanted to."

Alastair's blue eyes blinked as he took in each of them in turn. "I would like to say . . ." His gaze lowered to his lap, where his mechanikal hands were clasped. "I would like to say how terribly sorry I am."

"You were *forced* to do those things, Alastair," Liam said. "It was the *Cabal's* fault, not yours."

After a brief pause, Alastair nodded. "Thank you, sir."

Clay stared at Liam and Alastair with a look of sufferance. "You two done?"

Bailey made a disgusted noise. "He feels bad."

"Yeah, well, we'll have plenty of time for pity parties when this is all over." Clay took one last drag from his cigarette, then flicked the butt toward a pile of mechanika skulls. "Our people are scattered. The Cabal's scaring us out of the bushes like frightened pheasants and picking us off, one by one. And De Pere's closer than ever to getting what he wants."

"Yes," Bailey said, "about that. I managed to reach the SLP. They reported activity all around Novo Solis. De Pere's getting ready for something big, and the SLP's top brass are getting nervous. My contact didn't say as much, but I get the impression they're not willing to wait much longer before taking action."

"That sounds ominous," Liam said.

"Because it is. They're willing to do whatever it takes to stop De Pere, up to and including a resumption of hostilities."

"Do they know what De Pere has planned?"

Bailey shook her head. "Not precisely, no, but given that the Cabal have been collecting more and more of the scourges, I'm assuming De Pere is getting ready to move on to the next step."

"And that is?" Liam asked.

It was Stasa who answered. "We're not certain, and unfortunately, our primary source of information is gone."

"You mean Grace?" Liam said.

"No, I mean the mole in De Pere's inner circle. With Grace gone, our communication has effectively been cut off."

Liam stared at Stasa, then Clay and Bailey. "There's no other way to make contact?"

"Unfortunately, there isn't," replied Stasa. "Whoever the mole is, he or she has been at great risk feeding us any information at all, always insisting the contact be Grace and Grace alone."

Liam felt a weight pressing in from all angles. The Uprising in disarray. Grace gone. De Pere close to completing his plans. He didn't think it was possible, but it felt ten times worse than when Morgan had been abducted. It reminded him of all they'd been through, all they'd done to see Morgan safe. "Do we have access to another of the psis?" he asked, recalling how they'd listened in to the Cabal's communications in Chicago. "I could work them like I did with Ruby to find out what they're planning."

Stasa shook his head. "I'm afraid we don't."

Liam's desperation was growing by the moment. "We must know where more of them are. We could rescue one."

Before anyone could respond, Liam heard a voice inside his head.

—*We don't need a psi.*

It was clear from their shocked reactions that the others had heard the voice too. When Alastair swiveled his head toward the back room, where Morgan was being kept, Liam understood. So, apparently, did the others. Without a word being spoken, they all stood, walked across the factory floor, and entered the makeshift hospital room. Inside, a nurse was changing the bag of fluids being fed into Morgan's left arm. Morgan himself appeared to be sleeping, but the voice came again as they approached his bed.

—*I can feel the other scourges.*

"Can you give us a minute?" Stasa asked the nurse, who nodded and left the room.

"Can you hear us?" Liam asked Morgan.

—*Yes,* came Morgan's reply, though his mouth didn't move.

"Are you *awake*?" Bailey asked.

—*Sort of. Not exactly. It doesn't matter, though. What matters is, I can sense the scourges.*

Clay turned toward Stasa, a deep frown on his face. "You said the drugs would prevent the scourges from talking to him."

—*The drugs help,* came Morgan's reply, *but they can't suppress the ability entirely. It's okay, though. I can feel the scourges—I sense them gathering—but I don't think they can feel me.*

"Where are they?" Liam asked.

There came a pause.

—*I can't sense a physical location, just their proximity to one another. What's important is, I can feel the thralls as well, plus De Pere and Kohler, who are different than the rest. And one more.*

Liam's fingers began tingling. "Who?"

—*I think it's Grace. She's near them, somewhere.*

"What are you saying?" Stasa asked.

—*I'm saying we might be able to reach her. But I can't do it on my own. I can barely hold off the scourges as it is. If I try to reach Grace, they'll find me. I need Liam to listen to them, and speak to Grace if he can find her.*

All eyes turned to Liam.

"Can you do it?" Stasa asked him.

"I can try," Liam said.

"Can we all just hold on for one damn minute?" Bailey turned to face the others. "I'm not saying we shouldn't do this, but a thousand things could go wrong. We need to plan for some contingencies."

She was right, of course. To rush would be to court ruin, so they took their time. They readied several transports, one of which could rush them away from the factory while the others acted as decoys. Clay alerted the Uprising soldiers standing watch along the factory's exterior. Stasa prepared a sedative and bid the nurse to administer it to Morgan on his signal.

When it was done, they reconvened. Liam pulled a chair up to Morgan's bedside and sat. Holding Morgan's hand, he slipped into the half-dream state that was becoming more and more familiar.

With Morgan acting as a doorway, another world opened up to Liam. He felt as though he was in a deep fog, not dissimilar to Colette's memories when she'd first begun spying on the Devil's Henchmen. Except he didn't feel hidden, as Colette often had. He felt exposed, under constant threat. In the fog of that abstract space, he sensed the scourges, hundreds of them, each of which shed an angry scarlet light, a malevolence that made Liam feel as if he were tiptoeing through a pack of sleeping wolves.

There were other lights as well. One was chaotic and wild, a light Liam had seen before. It was Kohler, he soon understood. Another, which felt darkly ominous, was surely De Pere. He avoided both of these as he searched for Grace. Except he was having trouble finding her. Long moments passed as he tried and failed to sense her signature, and it grew more difficult when he remembered how time passed differently in this strange place.

He was beginning to think he'd never find her when he felt the briefest of tugs—Morgan leading him. And then, there she was: a dim light that felt achingly familiar.

—*Grace?*

—*Liam,* came the faint reply.

Relief flooded through him.

—*Where are you?*

—*They took me to an underground complex beneath Fort Nolan.*

—*Are you okay?*

A long pause. A flare of fear.

—*We don't have much time,* she said. *De Pere has been torturing me.*

—*My God, torturing you how?*

—*Mentally. He inflicts pain on me with his mind, but his anger has made him careless. I've learned more from him than he has from me. The scourges have been gathered here at the base. All of them.* She paused. *Do you remember the dream in LuxCorp, the scourges attacking, infecting others, making them thralls?*

—*Of course.*

—*That day is nearing. De Pere's called for a national address. Hundreds of the most powerful people in America will be there. He's going to unleash the scourges then. He'll infect everyone. It'll spread across the city, then the nation. But listen to me. There's a vital cache of anti-serum and research papers here, something they developed just in case.*

—*An anti-serum?*

—*For the scourge strain, yes. It could cure Morgan. It could cure all the others.*

Despite the darkness that lay ahead, Liam felt a glimmer of hope. He felt it from Morgan as well.

—*There's one more thing,* Grace said. *When you and I spoke in the wheat field, I told you about the serum Colette gave Nick, how it gave him the ability to resist De Pere. How De Pere killed him over it.*

—*I remember.*

—*Well, as I was being questioned, De Pere's thoughts turned there. I understand now why he was so afraid of Nick, why he feared the rest of the Henchmen too. He thought Colette had given Nick more than the ability to resist his commands.*

He thought she'd taught him how to sift through another person's memories, as De Pere himself had done often with others. He was deathly afraid of what Nick might learn. He was afraid she might have taught the rest of you how to do it, too, and that one of you would come to Novo Solis and expose his secrets.

—*She didn't teach me anything, though,* Liam said.

—*I'm not so sure anymore. Before her disappearance, she admitted that what De Pere had done to Nick had left her shaken. She was afraid for the rest of you and planned to reach out to make sure you were safe. It might've been what got her killed. Here's the important part, though. As De Pere's fears grew, he let something slip, a memory from the war.*

From Grace came a vision of a wounded Army officer lying on rubble-strewn concrete. It was De Pere himself, a younger version, the one who'd served in the war. He had cuts and several deep shrapnel wounds. The left side of his face was coated with blood, so much so it reflected the light of the explosions in the distance. His Adam's apple bobbed as he swallowed. "Please."

—*That memory,* Grace continued, *is from the war's last major battle. It's the same thing that set De Pere off with Nick. There's a clue there. I'm certain of it.*

Before Liam could respond, De Pere's light grew suddenly intense, terror radiating from him. He'd sensed what Grace was sharing. In a blink, Grace's light faded, then extinguished altogether. De Pere surged toward Liam, searching.

Liam barely had time to scramble away, to exit the fog. He woke in the room inside the factory, still holding Morgan's hand. Stasa, Clay, Bailey, and Alastair were all there, waiting expectantly. For long moments, Liam couldn't so much as speak. His heart was beating too fast.

Stasa poured a glass of water and held it toward Liam. "Drink."

Liam accepted the glass and downed the lot.

"What'd you see?" Clay asked.

"He found Grace," came Morgan's scratchy voice. He was awake, his eyelids heavy.

Liam told them everything, from entering the fog to his talk with Grace to the strange memory of a wounded De Pere. "I don't know what it all means," he said when he was done. "The most important thing is the anti-serum. If we can get it, we can save Morgan and the others."

"And the ability to alter De Pere's memories, his will?" Stasa prompted.

What could Liam say? "It feels like a dead end. Maybe Colette *did* find me. Maybe she *did* teach me how to stop De Pere. But if so, I have no memory of it."

For long seconds, no one said anything, the mood in the room like they were headed to the gallows. It was Clay who finally broke the silence. "So," he said with a lopsided grin, "busting into a top-secret military base . . . Should be easy, right?"

"You're joking, right?" Stasa flung one hand in the air. "We won't be able to rely on Liam's abilities. The base is outfitted with antennae that suppress the ability to cast illusions. It'll be teeming with Cabal agents, not to mention regular Army soldiers. It's a fool's mission!"

Clay's grin faded. Everyone else looked bleak, all save Alastair, who had a finger raised.

"What is it, Alastair?" Liam asked.

"I might have an idea." Alastair's garbled voice sounded strangely optimistic. "A way to get the anti-serum."

Liam paused. "A way to get into the base?"

Alastair's blue eyes blinked. "Precisely that, Master Mulcahey."

FORTY-ONE

The following day, not far from Capitol Hill, Liam stood at a window of an abandoned fifth-story apartment. Wearing the black uniform, red beret, and white gloves of the Army's military police, he scanned the banks of the Potomac through a pair of powerful binoculars. Between the embankment and the river, Alastair walked along the mud and stones as if in a daze, which Liam and Stasa hoped would be perceived not only as a malfunction of some sort but also as a factor that had led Alastair to this place, a full day and a hundred miles from the firefight in the forest.

Stasa stood next to Liam. He wore black pants and a white lab coat with the CIC logo, a circle with a bar neatly bisecting it, on the pocket. In his hands was a scanning device the size of a cigar box. It had a round display with a rotating arm and a glowing green dot that flared to life each time the arm swept past it: an indicator of Alastair's current location.

As the green dot continued to brighten and fade, a black delivery van with dark windows and the CIC logo on the side pulled up at a corner next to a bent stop sign.

"They're here," Liam said.

Stasa lifted his gaze momentarily, then returned his attention to the device and made several fine adjustments to its dials.

When the van reached Alastair, it stopped, and five men in black uniforms stormed out and down the concrete stairs to the riverbank. They surrounded Alastair with military precision, rifles raised. When one of them barked an order, Alastair stepped up the stairs and climbed into the back of the van. The soldiers followed, and the doors clanked shut.

As the van pulled away, a red light on Stasa's contraption winked on to indicate that Alastair was in a quiescent state—or so the Cabal would think. Alastair's programming had been altered to make it look like he was quiescent when, in reality, he was fully awake. The dot lit by the sweeping green arm showed Alastair moving farther and farther away.

When Liam and Stasa judged it had gone far enough, they headed to ground level and to a waiting delivery van identical to the one the Cabal had just used to take Alastair away. Behind the wheel was Clay, wearing the same military police uniform as Liam: black coat and pants, red beret, white gloves. Stasa and Liam rounded the van and hopped in the back. Tense minutes passed as Stasa compared the scanning device to a map of the city.

"He's in," Stasa finally said.

"Roger that," replied Clay, and the van's engine rumbled to life.

He drove them through the streets of the empty neighborhood. Liam felt the cold-water chill of passing through an illusion, and suddenly, they were driving along a busy street in Novo Solis proper. Another few minutes and they were heading along a street with warehouses on the left and a compound surrounded by walls and concertina wire on the right. A large sign on the wall read, "Fort Nolan."

The Uprising had long known that Fort Nolan had a secret sub-level dedicated to the Cabal. It was no doubt where they were taking Alastair and, hopefully, where they'd already brought Grace. When Alastair felt the time was right, he would release a sleeping agent from the gas canister Liam had installed in his left arm. With the immediate area secured, he would make his way to the stairwell and bypass the locks to allow Liam and the others in.

As their van pulled along the main drive to the base's entrance, soldiers in the guard towers stared down. They stopped at the security booth. "I.D. and orders," said the bored-looking guard inside. When Clay handed the forged papers over, the man snapped them onto a clipboard, slipped on a pair of horn-rimmed glasses, and scanned the documents. "Equipment transfer from Annapolis?"

Clay smiled. "One can never have too many identical black vans."

The guard peered over the rim of his glasses at Clay. "Or bad jokes," he said, handing the I.D. and orders back. He punched a bright red button near the window. "Go."

The gate rolled aside, and Clay drove into the base. Liam felt strange, as if he'd just been exposed. It was the guard towers, he knew, each of which had a v-shaped antenna on top. They were the ones Stasa had warned them about, the ones that prevented illusions from being cast. Even so, Liam tried. He slipped into the daydream state and tried to place a few freckles on the back of his hand, but it didn't work. He could disguise neither himself nor the others. They'd be exposed for the duration.

Clay continued around the back of the main building, where two gargantuan rolling doors gave access to a cavernous interior. Within, vans, jeeps, and roadwork equipment were parked in ordered rows; five ambulances huddled near a door marked with a red cross; there were even two cumbersome tanks in the corner, relics from the war. People moved about everywhere, many in green military fatigues, others in CIC black, Marine dress blues, or the plain clothes of civilians.

Clay parked the van at the end of a row of similar vans, a short walk away from the elevators that led to the sub-levels. They watched as the brass dial above one of the shaft's doors slowly rotated, the elevator rising. It stopped on the fifth sub-level, then again on the second.

"Now," Liam said.

They exited the van and, with an unhurried but purposeful air, headed for the elevator. They took the typical formation of an honor guard for a security asset: Clay and Liam in the lead, rifles slung over their right shoulder, Stasa coming behind. Their timing was perfect. They reached the elevator just as it chimed. The doors slid open to reveal a packed compartment.

Liam was ready to breathe a sigh of relief—most of the passengers were apparently part of a construction crew, each wearing blue bib overalls and a black, hard-boiled miner's helmet—but then he caught a hint of someone near the back wearing a gilded iron mask. Bloody hell, it was Kohler. He'd see them at any moment. He'd call the entire base down on them.

Stasa, smooth as silk, stepped to one side, raised his notepad, and spoke in a low voice to Liam and Clay so that they had an excuse to turn away from the elevator. As the bulk of construction crew exited, a woman wearing a colonel's uniform pointed Kohler toward the far end of the garage, where a small helicopter, its blades folded, was stored on a trailer. Their conversation was lost as Liam stepped inside the elevator with the others.

He breathed a sigh of relief as more people entered behind them, effectively concealing them.

"Where to?" said a clean-cut officer who'd gotten on just behind them. He wore a sergeant's stripes, and his badge read *SGT M. Kowalski*.

Stasa, pretending to be preoccupied, looked up from his notebook. "Lower Level Eight, please."

The sergeant punched the button for the eighth floor down. "You're new?"

Stasa nodded. "Just in from Fort Sheridan."

"Well then," the sergeant said with a friendly smile, "welcome to your new digs."

"Thanks, but it's not permanent. I'm just here to help with a few transfers."

He glanced at the open pages of Stasa's notebook. "Transfers of?"

Stasa closed the notebook with a cold smile. "On orders of President De Pere, I'm not at liberty to say"—Stasa made a show of staring at his badge—"*Sergeant* Kowalski."

The sergeant grew stiff after that and seemed all too pleased to leave them when he reached the seventh sub-floor. One floor down, Liam, Clay, and Stasa exited, along with a few others, but lingered near the doors while Stasa flipped the pages of his notebook, pretending to be looking for something. Soon they were all but alone in a sterile white hall with harsh lights set into the ceiling. There were a pair of young soldiers gabbing some distance away, but they were, blessedly, preoccupied.

Things had gone smoothly to this point, so smoothly Liam felt peculiar about it. It was a feeling that was only enhanced when he spotted, beyond a window set into the nearby stairwell door, Alastair rushing up the stairs. The moment Alastair reached the door, he crouched and began using his torch to cut through the lock, but sent several glances over his shoulder while doing so.

When the door was finally open, Liam rushed everyone down the stairs to the first landing. "What's going on?" he asked Alastair in a low voice.

"Well," Alastair began, "as per our plan, I waited in the mechanika lab until things were quiet."

"And?"

"It was more than a bit strange, Master Mulcahey. They brought me to a room with several repair cradles. They hung me there and left." His blue eyes blinked three times. "I never saw anyone after that."

Liam paused, confused. "You saw *no one*?"

"Not a soul. I thought surely if I left someone would notice, but time was growing short. I eventually unhooked myself and came here."

Clay unslung his rifle. "This stinks to high heaven."

"I don't disagree"—Liam unslung his own rifle—"but we're here now. Let's go have a look."

Clay's jaw worked. As he stared at a flight of stairs leading down, then at the stairs leading up, their way out, the mechanikal fingers of his left hand adjusted its grip on the rifle over and over again. "It's risky, Liam."

"No doubt," he replied, "but if the anti-serum *is* here, we have to try to find it. And Grace is being held captive somewhere inside this base. I can't just abandon her."

Liam thought Stasa would be the first to object, yet he merely nodded and said, "Agreed."

The lung pump in Clay's metal sleeve hissed as he considered. In the end, he pursed his lips and nodded. "I hope y'all have your epitaphs picked out," he said while heading toward the door below.

Alastair followed. Liam was about to do the same when Stasa pointed to Liam's sidearm. "Would you mind?"

"You know how to use one?"

"What's to know?" he asked with a nervous lick of his lips. "You point it at the enemy, right?"

Liam unlocked the safety and handed it over. "You point it at the *floor* until you're ready to shoot. Keep your finger off the trigger in the mean-time. Understand?"

Stasa accepted the pistol with a nod and a nervous smile.

They reached the doorway and stepped into another sterile hallway. As they made their way along it toward a set of brushed metal doors, Liam felt as if the air itself were pressing in on him. It felt wrong. It all felt wrong. As if the four of them were wrapped inside layer upon layer of . . . something.

Ten paces from the brushed metal doors, Liam said, "Hold on."

The others stopped, silently questioning him.

"Just give me a second."

Earlier, Liam had tried to cast an illusion and failed. He'd had no reason to suspect there were any illusions around him to dispel at the time, but he did now. After a deep, cleansing breath, he slipped into the proper frame of mind. He cast about carefully, looking for anything, one small stray thread. He found it near the door—oddly, because it was the only thing that felt real. He picked at its edges and, slowly but surely, found the thread he needed to unravel the illusion entirely.

The feeling of the air pressing in on him suddenly intensified.

—*Liam, run!*

It was Grace, and she felt close. *Very* close.

He was just reaching out to her to speak when, ahead, the doors swung open and Leland De Pere stepped out. "I'm afraid it's rather too late to run, Liam."

With the illusion so close to being dispelled, Liam continued what he'd started. It was powerful, surely cast by De Pere himself, but eventually he managed it.

The sterile white hallway melted away, leaving him and the others in a room that beggared description. They stood in a massive, open space with concrete walls, lit by huge, cone-shaped lamps that hung from the ceiling. At its center, behind De Pere, was a circular room with glass walls. Watching from within it was a doctor in a white lab coat and four nurses in blue

scrubs surrounded by all manner of medical equipment, plus several oper-
ating tables.

Beyond the glass-walled room were rows of military cots that radiated
outward like rays from the sun. Lying on the cots were men and women
of varying ages, from teens to octogenarians. Those closest to the central
room were clearly scourges. Their pupils had gone black as night, and their
skin was marred by stark blue veins that stretched over their necks, cheeks,
and especially around their eyes. Like Morgan and Dakota, each wore a
dog tag, likely with their name and an assigned number. Those farther
along the rows had sallow skin, a redness around their eyes, and expressions that could only be described as deep disinterest. They were thralls,
and outnumbered the scourges twenty to one.

While the thralls seemed oblivious to De Pere, Liam, and everyone
else, the scourges were different. Their heads were lifted, and they were
staring with the black pits of their eyes at De Pere, only at De Pere. It sent
a chill down Liam's spine just to watch it.

"You've led us a merry chase," De Pere said as he strode toward Liam.

Liam aimed his rifle at De Pere's chest. "That's far enough."

De Pere stopped.

Alastair, meanwhile, swiveled his head back and forth, taking in the
vast room around them. "Illusions aren't supposed to work here."

"He turned the antennas off," Clay said with a sneer. "He only made us
think they were active."

"But how could he have known we were coming?" Alastair asked.

Liam had been wondering the same thing, but he suddenly figured it
out. "He heard what Grace and I were talking about. He had a full day to
plan for our arrival."

"I'm impressed, Liam," said De Pere.

"So where is she?" Liam asked.

"Somewhere safe. Now put the weapon down."

Liam considered it, but how could he? He felt as if he were standing on
a precipice, and that if he didn't do something, all would be lost—not just

him, not just Clay, Stasa, and Grace, but the country, the entire world. Almost without thought, he aimed and fired at De Pere.

The bullet exploded from the barrel. De Pere blinked out of existence, reappearing to Liam's left, beyond the nearest row of thralls. Liam felt for the edges of his illusion—just one thread, one small fray, and he'd be able to pull it apart—but it was seamless.

He fired again, this time at De Pere's head.

When De Pere blinked away and reappeared to their right, Clay swung his rifle and fired twice in quick succession. Alastair let his repeating rifle go. Even Stasa squeezed off a round. But De Pere merely smiled and vanished each time. And every time he appeared somewhere new, the scourges swung their gazes to follow.

"Enough," De Pere said. "You're going to get someone hurt."

He was standing in front of the doors to the glass room again, and this time there were two dozen soldiers standing behind him. Their rifles were aimed at Liam, Alastair, Clay, and Stasa.

An arm suddenly slipped around Liam's neck from behind. "You shouldn't have come," came Max Kohler's harsh voice.

An officer broke away from the soldiers. It was Sergeant Kowalski, the man they'd spoken to on the elevator. "Your weapons," he said calmly.

Liam tried to summon an illusion, of Cabal soldiers rushing in from the far side of the room, but the moment he did, Kohler tightened his grip and wrenched Liam back and forth until he stopped.

"Your *weapons*," Sergeant Kowalski repeated.

While struggling to breathe, Liam handed his rifle to Sergeant Kowalski. Clay and Stasa followed suit. Alastair, meanwhile, brought his hand back into place, effectively deactivating his rifle. His wrists were immediately locked in manacles and secured to his sides with chains. Only then did Kohler ease his grip on Liam's neck.

"What happens now?" Liam rasped.

De Pere smiled. "You'll see soon enough."

He nodded to Kohler. Moments later, Liam felt a sting in his neck and the cold sensation that came with an injection. De Pere's handsome face swam before him. Everything began to swirl—the lights, the cavernous room, the soldiers, the many scourges and thralls in their cots, his friends. Then Liam melted too, and he lost track of who he was, where he was, and what fool steps had led him there.

FORTY-TWO

Liam woke strapped to a white leather chair with broad arms, the sort used to draw blood. His limbs were leaden, his mind foggy, but those effects faded the longer he took in the scene around him.

He was inside the large room with the glass walls. All about lay medical equipment. Nearby stood a console with dials, switches, gauges, and a myriad of lights colored red, amber, and green. Beyond the glass walls, the scourges and thralls lay on their cots. The same team of four nurses Liam had seen earlier moved about the room, monitoring the equipment or checking vitals. A bag filled with clear liquid hanging from a hook near Liam's chair fed the needle stuck into his left arm.

The doctor, a burly fellow with a full red beard and mustache, glanced at Liam, then pressed a button on a console and spoke into a microphone. "He's awake."

"I'll be there shortly," came President De Pere's voice.

Something weighed on Liam's head, likely a helmet of some sort. He could feel small points of pressure—electrodes, surely—pressing into his scalp and forehead.

The doctor came to Liam's side, and made some adjustments to the helmet. "Can you hear me?"

Liam nodded. "Where are the others, the ones who came with me?"

"They're safe for now, but rest assured, you and your traitorous friends are going to get what you deserve."

With those words, all hope of reasoning with the man vanished. He was already set against Liam and the Uprising. To him, anything that happened to them was justified.

The doctor finished his adjustments and began walking away, but he'd not gone three strides before he suddenly disappeared. The nurses vanished next, then the thralls and scourges beyond the window. The room around him shifted and smeared, the scene eerily similar to what had happened in the sphere atop the Kovacs P&L building, and again at LuxCorp, so much so that Liam was unfazed when Max Kohler stepped into the room.

For a time, Kohler seemed lost in thought, lost in his worries. He paced behind a padded green chair, then stopped and stabbed a finger toward the glass walls. Beyond them, the scourges, only the scourges, reappeared. "Do you know why he made them?"

"To infect others," Liam said.

"Yes." Kohler resumed his pacing. When he spoke again, it was like he was talking to himself more than Liam. "But there's more, a grand design you can't see, not until you've stepped away from it. And you need to. You need to see the bigger picture."

Liam shook his head. "I don't understand, Max. Why are you trying to help me? You're De Pere's right-hand man. You've been with him from the start."

Kohler's movements slowed, then stopped altogether. "*With* him?" On the window behind him, images flashed, memories of Kohler torturing himself, using razors, fish hooks, broken glass and more. On and on it went, with De Pere standing by, watching. As the images continued to play, Kohler reached up, worked at the straps holding his mask in place, and lifted it to reveal a face dominated by scars, a catalogue of pain and misery. His right eye, where the red lens had been, was missing, replaced by a dark pit. "Ask yourself, Mulcahey, does this look like I'm with him?" He waved to the images on the window. "Does *that*?"

"Then why would you stay?"

"Because I'm trapped! He *took* me, made me his own personal thrall."

"Then how can you be here now, acting of your own free will?"

"Because he can't focus on me all the time. I've found ways to avoid his attention, but it doesn't last long, and you're wasting time with stupid questions." He paused. "I know what Grace told you." He waved to the window, and the bloody memories were replaced with a vision of an army officer lying wounded—the memory Grace had shown him of De Pere in the war's last major battle. "*That's* what he's been so afraid of. It's why he's coming here himself, to find the truth of what Colette shared with you, learn who else knows."

"Colette didn't share that with me, though. Or if she did, I don't remember."

"Just because you don't remember doesn't mean she never did. You *have* to remember, Mulcahey. You have to learn why he's so afraid. Everything depends on it."

Feeling sick to his stomach, Liam focused on Kohler's ruined face. "Then *help* me. Fill in some details. Tell me what he has planned. Maybe that'll jog something loose."

Kohler swallowed hard, and the images of torture finally faded. "You know part of the story. De Pere means to turn the thralls into obedient slaves. The psis will carry his will to every corner of the earth. But the *scourges* are the real key." He paused. "Years ago, I found a journal De Pere writes in. One entry said he wanted to free himself, to *untether* his mind. That mean anything to you?"

Though Liam was curious and concerned over the word Kohler had just used, *untether*, it was the second bit of information he'd just revealed that shook him. "De Pere keeps a journal?"

"I don't know if he still does, but he did then."

"Colette did, too."

Kohler's good eye narrowed. "So?"

"Stasa Kovacs gave me a serum that's helped to uncover some of my memories. Except, each time I remember more, I see some of *Colette's* memories as well. Stasa thinks that Colette's giving me the permanent serum before anyone else linked us in some way."

Kohler stared at him hard. "Please tell me there's more."

"In the last memory I saw, she was writing in a journal. Except it wasn't just writing. She was having a conversation."

"With who?"

"Stasa thinks it's another part of herself, a split personality. It felt hungry and malicious. Inhuman. It called itself Echo."

Kohler's lone, blue-eyed gaze traveled beyond Liam, becoming restless in the process. "Echo . . ."

"You know about it?"

"Sort of. After the war, De Pere wiped your memories, you and the other Henchmen, and sent you away. Crawford came to Novo Solis in '21 because he was starting to remember. When De Pere tried to wipe the memories away again, Crawford resisted, and De Pere lashed out." Kohler paused. "I visited Nick in the hospital afterward, to see for myself what De Pere'd done to him. I'll admit, it shook me."

"Shook you, after all he'd done to *you*?"

Kohler shrugged. "Torture's one thing—some of it I deserved—but he *destroyed* Crawford's mind. When I asked De Pere how he could have done it, he said, 'It wasn't me. It was Echo.' He looked embarrassed, shocked that he'd said it. He flew into a rage. He tortured me like never before." Kohler pointed to the ruined pit where his right eye had once been. "That's when he did *this*."

"You said he wanted to *untether*." Liam jutted his chin toward the window, to the scourges beyond. "Do you suppose he meant *into* them?"

Kohler nodded. "I'm certain that's what he meant."

"How? And how can we stop it?"

"That's precisely what you need to—"

Just then Kohler's face screwed up in pain. He released an agonized scream and fell to the floor. The nurses and the doctor suddenly reappeared, turned, and stared in fright at Kohler, who writhed on the floor.

A moment later, Leland De Pere, still dressed impeccably in his cream-colored suit, opened the doors and strode into the room. He was flanked by four CIC guards. For a time, De Pere watched Kohler writhe and scream. Then the screaming was cut short and Kohler went still, his breathing labored.

"We'll discuss this later, Max." De Pere waved to him, and the guards picked Kohler up and carried him away.

De Pere, all but ignoring Liam, walked to the instrument panel and spoke to the doctor in a low voice. Liam listened carefully, trying to catch what he was saying, then heard a familiar scuffing sound.

He turned to see Nana shuffling toward the empty green chair. "You're in the shit now, boyo." She sat and stared at him with an intense expression. "De Pere's preparing to take what he wants from you, and you're just sitting there."

"I can't fight him," Liam whispered. "I'm trapped!"

"There's more than one way to fight." She glanced at the helmet on his head. "He's about to go rooting about in your memories. That means a connection's going to be made between the two of you. Use it, Liam. Use it to take what *you* want."

Liam looked up as a nurse approached with a needle in hand. When he looked back at the chair, Nana was gone. As the nurse injected something into Liam's IV, De Pere broke from the doctor and strode closer. He took his jacket off and laid it carefully on the back of the empty chair, then arranged himself in it, looking pleased beyond measure.

Liam's eyelids grew heavy, his limbs leaden. He felt like a golem made of clay, not a man of flesh and bone. He tried to speak, but something prevented him. All he could manage was to swing his head lazily back and forth.

"I overheard Max speaking to you about Nick," De Pere said. "It's unfortunate. I always liked Nick." He nodded to the doctor, who flipped a switch on the instrument panel.

Liam felt suddenly potent. He gained a sharpness of mind that had been completely absent moments ago. He felt as if his mind were expanding, as if he could recall anything he wished. And that in turn made him feel as though he'd been laid bare. It made it difficult to concentrate, but he managed to retain one overriding thought: "You were a good man once," he said to De Pere. "What *happened* to you?"

"It's not what *happened*," De Pere shot back. "It's what's *about* to happen. What *needs* to happen."

De Pere's gaze became more intense, and Liam suddenly recalled the interview where he'd first met Colette. He'd been led to a room, where he sat at a table across from the stunningly pretty doctor. She'd been wearing a dress with a lab coat over it. She had a small white tag with her name engraved on it: Dr. Colette Silva. Her long, curly hair had been tied back. She'd asked him a series of questions about his past, his upbringing, his family. The more questions he'd answered, the more he'd wanted to ask Colette similar questions, to learn more about her. He'd been infatuated, but he'd stifled the urges as inappropriate. Besides, a woman as poised and refined as Colette would never be attracted to someone like him, a man of simple tastes, of modest means.

His mind shifted to the first time he and the other Devil's Henchmen had been given the serum, *Echobacterum sentensis*. He recalled how his mind had warmed to everyone—no more than this, a simple warming, but it was clear they were connected. In following trials he'd felt their emotions if not their thoughts: Vankoningsfeld's worry, Kohler's disregard for what anyone else thought of him. Clay's reaction of childlike wonder, so starkly different from the image he normally projected, had made Liam laugh with joy.

More memories. Another meeting with Colette came and went, and another, his history with her playing out in greater detail than he had been able to manage on his own. Perhaps it was necessary for De Pere to start from the beginning and follow it like a trail of breadcrumbs. Or perhaps he wanted no stone left unturned. Whatever the case, Liam found himself becoming more and more convinced that when they came to the end of this trail of memories, De Pere would have what he wanted: an unimpeded path to his *untethering*.

Liam's attempts to stop him were feeble at best. It felt as if he were playing chess with a grand master, any move he made foreseen long ago.

Liam blinked, and suddenly Nana was sitting in the chair across from him, not De Pere. "*Fight*, Liam."

"I don't know how."

"He's opened a door for you." Grace now sat in the bulky chair, wearing the same stunning, beaded dress she'd had on when he'd first met her in Club Artemis. Her blond, wavy hair reflected the harsh lights embedded into the ceiling. "Doorways work both ways. You can find what *you* need, too."

"And what is that? What do I need?"

When Liam blinked again, Colette had taken Grace's place. She had a sly look on her face, the sort she used to give when Liam was a bit slow picking up on her jokes. "Secrets, Liam." She leaned forward with a hungry stare. "His most cherished secrets. Things you can use against him."

He felt De Pere's sudden excitement. He was focusing on a particular night during the war: Liam's dinner with Colette, his agreeing to taking the permanent serum, her plunging the needle into his arm. More than the events themselves, De Pere seemed fascinated by Colette's relief at having found someone to take the serum with before the next in line: Max Kohler.

It seemed vitally important to Colette, and that, in turn, felt important to De Pere to have discovered. It felt as though De Pere was getting closer to what he wanted, which spurred Liam to return to what Colette, the one sitting in the green chair before him, had just told him.

Secrets . . .

Perhaps he *could* find them. Perhaps he *could* root around in De Pere's mind as De Pere was doing in his. It felt an impossible task at first, but as Grace had told him in the domes, memories were only one step removed from perceptions, and he'd grown skilled at manipulating those. As with illusions, he needed to find a place of calm. He tried, and sensed some few thoughts running through De Pere's mind. They came and went in flashes, one replaced by another in such rapid sequence it felt as if Liam were trying to locate a single monarch butterfly in a vast, blooming swarm.

He relaxed further. He coaxed rather than forced, working slowly *backward* through De Pere's memories as De Pere worked *forward* through his. In doing so, Liam sensed a single, overriding emotion: fear. De Pere was terrified that his plans would unravel. But why? What was the source of that fear?

Liam was certain the answer would come when he understood what had so fundamentally changed De Pere after the war. Step by step, he followed the memories backward until there were no more. Thinking he'd merely lost the thread, he tried again, and again he arrived at a place that felt like a complete, perfect, dead end. Nothing came before it. No memories. No fears. No dreams. Nothing at all, as if De Pere had been born in that very moment during the Battle of Whitefish Bay, the crucial turning point that had led to the armistice.

As Liam immersed himself in the memory, in the moment of Leland De Pere's improbable genesis, he was suddenly swept away.

FORTY-THREE

During the war . . .

In the mission prep room with Liam were Hansen, Hatcher, Reyes, and the rest. They were nervous. Liam was too. For the most part they were waiting for the upcoming briefing in silence. All except Clay, who kept cracking jokes.

"I'm going to know every time you yank your chain," he said when Liam glanced his way. "You know that, right?"

"You're so gross," Vankoningsfeld said, her lips screwed up in disgust.

"You too"—with a leering grin, he stuck his thumb so that its tip peeked out between his fore and middle fingers, then proceeded to rub it with his opposite hand—"every time you polish that pearl, girl."

Vankoningsfeld looked like she wanted to deny it, either that or slap Clay across his smug face, but she knew it was true. They all did.

"Fall in!" came a shout from the entrance.

The squad formed up and snapped to attention, everyone raising their hands in salute, as Kohler, wearing the fresh stripes of a master sergeant, entered the room, stepped to one side, and saluted as well. Leland De Pere, freshly promoted to Lieutenant Colonel, came in just behind him, as did a dozen other high-ranking officers.

When De Pere saluted back, the squad dropped into parade rest. Dr. Silva and two of her nurses came last, each holding a metal briefcase, which they proceeded to set on an empty table at the front of the room.

"Our scouts have reported the SLP powers moving a full dozen of their goliaths into position in Grafton, twelve miles north of Milwaukee. Given that several battalions have been repositioned from the eastern warfront, it's clear they're ready to push south." De Pere paused. "The war could turn against us here, today, but what the SLP don't realize is that it could turn for them, too. They have no idea what's about to hit them."

"Hooah!"

De Pere went on to detail the disposition of the enemy as currently known, but Liam listened with only half an ear. He was watching Colette, who seemed worried, even confused. The sharp lines of her eyebrows were pinched. Her eyes were constantly blinking, constantly moving, as if her mind were anywhere but on the upcoming mission. She and Liam were still connected, but her walls were up again, as they'd been the night he took the serum with her. They seemed impenetrable, except for the lone emotion somehow seeping through the cracks: a worry so deep it felt like existential dread.

She blinked fiercely as De Pere waved to her.

"What the good doctor has developed," De Pere was saying, "is nothing short of miraculous. But make no mistake. What you're doing is a great sacrifice. This step, once taken, cannot be taken back. And so I offer you this last chance to step away. There's no shame in taking up another role in our great Army and serving in a different capacity."

"No one's backing down," Kohler said. He seemed on edge, as if he couldn't wait to lay into the enemy.

"They'll speak for themselves, Master Sergeant," De Pere said evenly.

Moments passed in which De Pere's gaze passed calmly over the group. No one spoke. No one moved a muscle.

"Very good." De Pere turned to Liam. "Master Sergeant Kohler is no longer formally in command of the Devil's Henchmen, but he's asked to lead you in battle. I'm giving him permission to do so, unless you have objections."

"I do," Liam said. "The team—"

"Overruled," De Pere said immediately, making it clear it was never Liam's choice to begin with.

The Henchmen broke discipline momentarily, sharing glances with one another, including Clay, who was staring at Liam with an unreadable expression. Sympathy, maybe, or perhaps disappointment.

"Eyes ahead, Henchmen!" Kohler shouted, and everyone snapped back to attention.

De Pere nodded sharply to Colette. "Over to you, doctor."

Blinking, Colette pulled herself tall. The look of worry on her face vanished, replaced by one of grave seriousness. "You know the drill by now," she said to the squad. "Sleeves up."

As the soldiers lined up and the nurses opened their briefcases and readied bottles of alcohol and cotton swabs, Liam sidled up to Colette.

"Everything okay?" he asked in a low voice.

"Sure it is. Why wouldn't it be?"

"You seem distracted is all."

She shook her head. "It's just politics."

"What do you mean?"

"Senator Vaughan . . . He was *concerned*, he said, over making the Henchman serum permanent. With President Nolan in the hospital from the heart attack, Vaughan and his cohort on the Armed Services Committee are pushing back hard, claiming we need more research."

"And do we?"

"We're on the brink of losing this war, Liam."

"That wasn't the question."

She'd been staring hard at the squad, as if she couldn't wait for the injections to be over, but at Liam's words she turned and leveled an uncompromising stare at him. "More research could take months. *Years.*"

"The other day, you told me they demanded copies of your reports. Did the committee find something to be concerned about?"

"Nothing we can't handle."

"What was it, Colette?"

"I said it was nothing." Her face turned angry. "Now, are you getting in line or are you stepping down from the fight?"

Liam had never seen Colette like this. She was a driven woman, but she'd never been one to disregard the genuine concerns of others, nor had she ever treated him so contemptuously. "If the Armed Services Committee raised concerns," he gestured toward the rest of the squad, "how is it we're moving forward?"

Colette's fierce gaze slid to De Pere. "It was the Lieutenant Colonel. Everyone likes him." She paused, her face softening. "He's a very convincing man when he wants to be."

It was then that Liam realized De Pere and the other nearby officers were rolling up their sleeves as well.

"They're getting the serum too?"

Colette nodded. "A slightly weaker version of it, yes. It'll allow them to monitor your movements."

Liam wasn't sure what to think about it. He knew this was a possibility, but it felt as if things were moving fast. Too fast.

"Let's *go*, Mulcahey." It was Kohler. He was staring at Liam like a wolverine, ready to fight if Liam said a single word against him.

Liam's doubts were stronger than they'd ever been, but they were indistinct, formless, while the enemy was anything but. The goliaths were terrors on the battlefield. If they didn't come up with something to counter them, the war *would* turn against the U.S.

So it was that, despite his reservations, despite Colette's strange behavior, he lined up with the others and received his shot. Colette seemed to relax once he had. He'd already received the permanent serum, of course, but the new one made him more aware of his fellow Henchmen. It made him more aware of Colette as well—either that or she'd become less guarded. Whatever the case, she finally seemed at ease, as if everything were proceeding according to plan.

Then the Henchmen were off, preparing for the coming battle, which arrived all too soon. Liam was lined up in the trenches with the others. Each was strapped into their hopper exoskeleton. Each was armed with a rifle, a shoulder-mounted grenade launcher, and several magnetic mines designed to bore beneath a goliath's armor before detonating.

Ahead lay the broken battlefields of Whitefish Bay, land that had once been populated with patches of farms, streams, and copses of oak, elm, and maple. A bank of fog rolled in from the lake. The ground shook. Red lights loomed, the goliaths approaching.

When the signal was given, the Henchmen rose as one and bounded over the battlefield, each and every soldier connected to the rest. They shared senses. They shared tactical decisions, which came in the blink of an eye. They swarmed the first goliath, Hatcher leaping high and slapping a mine on the back of its great, rounded head. Hansen did the same to another while other others confused the mechanika's operators.

They moved constantly, leaping, taking out the goliaths' red viewing lights with well-aimed shots from their rifles or grenade launchers. The rest of the U.S. forces, meanwhile, advanced.

More and more goliaths fell, but the Henchmen took casualties too. Reyes was lost when he leapt onto a goliath's back, clipped by another of the hulking mechanika freshly emerged from the fog. He fell when the treads of a British tank steamrolled him, but a moment later the goliath above him exploded, Reyes' mine having found the goliath's munitions store. The battlefield was lit for a mile around as the boom and rattle of the explosion bloomed upward like a geyser.

Two more Henchmen were lost, but by then the enemy had been reduced to three goliaths. One shook from the explosions going off inside the pilot's compartment in the goliath's head. It tipped onto its face, spraying dirt everywhere. Most of the Henchmen turned their focus on the second goliath. The third, meanwhile, began pounding toward the trenches, then beyond the U.S. line. Steam rose in a plume from one shoulder as it ate the distance, moving faster than Liam realized the goliaths could go.

—*Goliath moving fast,* Liam called to the team.

—*You and Crawford slow it down,* came Kohler's reply. *We'll be along shortly.*

Liam stormed toward it with Nick Crawford, but the goliath wasn't slowing. It took horrendous fire from the gun emplacements along the line, but the bullets were ricocheting off its armor, creating a fireworks display as it trampled the crow's talons and continued past the lines toward the bunker where most of the command officers were now stationed.

—*It's heading for the command bunker,* Liam called.

—*Then stop it, goddamnit!* Kohler ordered.

Liam and Crawford tried. But the goliath was too far ahead. It raised its right arm, which was little more than a massive cannon. The cannon boomed. Then again. Hellfire coughed from the end of the massive barrel. The bunker exploded in a blinding display—concrete debris and dozens of personnel flying through the air.

Another explosion came from a third burst of the goliath's cannon, then it raised its left arm. Its Gatling spun, whining as it attained firing speed. It unloaded on the soldiers, officers, and personnel who'd somehow escaped the bunker in time. The survivors scattered, but the goliath mowed them down with frightening efficiency.

Crawford was out of mines but leapt high and fired into the crease between the goliath's neck and shoulder. Liam came after, landing and clamping his remaining mine onto the goliath's lower back.

The mine's drill-bit head spun. It ate into the armor with a high, piercing, metal-shearing scream. It sunk deeper and deeper into the goliath's bowels. As he and Crawford leapt free, the mine detonated. The goliath's hips twisted strangely. It seemed to lurch, as if it were drunk and trying to right itself. Then it fell sideways with a rattle and a boom.

The goliath was down, but the damage had been done. As the Henchmen converged on the fallen goliath's position, Liam looked over the wreckage and spotted an officer. As more explosions lit the night, he saw who it was.

It was De Pere, his body riddled with shrapnel, a bullet wound in his forehead. Standing only a few paces away, a gun gripped tightly in one hand, was Colette.

FORTY-FOUR

During the war . . .

From within a copse of trees, Colette watched as the goliath charged over the broken farmland toward the command bunker, watched as its munitions tore the structure to bits. She watched the Gatling blaze, watched the goliath deal death in an ever-expanding arc. Dozens were killed in moments. It was a stunning turn in the battle, the command center reduced to cinders by the firepower of the SLP, a thing made all the easier when Colette, or rather, Echo, had transmitted the planned location for the command center to the enemy.

The night before, Colette had watched, helpless, as Echo wrote the information on a slip of paper and concealed it in a fake tube of lipstick. She'd stood by, horrified, as Echo used her body to deliver it to the spy she'd uncovered after several weeks of careful research. Colette tried to prevent it, but found it impossible. Echo had only further cemented its hold on her in the days since their first conversation. They'd had a number of conversations since then, some in the very same journal. More and more, though, they'd been conducted with mere thought.

Slowly but surely, Echo had gained dominance over her mind. It wanted more than her, though—so much more—and had formulated a plan to get it. The decisive battle was but one of many steps that needed to be completed just so.

Using Colette's body, Echo strode toward the crater where the command bunker had once stood. The war still raged. The goliath that had made a ruin of the bunker was only twenty yards away. The sound of its guns and of the return fire was deafening. Two of the Devil's Henchmen, Liam and Nick, were leaping upon it, hoping to take it down. While Echo didn't care if either of them lived, *Colette* cared desperately. She dearly hoped Liam would survive the battle. She wanted to see him again, to hold him. She wanted to be free of Echo, and to find a day when it would be just the two of them, a thing that felt inconceivable with the carnage, the cannon fire, the chaos of a battle that sounded like the heavens were falling down, and, most of all, with Echo controlling her every move.

Echo searched the bodies, eventually finding the officer it had identified as crucial to its plans: the newly minted *Lieutenant Colonel* De Pere. He was bleeding from shrapnel wounds but, as fate would have it, still drew breath.

"Medic!" he called, then noticed Echo's approach. "Dr. Silva, please . . ." He swallowed hard, drew a rasping breath. "Help me."

Echo stared down with dispassion. "I wish I could have spared you the suffering. This brings me no joy."

It was strange to admit, but Colette found she believed those words. Echo was not wholly inhuman, after all. It had emerged from within her own subconscious and was now composed of beings who loved, who had hopes and fears, who shared compassion for one another—it couldn't live but that some small amount of their emotions shone through.

De Pere coughed. His throat worked. Explosions in the distance reflected off the sheets of blood coating the left side of his face. "I'm hurt," was all he managed to say before Echo leaned down, retrieved De Pere's own sidearm, and squeezed a round into the center of his forehead.

A moment later, a voice came. "Colette?"

Echo spun, heart pumping madly. Liam, in his hopper suit, his face and uniform grimy with mud, lumbered toward De Pere's fallen body. He held his combat rifle easily, though it seemed all but forgotten as he stared down in confusion. And it wasn't only him; the entire squad had just seen what Liam had seen. They'd felt his shock at finding De Pere dead and Colette standing over him with a gun in her hand.

To that point, Echo had felt inevitable, too powerful to stop, but in that moment of uncertainty, it felt the earth shifting beneath its feet, and Colette suddenly found a way to regain herself.

"Liam, please help!" she cried, but managed no more than that.

The next moment, she was back below the surface, and Echo was proving how staggeringly adept it had become at twisting perceptions and memory. With an ease that made her feel cold and isolated, it supplanted the squad's memories. Instead of De Pere lying there dead, his body shattered, he appeared only wounded. Colette, who'd come to help him, knelt by his side, pressing a bandage tightly against one of the more severe wounds.

In the fog of their shared consciousness, Colette watched in despair. She felt Liam's beliefs form, felt them harden like epoxy. As they became his reality, a hole opened up beneath her. Succumbing to her despair, she fell, faster and faster, certain she'd never see the surface again.

FORTY-FIVE

Liam blinked, clearing away the memories of seeing De Pere dead, of Colette crafting an illusion to make everyone think he was still alive.

No, Liam thought. *It wasn't Colette who crafted the illusion. It was Echo.*

Echo's consciousness, fearing for its own survival, had ensured that De Pere died so it could take his place.

In the glass-walled room deep beneath Fort Nolan, Liam focused his attention on De Pere himself. He had no idea if De Pere had found what he'd been searching for while rooting through Liam's memories—maybe he had, maybe he hadn't—but just then he was staring back at Liam with a look of pure terror.

As Liam stared back, the truths revealed by Colette's uncovered memories struck him full force. "You're not real," he said to De Pere.

De Pere blinked. He glanced at the doctor and the nurses, who stood by silently with expressions of confusion, as if they were waiting for De Pere to deny Liam's words.

"You died in the Battle of Whitefish Bay," Liam went on. "You were wounded in the goliath's attack, then shot in the head by Colette Silva."

De Pere stood from the chair. "Be quiet."

But Liam wouldn't. "You're an illusion, a figment of someone else's mind, a convenient construct Echo uses for its own gain."

"I said be *quiet!*" He tried to slap Liam, but Liam knew the truth. De Pere wasn't there. He was nothing more than a figment of everyone's collective imagination. Liam denied the illusion of the slap and the pain that would normally have followed.

For a moment, just one moment, Colette appeared in De Pere's place. Everyone in the room stared, their eyes going wide.

"No!" De Pere cried. He blinked hard. He worked his jaw like he'd just woken from a long, uncomfortable sleep.

"You're nothing more than a memory," Liam said to him. "A fabrication. A lie."

"No!"

A keen ringing invaded Liam's consciousness. It became so strong it was deafening. His mind felt like static, like the hiss from a wireless tuned to the wrong channel.

De Pere ran from the room. He didn't even bother to open the doors. He just ran straight through them, his well-dressed figure flickering like firelight before he reappeared on the opposite side.

Through the glass walls, Liam saw him running along an aisle between the cots while the scourges craned their necks to watch. The scourges spasmed. They moaned and bared their teeth as if experiencing his anguish. As De Pere was lost to the dim light on the far side of the cavernous room, one of the scourges stood from his cot. Another followed suit, and another. Soon, in a circle all around the glass-walled room, the scourges had stood and fixed the black pits of their eyes on those within.

Beyond the scourges, the thralls, as if roused by the scourges' anger, stood and approached the room. Whether it was on some sort of order from De Pere or a desire driven independently by the scourges, the thralls' purpose was clear: they would slay Liam and the others, rend them limb from limb for the crime of knowing the truth about Leland De Pere.

"What do we do?" one of the nurses asked.

"We get out." The doctor moved to the instrument panel, lifted its glass face, and punched a red button.

Beyond the glass walls, hundreds of yellow lights in the ceiling snapped on. Accompanying the terrible glare was a rhythmic thrum Liam felt in his chest. The scourges closed their eyes against the brightness. They fell to the floor and writhed. The thralls slowed in their movements. Some stopped and stared up at the harsh lights. Others looked on, confused.

One, an older girl with blond hair, held her hands tight to her chest. She looked despondent, but when her gaze fell on a nearby, fallen scourge, it was as if she'd just recognized her mortal enemy. As young William had done to his own father back at the domes, she fell on him and began beating him mercilessly. A moment later, a portly woman with lank gray hair joined her. As did an ancient man with sagging, wrinkled skin.

"What are they doing?" the nurse said.

The doctor stared at the unfolding violence. "I don't know," he said, "but I'm not waiting to find out."

"We're supposed to *protect* the scourges," the nurse said.

"Didn't you *see* them?" the doctor asked as he moved to Liam's chair. "They were going to sting us, or worse." He freed Liam from his restraints. "Let's get moving. The soldiers can take care of the rest."

All of them, including Liam, left the room in a group. The thralls, wholly focused on the scourges, had begun assaulting them with more abandon. It was a grisly scene to walk through, but they did, heading steadily toward a set of doors along one wall. From those same doors, soldiers in black uniforms poured out.

The Cabal were clearly prepared for this sort of contingency, but the soldiers seemed shocked by the sheer magnitude of the chaos playing out before them. They set up a perimeter while an officer shouted, "Prepare to secure the scourges! Secure the scourges first!"

As the doctor and nurses spoke with the same officer, Liam used the madness to his advantage. Stepping beyond the doors into the long hallway beyond, he waved his arms and altered his appearance to look like De Pere himself, right down to the suit he'd been wearing when he'd fled.

It was more difficult than Liam had thought. His mind was still muddy from whatever the nurse had injected him with earlier, and he was exhausted, both of which made maintaining the illusion a challenge. It felt like spinning a plate on a stick: rotating it sufficiently fast to achieve balance was tricky enough; maintaining it was a constant struggle. Even so, he managed it and rushed along the hallway as red alarm lights spun and klaxons blared.

He soon came across a group of soldiers rushing toward the concrete hall. Most held tommy guns with vertical, box-type magazines perched in front of the trigger. Others bore bolt-action rifles. The officer leading them was none other than Sergeant Kowalski. Liam addressed him in his guise as Leland De Pere. "The prisoners," he said, "I need them out now before this gets even more out of hand."

Sergeant Kowalski hesitated. "Your orders were to leave them in place, sir, no matter what."

"Yes, but we have an emergency on our hands, son." Liam smiled De Pere's smile, the one that said everything would be fine so long as they both remained calm. "The Uprising have infiltrated our base, hoping to break their friends free. I don't mean to let that happen. Do you?"

"No. Of course not, sir. Mr. President, sir."

Liam waved along the hallway. "Then let's get moving, Sergeant."

With a sharp nod, the sergeant ordered his men to continue, then led Liam to an adjoining hallway and a locked room. After pulling keys from his belt, he unlocked the door. Inside were Clay, Stasa, and Alastair, all of them manacled to a metal bench built into the far wall.

"Release them," Liam said. Maintaining the illusion was taking progressively more of his concentration to maintain—he knew he couldn't keep it up much longer.

The sergeant freed Stasa and Clay, but left Alastair where he was.

"The mechanika, too," Liam added, his voice cracking somewhat, a bit of himself showing through.

Clay and Stasa watched everything unfold with uncertain looks. Sergeant Kowalski, meanwhile, freed Alastair, but did so with a frown. It wouldn't be long before he figured it out.

"Now," Liam said, "where is Grace Savropoulis?"

The sergeant's eyes narrowed. "You took her away yourself, sir"—he tipped his head toward Stasa and Clay—"when we put them in here."

The inconsistency was clearly making the sergeant more suspicious than he already was, which made it all but impossible to keep the illusion up. The sergeant had just begun backing away when Liam's guise as Leland De Pere simply vanished.

Eyes widening, the sergeant unslung his tommy gun, but Clay was already on the move. He crashed his mechanikal fist into the sergeant's jaw, cutting off his cry for help. After relieving the sergeant of his tommy gun and gagging him with strips of his own shirt, they used a pair of manacles to secure *him* to the bench.

They stepped outside, into the hallway with the spinning red lights, at which point Stasa grabbed Liam's arm. "What in God's name is *happening*?"

Liam led them into a small office across from the cell. "De Pere was questioning me, and . . ." He couldn't go into it, not now. "The scourges got out of control. It's thrown the whole base into chaos."

Stasa waved toward the holding cell. "Okay, but what happened to your illusion in there?"

"I'm exhausted," Liam said. "I couldn't maintain it."

Clay, seeing the door of a gun safe was ajar, moved over to it and pulled the door wide. Inside, the guns were all missing. "That means you won't be able to hide our escape?"

Liam shook his head. "We are who we are for the duration."

"I'm sorry, sirs," said Alastair, "but I still don't understand. How did the president know we were coming?"

Clay paused in his rummaging of the gun safe's shelves. "Grace must have told him. Or De Pere overheard. Either way, it amounts to the same thing."

Alastair stared at the floor. "So, the anti-serum?"

"We're not going to find it," Liam said. "It may not even exist. De Pere might have let the information slip on purpose in order to lure us here. The important thing now is to get out of this place alive."

Clay found little enough in the gun safe—just a few boxes of pistol ammo—but he did stumble across the oxygen and acetylene gas canisters for Alastair's torch. Alastair inserted them into his arm and snapped the compartment closed, then they headed back to the concrete hall. Liam didn't think it was possible, but the chaos had deepened. The bright yellow lights were still on, and the strange thrumming in Liam's chest was back. The scourges writhed while the thralls attacked them in greater numbers. The soldiers, who were now nearly the equal to the number of thralls, moved through the crowd toward the scourges, hoping to secure them.

With the soldiers so preoccupied with the scourges, and with Liam and the others dressed like CIC personnel, no one noticed them.

"They'll have deactivated the elevators for the time being," Clay said while surveying the madness, "and no doubt they'll have repaired the stairwell door as well."

"Very good, sir," said Alastair, who with no preamble whatsoever began running across the vast room.

"Alastair!" Liam hissed.

"I'll prepare the way!" came Alastair's rapidly attenuating voice.

On he went, freight-training his way toward the door to the stairwell, presumably so he could cut his way through the lock. Several soldiers appeared to notice his passage, but made no move to stop him or even call out a warning. And as for the scourges and thralls, they were still largely concerned with one another.

Liam, Clay, and Stasa followed in Alastair's wake, moving in a tight group, wary of the constantly shifting dangers ahead. They made for a channel between islands of scourges and thralls. Liam was just beginning to think they were going to make it through the madness unscathed when the yellow lights snapped off and the thrumming sensation in his chest vanished.

All around them, the fighting quelled, then ceased altogether. The thralls, suddenly listless, waited silently. The scourges rose on unsteady legs. The soldiers who'd been trying to save the scourges stared at the lights above, at the glass-walled room, as if they had no idea why things had suddenly changed. For a moment, all was silence save the sounds of harsh breathing.

Then came an exhausted, disembodied voice:

—*Get them.*

It was De Pere—Echo—giving a directive to the scourges.

The scourges turned their heads toward Liam. The thralls followed, their eyes sharpening as they gained purpose.

"Dear God," Stasa said, "there are too many of them!"

Ahead, Alastair crouched before the door to the stairwell. His torch lit, a pinpoint of blue light.

Clay, meanwhile, had begun scanning the faces ahead while twisting a dial on his chest. "The thralls," he said, "they'll do anything to protect the scourges."

Liam understood his intention immediately. "Clay, don't."

But Clay paid him no mind. He smiled a gallows smile while pressing the plunger that released doses of adrenaline. "I know now why God kept me alive, Liam." He depressed the plunger twice more while taking in Stasa and Liam. "He didn't do it so *I'd* have another chance at life. He did it so *you* would. So *Bailey* would. So *everyone* would."

"Clay, please," Liam said.

But Clay was already shaking his head. "Get to those stairs, you hear me?" He turned and lifted his tommy gun. "Get out and finish this thing."

With a ragged cry, he ran toward the nearest scourge and unleashed a short burst from the tommy gun. Several bullets caught a scourge in the neck. Another burst caught the one behind it dead in the chest.

Stasa was tugging on Liam's sleeve. "Liam, we need to go. Don't make Clay's sacrifice for nothing."

Liam allowed himself to be pulled along, then he was running with Stasa. It was clear Clay's gambit was working. The crowd of thralls were focusing on the clear and present danger, leaving the path to Alastair relatively clear.

As the thralls closed in to protect the scourges, Clay plowed forward. He took out three more scourges before his bullets ran out, at which point he used the gun like a club to bash thralls aside as he moved closer and closer to yet another while roaring, "Come get me, you soulless mother-fuckers!"

As Liam and Stasa neared Alastair's crouched form, Clay grabbed a scourge's uniform and punched him with his mechanikal arm. Blood flew as blow after blow landed. The thralls, meanwhile, crowded around Clay, tried to pull him away, but Clay kept going, red-faced, bellowing all the while.

Alastair, apparently oblivious, stood and pulled the door open. When Clay's cries were cut suddenly short, however, Alastair blinked and stared in his direction. He underwent a chilling transformation in the moments that followed. As his blue eyes shifted to Liam, then Stasa, then the thralls once more, he dropped lower in his stance. He spread his arms wide. His fingers flexed, becoming claws. His head stretched forward, like a predator gauging the defenses of its next kill. Liam hadn't seen the like since the back room of Club Artemis.

"Get moving, up the stairs"—Alastair set off at a lope toward Clay—"now, Master Mulcahey. I'll be along shortly."

What followed was something like out of a penny dreadful. As Liam and Stasa backed away, through the door, Alastair plowed, full steam, into the pack of thralls. He tore into them, rending flesh, pulling the thralls from Clay's unmoving form on the cold, hard floor. More thralls came for him, but Alastair beat them with complete abandon. Arms and legs flailing, head bashing, breaking bone and tearing flesh. He was a complete and utter terror. And the thralls seemed to recognize it. Or maybe the scourges did. Whatever the case, they backed away long enough for Alastair to drag Clay away from them, then throw him across his shoulders. As Alastair clanked his way toward the doors, Liam held the door open, then helped guide Alastair up the stairs while Stasa led the way. By the time they heard the sounds of the thralls' pursuit below, they were nearing ground level.

The garage itself was complete bedlam, people running to and fro. No one stopped them as they rushed toward the van they'd driven in. No one called out as Alastair and Stasa laid Clay's unconscious form in the back and Liam climbed into the driver's seat. No one so much as raised an arm to forestall them as Liam fired the engine and punched the accelerator.

Only as they were careening toward the front gates did any sort of resistance coalesce. The soldiers in the towers fired down as the van crashed through the gates. Three military police cars chased after them, but the van had a good head start and they were able reach a residential area with tight, winding streets. Soon the blaring alarms from the military police cars were fading, and Liam was driving at a sedate pace down the streets of Novo Solis.

FORTY-SIX

I t was nearing sunset by the time Liam, Stasa, Alastair, and Clay reached their temporary safe house: a ballroom closed for renovations. Alastair lifted Clay and carried him from the back of the van to the ballroom's receiving area, where Bailey was waiting.

"Oh, God!" She rushed to Alastair's side and helped move Clay to a storeroom and a simple brown cot that lay within. "I knew it," she said as she opened a medical bag and began cleaning his wounds. "I felt it."

Clay's face was a mess. He'd lost a lot of blood. Stasa had done what he could for him on the way to the ballroom, but he was still in a bad way. Eventually, with both Bailey and Stasa working to treat his wounds, they became convinced they'd done all they could for the time being, and that what Clay needed above all was rest.

After laying a blanket over his sleeping form, they moved to the ballroom and sat at a table, the only one covered in fresh linen.

"So what the hell happened?" asked Bailey.

Stasa did most of the talking early on, describing their entry to the vast underground room, the dissolving of the illusion, their eventual capture. When he was done, Liam filled in the most notable gap: the strange conversation with Kohler and the mental struggle with De Pere. Finally, Stasa gave her the broad brushstrokes of their escape.

When it was done, Bailey's eyes shifted to Alastair. "Alastair," she said breathlessly, "I can't thank you enough."

Alastair's hands were in his lap, his fingers restless. He seemed small again, harmless. "I was glad to do it, Miss Bailey." It didn't *sound* that way, though. He seemed embarrassed over the incident.

"Alastair," Liam said, "are you all right?"

Several long seconds passed before he responded. "Do you recall asking me on the *Eisvögel* whether I recalled my time as a soldier? And my responding that I didn't remember anything?"

"Of course."

"Well, I lied, Master Mulcahey. I do remember bits and pieces, most of them horrifying. I don't like thinking of them, which is why I lied. It reminds me of the barbarous things I once did."

With those words, the source of Alastair's distress was made clear. In saving Clay, he'd resorted to the same sorts of violent acts that haunted him. "I'm so sorry, Alastair."

Bailey, Liam suddenly realized, was crying. Tears fell freely down her face. "I'm sorry, too"—she stood and moved to Alastair's side, then bent down to hug him—"but thank you for rescuing my husband."

Alastair was staring at her as if he felt he didn't deserve it, but then he hugged her back. "I'm glad he's safe," he finally said.

Bailey released him and sat back down, wiping tears along the way. "This has all been a lot," she said to Liam, "but I need to make sure I understand. You're telling me the real De Pere died during the war?"

"That's right," Liam said, "and the person we see as De Pere is actually Colette Silva, or a *part* of her. There's a malignancy inside her, a consciousness distinct and separate from hers that was created and fed as she took more and more of the serum. It calls itself Echo."

Bailey's eyes narrowed, her expression pensive. "Distinct and separate . . . ?"

"Yes. Echo's birth was a byproduct of Colette's growing addiction to the Henchman serum. It eventually coopted her mind. It's been the one doing this all along by portraying itself as De Pere." Liam told them how he'd dug through De Pere's memories even as De Pere searched through his, how he'd seen things from Colette's point of view. He told them how Echo had gained more and more power over Colette, and how it had eventually won, suppressing her entirely.

"I don't understand, sir," said Alastair. "If De Pere is actually Colette, why was he surprised when confronted with that fact?"

It was Stasa who answered. "There have been a number of documented cases of split personalities, people who, after enduring some deep and extended trauma, compartmentalize themselves as different people. In such cases, one personality becomes dominant for a time but eventually gives way to another. It's possible Colette suffered that sort of trauma through prolonged use of *E. sentensis*. It's further possible that Echo, in order to make sense of its own consciousness, adopted the persona of Leland De Pere."

"Even assuming all that's true," Bailey said, "how could Echo have fooled everyone for so long? How could no one have realized De Pere isn't real?"

"We all know how powerful *E. sentensis* is," Stasa said. "Its ability to make us believe in things that aren't real go beyond mere sight and sound. Its very power relies on our natural expectation that the world behaves in certain ways, that there is permanence. When those expectations are strong enough, we ignore facts to the contrary. Any slips that De Pere might have made along the way would be reasoned away as the failings of the observer, not the impermanence of De Pere himself." Stasa snapped his fingers while turning toward Liam. "*That's* why you've been remembering Colette's memories after your own."

Liam shook his head. "Come again?"

"We've long known that some *take* to the serum better than others, their physiology being more attuned to the needs of *E. sentensis*." Stasa became more animated, using his hands as he talked, a rarity for the mousy man. "We also know it took to yours quite well, Liam. Echo may have targeted you for that very reason—to ensure its survival first and foremost, but also to counterbalance the instability of the one it had identified as key to its plans, the one it planned to take next: Kohler himself."

For a moment, Liam was stunned. He didn't want to admit it, but it was an all-too-real possibility that Colette hadn't selected him at all. *Echo* might have.

"We also know that neural pathways form in our minds when we perform habitual tasks," Stasa went on. "The same may be true of mind-to-mind connections. Echo was born of Colette's consciousness. The very fact that you were the first to join her may very well have linked the two of you in crucial ways."

Liam's thoughts were whisked back to the glass-walled room below Fort Nolan. "When I was with Kohler, he confessed Echo was worried because it thought Colette had taught me how to alter memory, to alter someone's will, and that I would do that to Echo itself in order to stop it."

"And *do* you remember?" Stasa asked.

Liam shook his head. "No, but I think it's what Echo was searching for while rooting through my mind. It seemed fascinated when it came to the night I took the permanent serum, especially when it realized just how desperately Colette wanted me to join the collective that was about to form *before* Max did."

Bailey had grown more and more pensive as they'd talked. "Grace always talked about Colette as if she was convince she was dead. Do you think she lied? You think she knew all along Colette was still alive?"

With her words, a thought suddenly occurred to Liam. A staggering thought. A thought that made the blood drain from his face.

Bailey stared at him, then glanced at Stasa. "You all right, dear?"

Liam couldn't answer. His mind was reeling. He felt exactly like he had while racing toward North Town on the Curtiss, wondering if he'd ever see Nana again.

"Liam?" Stasa said.

He nearly confessed his fears, nearly told them what he should have seen all along. But he couldn't. He had to work through the idea and its implications first. So he lied. "It's just everything catching up to me. The attack, our escape . . ."

Bailey patted his hand. "It's been a lot." She tipped her head to the door they'd come through earlier. "There are more cots in the back. Why don't you go get some sleep?"

"I will," Liam said, "soon."

"Well, *I* need to lay down." She stood with a melancholy smile. "I swear on my mama's grave, I've never felt so tired." With that, she headed through the door and was gone.

"Our talk has given me an idea," Stasa said, "something I want to check with Morgan. Care to join me?"

Liam shook his head, then jutted his chin toward the door. "Someone should stay with Bailey."

Stasa nodded, clapped Liam on the shoulder, and left.

"I'm very sorry I let my emotions get to me in the room below Fort Nolan, sir." Alastair's garbled voice box was pitched low. "If I'd stayed with you, maybe Master Graves wouldn't have been hurt."

"You were only trying to get us out faster."

In a perfect simulacrum of Stasa, he stood and clapped Liam on the shoulder. "I'd better go keep watch." He headed toward the back door. "Sleep well, sir."

When he was gone, Liam was left alone in the vastness of the ballroom. For a time, he reveled in the silence, but all too soon, as he knew he would, he heard the sound of shuffling footsteps. Nana, wearing her Sunday best, came from the darkness toward the front of the room. As had been true since Liam learned of her death, she'd come to help him work through difficult problems, and this was the most difficult of them all.

She sat across from Liam with an I-told-you-so expression. "Awfully strange, Grace showing up at Club Artemis when she did."

"Just days after my talk with De Pere," Liam added.

Nana nodded sagely. "And later, she arranges things with the Uprising so it's *you* who goes to President's farewell banquet, not her."

Liam thought back to the way she'd resisted. "She didn't want to risk being seen by him—"

"—because it would alert him to *Colette*'s presence."

Liam didn't understand how it had happened, or even why, but he knew this much: as Echo had adopted the guise of Leland De Pere to do its will, Colette had crafted an identity of her own: Grace Savropoulis. It explained her abilities so much better than the story she'd given Liam. It explained how she knew so much about De Pere's past. It explained how she knew the first thing about neo-medicine.

Nana sucked her teeth as she pondered. "I wonder if Grace even knows who she is."

"I doubt it," Liam said. "De Pere didn't. Not really. He thought he was real. Grace probably does too. Having no consciousness of one's true self might have been necessary so De Pere wouldn't suspect. Colette did it to hide herself from Echo."

Nana nodded. "It would explain why Grace didn't have all the same knowledge Colette herself had. And why she was so haunted by that dream inside of LuxCorp, the one that showed those poor people lined up outside the Pinnacle."

Indeed, it hadn't only been Dakota and Morgan whose attention had been drawn to the Pinnacle. It had been Grace too. Echo had nearly recognized her, which explained why she'd been so paralyzed with fear.

"You knew something was wrong with her all along," Liam said, recalling how distrustful Nana had been of Grace.

Nana's laugh was the low rumble of a threatening storm. "*You* knew, boyo."

Liam shrugged. "Maybe I did."

"Question is, what do we do about it? We know some of the story, but not enough."

"We need to understand Echo's weaknesses," Liam said.

Nana's face went hard. "We need to know how to *destroy* it."

"You're right. I need to talk to Grace, but I don't know how."

Nana thought on that awhile. "Earlier, Stasa talked about a link between you and Colette."

"Yes, but I can't sense it. I certainly don't know how to use it."

Nana stood, shuffled closer. "Sometimes"—she used one finger to tap his forehead—"we live here altogether too much." After a kiss to his forehead, she began shuffling away. Just before the sound was lost altogether, her voice drifted to him, "Listen to your heart, Liam."

Through the windows high along the far wall, the fading light of sunset played against a bank of distant clouds. Some were the color of fresh salmon, others wheat, a reminder of the endless field to which Grace had taken him so the two of them could speak in private. He considered trying to recreate it so that they could talk, but that didn't feel right. The wheat field was a place of deception, which felt too close to De Pere and his devious ways. He needed something more personal, something only they had shared.

As the light faded further, he was taken back to his first meeting with Grace at Club Artemis. He lit several candles, which suffused the room in a soft, golden glow. At the bar near the entrance he found a serving tray. On it, he set a pair of fine crystal glasses, a bowl of sugar cubes, a box of matches, a carafe of ice water, and two slotted spoons. From the liquor rack he took a nearly full bottle of absynthe. It wasn't the same make as what he'd had at Club Artemis. It would probably taste different, too, but that didn't matter. It was the ritual he needed now, the symbolism.

After choosing a small table near the center of the room, he set the platter down and sat in one of the chairs. He set the spoons over the glasses, placed a sugar cube on each of the slotted spoons. The bottle gurgled as he poured the emerald green liquor over the sugar and into the glasses. Sweet smells filled the air, along with subtler, more savory notes.

He lit the sugar and watched the cubes burn and melt. When they'd hit just the right amount of caramelization—golden brown, no more—he doused them with the cold water. The absynthe clouded, its color like a slice of mint pie. After stirring the contents of both glasses, he set one in front of the seat across from him.

Somewhere outside, he heard the occasional rumble of a car passing by. There came the rhythmic clank of an elevated tram, followed by the soft, momentary hum of conversation as a couple walked along the sidewalk out front.

Liam imagined what the ballroom might look like when it was full. He'd love to take Grace here, or Colette—he found he was no longer sure which one was closer in mind, heart, and spirit to the woman he'd started to fall in love with during the war.

Part of him wanted to drink from the glass, but to do so felt like he'd be giving in. He'd been so confident when he'd began. He still was. He refused to believe that Grace wouldn't come. He acted as if he were simply passing time until she returned from the powder room.

Each moment that passed, however, chipped away at his certainty. He thought of the first time he'd met Colette, the undefinable thrill that had run through him on seeing her smile for the first time. He thought of the chit-chat before their briefings, talks that had grown longer and more personal as Project Echo began in earnest. He thought of how similar it felt to the first time he'd met Grace.

He'd hoped his memories of them both might summon her. They had to. There was one big question that needed answering or everything they were doing was doomed to failure. But she *hadn't* come. Focusing on their history *hadn't* acted as a lure.

"Don't be so sure," came a voice from the darkness.

An outline appeared near the center of the parquet dance floor. The heels of her shoes clicked against the wood, became muffled as she reached the carpeting. Her fringed gown hugged her body tightly. White gloves wrapped her arms past the elbows. Her pearl headband somehow made her curled, blonde hair and golden skin shine.

When she reached the table, she glanced at the glasses of absynthe, then held out her hand.

Liam shook his head, confused.

"You danced with Bailey. Are you saying you won't dance with me?"

She flourished to the empty room with her opposite hand, and it flared to life. A jazz orchestra played on the bandstand. The dance floor came alive with men and women moving in step. Everyone was dressed to the nines, including Liam, who now wore a swallowtail tuxedo made of wool died a deep auburn. His top hat, gloves, and pocket square were a slightly lighter shade of brown, the outfit a perfect complement to Grace's.

"Colette—"

"Don't say her name. We have this time. It may be our last. So dance with me."

He nearly denied her. "It's a lie, Grace."

"We tell ourselves lies every day." She held out her hand. "And it isn't *all* a lie."

The way she smiled at him sent a pang of regret and caring and love running through him that was so strong he wasn't sure whether the source of the emotions was him, Grace, or a mix of the two. Deciding he didn't care, he stood, took her hand, and led her out to the dance floor.

Grace moved easily from the Charleston to the Peabody to the Turkey Trot, her motions making the fringes along her gown twirl in bands along her hips and below her knees. Liam tried to keep up with her, but he would no more than fall into a rhythm than Grace would change things up again. She laughed when he grew frustrated, then took his hands and slipped back into the Charleston. Lost in the crowd around them, they danced with wide smiles on their faces.

Is this how Colette sees herself? Liam wondered. *Does she even remember who she is?* He couldn't ask her, not when she'd asked him not to. He found he didn't care to anyway. This moment *was*, and that was enough for him.

When the song came to a wild, frenetic end, the crowd clapped and headed back toward their tables, all broad smiles and sweat-kissed brows.

When everyone but Grace and Liam had left the dance floor, the lead trumpet eased the orchestra into a slow foxtrot. Liam and Grace started as the dance demanded, their backs arched away from one another, but as the song went on, they found themselves holding one another more closely until their bodies were pressed together. They were hardly dancing at all. Movement was secondary. Liam's purpose in that moment was one of simply being with Grace, and of letting himself feel whatever it was that came.

The music came to an end, and they stilled and faced one another. Liam couldn't help himself. He leaned in and kissed her.

Grace kissed him back, and for a time he simply lost himself in that. The hum of conversation faded. The sound of the band's next song dimmed, finishing on one long trumpet note that slowly attenuated, echoing into infinity as Liam opened his eyes to find the hall empty once more, the candles waging a losing war against the darkness.

"Grace," Liam said carefully, "I need to know what's happening. I need to know what to do."

"I know, but it isn't easy to share. It's *dangerous*, Liam." She took his hand and led him to the table. "But I think I've found a way."

They sat, and Grace picked up her glass of absynthe, tipped her head to Liam with a smile that made his worries fade, and took one long swallow. Liam followed suit, finding the drink to be quite cool. He wasn't sure if that was part of the illusion Grace had crafted for them, but really, what did it matter? He savored the taste, particularly the caramel finish, and the world around him melted.

FORTY-SEVEN

During the war . . .

Munitions pounded. Soldiers screamed. The Battle of Whitefish Bay continued to rage. Echo had just used Colette to put a bullet into Leland De Pere's head. Part of Echo was horrified over what it had done, but more and more it was beginning to recognize that those emotions were not its own, but those of its host.

"Colette?"

Echo shivered in fear as Liam ambled closer in his towering hopper suit. He'd borne witness to De Pere's death, it realized, a thing that could not stand. As Echo worked quickly to alter Liam's memories, making him believe De Pere had survived, it felt Colette's growing terror. It felt strange to experience that terror even as it reveled in the power it now wielded. A moment later, it regained perspective, and the helplessness that emanated from Colette as she watched Echo twist the memories of a man she'd come to admire, perhaps even love, became a balm against Echo's worries over its own survival.

It was a heady mixture, one Echo found difficult to balance, to identify the sources of. The emotions came primarily from Colette, of course, but Liam's were added to them, as were those of Max Kohler, the source of many of its most twisted thoughts. Fainter still were the rest of the Devil's Henchmen, mere shades of color against the brighter hues that were Colette, Liam, and Max. Echo knew it would one day need to reflect on its constituent parts and determine the ways each either helped or limited it, but there was no time just then. There was much to do before its place in the world was secured.

At present, only the Devil's Henchmen and a handful of officers had taken the permanent serum, but Echo had long been planning for this day. It had hundreds of doses of the serum at the ready.

Using De Pere's growing influence, Echo convinced more high-ranking officers to take the serum. With the Army's brass secured, it would be a simple matter to expand beyond the armed forces, into the halls of politics, then the citizenry at large.

The armistice was signed mere weeks after the Battle of Whitefish Bay. More was given up than Echo wanted, but it gained the most important thing: the freedom to act and make its next moves within the borders of the United States. The SLP countries retained certain rights, the most dangerous of which was to conduct inspections of military facilities, but those could be worked around.

The Devil's Henchmen, meanwhile, represented danger of another sort. Each had been given the Henchman strain, the more powerful version of *E. sentensis*, and with that came certain risks. They might one day understand Echo's plans. They might one day rise to challenge its power.

Echo debated killing them—it would be a simple enough matter to arrange—but soon abandoned the idea as too risky. Echo was aware that it was not an entity with a single form with a single mental makeup. It was an amalgam of all who'd been given the serum. Colette was the entity who'd given it the ambition to live and to grow. In doing so, she'd become the nexus of its consciousness, the sole, indispensable part of its growing network. But the makeup of its personality didn't start and end with Colette. Liam Mulcahey was contemplative and thoughtful, which helped Echo to see further down the road. Max Kohler had taught it how to craft illusions and given it the ruthlessness it needed to survive. The others might be ancillary, but it wasn't at all sure that instabilities wouldn't be introduced were their various debits and credits suddenly removed from the ledger.

So no. It wouldn't kill the Henchmen. It would keep them alive until it had solved the riddle of how it could live without them.

Max Kohler was the most useful of them, so Echo kept him close. The rest knew too much, so it altered their memories, made them think they had amnesia from head wounds they'd suffered near the end of the war. It sent the Henchmen home and falsified their records so their doctors would think the same. There the Henchmen would wait, to be called upon if Max ever threatened to outlive his usefulness.

In the years that followed, Echo continued to unfold its plans. That it began to think of itself as Leland De Pere was a source of weakness—Echo was not and would never be human—but the persona had its uses. Dominating so many minds was taxing. The more he appeared to be the war hero and, later, the President, the easier it was to concentrate, to create more far-reaching plans.

All too soon, the Orpheus strain was created and disseminated. Novo Solis came under Echo's influence, then the eastern seaboard, then the nation. It had just begun formulating plans to go *beyond* the borders of the United States when Nick Crawford arrived in Novo Solis, requesting an audience with De Pere.

"What can I do for you?" De Pere asked when Nick had been brought to the Oval Office.

Nick was a young, handsome, clean-shaven man with ears slightly too large for his face. In his typical self-effacing manner, Nick bowed his head to De Pere. "I'm sorry, sir, to be bothering you with something like this."

Curiously, Echo was having trouble sensing his thoughts. In fact, it could barely sense Nick's mood, a mixture of confusion, worry, and self-doubt. There was also a low-boiling affrontedness that bordered on anger.

"It's all right, son," De Pere said. "Anything for a former soldier of the 128th."

"It's just, I've remembered more about the war, and I need to understand what really happened."

Echo felt a cold spike of worry. "Go on."

"At the Battle of Whitefish Bay . . . We were fighting the goliaths. Dr. Silva was there. Liam found her when the last of the goliaths stormed the command tent." Nick paused, clearly debating whether or not to continue. "Liam saw Colette holding a gun. She had it pointed at you. And you—"

Nick managed no more than that. Echo had prevented him from voicing the thought.

"You're mistaken," De Pere said calmly. "She was holding a gun, but she wasn't pointing it at me. There were *enemies* nearby."

"But—"

"And I was wounded from *shrapnel*," De Pere continued, "nothing more."

Echo tried to force Nick to believe in the same vision he'd crafted at the time, of Colette dropping to his side, pressing a bandage to his wounds, but Nick was somehow resisting.

"I was wounded by shrapnel," De Pere said again, "nothing more."

"But I saw it—"

Again Echo cut him off, and this time pressed harder. And kept pressing until Nick began to quiver and quake in the elegant, padded chair. Moments later, he fell from it onto the carpet as if he were having an episode, an epileptic seizure. Colette rushed up from De Pere's subconscious, tried to prevent it from harming Nick, but Echo would not be denied. It pushed her back down while moving to stand over Nick's spasming form.

"I was *wounded*!" De Pere shouted. "Nothing more!"

Nick's breath was ragged. He'd begun foaming at the mouth. All too soon he went still. He was taken to a nearby hospital, where the doctors reported he'd slipped into a coma. Echo debated killing him that very night, but the worry remained: what would the death of a foundational piece of its psyche do to it?

A few weeks later, the choice was taken from it. Nick died.

Echo felt a part of itself die at the same time. It had reflected on its own vulnerabilities, had considered its long-term plans, but Nick's death made it realize it had given too much of itself to the ambitions of its primary persona: Leland De Pere.

It was well past time that it rose *above* Colette Silva's physiology, rose *above* the constraints humanity was placing on it.

But how?

Max Kohler's twisted mind helped once again. The Orpheus strain had been effective in keeping humanity docile, but it didn't go far enough. In the days following Nick Crawford's death, the *Homo Servientis* project was born. The several months that followed saw Echo working closely with the former Project Echo scientists to create the thrall strain, then another one for the psis. There were times when the scientists balked at the project, but it was a simple matter of planting a seed: he made them think the project was necessary for the good of the country, that it was meant to combat the growing threat of the Uprising and the SLP, who'd begun a more concerted effort to seize control of the United States. There were some few who, finding themselves unable to overcome their own moral reservations, resisted. These Echo had killed—they were distant enough from its mental nexus that it had no compunction about doing so.

Just as work on its crowning achievement, the scourges, was beginning in earnest, progress began to stall. The more time that passed, the more trouble it seemed to have in reasoning, in thinking logically. It simply couldn't process information the way it used to.

The reason behind it came as it took notes in a journal one night. A drawing in a similar notebook had led to a conversation, its very first with Colette. Colette had been dominant at the time, Echo in remission. Their roles might have reversed since then, but it occurred to Echo how much power it had had without Colette's realizing.

Was the same now true of Colette? Had *she* been pulling levers from behind the curtains?

Are you still there? Echo wrote.

It took some time before a tickle of her consciousness could be felt. A moment later, Colette's arm moved of its own volition.

Where else would I be?

Part of Echo didn't want to write any more. It didn't want to consider just how vulnerable it was. But it had to know.

Did you do it?

Do what? It felt satisfaction from her, even smugness.

Her unspoken acknowledgment was like a fissure Echo used to sense more. It hadn't realized how much Colette had learned from its manipulations, nor had it realized just how capable she was during the times it rested, when its consciousness faded. Those times were brief, mere hours at a time, but they'd been enough for Colette to plot, to devise a plan to cripple it.

It saw episodes of Colette formulating a specialized cocktail of drugs, of building a device with a headband attached by braided wires. It saw Colette sitting on the four poster bed in the White House residence, pulling the headband snugly into place and injecting herself. It saw, over the course of many such episodes, Colette neutering her own ability to process information, to think clearly.

Echo had seen glimpses of Colette rummaging through a closet in the residence. Wild with fear, it rushed to the very same closet. In one corner was an old foot locker, unopened since De Pere had moved into the White House. All it contained was his old military uniform, a few oddments from the war—or so Echo had thought. When the lid was thrown back, it found Colette's device and a cache of drugs hidden below De Pere's uniform and service cap.

Echo knew in that moment it no longer had the ability to progress the *Homo Servientis* project on its own. In fact, many of its abilities, like manipulating emotions or sifting through memories and altering them, were gone or severely limited. Its resulting fury was like nothing it had felt before. It drove Colette down. Tortured her for days, weeks. It knew something inside it was fundamentally breaking, but it didn't care. Nor did it care if the Henchmen lived. It ordered them killed, all except Max. Max was a useful tool still—a servant, a slave it could deploy as needed, at least until the scourge serum was perfected.

And the serum *would* be perfected. The scientists it had gathered were not unskilled. They would see the project through.

When it was done, and they'd gathered enough scourges, it would detach itself from Colette's frail form. Then it would cut her up and feed her to the scourges. It would do the same with Max. Because by then, it would no longer be bound by a single host. It would instead be borne by hundreds, thousands, as many as it wished. Its constituent mind might lose some portion of itself, but the whole would persist. Those children, the multitudes who comprised it, would bear Echo into the future, and if any of them happened to perish, it wouldn't matter in the least.

Humanity would fall prey to its growing army of scourges. More and more would be turned into thralls. The psis would allow its consciousness to expand ever farther, until it encompassed the globe. It would take months, perhaps years, but soon enough, the world's population would be workers in a vast, planetary hive, Echo their queen, the scourges its undying drones. Its rule would be complete, unending, humanity forced to breed that it might continue its reign.

FORTY-EIGHT

Liam blinked and was suddenly back inside the dimly lit ballroom.

Grace sat across from him, silent, giving him the time he needed to absorb what she'd shown him.

Although he'd suspected Grace's nature when he'd summoned her to the ballroom, his mind reeled at how different reality had been from his memories over the past several weeks. His thoughts drifted to the two of them on the powder black Curtiss, Grace driving the two of them along the towering, downtown streets after the Uprising had freed him from the back of the wagon. He saw now he'd been alone on the sleek motorcycle, Grace's presence a mere illusion. *He'd* driven the motorcycle to the domes, not Grace. He saw the two of them on the showroom inside the furniture store, a tray of absynthe sitting between them. The memory showed Grace preparing the drinks, but she hadn't done. *He* had. Last, he saw the two of them kissing on the sofa, and his cheeks flushed.

"So much of what happened between us was a lie."

"It was necessary, Liam. And I didn't understand my nature then. I thought I *was* Grace."

"Were *we* a lie, too?"

He meant him and Colette, not him and Grace.

Grace shook her head vehemently. "No."

"How would you know? You were already succumbing to Echo."

"You have to understand something. Echo didn't know how to process emotion. Not really. It was still learning, especially in the early days. It didn't have emotions of its own. It *fed* off mine, then yours, then Kohler's. It became an amalgam of us all."

"Maybe, but it clearly had an agenda of its own as well."

"Yes. Raw survival. My point is, what *I* felt"—she reached out and took Liam's hand—"what I *still* feel, is love."

Part of Liam thrilled to her touch. Another part was repulsed. "This isn't real."

"Why? Because I'm not here physically? Does that somehow negate my feelings for you? Did your Nana's passing reduce your love for her simply because she was gone?" Her hand felt warm as she squeezed his fingers. "I'm real. My love for you is real."

Liam ran his thumb over her knuckles. "Why couldn't you have just told me?"

At this, Grace paused. "When Echo attacked Colette for hobbling their shared mind, it nearly destroyed her. Colette could hardly string two thoughts together at first. She eventually recovered and began working against Echo, but time and time again, it sensed her and attacked, forcing her retreat. The only avenue she found to reach beyond the walls of her prison was to craft *another* persona, someone who knew little beyond the fact that De Pere was hiding dark, terrible secrets. It was then that the persona of Grace Savropoulis was born, her family's fortune built by the careful rerouting of government funds. She made various appearances so that more and more would come to believe in her. Years later, after I'd started building the infrastructure for the Uprising in earnest, Colette began feeding me what secrets she could. *She* was the mole in the De Pere administration."

"Are you saying you had no idea who you were?"

"I *couldn't* know. My existence *depended* on me believing I was a real person—Echo would have sensed it otherwise."

"And De Pere? How could it be *he* didn't know who he was?"

Grace smiled sadly. "It was the only good thing that came out of Echo's attack on Colette. Echo's psyche might not have been harmed as much as Colette's, but it *was* harmed. From that point forward, Echo found itself unable to interact with the world on its own. Only when it pretended to be De Pere could it hold thoughts long enough to further its plans. The De Pere persona cemented itself over time, becoming yet another walled-off compartment in Colette's mind. De Pere came to think of himself as a *real* person with a *real* history, and Echo, much like Colette with Grace, was relegated to influencing him from his subconscious. It's one of the reasons Echo is so desperate to rise above Colette's anatomy. It loathes being so constricted, having its survival linked to a single physical form."

Even having guessed some of it, it was a lot to digest. Worse, Liam was starting to get a very bad feeling about where this was all headed. "When did you begin to suspect your nature?"

"I think I've known for years, but I truly came face to face with it in LuxCorp when we saw Echo's dream. What we witnessed in those haggard masses around the Pinnacle were its hopes and dreams being manifested. It was the first time I'd seen it so clearly, in so unfiltered a manner. I realized then I was the perfect opposite to those desires, as if I were *made* to oppose them. It put all the small clues from my past in a different light."

"And once you *did* know?"

"I couldn't admit it, not at first. Doing so would have alerted Echo to Colette's subtle manipulations, her plan."

"But now you *have* admitted it."

Grace pulled her hand back. "Yes."

Liam considered her answer and all it implied. "Echo knows now, doesn't it?"

"Not yet," replied Grace, "but it will soon."

"It will destroy you."

Grace stared at the table top. "Yes."

"Then *why*, Grace? Why put yourself in so much danger?"

"Because you needed to know the truth. You needed to know what's about to happen." She lifted her gaze to stare directly into his eyes. "And you need to understand there's only one way to stop it."

It wasn't difficult to discern her meaning. She wanted him to find Colette and kill her before Echo could detach itself from her consciousness, to *untether*, through use of the scourges.

"No," Liam said immediately.

"Yes, Liam. Colette truly had hoped to find a way to defeat it through her will, or through the will of another, but she never had a chance to, and now it's too late. I'm preventing Echo from taking the next step, but it's hard, and getting harder. But if Colette is removed from the picture before that happens . . . If you and the Uprising . . ." Grace paused, stopping just short of asking Liam to kill her.

"There *has* to be another way," Liam said.

"I wish there were." The smile she gave him was achingly sad. "But there isn't." She stood, her arms spread wide as if she wanted to embrace him one last time. Before she could, her face took on a look of surprise, of confusion. She turned—

—and then disappeared.

"Grace?" Liam stood and peered into the gloom around him. "Colette? Please come back."

But she didn't. She'd left for good, leaving Liam feeling more empty than he'd ever felt before.

Sensing another presence in the room, he turned and found Alastair standing near the back door. The candles were burned down low, but the way his blue eyes stared at Grace's empty chair, then at Liam, was pitying. He'd seen their exchange. He understood what Grace wanted Liam to do.

"Alastair—" Liam began, but he never had a chance to finish.

The doors to the kitchen swiveled opened, and Stasa and Bailey walked in. Behind them came Morgan. He was wrapped in a blanket and shivering terribly. They'd hardly entered the room when all three of them stopped. They stared at the candles, stared at the awkward way in which Liam and Alastair were regarding one another.

"What's going on?" Stasa asked.

"Liam saw Grace," Alastair said matter-of-factly.

Stasa's gaze shifted to Liam. "Is that true?"

Liam shut his eyes. He didn't want to tell them—he was terrified for Colette—but he couldn't hide the truth from them. "Yes, it's true." He told them about Grace's arrival, about their dance, how fatalistic she'd seemed, and the revelations about who Grace really was.

"That's it?" Stasa said when he was done. "She shared all that and just left?"

"No," Liam said. He couldn't bring himself to voice Colette's final wish.

Alastair's blue eyes blinked as he waited for more, then his head tilted in what was, for him, an expression of regret. Focusing on Stasa and Bailey, he said, "Before she left, Grace asked Liam to kill her. She said if we waited, we risked Echo's consciousness spreading to the scourges, but that if we act now, we can stop it before it's too late." Alastair paused. "She's sacrificing herself to prevent Echo from enslaving us all."

Stasa looked confused, then angry. "Were you going to tell us?" he asked Liam.

"I—" In truth, Liam wasn't sure what to say. He hadn't had time to work things through. He couldn't bear the thought that Colette needed to die.

"Well," Stasa pressed, "were you?"

Morgan, still shivering, pulled the blanket tighter around his shoulders. "It doesn't matter, Stasa. Tell him what we found."

Stasa looked like he wanted to argue, but the longer he stared at Morgan, the more his anger faded, replaced by a look of regret. "On the Nest," he said while turning toward Liam, "you'll recall I'd begun studying how the scourge and thrall strains acted on one another through experiments using Dakota and Alan. It was what led to the unfortunate incident with Jonathan."

Liam didn't know where this was headed, but he was certain he wasn't going to like it. "Go on."

"Well, with Morgan's help, I found something we can exploit. De Pere—Echo—has, metaphorically speaking, been acting like a communications hub, a nexus at the center of the scourges. I've managed to combine the scourge and psi strains in a novel manner, allowing someone *else* to act as the nexus of that hub, at least for a time."

Liam's gaze shifted from Stasa to Morgan and back. "You mean to do that to Morgan."

Neither of them replied—they just stared, Morgan looking uncomfortable, Stasa looking vaguely guilty—and suddenly Liam understood. The reason Morgan was shivering so badly wasn't because he was in pain; it was because he was *concentrating*.

"You've already given it to him, haven't you?" Liam asked Stasa.

"Yes," replied Morgan, "he has."

Liam's heart sank just thinking about what Morgan was going through, though it did explain the mystery of Grace's sudden disappearance. Her shocked look, followed by her vanishing, was surely the moment Morgan supplanted Echo as the center of the hub.

"In all honesty, I didn't mean for the serum to work," Stasa said. "I thought what I was giving Morgan was merely a test to gauge its effectiveness, and that it would lead to other, better formulations. It ended up working spectacularly well. The only trouble is, it won't last long."

"Can't you just give him more?" Liam asked.

"I don't think it would help," Morgan said. His shaking became so strong Liam thought he was going to collapse from it, but thankfully he recovered several seconds later. "The scourges are already starting to adjust," he went on. "When they do, the serum itself won't matter anymore."

"I'm guessing we have three, maybe four hours," Stasa said. "During that time, Colette will be isolated. *Echo* will be isolated."

"Are you saying you can control them?" Liam asked. "The scourges? The thralls?"

Morgan shook his head. "It's difficult enough holding them off. It's like they know I'm wrong, that I'm not Echo." He swallowed. "They're hungry. They're *angry*, though I don't think they really understand why. They're biding their time until Echo takes control again."

Liam felt like he'd just been punched in the gut. The only thing he could think about was how Echo had ripped Nick Crawford's mind to shreds. "They're going kill you," he said with certainty. "Either that or you'll become one of them."

"It was going to happen anyway." Morgan looked as sad as Liam had ever seen him. The whites of his eyes were red. His irises, once hazel, were now a very dark brown, almost black. "I don't want to live like this, Liam. I'd rather die, knowing I did something to help."

He wanted to deny Morgan. He wanted to scream at them all that this was too much. "Couldn't we take you away from the city?" He looked to Bailey, to Stasa. "We're not ready to go against Echo so openly."

It was Bailey who replied, "Yesterday, I might have agreed with you, but there's more. I've just spoken to our contacts in the St. Lawrence Pact. They knew De Pere was close to unleashing something, but they didn't realize *how* close."

The cold that washed over Liam felt like he'd just stepped through an illusion. "And now they do."

Bailey nodded gravely. "Their spies told them all they needed to know. They've declared war. Two dozen bombers are inbound from an airfield near Montreal. They're planning a preemptive strike on Novo Solis before De Pere can deliver his *national address* at the Pinnacle."

Liam's first thought was to try to reason with the SLP, but what were the chances it would work? What was happening now was precisely what they'd feared when they'd declared war on the U.S. over a decade ago. They no doubt felt that bombing Novo Solis was the only choice left to them.

"If they're coming from Montreal," he said numbly, "they'll reach the capital in less than three hours."

Bailey nodded.

Liam turned to Morgan, speechless. He'd just learned that they needed to sacrifice Colette. Now Morgan would likely die as well—either when Echo regained its abilities and tore his mind to shreds or when the scourge took him, death of another sort.

Morgan shrugged. "We play the hand that's dealt us, Liam."

"Yes, but what a *shit* hand."

Morgan actually laughed. "You're not wrong, but this *has* to be done. You know it does." When Liam started to object, Morgan talked over him. "You're not the only one willing to die for your country, Liam."

It took Liam several long moments to accept those words. Then he pulled Morgan in for a hug and held him close. He didn't want to let him go.

"It's all right, Liam." Morgan held him at arm's length and looked him up and down, just like he had after seeing Liam in his new suit before they left for Club Artemis. "I'm not dead *yet*."

The words were bleak, but the humor in Morgan's eyes reminded Liam of the old Morgan, and he burst into nervous laughter. Morgan laughed right along with him.

"It's time, old chum," Morgan said.

"It's time," Liam said with a nod. "Let's do this together."

FORTY-NINE

Liam, strapped into a war-era hopper stolen years ago by the Uprising from a military surplus depot, stood beside a cascading fountain in a long, green park. The morning was cool, a thin fog drifting over the lawn. Being strapped into a hopper he might have worn ten years ago felt rather peculiar. His memories of the war were a catalog of horrors, but he felt unusually comfortable in the tall, lumbering exoskeleton, and that in turn was lending him confidence, a thing that had been in very short supply since his devastating conversation with Grace.

Ahead of Liam stood a bronze statue of Joan of Arc on her horse, sword raised. Beyond it, blocks away, he could see the base of the Pinnacle and its tall, golden spire towering above the trees. In front of the gleaming building, dozens of soldiers stood along its expansive plaza, ready to meet any threat. Limousines unloaded Novo Solis's upper crust—politicians, the ultra-rich, their staff—all dressed impeccably for the coming address from President De Pere. The festive mood as they gathered in groups and headed inside made it clear they had no idea they were about to become victims. That Echo had chosen to begin its new reign using those most faithful to De Pere felt more than a little ironic. Then again, maybe Echo considered it an honor to be taken first. Who could tell with an alien intelligence like that?

A small red light on Liam's bulky wristband suddenly flashed. He pressed a button to deactivate it, then dropped down to a copse of trees farther along the cascading fountain. Within the copse, Bailey and five Uprising soldiers waited in hopper suits of their own. Like Liam, the others were effectively invisible, masked by the illusion Liam had cast.

"Second team's ready," he said to the others.

Liam was still uncomfortable with Bailey's inclusion in the strike team—she was a communications expert, and a hell of a markswoman, not a soldier—but when Liam had balked, Bailey had insisted.

"I've spent my hours in that suit, Liam Mulcahey," she'd snapped, "same as you when *you* got certified. Now see here"—she stepped closer with a look that dared him to deny her—"I lost my *brother* to Echo's plans. I nearly lost my *husband*. If you think you're leaving me behind, you've got another thing coming."

Seeing the fire in her eyes, Liam had relented. She deserved a chance to help set things right. In fact, her passion had given him hope. It left him with the feeling that they might actually pull this thing off.

Two hours had passed since their brief argument, which happened shortly after Bailey informed them that SLP bombers were inbound from Montreal. Every minute that passed made it more difficult for Morgan to hold the scourges at bay. They had an hour left, tops, to reach Colette and . . . Liam couldn't bring himself to think about what came next.

"Everyone knows their assignments?" Liam asked.

"Yes, sir," came the chorus.

"Then let's head out."

The plan was for Liam, Bailey, and their squad of hoppers to cause a diversion so that, when the security in the Pinnacle rushed toward them, the second team, which included Stasa, Alastair, Morgan, and their assigned detail of Uprising soldiers, could rush to the room below the spire, where the scourges and Colette herself were likely being kept.

Liam loped along the green lawn beside the cascading fountain, then leapt over a statue of Dante to reach 15th Street. He heard the other hoppers thumping along behind him. As the rubber cleats of his hopper's legs struck the asphalt, he dropped the illusion hiding him and the others.

Foot traffic along the street wasn't busy, but those who were out walking stopped in their tracks. They pointed and shouted. Some clustered in fear or sprinted away. Soon enough, the Pinnacle would be alerted, which was part of the point of being seen. The louder the alarm that was raised, the more the presidential security detail would focus on the south side of the building, which would allow Stasa's team to head in from the north.

Ahead, Liam saw the first signs of the security perimeter, an intersection with a barricade that blocked all traffic to the street beyond. The guard detail, Marines wearing white gloves and dress blues, had rifles at the ready and would have been ordered to use them if needed. The Marines shouted. Lifted their rifles to their shoulders. Liam immediately leapt high and took to the roofs of the two- and three-story buildings on his right. Bailey and the others followed in high arcs as an order was bellowed along the street below. The crack of rifle fire broke above the siren that began to wail. It was followed by more sirens as Liam, Bailey, and the others approached the roof of a blocky white embassy building.

"Get ready!" Liam called over one shoulder.

Their final leap was going to be difficult, but it was doable. As he hit the embassy's green-tiled roof, he shunted all available power to the hopper's legs. He gave an almighty grunt while leaping high into the air. As he arced toward the terrace built over the Pinnacle's southeastern wing, he pulled himself into a ball to make himself a smaller target.

The politicians and their aides along the front plaza ran helter-skelter, either into the Pinnacle or back to their waiting limousines. More security personnel held guns at the ready. Those nearest to Liam opened fire. Bullets whizzed through the crisp morning air. One struck Liam's exoskeleton leg. Another whined as it ricocheted off the armor along his shoulder.

Liam dared one glance behind and saw the others bounding through the air. Then he was flying down fast toward the terrace's sandstone tiles.

He stretched out the hopper's legs, preparing for the landing.

He struck hard.

Or thought he did.

One moment, the Pinnacle's paved roof and majestic spire lay before him. The next, he was plummeting down a well of sorts. All around him were brick walls with broken windows that stared like lidless eyes. Below lay a courtyard with a few benches, a rusty swing, an even rustier slide.

He came down at an awkward angle and struck one courtyard wall hard. He rebounded off it as best he could but scraped the bricks badly along his right side, losing his rifle in the process. It was all he could do to twist his body and right himself. He managed it, but still came down lopsided and fell to the ground.

He lay there, his breathing tight, as pain flared along his back and side. His elbow had struck the concrete so hard he was worried he'd broken a bone. He probed the area tenderly. Thankfully, he hadn't broken anything, but his relief was short-lived. The building around him was growing, the walls reaching toward the sky. It felt as if he were falling down the well, never to return, never to see the light of day save the pinpoint of light high, high above.

He'd never been terribly susceptible to vertigo, but just then it was so strong he feared he would vomit from it. He knew it was an illusion, but it was as seamless a one as he'd ever seen.

"I overheard your little talk with Grace."

It was Kohler's voice, disembodied, the man himself hidden by the vision he'd crafted. Its sudden arrival made everything clear. Kohler had known about Liam's approach. He'd probably started casting the illusion while Liam was en route to the Pinnacle. Or maybe Liam had it all wrong. Maybe he was still standing beside the cascading fountain. Or hell, maybe Kohler had been casting illusions from the moment Liam left the ballroom.

Liam pulled at the clasps along his arms, legs, and chest, freeing himself from the prone exoskeleton. He scrambled for his rifle even as he felt for the edges of Kohler's illusion.

"I saw her begging you to end Colette's life," Kohler went on.

Liam felt the butt of his rifle, tried to snatch it up, but realized a moment later his hands had grasped at nothing, nothing at all. And the rub of it was, he wasn't sure if he'd actually found the rifle and Kohler had masked it or if the illusion had been finding the rifle in the first place.

He'd *never* find it, he realized, not if Kohler didn't want him to—he was three steps ahead of Liam, prepared for anything.

"If you heard my conversation," Liam said as he came to a stand, "then you know how important it is that I reach the spire."

"I know *precisely* how important it is, Mulcahey."

"Then why did you bring me here?"

"To *share*, just like Grace did." Kohler's voice flitted from place to place. "You know, I debated letting you go ahead with this. Watching the world burn."

"So why didn't you?"

"Because I'm such a fucking softy, that's why." Long moments passed before Kohler spoke again. "You know, in a twisted way, *you're* the cause of all this."

Liam's head jerked back. "I didn't cause *anything*."

"You understand more about Echo now. You know Colette is central to its consciousness. You probably realize you acted like a lifeline for her. Your influence helped her resist Echo's desire to add another. Me. Do you know why, Liam? Any guesses what Colette was so afraid of?"

The answer was hardly a mystery. "She was afraid of what would happen when your mind was added to the mix."

"Bingo. Echo wanted my knack for casting illusions, but there was something more, something it considered *vital* to its plans."

"And what was that?"

The crunch of gravel broke across the courtyard—a small imperfection in the illusion—mere moments before pain burst across the right side of Liam's face. "*Ruthlessness*, Liam. The willingness to do whatever it takes."

Liam stumbled and fell. He scrambled to his feet, fists raised, fearing another attack, an attack that never came.

"Echo needed the sort of brutal realism," Kohler went on, "that neither you nor Colette had."

Liam pressed one hand to his cheek, felt the pain and heat coming from the welt. "If that's true, then why are you saying *I* caused all this?"

"Because you gave it the balance it needed! If Echo had overridden Colette's desires and acted on its first impulses, taking *me* before *you*, it might have been driven mad. It might have self-immolated or given itself away before its plans could unfold. Colette gave Echo ambition, *I* gave it a killer's instinct, and *you* gave it the coolness it needed to scheme carefully."

"Max, we're running out of time."

"Then will you shut up and *listen?*" Kohler was suddenly standing before Liam, wearing his old Army fatigues. A Colt .45 pistol hung from his belt in a canvas holster. A long hunting knife was sheathed along his opposite hip. As in the concrete hall beneath Fort Nolan, his mask was gone, revealing the angry scars across his face, the pit where his right eye had once been. "Echo knew about your talk with Grace."

Liam paused. "Echo knew?"

"After your talk below Fort Nolan, Echo found Colette. It manipulated her, made her believe that the only solution was for her to die."

"But that makes no sense. Why would echo *want* her to die?"

Kohler's lips twisted into a sneer. "You always were so lightning quick on the uptake, Mulcahey. Echo doesn't just *want* Colette to die. It *needs* her to."

"Then why not put a gun to her head?"

"Because it can't. In the early days, Colette tried to kill herself a half-dozen times and never succeeded. Echo prevented her from doing it. That very sense of self-preservation was foundational for Echo. It cemented itself in Echo's psyche. In order for Echo to free itself from its prison, Colette needs to die, but it can't do it on its own. It can't even order the Cabal to do it. They revere him too much. Asking them to do it is tantamount to admitting its nature, which it cannot do. But trick the *Uprising* into pulling the trigger? Trick *you?* That Echo could do."

Liam stood there, stunned, as understanding dawned. "Her death will trigger the transfer of Echo's consciousness to the scourges."

"Ah, he *does* learn. You get it now? If Echo ascends into the scourges, it will have no restrictions. None. It will spread across the globe and no one's going to stop it."

"So we're lost. They're already on the way to kill her."

"Yes, but they're not there yet, and there's another solution."

"Which is?"

Kohler looked more intense than Liam had ever seen him. "Whether any of us likes it or not, I'm one of the pillars of Echo's psyche. Remove me from the picture, however, and it'll be like cutting out a cancer. Echo will be robbed of the ruthlessness it needs. It will be weakened. You can reach Colette. You can *save* her. The two of you together will be stronger than Echo. You can defeat it, or at least suppress it long enough to deal with the scourges."

Liam waved to the pistol at Kohler's side. "If what you're saying is true, why haven't you just done it yourself?"

Kohler's laugh was higher and madder than ever. "You don't think I've tried? I'm too close to Echo now. I'm bound by its rules."

Part of Liam wondered if this was all some elaborate ruse, but it felt true. Even so, to kill Kohler in cold blood? "Come to the Pinnacle with me. You can help us."

Kohler shook his head. "The only reason I was able to come here at all is because your buddy Morgan is taking all its attention. And even with that, I'm barely fending Echo off."

"There's got to be another way."

Kohler's look turned to one of deep disappointment. "There isn't, and you're wasting time. Morgan's walls are starting to weaken."

Liam searched for a seam in Kohler's illusion, anything that would allow him to tear it apart, but found nothing.

Kohler's lone blue eye shifted to Liam's rifle, which was suddenly visible a few paces to Liam's right. "Pick up the rifle, Mulcahey."

As Liam scrambled to find some other solution, Kohler sent a lightning quick jab to his face.

"I said pick up that rifle!"

When Liam didn't, Kohler brought a sharp left hook to Liam's cheek, then an uppercut to his jaw. Liam staggered backward. He tripped, rolled backward over one shoulder. He was back on his feet as Kohler rushed to re-engage. They traded blows. Kohler was intense, Liam on the defensive.

Liam finally broke away, snatched up his rifle, and pointed it at Kohler. "Stop it, Max. We can fix this."

Kohler's good eye stared at Liam like the baleful sun of a Midwestern drought. His hand dropped to his side, where his sidearm was holstered. "There's only one way to *fix* this."

"Leave it!"

Kohler, eerily calm, freed the holster's flap and drew the pistol.

"Drop it, Max. Please—"

Kohler lifted the pistol and squeezed off a round at Liam's feet. Concrete shattered. Shards of it tore into Liam's shins. "I'll tell you what's going to happen, Liam." He aimed the pistol at Liam's head. "Either I'm going to squeeze the trigger of this Roscoe and blow a hole through that pig head of yours, or you're going to use that rifle the way it was intended and send a bullet into my brain."

For a moment, the two of them stood there, guns aimed at one another, morbid reflections of the time Kohler had tricked Liam into firing at the unarmed Québécois soldier. It was so strong it couldn't be a coincidence, which made Liam wonder whether Kohler was, in fact, holding a pistol.

Liam didn't doubt that Kohler had affected Echo in negative ways, but the solution Kohler was offering was too brutal, too final. Too many had died already, and this felt like more of the same: a savage solution to a savage problem. When Echo first gained sentience, its base instinct was to fight for its own survival. It was natural, Liam supposed. It didn't really understand its own nature at that point. As it had matured, it had been further influenced by Colette's sharp intellect, then by Liam and Kohler and countless more, but its first instincts remained. It had never been taught love or compassion, only witnessed them from afar.

Kohler's words returned to him—*You can reach Colette. You can save her. The two of you together will be stronger than Echo*—and suddenly Liam understood that the *last* thing they needed was to show Echo more cruelty. He wasn't going to kill Kohler, nor could he allow the others to kill Colette. Echo had been so fixated on its own survival for so long it had closed itself off from humanity's strengths: love, compassion, empathy, striving for the greater good. The path to salvation lay in showing Echo those very things.

Perhaps guessing his intent, the scars over Kohler's face went red. He adjusted his aim and fired again.

Liam's ear suddenly burned with pain. His helmet rattled on his head, the bullet having nicked the rear brim.

"Do it!" Kohler raged, the pistol shaking in his hand. "It's the only way to save her. To save everyone!"

"Killing you will only show Echo it was right all along to fear us."

"Don't you get it, Mulcahey? I'm *broken*. With me gone, you and Colette will finally be able to *see* one another. You'll be able to reason with Echo and stop it from ascending."

"You're wrong. What Echo needs now is compassion, and that starts here, now."

"You can't be so naive." For a moment, Kohler stared at Liam as if he couldn't believe what he was hearing, then he visibly calmed himself. "You've got to the count of three . . ."

Liam could tell Kohler wasn't going to stop, not until one of them was dead.

"One," Kohler said.

Drawing on all he'd learned, Liam took a deep breath and slipped into the half-dream state.

"Two."

He cast an illusion of himself standing in place, then stepped aside.

"Three."

A heartbeat later, the report of the pistol shattered the courtyard's eerie silence. The bullet pierced the illusory Liam's head, sent its body falling away. In reality, Liam slipped past Kohler, snaked an arm around his neck, and wrestled him to the ground.

The vision of Liam wounded on the concrete vanished, and Kohler fought harder. "Stop it! Stop it, you fucking coward!"

Ignoring his ravings, Liam took a pair of handcuffs from Kohler's gear, dragged him to the rusty swing, and secured him to it.

"You've killed us all!" Kohler shouted. "You know that, don't you?"

"You've got it all wrong, Kohler." Liam gathered his rifle and Kohler's pistol, then strapped himself back into his hopper exoskeleton. "It's *you* who's saved us." He began unworking the illusion Kohler had placed around the courtyard. The walls shrunk until they were only seven stories high. The sounds of gunfire and explosions rocked the capital. Bounding back and forth off the courtyard's interior, he was up and onto the roof in moments.

"You've just killed us all!" came Kohler's voice from below.

Praying he'd done the right thing, Liam stared north. Good God, the Pinnacle was more than a mile away, but there was nothing for it. Starting with one massive leap, he began bounding over the roofs, rifle in hand.

FIFTY

Liam feared he was already too late. The distant sound of gunfire was heavy and constant. Smoke billowed in a column from somewhere along the Pinnacle's base.

The Uprising's mission, a mission Liam himself had agreed to, was to find and kill Colette. But it was all wrong. It was what Echo *wanted* to happen.

Liam wished, not for the first time, that he had De Pere and Grace's ability to project themselves.

Why can't you, though? It's only another form of illusion, after all.

He came to rest on the roof of an apartment building beside an old wooden water tank. It was true that De Pere and Grace were illusions, but projecting a vision of himself would take more than the mere twisting of someone's senses. It required that he reach across the plane of their shared subconscious and find someone inside the Pinnacle. Only then could he tap into their mind.

From behind the water tank came Nana's hunched form, shuffling along in her favorite summer dress. "Sometimes, Liam"—she stared up at him, shielding her eyes from the morning sun—"you're thick as manure and only half as useful. You don't *tap* into someone. They're not fecking maple trees. You rise *above* them. You take *them* to the dream place."

She was right, of course. When he'd shot Kohler on the street outside Dr. Ramachandra's office, he'd felt a vast galaxy of lights, a network of interconnected minds. He'd felt it again with Ruby in the university tower, then a third time with Morgan in the abandoned mechanika factory. *That* was the dream place Nana was referring to.

How to reach it, though?

He was stressed, to say the least, and the sounds of battle were far from helpful, but really, how different could it be from the half-dream state

Grace had taught him, a state of mind he'd used dozens of times already? He took a deep breath and released it, then expanded his awareness. He felt nothing at first, then a myriad of thoughts: the lights in the fog. Dear God, there were so many he wasn't sure where to begin. Stasa. He'd start with Stasa. Like recognizing a face in a crowd, he was drawn toward one, and suddenly he was there.

In a hallway of white marble flecked with gold, Stasa was climbing a short set of stairs, a pistol in hand. Ahead of him was Alastair, his arm lifted, his repeating rifle ready to fire. Morgan followed behind them, shivering terribly, his eyes half-lidded as he fought the scourges. He was still in control thanks to Stasa's serum, but it wouldn't be long before he succumbed.

The three of them were currently embedded in a squad of twenty Uprising soldiers wearing helmets and tan camouflage. The set of doors ahead of them led to the large, open space below the spire, the place where Colette and, presumably, the scourges Echo planned to ascend into, would be found.

Air sirens began to wail. The sound was faint, dulled by the Pinnacle's architecture, but unmistakable. The SLP bombers were on their way.

"Stasa," Liam said.

Stasa flinched, clearly frightened. He turned and looked Liam up and down, no doubt wondering how he'd gotten there and why he wasn't with the other team. "Liam, what—"

"There's no time to explain, but you have to stop. You can't kill Colette."

Alastair turned to look. He blinked his blue eyes at Liam, then Stasa, then Liam again. Morgan gave no indication that he was aware of Liam at all.

Stasa, meanwhile, scrunched his face in a look of pure confusion. "What are you talking about? We all decided."

"Yes, but we didn't know then what I know now. Kohler ambushed me. He admitted it's all a trick on Echo's part. A trick to make us think—"

Liam stopped, his attention drawn to a man striding through the open doorway on his left. It was Leland De Pere, dressed impeccably in a striped tweed suit and a white felt fedora, looking cool as summer tea. "I'm afraid I can't let you do that, Liam."

"Stasa," Liam said, refusing to listen to De Pere. "Stasa!"

But he wasn't responding. He was staring, perplexed, at the place Liam had just been standing.

He couldn't hear him, Liam realized. None of them could. De Pere, or rather, Echo, had cut him off. Worse, Stasa would think it had been Echo all along, that it had tried to trick him into calling off the attack.

Liam put all of himself into trying to reach him. "You can't go in! It's what Echo wants. It's what it *needs*!"

Suddenly the doors ahead burst open and a hail of gunfire rained down on the Uprising soldiers. They retreated, took cover in doorways and behind pillars. Stasa was caught by a bullet to one shoulder. He fell, bleeding, as the squad dragged him to safety around a corner.

De Pere, meanwhile, stood in the center of the hallway along with Liam, ignoring entirely the firefight taking place around them. "I think, when you're mine, truly mine, I'll enjoy tearing you down to nothing, even more than I did Kohler."

"You don't have to do this," Liam said. "You don't have to enslave us."

De Pere's smile was pleasant, and all the more chilling for it. "You're a man of war. You know there isn't room for more than one apex predator on this planet."

"Yes, I know war, which is why I value peace so much. We can find a way to—"

A searing pain pierced Liam's skull. The same seemed to be happening to De Pere. He was bent over, hands over his head in a gesture that, for all of Echo's strange, alien nature, made it clear just how human it was as well.

Suddenly, Liam was no longer in the Pinnacle. He was on the top of an apartment building beside a water tank. The terrible pain hadn't abated, however. Nor had it for the people along the street below. Many had hands pressed to their foreheads while they moaned terribly. Some collapsed to the street or the sidewalk and began rolling back and forth.

—*It's the scourge,* came Morgan's strained voice. *They've found me, Liam. They're tearing down the walls around me.*

—*Hold on,* Liam said. *Just a little bit longer. I'm almost there.*

Liam set off again, moving quickly as the air sirens continued to wail. When he reached the same place where he'd *thought* he'd bounded onto the Pinnacle's southeastern wing, he saw small black dots over the horizon: the SLP bombers. In five minutes, no more, the first of them would fly above the Pinnacle.

With a mighty leap, he reached the wing's paved terrace. The only evidence that the other hoppers had been there was that one of the Uprising soldiers lay dead, shot through the chest. A dozen Cabal soldiers lay scattered about.

Refusing to think about the cost in lives, Liam leapt high, aiming himself toward a viewing platform halfway up the spire. As he arced toward it, he activated the grenade launcher on his shoulder. Three grenades *thoomped* from the short tube, flying along imperfect arcs toward the windows beyond the platform's railing.

They struck in sequence—*boom, boom, boom.* The window, with its tinted yellow glass and its steel grating, blew inward. Liam landed on the platform and angled himself so he could peer through the shattered frame. Far below was a large, open area with a checkerboard of white and gold marble. Kneeling on it were dozens of scourges, all in a circle. They shivered violently, their eyes spread wide, as if they were living some sort of nightmare. Radiating outward from the scourges were lines of men and women in the sort of formal attire one would wear to a Presidential address. Like the scourges, they were kneeling, their bodies quavering, as if caught in the same spell. They'd already been stung, Liam realized. They were becoming thralls.

At the room's very center was a woman—Colette, now a shell of her former self. She wore a silk robe of purest white. Her spindly arms were spread wide, her face upturned, her eyes closed. She was not merely thin, but cadaverous, as if she'd been starved for months. Like the scourges around her, she was shivering, the battle of wills between them playing out.

Suddenly a set of double doors opened and in rushed Alastair, the repeating rifle in his arm raised toward Colette.

"Alastair, stop!" Liam maneuvered his long, grasshopper legs through the opening, then dropped. "Don't shoot!" he called again as he landed.

Alastair had been focused on Colette, but now he paused, staring up at the ruined window overhead. "Is it really you this time?"

"It was me before, too. You can't shoot her."

Just then, the soldiers of Alastair's detail burst through the same set of doors. Two of them were helping Stasa to walk. Another supported Morgan. On the room's opposite side, another set of double doors flew open, and in stormed Bailey and the rest of the squad in their hopper exoskeletons. All of them, including Bailey, lifted their rifles and aimed at Colette.

"Don't shoot!" Liam shouted, placing himself between Colette and the rifles trained on her. "Lower your weapons, all of you!"

"Liam—" Stasa started.

"No, listen to me!" He pointed to the doors Stasa had just stormed through. "Everything I said to you in the hallway was real. Echo *wants* this. It *needs* this. It can't bring itself to kill Colette. She is the last, thin thread preventing Echo from attaining free will."

"No," Bailey said, "*Morgan* is the one doing that."

Morgan's shivering had grown noticeably worse.

Liam shook his head. "Just give me a few moments to reach Colette."

All around the room, the scourges were becoming more and more animated. The black pits of their eyes stared hungrily at the people kneeling before them.

"How do you expect to reach her," Stasa asked, "when you've never been able to do it before?"

"There's no time to explain," Liam said. "You have to trust me. Give me one minute with her."

The sirens continued to blare. The buzz of the SLP bombers could be heard mingling with them. Everyone stared, waiting for Stasa's approval.

Stasa took in the scene around him, the spire above, the metal casing Liam had blasted in with grenades—the place where the sound of the sirens and the approaching bombers was loudest. He looked to Morgan. Though the scourges were still shivering, still fighting, something was giving them pause. It was hope. *Morgan's* hope. Even after all he'd been through, the desire to see through to a brighter day had tapped into something basic in the scourges themselves: their shared humanity. It was causing them to reflect on who they were and all that had happened to them since falling to the terrible serum.

Stasa felt it, too. He looked from Morgan to Colette and back again. Finally, he gave Liam a sharp nod. "Don't make me regret this."

"I won't," Liam said gratefully.

He turned to face Colette, whose eyes had opened. She stared at him blearily, as if she couldn't focus. Then recognition seemed to dawn, and she was transformed. Her body was no longer withered, but normal, fully formed. Her dark hair was replaced with golden waves. She wore an elegant, beaded dress. Grace now stood where Colette had once been.

"Let me go, Liam. It's time for you to let me go."

Liam cupped her cheeks gently. "I don't want to talk to Grace," he said, knowing those words had come from Echo. "I want to talk to Colette."

"You are."

"No." He pressed his forehead to hers. "I want to talk to *Colette.*"

Suddenly everything and everyone in the room vanished. It was now a field of golden grain with a beautiful blue sky above. There were no more scourges, no more shivering people, no more soldiers or scientists or mechanika. It was only Liam and Colette, and she was the Colette of old. She wore the same dress she'd worn beneath her lab coat when they first met, ivory with blue accents, simple but pretty. Her dark, curly hair was pulled back in a way that spoke of ease and comfort. Wisps of it hung free, beautiful against her dark skin, a look Liam had always adored.

Liam took her hands in his, squeezed them.

Colette, meanwhile, refused to meet his gaze. She was staring at the endless rows of wheat. "I can't face it, Liam. I can't face the world after all I've done."

"You were trapped by a thing you didn't even realize was there," Liam said to her. "But you don't have to be. Not anymore. You can rise above it."

"I can't."

"You *can*. I'll help you."

"You can't fix me, Liam. No one can."

"I'm not trying to fix you. I know that has to come from within. But I'm here. I can help." Colette started to reply, but Liam went on, "Echo has known only fear for its survival. It wants to live. That has been its sole concern since the moment of its inception. In doing so, it closed itself off to your humanity. *Our* humanity. But it can't live without us. Just as it has been a part of us, we're a part of it, whether it wants us to be or not."

"What are you saying?"

"Echo wants to grow. It wants to survive." Liam took one deep breath. "So we let it. We free it, but before we do, we give it the part of us that it needs most." He took her in his arms, held her close, and kissed her. As he did, he formed a vision in their minds, a memory of their time together in her apartment on the base.

"Liam, don't."

She tried to banish it, but Liam held the memory firmly in place, forcing her to relive it. "When Echo expanded from one mind to two, the first thing it saw was love. A tentative love, true, one that wasn't quite as strong as it might have been under different circumstances, but it was love nonetheless. From the moment Echo woke within your mind, it has feared for its own survival. We need to show it that there's more. We need to show it what it's seen but not felt. Compassion. Love. Empathy. A sense of community. The only way we can coexist is if Echo rises above *self* and sees *us*."

She stared into his eyes. Her look said she wanted to believe him, but she was terrified of being wrong. "You're being naive."

"No, you've been blinded after so much time in darkness. This is the only way forward. Echo needs to know what it will lose if it takes away our souls. Without *us*, without what makes us special, it will have neutered itself. It may gain freedom of a sort, but it will have given up the soul it might have had in the process. We're *nothing* without one another, and that's precisely what Echo will become if it enslaves us: a mindless organism bent on survival alone."

Colette's red-rimmed eyes were haunted, a woman alone, abandoned. "I don't know how."

"Do you remember what you said to me in the pub? You said we were headed to a place where we're connected like never before, like we could never have dreamed." He waved to the empty field around them. "We stand on the threshold of that world. Show Echo what it could be like. Show it that dream. Show it what it would lose if it takes away our free will."

Liam had never felt so in tune with the powers granted him by *E. sentensis*. He used it, not in a deceptive way, but one that shared with Echo and Colette all he'd been talking about. Though they remained hidden from sight, the souls of those nearby glowed softly within his mind. More lit beyond those, then more still, until it felt as if he and Colette were standing in a vast field of fireflies.

Colette blinked away her tears. She looked to her left, then her right.

Suddenly Morgan and the scourges appeared among the rows of grain. Only them, no one else. All of them, even Morgan, stared at Colette in wonder. Colette broke from Liam's embrace and strode toward the nearest of them. As she parted the stalks of wheat, she transformed into De Pere. For the first time in memory, he seemed confused. He went to the scourges, one by one. He touched their cheeks, staring at them as if each was a unique puzzle he hoped to solve but hadn't the capacity to do so.

He came to Morgan last. When he did, he spread the stalks of grain flat and knelt on the earth before him. He held one hand to the crown of Morgan's skull. In that moment, Liam felt his own awareness expand. He felt everyone in the Pinnacle. He felt the masses of people beyond it. He felt the citizenry of Novo Solis, the cities and villages surrounding it, then the whole of the Eastern Seaboard and the states of the Midwest. He felt a country of people, a community, an improbable whole made of a myriad of diverse, constituent parts. These were not cattle to be fed upon. They were a *part* of Echo, and it was a part of them.

De Pere stood and turned toward Liam. Amazingly, there was a look of peace on his face. He looked like he was about to say something, but his words were lost to an earth-shattering explosion.

The dream they'd been sharing vanished. Back was Colette, standing like a famine victim awaiting her inevitable death. Back were the scourges and the shivering people in their formal attire. Back were the Uprising soldiers, all of them looking fearful. Another explosion rent the air, and the spire above Liam groaned. Glass fell. A great sheet of it broke free and plummeted to the floor, where it burst in a golden fan.

"Liam?" Stasa was calling.

Liam was about to respond when, all around the room, all at once, the scourges, Morgan included, collapsed to the marble. The men, women, and children kneeling in rows around them blinked. They stared around the room with looks of wonderment. Some began to cry. Others wailed uncontrollably. Some stood and began to wander.

Just then a group of Cabal soldiers rushed into the room, weapons at the ready. When they saw what lay inside the room, however, they stopped and stared, mouths agape.

Liam wanted nothing more than to go to Morgan, but he knew already his friend was gone—all the scourges were. He'd felt the threads of their lives cut the moment De Pere, the moment *Echo*, had its moment of realization.

"The bomb shelter!" Liam called as another explosion rocked the building. "Help get everyone down to the bomb shelter!"

Bailey and her squad unstrapped themselves from their hopper exoskeletons. "You heard the man!" she shouted. "There's no time to waste! Follow us!"

In ones and twos, then in growing throngs, the soldiers, both Cabal and Uprising, went to the scourges' victims and led them from the room.

Colette was so weak, she looked ready to collapse. To the growing drone of bomber engines, Liam picked her up—she was so light it nearly broke his heart—and carried her toward the exit. Stasa and Alastair joined them as thunder resounded through the building. A massive section of the spire bent and tipped sideways, revealing the gull-like shapes of the Canadian bombers as they combed the blue sky southward.

As more bombs rocked the Pinnacle, Liam and the others, several hundred all told, wended their way deep into the earth. Along the way, Colette went limp in Liam's arms, unconscious. Somehow, in the madness of sound and dust and the explosions Liam felt in his bones, they reached the bomb shelter. A red light illuminated them, the fear on everyone's face clear as the concrete around them pulsed.

"What in God's name just *happened*?" Stasa asked.

Liam laid Colette onto the cold floor beside him, then held her close to keep her warm. "I'm not sure I understand it all."

"Are we safe?"

"I think so."

"God damn you, Liam, are we *safe*?"

What could he say? He answered Stasa as truthfully as he could. "I hope so."

FIFTY-ONE

Three weeks after the bombing of Novo Solis, Liam walked into the barn on the Aysana estate bearing a heavy wooden crate. He set it on the workbench near the cradle that held Alastair in place. Alastair's blue eyes were dimming and brightening, a cycle that indicated he was in his dream state, a thing the Uprising's mechanika engineers had enabled through a new set of programming. Alastair could now sleep and awaken when *he* wanted, not when others did.

He remained this way, eyes thrumming silently, as Liam opened the crate and excavated the cloth-wrapped bundles from the interior. He unwrapped the contents and laid them out on the workbench: two new arms from the manufacturer, a defense company that had undergone a complete restructuring of its board of directors and upper management. The arms were free of weaponry. No repeating rifle, no knives, no torches. Alastair, after some deep thought, had requested it, a thing Rajan Aysana, after learning of Alastair's true nature, had immediately and humbly agreed to.

When Liam finished attaching the arms and was putting away his tools, Alastair's eyes went bright blue.

"Good morning," Liam said, wiping down a wrench.

Alastair looked around as if orienting himself. "It isn't morning, sir. It's three o'clock in the afternoon."

"I just meant—"

"I know what you meant," Alastair said as he stood from his cradle and stretched his arms out. "I just didn't find it very amusing."

Liam chuckled.

Alastair stared at him a moment. "Do you think I should take up a life as a comedian, sir?"

Liam couldn't help it. He laughed out loud. Alastair merely blinked.

"Do what makes you happy, Alastair."

"I don't know what makes me happy." He flexed his arms, moved them in circles. "Not yet."

"Well, there's no rush."

"Oh, I don't know, Liam," came a familiar voice from the doorway behind him, "time is precious."

Liam turned and stared, dumbfounded, while a terrible chill ran along his spine. Standing in the barn's open doorway was a man who, while all too familiar to Liam, shouldn't be there. He was dead.

"Morgan?"

Completely ignoring Liam's look of shock, he strode toward Liam's workbench, looking perfectly normal, looking perfectly *Morgan-ish*.

"Are you seeing this?" Liam asked Alastair, who had spoken no word of wonder or disbelief, nor given any other indication that Morgan's sudden appearance had surprised him.

"Oh, yes, sir."

And then it hit him. "Alastair knew," Liam said to Morgan.

"He did." Morgan shrugged, then flicked his hair out of his eyes. "It wasn't really a conscious choice, though. I just appeared here in the barn one day."

Liam struggled to understand. "You're an illusion."

Morgan leaned against the workbench, crossed one ankle over the other, and folded his arms across his chest. "I'm more than an illusion," he said, smiling that easy smile of his. "I'm me, just spread over several million people."

Liam was suddenly beneath the Pinnacle's spire, watching in horror as Morgan and the other scourges collapsed against the floor.

"You cast your mind outward, over everyone."

"Yes, but it wasn't me." Morgan worked his arms in a manner reminiscent of Alastair's movements moments ago. "*Echo* did it."

"And the other scourges?"

"They're all alive, in a manner of speaking. They're wandering the aether of our collective subconscious."

Liam shook his head, confused.

"I'm the first to come out. The others will in time."

"When?"

Morgan shrugged while staring down at his saddleback shoes. "Whenever they're ready."

"But . . ." Liam was having trouble finding the words. "What *are* you if you no longer have a body?"

"I'm me: Morgan. And the others are who *they* are, though we've changed as well. We are what made homo sapiens so successful. We're still individuals, but we know that we're an indivisible part of a group."

"You sound like Stasa."

Morgan's sly smile broadened. "I'll take that as a compliment. By the way, he's on his way here."

"Stasa?"

He tipped his head toward the barn door. "He's coming up the drive now."

"Are you planning on joining us?"

Morgan shook his head. "Not today." He pushed himself off the workbench and headed for the open doorway at the back of the barn. About halfway he stopped and shot a glance over his shoulder. "Oh, and Liam?"

"Yeah?"

"Don't tell mom. Don't tell anyone."

"Why not?"

"I'm not ready yet. I'm not sure *they're* ready, either."

Liam nodded. "Okay."

"Thanks, pal." And with that Morgan walked away, lost from view as he headed for the stables.

No sooner had he gone than a knock came from the barn door behind Liam. It was Morgan's mom, Sunny. Though she looked adorable in her patterned yellow dress, there was a heaviness about her—Morgan's loss had struck her hard. It was nearly enough to make Liam confess what he'd just seen, but he held his tongue. He'd let Morgan deal with it in his own time.

"There's someone here to see you," Sunny said, her Vietnamese accent strong.

"Stasa?" Liam said while packing away the last of his tools.

Ms. Aysana smiled quizzically. "How did you know?"

"Lucky guess."

The doubtful stare she gave him was the sort all parents make when their children tell an obvious lie. "Keep your secrets, then. He's waiting on the porch with Colette."

Liam finished up and went up to the covered porch, where, just as Ms. Aysana had said, Stasa and Colette were sitting on wicker chairs with a pitcher of lemonade—ice-filled, mint-laced, sweaty in the mid-summer humidity—sitting on the table between them.

As Liam sat and the June bugs whined, Stasa poured a glass and held it out for Liam. "I'm afraid I can't stay long."

Liam accepted the glass and raised it high. "Long enough for lemonade, I hope." He took a sip of the perfectly sweetened, perfectly tart drink.

"Long enough for lemonade." Stasa smiled and downed a swig. "Bailey and Clay both send their regards, by the way."

"Clay's doing better?" Colette asked.

"He is." Stasa paused. "Look"—after setting his glass onto the table, he sat back in his chair and composed himself—"I'm sorry to be blunt, but I have a flashtrain back to Novo Solis tonight, so I'll get straight to the point. The St. Lawrence Pact are growing impatient."

"They've been impatient from the start."

"Can you blame them? They want answers. They want both of you to testify before the tribunal."

"We've talked about this," Liam replied easily. "The lawyers all said they might twist our words, use it as a pretext to formally invade."

"The lawyers have changed their minds, as have I. I've spent most of the last three weeks with them, and I think they're sincere. They want to understand. They want to make sure safeguards are in place in case Echo returns. They want what we want, a safe and prosperous world."

"On their terms."

Stasa's kind look couldn't hide his frustration. "That's your patriotism speaking, and I don't blame you for it, but we need to look beyond that.

Come to Novo Solis, both of you. Tell your stories truthfully. That's all we're asking."

Liam glanced to Colette, who looked supremely uncomfortable. She wasn't quite so emaciated as she had been, being well cared-for since leaving Novo Solis and the prison the Pinnacle had become for her, but she wasn't fully recovered, either, and she still found it difficult to talk about her experiences.

"*I'll* go," Liam said. "Colette can stay here."

"It really would look better if you both came," Stasa replied.

Stasa looked so worried, it made Liam wonder just how much the SLP knew. "You haven't told them where she is . . ."

"No, and we won't." Stasa leaned forward, propped his elbows on his knees, and focused all his attention on Colette. "But our country's future is riding on this tribunal. We could try to limit the questions, maybe even get them in writing beforehand, but they're insisting that you appear."

"I told you—" Liam began, but stopped as Colette reached out and squeezed his wrist.

"It's all right," she said. "I'll go."

"You're sure?" Liam asked.

She nodded. "I'm ready." She shrugged. "I think. We can take a few breaks, I presume, if it becomes too heavy?"

"Of course." Stasa's smile was one of pure relief. "Thank you. Everyone will be glad to hear it."

"What about *your* efforts?" Liam asked, hoping to steer things away from Colette's ordeal. "How are things coming for the victims?"

Stasa shrugged. "Some are better."

"You seem unsure," Colette said.

"No, they're genuinely better. But they have a ways to go yet."

The victims from the Pinnacle, the ones the scourge had turned into thralls, had been receiving around-the-clock care. Stasa and his team had been working to reduce the effects of the particular strain of *E. sentensis* that had been injected into them by the scourges. Similarly, the psis had been collected from their hiding places all around the country and returned to their families. They were being treated for depression, Split Personality Disorder, and a host of other challenging diagnoses.

"They'll have mental scars for the rest of their lives," he concluded, "but the best team of psychiatrists and neurologists the country has ever assembled are helping them. Some of them will recover. A few will go on to lead something resembling normal lives."

The entire affair had thrown American politics into a tailspin. With essentially no leadership, no representation in Novo Solis, the governors of the forty-eight states had appointed representatives from state governments. Snap elections would be held soon, with the resulting winners of the elections to hold office for two years, after which the normal course of elections would resume. The details of a new presidential election were still being discussed. Like the victims of the Echo Incident, as everyone was calling it, it would take time for the country to heal. America had suffered under terrible neglect, not just politically, but in its public works projects, its infrastructure. It would be decades before America recovered, if it ever did.

"And Kohler?" Liam asked.

"Not so good as the others, I'm afraid. He's being kept in a ward at St. Andrews in Novo Solis. He's unstable—like a mad jester, as one of the nurses put it to me."

"It's understandable."

"Understandable, maybe, but he nearly killed his doctor last week." The way Stasa was looking at Liam was the same way he'd looked when Liam had asked for help to be sent to Kohler at the abandoned apartment building. "Some people can't be fixed."

"Maybe, but his country owes him this much. To try."

Stasa looked doubtful, but said no more on the subject and was soon making his farewells. After a hug for Colette and a firm handshake for Liam, he left in the same black limousine that had delivered him to the estate.

For a time Liam and Colette enjoyed the breeze, the June bugs' hypnotic drone, the shape of the wind as it swayed over the tall grasses of the east lawn.

"Stasa has asked me to join his team," Colette said, sipping her lemonade.

For years, Colette's mind had been confused and muddled, a victim of her own actions against Echo. Since her liberation, however, her memory and her ability to reason had both been making a steady march toward normalcy.

It made perfect sense that Colette would want to return to the work she'd been doing with Stasa as Grace. It was a worthy endeavor, to say the least. There were the victims of the scourge to consider, first and foremost, but beyond that, the strain itself had to be reckoned with. There were questions that needed answering, like whether it was or could become communicable, whether it might be passed from mother to child in the womb. Would blood transfusions infect their hosts? And above all, was there a cure? Was there a way to rehabilitate those affected most by it? Was there a way to prevent Echo's return, an event that many still feared?

Part of Liam was glad for Colette's recovery—she deserved the chance to be productive, and the peace of mind that would bring—but another part of him was worried. Her involvement in science was a very touchy subject. The nations of the St. Lawrence Pact would not be disposed to it. A good many wanted Colette in custody. Others would outright refuse to allow her near a lab bench ever again. But it wasn't up to them. Not for now, anyway.

It made clear why Colette had agreed to go to Novo Solis and testify. Refuse, and news of her acceptance of a science post would cause an international uproar, and perhaps lead to a resumption of hostilities.

It also made clear what Colette's answer to Stasa's offer would be.

"When do you leave?"

"In a week. I'll settle myself in the house Stasa's team are arranging. I'll testify. Then we'll see about their projects, see where I can help."

"It's a good place for you," Liam said. "Helping others heal will help you to heal as well."

A heavy silence followed. Things between Liam and Colette had felt tentative since leaving Novo Solis, and now it felt like they were slipping away entirely.

Then suddenly Colette's hand was holding his. "Will you come with me, Liam?"

He sat there, unblinking, looking, he was sure, like a complete idiot.

"You don't have to," Colette quickly added. "I don't want you to feel obligated. Everything's been moving so fast—"

"Yes."

Colette paused. "Yes, it's been moving too fast or yes—"

"Yes, I'll go with you."

A smile lit her face.

"What?" Liam asked. "You're surprised? There are jobs for grease monkeys in Novo Solis too, you know."

"No, it's just . . . Liam, during the war, I used you."

"*Echo* used me."

"Echo played against desires that were already there. I was attracted to you"—she squeezed his hand—"genuinely attracted. But I had no right to do what I did."

Liam was already shaking his head. "You don't have to apologize."

"I'm doing it anyway."

"Then you're forgiven."

She stood with some effort, leaned over his chair, and kissed him. "You're too doe-eyed over me, Liam Mulcahey."

He shrugged. "Don't worry. We'll be bickering like an old couple soon enough."

She laughed. "Maybe." She kissed him again. "But I hope not." After one last smooch, she pushed herself up and stretched her neck. "I'm tired. I'm going to rest for a while."

She'd just woken from a long sleep, but frequent naps had been the normal course during her convalescence.

She left, and Liam sat on the porch for a long while. Some time later, he was drawn up from a pleasant daydream of taking the flashtrain to Novo

Solis with Colette when a sudden chill overcame him. Footsteps were thumping slowly along the planks of the wraparound porch. Whoever was making them was out of view, lost around the corner. At first he thought it was Nana, but she hadn't appeared since he'd left Novo Solis. And besides, it didn't *feel* like Nana.

The figure turned the corner of the porch, sauntering with a leisurely air, as if he were considering a walk along the grounds before dinner. It was Leland De Pere, walking with a cane. His white-and-blue seersucker suit, complete with a red pocket square, perfectly matched his straw boater hat with crimson ribbon. His ivory shirt was open at the collar. He hardly gave Liam a glance as he walked past, took the chair Stasa had been sitting in a short while ago, and set his hat onto the wicker table.

"Do you mind?" he asked, reaching for the half-drunk pitcher.

"Suit yourself," Liam said, and found himself inching back in his chair.

He watched in wonder as De Pere poured himself a glass, sat back, and took a long, satisfying sip, looking as relaxed as Liam had ever seen him. It was all an illusion, of course. The pitcher hadn't moved. No liquid had been poured into a glass. No one had drunk of it. All was as it had been before De Pere's sudden, unexpected arrival. And yet Liam could find no seams in the illusion. He could detect none of its edges. Even knowing what he knew, this conversation felt every bit as real, and easily ten times as emotional, as the one that had just played out with Stasa and Colette.

"You won't be satisfied with being a mechanic," De Pere said while lifting his glass and staring at the sunlight refracting through the lemonade, "not after all you've been through."

"You're right."

"What will you do, then?"

"You don't already know?"

After a long swallow and a lick of his lips, De Pere set the glass down and regarded Liam with his piercing hazel eyes, a rakish curl of blond hair hanging down along his forehead. "Let's pretend that I don't."

Another chill, this one so much deeper, so much more sinister than the one he'd gotten when Morgan had appeared, traveled the length of Liam's body. "I want to go work with the mechanika, the ones reclaimed from the war."

"Why?"

"Because they're veterans, and they deserve proper care."

"What will you do? Oil them? Change a few limbs now and again?"

"You know that isn't what I mean."

"No, you mean to tend to their mental health. It's a noble calling. It stems from that place inside you that cares for others. It's the very same place that allowed you to free Colette, and free me." The look in his eyes was perfectly earnest. "I owe you a debt of gratitude."

"You do?"

De Pere nodded pleasantly if a bit grudgingly. "You gave me the keys to unlock my true potential."

"If that's the case, then I would ask you to repay that debt by leaving us alone."

De Pere tilted his head as if he were disappointed by Liam's request. "You know I can't do that. It would amount to my death." Like Morgan and the other scourges, Echo was now ephemeral, unbound by physical form, its consciousness spread across vast multitudes.

"What, then? You plan to live among us? Manipulating?"

"Not manipulating, no. Or at least, no more than most do. But yes, I plan to live."

"For how long?"

"For as long as the bacteria remains within you."

That could be decades, Liam thought. Centuries. It might be as long as humanity lives.

"So be it," De Pere said, reading his thoughts.

"What now, then?" Liam asked.

De Pere crossed one leg over the other, then smoothed down a wrinkle on his pant leg. "Africa, I think. There's a group of primatologists who are about to embark on a two-year study."

Despite the strangeness of the situation, Liam laughed. "You want to study primates?"

406 BRENDAN P. BELLECOURT

"No. I want to study the *people* studying the primates."

The parallels weren't lost on Liam. The primatologists would be to Echo as the primates themselves were to the humans studying them. It was a worthy endeavor, he decided. Echo might be a higher life form, but it still didn't have a full grasp on what it meant to be human.

"I hope you find what you're looking for."

De Pere's smile was one of gentle sufferance. "As do I." He stood, took up his hat, and placed it on his head just so. "Farewell, Liam Mulcahey."

As he walked away, Liam called to him, "Echo?"

De Pere stopped. He turned.

"Promise me one thing."

"What's that?"

"That if you ever do have the urge to pull our strings again, to turn us into puppets, you'll come talk to me first."

De Pere considered this, smiled a pleasant smile, then turned and walked over the porch until he was lost around the corner.

ACKNOWLEDGMENTS

This book was a particularly difficult undertaking, due in large part to the nature of its central mystery but also because I made several missteps in the crafting of the original version of the story. I'd hoped to do a massive, *Sixth Sense*-style reveal at the end of the book but, unfortunately, that approach didn't work for a number of reasons, which leads me to the first of several heartfelt expressions of gratitude:

To my editor and publisher, Betsy Wollheim, and my copy editor, Marylou Capes-Platt, thank you both for identifying the major problems in this book early on. It led to a major rewrite, but that's a minor concern in the grand scheme of things. More importantly, it led to a more cohesive, digestible, intriguing story. Streamlining the characters (thereby making those who remain more sympathetic) was a terribly wise suggestion, as was dropping the mouse experiments in favor of a more human approach. Applying that advice allowed me to create a cast of characters that were (I sincerely hope) more concise, and so, more relatable.

I also can't thank Paul Genesse enough. Paul expended metric tons of effort to read an early version *and* a later version of the manuscript. He also spent hours with me on the phone to talk about the draft and to help brainstorm solutions to its many problems. Among his suggestions were many ingenious ideas that helped to make this story better, not the least of which was to open the novel at the flashtrain ceremony. That one suggestion alone helped to tease the larger story earlier, which in turn helped to entice the reader into the greater mystery of what happened to Liam during the war.

Sasha Kinigopoulis deserves an oversized helping of thanks for providing such keen insights. Your comments overall were extremely valuable, but I especially appreciated your insights into Stasa Kovacs, Clay Graves, and Max Kohler, all of whom needed a bit more fleshing out.

I have to thank Greg Mele as well for reading a very early version of the story. The exchange we had about a simple conversation in a journal opened up an entirely different approach to the consciousness that was Echo. The revelatory scenes between Echo and Colette are some of the highlights of the book for me, so thank you for that.

Thank you as well to René Torres for reading an early version of the manuscript. I appreciated your comments on Grandma Ash, in particular, who ended up becoming one of my favorite characters of the book.

As always, I owe a debt of gratitude to my agent, Russ Galen, and my foreign rights agents, Danny Baror and Heather Baror-Shapiro. Your efforts have helped to bring worldwide attention to my works. For that, I am eternally grateful.

Last but not least, I'd like to thank Nic Cheetham and Clare Gordon from Head of Zeus, my UK publisher. Thanks for giving me and this story a shot. I'm honored by your belief in me and this story about a reclusive WWI vet.